Praise for *Secluded Cabin Sleeps Six*

"A stellar thriller, packed with tension and twists, but also laced with nuanced insight and characterization."
—Gilly Macmillan, bestselling author of *What She Knew*

"*Secluded Cabin Sleeps Six* is a deliciously tense ride that takes a deep dive into the meaning of family and the price we'll pay for those we love."
—Ruth Ware, *New York Times* bestselling author of *One by One*

"An adrenaline-fueled plot and an expertly drawn cast of characters. I still can't catch my breath."
—Heather Gudenkauf, *New York Times* bestselling author of *The Overnight Guest*

"Hidden history and 21st-century technology collide in a breathtaking thriller."
—*Kirkus Reviews*, starred review

"Genetics and nature-versus-nurture take the spotlight in Unger's 20th novel… Readers will revel in the search for genealogical justice amid best-kept secrets, while wondering who will live and who will die."
—*Library Journal*, starred review

"Terrifying… Keep the lights on."
—*People*

"Unger is a virtuoso of the psychological thriller."
—*Tampa Bay Times*

"Astonishing."
—*South Florida Sun Sentinel*

"Secrets abound in Lisa Unger's latest thriller, which is so well crafted, you'll be tempted to read all 400 pages in one go."
—*BookPage*

SECLUDED CABIN SLEEPS SIX

LISA UNGER

PARK
ROW
BOOKS

PARK™
ROW
BOOKS™

Recycling programs
for this product may
not exist in your area.

ISBN-13: 978-0-7783-3422-4

Secluded Cabin Sleeps Six

First published in 2022. This edition published in 2023.

Park Row Books
22 Adelaide St. West, 41st Floor
Toronto, Ontario M5H 4E3, Canada
ParkRowBooks.com
BookClubbish.com

Printed in U.S.A.

A writer is nothing without the people who take her words, characters and stories into their hearts.

My twentieth novel is dedicated to the devoted readers, booksellers and librarians who have made possible this writing life.

Some of you have been with me from book one— you know who you are!

Thank you for joining me on this wild, wonderful ride.

PART ONE

origins

Happy families are all alike;
every unhappy family is unhappy in its own way.
—Leo Tolstoy, Anna Karenina

prologue

Christmas Night 2017

The carcass is splayed in the middle of the table. Carved, flesh torn away, eaten, ribs exposed. The turkey, brown and glistening when it was removed from the oven, is now just a pile of bones. Plates are smeared with gravy, wineglasses empty, stained red. A swath of maroon lipstick mars a white cloth napkin. The lights from the towering Christmas tree blink, manic.

The holiday, in all its glittering, wrapped promise, is over.

And there's that moment, which Hannah remembers since childhood. After all the weeks of anticipation, the preparation, meals planned and served, gifts purchased, wrapped, torn open, surprises revealed and enjoyed, the inevitable time comes when it's all done. There are no more presents to give or to get, just the mess to clean up, the dishes to do. When she was little, she always felt this moment, its quiet, its subtle sadness, keenly.

Now that she was older, she knew it for what it was—the flow of life. The calm after the storm where you were meant to re-calibrate, reset before the onset of the next event—good or bad.

"Too much," says her mother, Sophia, pushing her plate away as if *it* were the culprit of this excess. "Too much food."

Sophia is well and truly drunk. Not in a sloppy, word-slur-ring, falling down sort of way. No. Never that.

It's subtle.

A sharpening of her tone. A hardening of her expression. How much has she had? When did she start drinking? Hard to say. She's rambling now, sitting to the left of Hannah's father, Leo, who resides at the head of the Christmas dinner table. Leo smiles indulgently as Sophia goes on.

"That's the problem with this country, isn't it? People don't know when to stop—stop eating, stop buying."

Hannah feels a slight tension creep into her shoulders. It's only a matter of time now before Sophia puts out the first barb, or before a casual comment from someone, probably Leo, will ignite her mother's temper.

Hannah decides to get up and start clearing the plates. Better to keep moving.

"Leave it, sweetie," says her father as he draws a big hand though his still thick, snow-white hair. "Bruce and I will get it. You and Liza did all the work."

Sophia tugs at her sky blue cashmere wrap with ringed fin-gers; the color matches her eyes. "I supervised," chimes in her mom, still light.

Hannah's mother hadn't really wanted to host Christmas, mentioned multiple times in different, subtle ways how much work it would be. So Hannah and her sister-in-law, Liza, did all the shopping, all the early prep work, and all the cooking today to make it easier on Sophia. Now, the meal a success, her mother wants some of the credit.

"We couldn't have done it without you, Mom."

Hannah always knows what to say. She's an expert on navigating this terrain. She earns an adoring smile from her mom, blue eyes slightly bloodshot, glistening.

"*Your* recipes, Mrs. M," says Liza.

Actually, they'd used recipes from Dad's side of the family. There was an old bound notebook, full of handwritten recipes for everything from lasagna to tripe, from white clam sauce to eggplant Parmesan, from mashed potatoes to the perfect roasted turkey, to standing rib roast. Recipes Dad said were collected from his Italian mother and his aunts, recipes from the old country and the new, expanded over time, splattered with decades-old stains, pages torn and creased. All of it tied together with a rubber band. It was a long-held family aspiration to enter everything into a document and create a self-published book. But this has never happened, everyone always too busy, and the project forgotten until the holidays rolled around, then forgotten again in the New Year.

"That book," says Liza, still trying. "It's a treasure."

Hannah glances at her dad, who is relaxed at the head of the table, wearing his usual patient half smile, hands folded on his belly. Mom gives Liza a noncommittal hum. Liza clears her throat, casts a glance at Hannah. Her sister-in-law can't win. She should know that.

Liza hasn't been asked to call Hannah's mother "mom," or even to use her first name. Liza has been married to Hannah's brother, Mako, for a year and has still not been welcomed by Sophia, not really. It's all very cordial though. Polite. Until it isn't. Why Sophia is like this, Hannah has no idea. Liza is lovely and kind, a good wife, a dutiful daughter-in-law. Hannah and her mother haven't discussed it.

Hannah's husband, Bruce, puts a comforting hand on her thigh. She glances over at him, his dark eyes, strong jaw, that smile. It calms her; *he* calms her. Together they peer at the video monitor on the table between them. Their nine-month-old daughter, Gigi, sleeps peacefully, a cherub floating on a pink cloud.

"She's a good sleeper," says Hannah's mom, leaning in for a look as she gets up to pour herself another glass of wine. Hannah glances at her dad again, who still wears that pleased but somewhat blank expression. He's a large man, standing over six feet tall. *I have big bones*, he likes to say. His doctor wants him to lose twenty pounds. That's probably not going to happen.

Bruce calls Hannah's father "The Space Cadet," which always annoys Hannah more than it should.

He's not all there. Like, he checks out.

It's true, even though Hannah doesn't want it to be. Her dad is loving, present for her—always has been. But he *does* sort of blank out and drift away when things get hot; even when they don't. He's in his own world a lot of the time—on long walks, or zoned out in front of whatever game, the computer.

But you know, Bruce is quick to add, *if I were married to your mom, I'd check out, too.*

Mako, Hannah's older brother, left the table after he'd finished eating and has noisily fallen asleep on the plush sectional beside the towering Christmas tree, visible in the huge open-plan space. An explosive snore draws all their eyes.

Hannah laughs; she's always been close with her brother, closer than most siblings. They're friends, confidants. They've had each other's backs as long as she can remember. In fact, she can't imagine who she'd be without him.

"He's put on weight," says Sophia.

Hannah glances at her brother. He looks bigger around the middle maybe, but still fit, virile. He doesn't look unhealthy. He works too hard, driven by things Hannah doesn't always understand. He barely sleeps. Eats way too much junk food.

Sophia's comment is directed toward Liza, Mako's wife. As if somehow it's her fault. Liza, a part-time vegan, yoga influencer—whatever that means—is a size zero. Hannah is happy to have dieted and exercised herself to a size twelve after the baby. She's been bigger. All the people on her father's side of the family are bigger, as her mother rarely fails to point out. Sophia is so thin that her collarbone looks like a shelf.

Mako has consumed at least twice as much food as everyone else. While Liza has eaten precisely one paper-thin slice of turkey, a small helping of Brussels sprouts, no bread, no potatoes, and three glasses of water. Not a drop of alcohol. Not that Hannah was paying attention, or trying to mimic Liza's choices and portion sizes. Even if she had, it really wouldn't matter. Hannah would never be a size zero. Which was totally okay.

"He's under a lot of stress," says Liza, her shoulders going a little stiff. "He's a stress eater."

That was true. Hannah knew the feeling—anger, sadness, frustration, worry and all she wanted were carbs.

"The new game is about to launch and he's working twenty-four-seven," Liza continues, glancing over at her husband with a worried frown. "His personal assistant quit without notice. And this is his first day off in weeks."

"Did she?" asks Hannah. This is news to Hannah. She wonders what happened there though she can probably guess. She looks down at her plate.

"Yes," says Liza. "Anyway—good riddance. She had very bad energy."

Hannah agrees. The young woman had always been snippy with her on the phone, a bit frowny when Hannah came into the office. She'd been tall and stunning—not beautiful exactly, but exuding a kind of raw sexual energy. *Yeah*, thinks Hannah, *good riddance*. Hannah is going to suggest that her brother hire a male assistant next time.

Mako has also had too much to drink. He's had five bourbons. *Five*. Hannah, if she drank five bourbons, would need to be hospitalized. She decides to rise to clear the plates after all. Her father seemed to have forgotten his offer, but Bruce and Liza rise as well to help.

"Maybe if he had a home-cooked meal every now and then,

he wouldn't eat so much junk," says Sophia, an edge to her voice.

There it was. The opening shot. Hannah realized that she was literally holding her breath. She forced herself to release it.

But Liza just offered a polite smile. She was, in many ways, a lot like Hannah's dad. Even. Slow to anger. Mako, and even Hannah on a bad night, might engage with Sophia, leading to an all-out battle. Which was exactly what Mom wanted; it was sadly the only way she knew how to be intimate. It had taken a couple of years of therapy for Hannah to come to that particular realization.

But Liza just deflected.

"Mako doesn't like my cooking," she says, casting an amused glance at Hannah. Hannah feels a rush of gratitude for her sister-in-law. "He likes Taco Bell. That's his go-to."

"And yours." Hannah nudges Bruce. "You two eat like teenagers when you're working like this."

Sophia seems amused by the three of them and the moment of ignition passes. They all finish the kitchen while Mako snores on, then gather in the living room. Mako stirs to seated, rubbing at his eyes like a kid. "What did I miss?"

"Only everything," says Liza.

He drops an arm around her shoulders and she slides into him, looking up. Pure adoration, that's what Hannah sees. Her brother always inspired that in women. It's not his looks, though that's part of it—a kind of boyish beauty, thick lashes, big, strong arms, wavy dark hair that he's always worn longish. There's something about her brother that makes girls want to take care of him. Liza loves Mako; Hannah sees that clearly.

"What's this now?"

Hannah's dad is behind the tree. This is an old Christmas trick of his. Hiding his presents until the end of the night, after everything else has been opened and you thought there was nothing left. Hannah loves this moment, when she thinks the holiday is over, but then there's one more surprise.

Leo comes to the sectional with a stack of neatly wrapped boxes, starts looking at labels and handing them out.

"From you, Dad?" asks Hannah.

"No," he says, glancing at the tag. "From Santa."

She can't tell if he's kidding or not. She'd thought his surprise gift had been cash this year, a thick red envelope he'd handed to each of them with a warm embrace. *You're such a wonderful mother*, he said to Hannah. *I'm so proud of that and all you've done.*

Her dad was always proud of her, even though she hadn't accomplished nearly what she thought she would have by this point in her life. And now there was Gigi.

When they all have their boxes, Dad included, they rip at the red wrapping.

"Oh," says Hannah, staring at the rainbow helix on the box, the foil-embossed lettering.

"Origins," reads Bruce.

"What *is* this?" asks Sophia, looking at it with disapproval.

"Huh," says Mako. "It's one of those DNA testing kits. Dad, I'm impressed. I wouldn't have thought you'd be into something like this. Too sci-fi."

Dad shakes his head, offers a light chuckle. "Seriously, guys, this *isn't* from me."

"Then who?" asks Liza.

They all look around at each other, offering clueless shrugs. Hannah feels a little tingle of unease. Somebody is not being honest. Otherwise, where did these boxes come from?

"It *has to* be from Mickey," says Mom, holding up her box and pointing it at Hannah's brother. Something is going on between them; they've been glaring at each other like rival gang members all night. "Believe me. I know when my son is up to his tricks."

"*Mako*, Mom," says Mako, whose given name was, in fact, Michael. Mickey all his life until he went off to college, where he decided he needed to shed his childhood self.

Mako. Like the shark.

"Oh *that's* right," Sophia says. "The name *I* gave you wasn't good enough. Like everything else. Never enough."

She drops the box, bends over to pick it up. Hannah keeps her eyes on Mako. An angry flush is working its way up his neck.

"So," says Dad, interrupting Mako's reaction again. "What *is this* exactly?"

Hannah's waiting for it but Mako doesn't blow. Instead, he casts an annoyed look at Mom, then turns to their father.

"It's a kit. There'll be some kind of saliva collection vial. You register online, then send it in to this company. And it will give you any number of different reports about yourself—health, ancestry, genetic predispositions, etc. It might even connect you with long-lost relatives."

"Huh," says her dad, inspecting the box. He seems vaguely interested, but wary. Hannah's guessing it did not come from him. "*That is* a little sci-fi."

Sophia blazes a hard stare at Mako, her expression unreadable even to Hannah who knows all her mother's many moods. "At this age, I assure you I know as much about my family as I care to. Thanks for the gift, *Mickey*. But I'm not interested."

She rises unsteadily. Hannah stands to keep her from toppling over.

"I'm fine," Sophia snaps, grabbing her arm away.

Hannah sits and Bruce takes her hand, gives her an apologetic look. *Your family. Wow. Were you switched at birth?* That's what he said the first time she brought him home.

"It's not from me," Mako says.

"Whatever you say, son," says Sophia. "I'm turning in. Merry Christmas to all and to all a good night."

"It's *not* from me," Mako says again, this time looking at Hannah. "Did you guys do this?"

"It's not from us," says Hannah, with a brisk shake of her head.

Everyone looks at Liza, who raises her palms. "Not me. I would hesitate to share my personal data with a corporation like that. Who knows what they'll use it for? And you guys should think twice about it, too. When did everybody just decide to give their privacy away?"

"Okay," says Mako impatiently. "Then *who* is it from? Where did these boxes come from?"

Hannah looks at the gift. The tag has been printed from a label maker, no handwriting to inspect.

To: Hannah.

From: Santa.

No clue from the paper, a glossy red foil. She'd seen rolls and rolls of it at Target.

"Dad, did these come in the mail? Or did someone drop these off?"

Since his retirement, her dad was in charge of the mail— going to the mailbox, bringing in packages. He also did the grocery shopping now, took out the garbage, ran all errands. The hunter-gather.

He lifts his palms. "No, they were not delivered by mail. Someone brought them in and hid them behind the tree. They weren't there yesterday."

"Huh," says Hannah. "Some Christmas intrigue."

She was trying to keep it light. But it *was* odd wasn't it? She didn't think her brother was lying. She knew *they* hadn't brought the gifts. So did someone else have access to the house? Had someone snuck in? That was silly. The only one who broke into your house and *left* gifts was Santa.

"Doesn't anyone else find this strange?" asks Hannah.

"Someone's having fun," says Bruce, stacking his and Hannah's together, putting it on their pile of presents.

Mako frowns another moment, then gets up and pours himself a sixth bourbon from the wet bar. If Liza is concerned about Mako's drinking, it doesn't show. She looks at her box.

"Sorry, I'm not sure who left this or why. And I don't want to be rude. But this whole thing is a little creepy. Thanks, but I'm putting mine right in the trash," she says.

Then she rises and does just that. Hannah hears the garbage open and close in the kitchen. Then Liza returns to the couch. Hannah tries to catch her eyes, but Liza is looking at Mako with a slight frown.

"Good idea," says Hannah.

She searches for something more to say, a way to connect with Liza. But there's nothing. They are friendly, but not friends—though Liza is always unfailingly polite and warm. There's something between them, a barrier which Hannah can't seem to break through. Hannah suspects that Liza keeps her guard up because of Sophia. Hannah vows to talk to her mom about being less brittle, more welcoming. Sophia has her issues, but she's not always awful. Sometimes she's warm and funny. Maybe she feels threatened by Liza, though Hannah can't imagine why.

Hannah scans the room again, feels that deflation, that current of sadness that always seems to undercut the holiday, that awareness that nothing that glitters can stay. Darkness must always come. She tries not to think about the gifts, who gave them, why. Someone in this room, of course. But why play this game?

She gives her brother another glance, but he is blank. Her gaze drifts to the locked front door, to the windows that only reveal darkness. Strange.

Hannah gets up to gather the remainder of the mess while Liza and Mako collect their things. Hannah and Bruce are staying. Liza and Mako never spend the night; which Hannah gets. Mom doesn't make it comfortable. Even Bruce would prefer not to stay. But they do. And Gigi is sound asleep in the bassinet in the spacious, beautifully appointed guest suite.

This is what they've got. Except for his mom, Bruce doesn't have much family. Any family, really. So Hannah's will be everything to Gigi. It's not perfect.

What family is ever perfect?

In the driveway, Mako pulls Hannah into a big hug.

"But did you bring those gifts?" she asks quietly.

"Why would I do that?"

"Right," she says. Why would he?

"Well, don't let mom get to you," Hannah whispers, holding on to him.

"You're right. She is who she is."

"That's true of all of us, isn't it? No one's perfect."

He puts a hand on her cheek. "Except for you."

She puts her hand to his. She's lucky to have a brother like Mako.

"We still good for that long weekend this summer?" he says, moving away. "I booked the house already."

Why he was *so* into this idea, she did not know. He'd brought it up multiple times—his birthday present to Hannah, a bonus to Bruce for all his hard work. He was like this, got an idea in his head and wouldn't let it go. There was something else, too, some other reason. But Hannah didn't know what.

When the time came, though, the chances of him canceling were high; or Bruce may or may not be able to get away. Grown-ups only, Mako had insisted. So Hannah and Bruce would have to make arrangements for Gigi—when they hadn't even left her for an evening yet. She wasn't sure she would be ready for that.

But her brother kept talking about a stunning house deep in the woods of Georgia, a kind of self-styled wellness retreat— hiking, yoga, massage. He had a way of painting a picture—an idyllic weekend in nature, a fireplace, her and Bruce reconnecting with their couplehood, maybe an opportunity to grow closer to Liza. *We'll invite Cricket*—Hannah's best friend, who was more like part of the family.

Hannah had agreed and put the weekend in the calendar— six months from now. A lifetime. Anything could happen between now and then. Truly, there was almost zero chance they'd pull it off.

"Sure," she says, looking back at Bruce, who is looking at

his phone, frowning. Hannah feels a familiar jingle of unease. "Of course."

"Don't let this guy talk you out of it," he says, throwing a glance at Bruce, who looks up and shrugs amiably, frown dropping.

"We're in," he says, and Mako gives him a satisfied nod.

"It's isolated but there's Wi-Fi," Mako goes on. "We can check in to work if we have to. You can keep your eye on that baby monitor."

"I *could* bring Gigi," she said.

"But then it's not a vacation for you and Bruce, right?"

That was true. But his statement annoys her. Once you have a baby, you see it. The world is divided. There were people with kids. And then there were people without kids. Parents remembered what it was like before. But people before parenthood had no idea what it was like afterward. It was an abyss between Hannah and Mako, would be until he had kids of his own and maybe even then.

Hannah glances at Liza who stands by the car watching them impassively. Hannah can't imagine the tiny woman pregnant, mothering. Which was a silly thing to think—judgmental and not nice. Hannah has more of Sophia in her sometimes than she cares to admit.

"Where did you hear about the house?" asks Hannah. He wasn't normally a vacation rental type.

"I'll send you the link. It's—amazing."

Of course it would be. He wouldn't be gunning for some shack in the middle of nowhere. That wasn't how Mako rolled. Go big or go home. That was all.

Obviously, Liza is driving. Hannah moves over to her and Liza offers a quick, bony hug,

"Thanks for everything today," Liza says.

"I really couldn't have done it without *you*," Hannah says. And Liza smiles, sweet, warm. Hannah decides that she is going to work on getting closer to Liza this year.

Liza climbs into the driver's seat of the new Tesla.

"Take care of yourself," Hannah says to Mako, moving away from the car. "Don't work too hard."

He laughs, runs a hand through his hair, looks at Bruce who stands beside her. "I'll try not to."

Bruce has joined them at the car. Mako claps Bruce hard on the shoulder.

"Anyway, things are a lot less stressful now that Bruce has saved my ass."

She's not sure what that means. Some glitch in the game that Bruce found and fixed. But sometimes the two of them are speaking a language she can't understand. She knows they'll both be working around the clock until it launches. Such is the nature of tech.

As the car glides away, silent and smooth as a shark, Bruce stands behind her, and they wave until the car is out of sight. The air is cool but balmy, palm fronds whispering. Somewhere a halyard clangs, a neighbor's boat rocking in one of the docks behind the houses. Christmas in Florida.

Bruce stares after the car a moment, something strange on his face.

"What?" Hannah asks.

He shakes his head, seems to snap back from his thoughts. "Nothing. All good."

Later, her parents and Gigi sound asleep, Bruce in front of his laptop "just checking in on a few things," Hannah takes a moment to sit in front of the tree. Its lights glimmer and shine. She stares at the ornaments—some handmade by her and her brother from their childhood, collected from family vacations, tiny framed pictures of Gigi—gifts Hannah made for her parents this year. It's peaceful. Now that she's older, she gets it. The quiet space after the storm can be a blessing.

Hannah picks up the Origins box. It probably *was* Mako. Just like him to give a gift that causes trouble. He's always been a mischief maker. And really—who else?

"Was it you?" she asks her husband who sits at the kitchen island, face glowing blue in the light of the screen. He glances over at her blankly.

"Huh?"

She reaches for the box, holds it up to him. "Was it you?"

"*Me?* No, no, no. I say let sleeping dogs lie."

"What does that mean?"

"Just—you know." He lifts his shoulders, shoots her an innocent look. "Don't go looking for trouble?"

There's something funny about the way he says it. She's about to press.

"Give me a minute okay? I'm almost done here."

When she gets up to turn in, Bruce still working, she takes a final bit of wrapping to the garbage. She digs in, looking for the box Liza threw away. It's a waste to toss it, right? It's expensive. Maybe if it was Mako's gift, he can send it back. But she doesn't find it.

The Origins box is gone.

She puzzles over this a moment, then she walks over to the front door. It's locked. Bruce has set the alarm. She knows there's a motion detector in the doorbell, that sets off a chime on her father's phone when someone arrives there. There's no way those gifts were delivered without his knowledge. There's no way someone could get in now, while they were all sleeping.

They are safe. She'd always been concerned about that. Captain Safety was her family nickname growing up. Since motherhood, that quality (flaw?) has edged toward paranoia. She peers out onto the street and sees a black BMW parked there. There are other cars lining the street as well, people visiting for the holiday. The houses on the street are all decorated wildly for the holiday—blow-up Santas and lights in the palm trees, glittering reindeer on lawns. She watches for a moment. All is calm. All is bright.

Hannah moves over to her husband, and slips her arms around him, puts her lips to his neck. He shuts the laptop lid—a little too suddenly? She pretends not to notice. He spins around on the stool and she moves into him. He puts a hand to her cheek, leans to press his mouth to hers.

"Really?" he whispers, as her hands start to work at the buttons on his pants. "I thought you didn't like to—you know—in your parents' house."

She doesn't care tonight. Something about her brother, the Origins test, the wine she's had, Liza, her mother, the tension of the holiday, of family. The sadness of a joyful moment passed. She wants to push that away. She wants to be with the person she chose in this life, her husband. She wants to *show* him what he means to her.

She drops to her knees.

"Hannah," he says, voice just a moan. He glances uneasily in the direction of their bedroom. "Your parents."

She gives him a wicked smile before she takes him in her mouth; he groans, grips the bar.

Discussion closed.

In her family, Hannah is always the good girl, the responsible one, the fixer, the mediator.

Sometimes, though, it feels so nice to be bad.

1

HANNAH

June 2018

The night-light stars spun on the ceiling, and Hannah lay on the plush carpet watching them glimmer and turn. She listened to Gigi's measured breathing. The baby—almost a toddler at fifteen months—had just, *just* drifted off in her crib.

Hannah stayed still though her arm was falling asleep, tingling unpleasantly beneath her head. One wrong move and those angelic eyelids would pop open and Hannah would be on the floor for another half hour at least.

She breathed. Gigi breathed.

Outside the door, she could hear Bruce's low, rumbling voice from his home office down the hall. He was on the phone, working too late as usual. Hannah pricked her hearing in his direction. Did his tone sound slightly off? Did he sound angry? Or was there something a little desperate, pleading there?

But then it was quiet again. After a few minutes, she heard

him walk outside, the back door chiming as it did whenever it was opened.

She felt an unease that was becoming too common.

He had been coming home late. Twice she'd awoken to find him gone from bed, at his desk. Laptop lid gently closed as she entered his office. There had been phone calls that he'd taken, leaving the table, or the living room.

Hannah wasn't the jealous type. And her husband was loving and devoted, a wonderful father.

But.

She heard him come back inside and her attention returned to her lightly sleeping daughter, who turned over onto her side.

Hannah and Gigi had fallen into one of those bad nighttime rituals that pediatricians and parenting books were always going on about. It had started with a storm last month, a violent shaking thunder and lightning show that rocked the house. Bruce had been out of town and Gigi had been wailing.

Hannah stayed on the floor until the storm passed, and the baby had finally drifted off, too.

Stay, Mommy, Gigi begged the next night.

Of course then it was the next night, and the one after. It was a habit now, one that would have to be broken. Every parent knew the epic amount of energy it took to change a bad habit. Energy that Hannah did not have. Easier sometimes to just do the thing.

And anyway—who *cared*?

Was it the worst thing in the world to lie on the ground while your tiny daughter pinned you with her gaze, eyelids fluttering, closing, then opening to make sure you were still there? Who else ever loved you that much? And how long before her daughter didn't even want Hannah in the room anymore? The space, dim, with glittering stars and the face of her baby, and the shelves of toys and books, and walls she and Bruce had painted themselves. It was, truly, one of her favorite places in the world.

Her husband's voice again, this time louder. His tone *was* off. Not his usual professional cadence.

She was ashamed to admit that recently, when he got in the shower, she'd checked his work phone. He had two phones—the life phone as they called it, which was always lying around not password protected, an open book. And his work phone; it was a known but unspoken thing that she should not look at it. He had clients—military, government, security contractors—whose business was classified. And never before had she even thought to breach that boundary.

He had a habit of deleting all his texts immediately, a fan of the whole inbox zero thing. So there was nothing there. But in the chain of mostly unfamiliar but some known contacts—the office, Mako, Bruce's virtual assistant—in his recent calls, there had been three from someone named only UNKNOWN. No number. No way to call back. She almost asked him about it, prepared to admit that she'd been snooping. But she knew what he'd say. What he always said: "Difficult client."

Many of his clients he couldn't discuss, and it probably *was* that.

But.

Hannah was trying to be *kind to herself*—the way you were supposed to be now, self-care and self-compassion and all of that—but she was not in love with her post-baby body. (In fact, she had not been in love with her *pre-baby* body.) And sometimes she was in her pajamas when Bruce left for work, and still in the *same* pajamas when he came home. The sex was always good—but it was hurried, rushed, lately, prone to interruption from Gigi, both of them overworked in different ways, exhausted, passing out right after.

Maybe there was some hot young thing at one of his clients' offices.

Someone not wearing pajamas.

Someone who had a daily shower.

Her husband—simply put—was a hottie. Broad, tall at six

feet, he towered over her brother. Chiseled jaw and bedroom eyes, which gleamed with intelligence and warmth. He could be a bit brooding, a bit severe maybe. But he was in great shape from running, and always well put together, groomed. He was a catch.

She'd known *that* the night they met. Even though Hannah had been rebounding from an ugly breakup, she knew it right away. Bruce was at one of Mako's epic, pre-Liza blowouts at a hot new Saint Petersburg restaurant he'd invested in. In fact it had been Mako who'd introduced them. "This is my sister, who also happens to be my best friend," said Mako, dropping a protective arm around her. "And Bruce—well, he might just be the smartest guy I know. And the most honest."

He's safe, that's what Hannah remembered thinking when they shook hands, Bruce's grip warm and firm, but not too tight like some men who seemed to view the handshake as a statement piece. She was still reeling from the cheating, border-line verbally abusive man she'd just dumped. He'd been calling all night—leaving messages that alternated between desperate and nasty. Chad. Another friend of her brother's—though not anymore after the way he'd treated Hannah. FOMs—Friends of Mako's, as her best friend, Cricket, liked to call them. All smart, successful leaders in their field, but many of them also entitled assholes. That particular trait seemed to come with power, didn't it?

But this one seemed different. A measured coolness to him, an elegance.

And those eyes. He'd worn an understated watch, analog with a blue face and silver dials. It caught the lights overhead and glinted. She liked it because it wasn't the usual Rolex that most men wore to telegraph their wealth. Bruce, she'd learn later, had a love of watches, precision machines with only one function—to mark the passage of time. A funny passion for a tech guy.

They'd started talking and didn't stop, drifting from the

party and out to the deck into the cool night. The bay glittered and across Beach Drive, the small Museum of Fine Arts sat white and glowing.

"You can't be related to Mako," he said after a while.

"No?"

"You're too—real."

She didn't ask him what he meant. She knew. The Mako Show. It was always running.

That night, Hannah had been threaded, manicured, waxed, and coiffed. When she met her husband, all her assets were well managed. She'd been working for Mako—event planning, client schmoozing, booking corporate retreats, researching all the best hotels and restaurants wherever Mako traveled, making reservations. It wasn't what she ever planned to do with her life. But.

Now Bruce's voice carried down the hall again. She listened but still couldn't hear the words.

During last week's brief and mainly unhelpful visit, her mother had gently intimated that Hannah needed a haircut, maybe a manicure. *We do need to continue to take care of ourselves, dear, even with a baby around.*

Sophia had stopped short of offering to watch Gigi so that Hannah might do that. No, Sophia's visits consisted of getting a picture with the baby that she could text to all her friends, handing Gigi back immediately after that. Hannah sensed that her mother wanted to be closer to Gigi, but that she was a little afraid. *She's so tiny,* she'd said more than once. *So fragile.*

Even when the visits were good, and Sophia did some cleaning or cooking, Hannah often felt more insecure, frazzled, and exhausted than ever after she left.

When Bruce went out for a run that night of Sophia's last visit, Hannah tried to get on his laptop and found it password protected. She tried Gigi's birthday, their anniversary. She was afraid to try a third time, knowing she'd activate the lockout feature.

Had it always been password protected? She honestly wasn't sure because she'd never tried to spy on her husband before.

She was becoming one of those women.

Finally, after a hard look in the mirror, Hannah had asked her mother-in-law, Lou, to come last week to watch Gigi for a while. Lou was the exact opposite of Hannah's mother; she literally *demanded* that Hannah sit and put her feet up while Lou made coffee, and did a load of laundry, and played blocks with Gigi. She took pictures of the baby; but not selfies. Lou was not on Facebook. There would be no posts for Hannah to look at annoyed: *Just little Gigi and Grandma today! She's the light of my life!*

Lou happily stayed with Gigi while Hannah got a Brazilian bikini wax that hurt so much she saw stars in front of her eyes. Mani, pedi. Cut, color, and blowout. She bought some new underwear, some elevated lounge wear.

Okay, yeah, she'd needed a little cleanup.

Hannah shifted now, watching Gigi.

Her beloved face: Gigi's eyes were firmly Bruce's—big and innocent; her high, intelligent brow belonged to Bruce as well. Gigi's cupid's bow mouth and button nose, her wide smile and her high cheekbones, were a mirror of Hannah's face. Hannah who favored her father, Leo. Everybody always said that. Hannah had been staring at her daughter a lot over the last couple of weeks, analyzing her features.

She'd been staring at herself as well, wondering about the ungroomed woman she saw in the mirror. Did she really look like her father? She saw a lot of Sophia, even though their coloring was different.

She was lost in thought about all of this when Bruce pushed in at the door softly. Finding her on the floor, he gave an indulgent smile. Then he made the motion of tipping a glass to his lips.

Yes, she thought. That would be nice. She gave him a nod and he moved away into the shadows.

She got herself to all fours, arm aching, and she crawled—yes, not ashamed to admit it—she crawled from the room, only coming to her feet outside the door. She could already taste the cabernet Bruce was probably pouring.

She stood in the dim hallway, waiting, breath held.

Gigi released a little moan, shifted onto her back. One. Two. Three. Silence.

Mission accomplished.

Child asleep.

Hannah released the sigh native to motherhood, only issued when the baby was down for the night, safe in her bed.

A free woman, Hannah padded into the adjacent open-plan living room when the lights were low, and soft music played. Bruce's jazz station. He stood in the kitchen, two glasses waiting, cab decanting.

"Down?" he asked.

She nodded. "Done working for the night?"

He smiled at her, poured the glass. "Knocking off early." It was nearly 9:00.

He poured, then handed her a glass; they strolled to the living room where he flipped on the faux fireplace which was all light and no heat. It was Florida, after all. A real fireplace was a silly feature in a house where the air-conditioning ran ten months out of twelve. Hannah sank into the plush sectional. She wanted to pop on the television and turn off for a while.

"Who were you talking to so late?" she asked lightly. "You sounded angry."

He rolled his eyes. "Difficult client."

She searched his face for signs of deception, but there was nothing—just fatigue.

"Want to talk about it?"

"I'd rather talk about *anything* else, to be honest," he said, putting down his glass on the coffee table.

She put a hand on the back of his neck and rubbed; it was where he held all his tension.

"Do you really think you're going to be able to unplug this weekend?" she asked.

She highly doubted it. Even in Hawaii last year he hadn't been able to fully disconnect from his company, working most mornings while she and infant Gigi played in the kiddie pool. She never complained or gave him a hard time. She knew who he was when she married him.

"I'm going to try," he said, slipping his phone from his pocket and taking a quick glance. "What about you?"

Anxiety bubbled. "It's our first time away from her."

"My mom's good with her." He put a comforting hand on her leg.

"She is," said Hannah. Gigi absolutely adored her Lulu. "And that's the only reason I even considered it."

"The only reason?"

He moved in, took her glass and placed it on the distressed wood. She slid into his heat.

Truthfully, she didn't feel like fooling around, but she made a point not to push him away. They needed the connection, the closeness. His lips on her neck. The strength of his arms. The light scent of his cologne.

Hmm. Maybe she *did* feel like fooling around. And there was that new Brazilian to show off. They'd had the lights out last time. She met his mouth with hers, let the moment, his desire, take her.

Gigi issued a little cry. They both froze, staring at the monitor on the counter. Hannah made a move to get up. Bruce gently held her back. "Give it a moment, see if she settles."

Silence. Outside the distant rumble of thunder, a flash of lightning. Then, the soft hiss of Gigi's sleeping breath. Hannah's shoulders, which had hiked up high, melted.

"I swear she knows when I'm about to get lucky," he said, picking up his glass, giving her a wry grin.

The kid was a cock-blocker, no doubt. Any stirrings of desire dissipated. No wonder Bruce was fooling around with the hot woman from his client's office. He *wasn't*. Of course, he wasn't. She knew her husband. Didn't she?

Hannah grabbed her glass and slid into the crook of his arm, stared at the dancing orange faux flames, took a long swallow. He placed a tender kiss on the top of her head.

"There will be plenty of time and space for us at the cabin," she said, comforting him as well as herself.

"Sure about that?"

"We'll *make* time."

"The agenda your brother sent looks pretty packed. Hiking, zip-lining, yoga, massage, facial."

"He's not the boss of us." Actually, Mako *could* be enthusiastic to the point of overbearing. And it was true, that she did sometimes feel powerless against his will. But he was essentially sweet, most of the time; though he had his moments. He just had a big personality and he wasn't for everyone.

"Technically," said Bruce. He drew his hand through his curls. "He *is* my boss. At the moment anyway."

Bruce was a wizard coder with his own freelance company. Mako owned a growing game software franchise Red World. Her husband had established a niche for himself in the tech industry. He was a fixer. He found bugs, security breaches, errant code that caused glitches eluding even the original developers. He was like that at home, too. Always inspecting, repairing, cleaning up—the running toilet, or the chip on the baseboard, the light out in the shower. She never had to ask him to do any of it. He always saw what was wrong and fixed it.

He's kind of a whisperer, Mako told her. *He lives inside the code; it speaks to him.*

Bruce had worked for Mako a handful of times over Hannah and Bruce's five-year marriage, and had recently saved her brother from a major error right before a big launch. Mako wanted Bruce at Red World full-time; it had come up a couple of times since Christmas. There was even a formal offer, a big one, to be his CTO. But Bruce liked to do his own thing, had built his company, and wasn't looking to sell it and go to work for Mako. Maybe there was a little tension about it. Because Mako usually got what he wanted. But it was a friendly tension. They were friends, had been for years. So, Hannah stayed out of it.

"*You* are the boss," she reminded him.

"Actually, you are," he said, kissing her on the head.

A chirp from Gigi crackled out of the monitor. They looked at each other and laughed. Everyone knew who the boss around here was.

"Anyway," she went on. "The weather is supposed to be bad. A big storm in the Atlantic, supposed to come ashore on Friday. By the time it gets to us up there inland, it will be mostly dissipated. But still, not hiking weather. So, lots of time to laze around, right?"

Bruce picked up his phone and opened the weather app. "Weather looks fine here. Gigi and Lou will be all right."

"Other coast. Looks like it will hit land around St. Simons Island as a tropical storm."

Many miles away from their Sleepy Ridge destination.

Her phone pinged. Mako.

You guys ready? This is going to be epic.

That was Mako's favorite word. Everything was *epic*.

What time are you heading out?

She typed: Bruce's mom gets here at 7. The car is packed. We'll head out then.

A rush of anxiety. Three nights away from Gigi. She quashed it. It was okay. She needed this break. Bruce did. Gigi and Lou had a relationship that should be given space and room, too. It was good for everyone.

So why did she feel sick?

Awesome. Cricket and beau of the moment—what's his name—will get there around the same time. We'll all be there in time for the dinner the private chef is preparing.

Bruce blew out a breath, reading over her shoulder. "A private chef? I thought this was going to be more chill—like grilling out," he said. "Burgers, ribs."

Hannah felt the familiar urge to mediate, tried to call her brother but only got voicemail. Mako almost never picked up. He liked to distill communication to its most efficient form—or so he said. Hannah suspected that he just didn't want to be bothered with the messiness and unpredictability of actual human interaction when he could help it.

Another ping from her phone: Tell Bruce the chef is grilling. I know what a carnivore the big guy is. But you know Liza.

He didn't even acknowledge that Hannah had just tried to call.

Hannah wasn't sure what Mako meant in this context but was he implying that Liza had put up obstacles to a casual cookout? True, she was not a beer from the bottle, paper plates kind of girl. But also, she was mostly vegan, munching on salads or black bean burgers when meat was served. If she were calling the shots, they would not be grilling meat. Hannah suspected this was a Mako thing. *Mako* wanted the private chef. It was showy in a way that appealed to him and made Bruce uncomfortable. The two men could not be more different, really.

Hannah and Bruce exchanged a glance. Family. What were you going to do?

All good, she typed. Thanks again for this.

This whole "private wellness retreat" at the huge, beautifully appointed, and totally remote cabin was all Mako's design, and his treat. It was like him to be expansive this way, showy and generous.

Least I can do after all you guys do for me.

Love you, she wrote. **See you tomorrow.**

Love you both. Can't wait to just chill and connect.

She almost wrote him back right then. Can we find some time to talk? Alone?

But if she did that, he'd hound her until she told him what was on her mind. He was not a patient guy. And she wasn't even sure she *wanted* to talk. She wasn't sure if it was a good idea.

"What's wrong?" Bruce asked, as always reading her expression, her mind.

"Nothing," she said. "Just tired."

It probably *was* nothing.

"We should be paying our own way. It's not like we can't afford it," said Bruce.

"He wants to do this for you, for us. Let him," said Hannah.

Bruce made an assenting grunt. She snuggled into him. The fake fire danced; Gigi breathed.

"And you're going to tell him, right?" said Bruce. She looked at up at him, feeling a little jolt of surprise. Did he know?

"Tell him what?"

He frowned. "About the house?"

They were currently renting and living in Mako's old house. They hadn't been ready to buy their own place when Mako upsized. Bruce and Hannah had moved into the spacious waterfront home, Mako's old bachelor pad—complete with hot tub and outdoor kitchen—just after they got married. But they were ready to buy their own place now, Gigi's home, the place where she would grow up. It was in the same neighborhood, but at the end of the finger island with expansive open water views. Their bid had been accepted and they were under contract. She was uneasy about telling her brother. But why should she be? He'd sell this house and make a fortune.

"Yes," she said. "I'll tell him this weekend."

Bruce looked at her, seemed about to say something, then didn't.

His quietude was one of the things she first loved about him. The way he waited before he spoke, the way he listened when she talked. But he had a way of keeping things in for too long; he ruminated. He'd had a hard childhood—father left him and Lou when Bruce was just a kid. Lou, she knew, had worked two jobs to keep them afloat. And Bruce grew up feeling like he had to be strong, take care of his mom. Hannah thought he never really had a chance to be a kid; Hannah tried to make up for it—big parties for his birthday, an Xbox on the television in the den. He was stoic. Pushing him didn't work; she had to wait for him to open up.

Which he would eventually.

She hoped.

Unless.

"It's going to be great," she said, looking up at his presidential profile—square jaw, ridged nose. He looked so tired. Even in the orange glow, she could see his fatigue.

He needed this getaway. She needed this. *They* needed it.

But there was something.

She chalked up the rising tingle of unease to leaving Gigi for the first time. It was normal, wasn't it? Of course it was. Perfectly normal.

They finished their wine in silence.

2

TRINA

I watch. I am the watcher. From my place in the shadows, I see it all.

Tonight, the humidity is brutal, raising sweat on brow, on the back of my neck. The lights across the street go out one by one, until the house is sleeping.

You all have a long drive tomorrow.

So do I.

I stand beside a towering queen palm, blending in with the night. I've set this thing in motion, a great boulder that I leaned my weight against and now it's tumbling down, ready to crush everything in its path. It has taken time and planning. More than six months. Multiple moving parts.

I sigh, listen to the singing of the frogs, the whisper of wind in palm fronds.

Do you remember the day you first met me? I certainly do. It was one of those perfect Florida mornings when the air is neither hot nor cold, where the sky is a crisp baby blue and the clouds happy white mountains in the air. This dank blanket of humidity that comes in late spring and lingers into late autumn hadn't fallen yet.

The world felt clean.

I felt clean. Electric with purpose.

There was a lot of birdsong that day, if I recall correctly. More than usual, maybe. Yes. I remember thinking that when I woke up just as dawn was breaking. How happy the birds sounded outside my window. A mockingbird trilled, his call an overture of other birdcalls. It felt like a good omen.

That morning I practically leapt out of bed, got in the shower right away, not wanting to be late for the job interview that hadn't been easy to get. I was determined to ace it.

I wanted you to want me as much as I wanted you.

And you did.

As soon as we were alone in that posh office of yours at the very top of one of the few tall buildings in the area, I could see it on your sculpted face. I was just your type.

Your walls were windows; all around us was the city, the glittering bay, the shipping yards, the marina where the giant cruise ships roll in. To the west, off in the distance, I could just see the white sand beaches cut into jewel-green water.

People make fun of Florida, and this area takes a particular hit. Perhaps it lacks Miami's more obvious glitz, luster, and culture. But there's a secret beauty here; something that breathes in morning, and sings at sunset. There's a violence, a wildness. A peace. Florida hides its predators well—beneath the still lake water, in tall grass, under the foamy waves. Foliage blossoms, grows fecund and thick. The stars glitter and the music wafts; drinks flow. You never see it coming, the darkness.

But I did. I saw that darkness in you—beneath your glittering star eyes, your musical smile. Your ebullient charm, booming laugh, and ready smile. That's the best trick of the predator, to glamour his prey so he can get in close. Once he strikes, they don't have a chance.

You enthused over my résumé. My experience, my glowing recommendations. We laughed—at your silly jokes, your self-deprecating comments. I didn't want to be impressed by you, honestly. But I was. Your intelligence, your obvious passion for the work, the local environmental causes your wealth allowed you to support.

"At heart I'm still a Florida kid, tramping around beaches, kayaking through the mangroves. I want that Florida to be here for my kids—clean and wild."

Your earnestness. I didn't expect that.

You showed me around—ushering me from the coders to the testers, from the marketing to publicity departments. The people at their desks were heliotropes and you were the sun, everyone turning a worshipful face to you as you strolled through. By the time we got to the break room—a comfortable space with colorful couches, a generously stocked snack area, Sub-Zero full of beverages, a coffee maker that cost more than a used car, Ping-Pong table, gamer consoles—you had already put a gentle hand on my arm. Just a brush really.

We communicate so much with so little. It was just the slightest breach of professional boundaries. I was sure not to pull away or react with anything but a sweet smile, even though your touch revolted me for a hundred reasons.

The space was expansive with tall ceilings, bright lighting, furniture white, big iMacs gleaming, expensive ergonomic chairs, glass-enclosed conference rooms with screens on the walls. Most of the employees seemed young, not a wrinkle or a gray hair among them. The women were mostly stunners—tall and svelte, or busty, stylish, or quirky. But all shiny hair and the plush skin of youth. Like me. Almost everyone had AirPods in or big Beats making them look like air traffic controllers.

"Family in the area?" you asked.

It was a throwaway question but something that people ask

often, as if maybe you wouldn't come here for any other reason. It's not New York or San Francisco, or Los Angeles, or any of the places people most often go to hustle and make their dreams come true.

"Some."

I didn't go on and you didn't press.

"What do you think?" you asked. And I saw your boyish need for praise, for people to be impressed by what you've shown them.

"It's—amazing," I answered, suitably breathless. I tilted my head up, hoped my eyes were gleaming.

The male gaze. It slides, just glancing over the objects in its field. Rarely seeing what is there, merely confirming what it already believes to be true. It only rests on the thing it desires, only notices what whets the appetite.

You must be so proud, I said, *to have built this.*

I've been lucky, you said. *That's all. I had lots of help.*

This surprised me.

You took me to lunch in the building's cafeteria which was surprisingly upscale—we had sushi rolls and seaweed salad, sitting outside in the fresh air while you talked about Red World, and gaming, and how you're just a geek at heart who got to do the thing he loved the most.

You talked about how after graduating you could have gone anywhere to start your company, but you *wanted to come home.* You made it sound so meaningful, so emotional.

And I could see why women responded to you. I even felt a little tug myself. You're that good. That handsome. Virile but boyish, intelligent but sweet.

"I guess what I'm looking for most in a personal assistant is something I like to call 'The Three I's.'" You used your fingers to make quotations marks. "Intelligence, integrity, and initiative. The person who had this job was smart, but lacked foresight, failed to learn how to be in step with me, or even one step ahead."

You want someone to read your mind, to anticipate your whims, to cover for your shortfalls, to make you look good, to laugh at your jokes. In other words, you want someone to stroke your enormous ego, daily, in ways that you don't even notice.

"I understand," I said. "Engagement is key. You have a huge job; your assistant needs to be like a second brain, sharp and responsive."

It was the right thing to say. Your smile was wide and sincere. "Exactly."

My offer letter came via email later that night with a salary that was a little too high for an assistant job, good benefits, 401K matching, stock options. *We like to make a financial commitment to our employees because we want to earn their loyalty. We want people to stay so that we can grow together.*

How nice.

I happily accepted.

I texted my half brother right after: I'm in.

Was there ever any doubt?

This is the last one.

You've said that before.

I mean it this time.

I did mean it. I have tired of this enterprise. In fact, I'm not even sure I have the energy to see it through. Life, choice, the actions we take—it's so much more complicated than we imagine as younger people. People are layers of light and dark. There are few true villains and justice is a shape-shifter. But here we are. One last time.

That day seems like so long ago.

It wasn't.

Tonight, I watch a while longer from my place across the

street. Then I head back to the dark of my car. I recline a bit, not quite ready to leave.

What is it that they say? That thing about happy and un-happy families? That happiness is all the same, but misery is unique? It makes a kind of sense. When you think about the people you know who love their families and who are in turn loved, cherished, respected, honored—it's a bit dull, isn't it? I mean, there's not much to it. You're born, you're loved, you die. Where's the excitement, the drama? Where are the blow-out fights, the tentative makeups? The estrangements? The seeth-ing bitterness? The dysfunction?

Happy families. Unhappy families.

Actually, it's all pretty dull, isn't it?

What's interesting is the families that *pretend* to be happy, that have a carefully constructed facade, just barely propped up by secrets and lies.

One breath and it all falls down. I can't wait to see yours crumble.

3

HANNAH

Later Bruce slept, the full moon casting the room in silver through the thin drapes. Gigi's breathing was deep and even over the monitor. And Hannah tossed and turned—couldn't get comfortable, couldn't quiet her mind. The unknown caller, her worries about leaving Gigi, the fictional affair she'd concocted for her husband—all of it on spin cycle in her overtired brain. Hannah finally gave up on sleep and took her laptop to the couch.

She clicked on the link to the place where they'd be staying, a cabin called Elegant Overlook. *This secluded cabin sleeps six. Peaceful, luxurious, every detail from the original art to the chef's kitchen has been carefully considered.*

Click. Click. Click. She scrolled through the images. It was stunning—at least in pictures—with three bedrooms, a huge great room, fireplaces, a hot tub, hiking trails from the property, another cabin.

But yesterday, she'd pulled it up on Google Maps and noted with a tiny bit of panic that it was totally isolated. The satellite photos showed a huge house in a clearing, surrounded by acres and acres of trees, one thin, winding road, miles long, leading to the home. No neighbors at all, not another structure in sight—except for the small second cabin. The nearest town was almost twenty miles away.

She had cast about for ratings and reviews, but it wasn't offered on any of the usual vacation rental sites. So there wasn't the comforting catalogue of star ratings, and comments about the good sheets, or complaints about the noisy neighbors, judgments on cleanliness and comfort, proximity to sites and attractions.

It was managed by a company called Luxury Cabin Rentals of Sleepy Ridge. The website was elegant and expensively designed, showing the five cabins it offered, plus one under construction. Elegant Overlook was the grandest among them—of course. There was another smaller one called Peaceful Retreat, which looked like it might have served just as well for half the price. But the pictures of the trails from the Elegant Overlook property, the bubbling hot tub, the roaring fireplace, were enticing. The site also offered a list of possible services: the private chef, an in-house masseuse, private yoga instruction. These offerings had clearly been Mako's—or Liza's—guide to setting up the itinerary.

There were a slew of five star reviews listed on the site.

The perfect getaway!

Elegant and comfortable!

Secluded and peaceful!

But the listings seemed curated. Nothing negative at all. Someone was always negative, right? People these days did nothing but complain, especially online.

She scrolled through the website and clicked on the *About Us* tab. An attractive bearded man with a smiling face and outdoorsy, lumberjack look to him grinned back at her:

Bracken Jameison, owner and operator of Luxury Cabins of Sleepy

Ridge, built all of these cabins with his bare hands, sourcing local materials, and with the help of local craftsman. Every cabin is designed for comfort, luxury, seclusion, and a return to nature as a way to restore and revitalize. He considers each and every person a special VIP guest, and it is an honor to serve and provide the best possible experience at his cabins.

She found herself staring at him, the roundness of his face, the ruddiness of his skin. He seemed like one of those salt of the earth types—nice, honest, friendly. Exactly what you want from a host.

Hannah entered his name into the search bar. But there was very little else about him. No social media profiles, which usually popped up first. Nothing on ConnectIn, which was odd for a businessman. As she continued to scroll, she found a brief article about him and his new cabins in the *Sleepy Ridge Gazette*. It was from a few years ago and hid behind a paywall. All she could see was the headline: Native Son to Restore Old Properties for Vacation Rentals, a Boon for the Revitalization of Sleepy Ridge.

Outside Hannah's glass doors, a great blue heron squawked, loud, annoyed by something. She looked up in time to see it flapping from his perch on the neighbor's boat hull. His long wings and limbs in graceless flight were cast against the silvery gray moonlit sky.

Hannah went back to scrolling through images of the cabin, looking at the palette of green and brown, the towering old growth trees. She could almost smell the crisp, cooler air. It was already blazing hot here. She, her dad, and her brother had camped in the Sleepy Ridge area often when she was younger. Maybe that was it; Mako wanted to reconnect with those peaceful times when it was just the three of them (Sophia was *not* the camping type), the air cool, the green trees, the fire crackling. It *would* be great. Wouldn't it?

Her phone pinged and Hannah knew it could only be one person since it was after 1:00 in the morning. Her longtime best friend and fellow insomniac Cricket.

You up?

Yeah. You okay?

Packing for the big weekend! Can't wait!

Me, too.

She clicked over to Cricket's Instagram, saw a post of her lunch that day—a yummy-looking cobb salad which made Hannah's stomach groan. She thought about snacking but then stopped herself. She was trying not to eat for twelve hours at least between dinner and breakfast.

How's the new guy?

Dare I say it: Dreamy. I'm—gaga. He might be special, Han!

Hannah scrolled through Cricket's feed for a picture of the mysterious new boyfriend. They'd been seeing each other for a while, and Cricket had yet to post anything. Usually she was the queen of oversharing. She was quiet about this one. Maybe that was a good sign.

Can't wait to meet him! xo

Worried about leaving Gigi?

A little.

Don't be. I have a feeling. This is going to be amazing—for all of us. Get some sleep so we can stay up late and party tomorrow night. That hot tub is calling my name!

Mine, too!

See you tomorrow, bestie.

Hannah smiled, imagining Cricket's ebullient laugh, her infectious enthusiasm for food, music, games, gummies, cocktails—anything and everything that augmented fun. Hannah *needed* a good long catch-up with her old friend, and hoped the new guy wasn't clingy, or a dick, or—whatever. But the chances were good. Cricket had legendary bad taste when it came to the men in her life.

Whatever—they'd make the best of it. They always did.

Just on a whim, Hannah entered "Elegant Overlook rental cabin in Sleepy Ridge Georgia reviews" in the search bar.

There was a whole long list of entries that had nothing to do with the place where they were staying—other listings on common vacation rental sites. She scrolled through page one, page two, page three—the way her brother had taught her. *Sometimes the things you want to know are buried deep—fixers and hiders have gotten very good at burying bad press deep beyond where anyone has the attention span to look.*

There on the fourth page of listings, was a personal travel blog: Ben's Vacation Adventures. She clicked on the link. The site looked homespun, not laid out well, poor images, typos, background just a dull gray. The date of the entry was a couple of years ago. A *cob-website*, Bruce would call it. Something someone set up and then forgot.

There was a short entry about one of the smaller cabins, next to a few poor-quality pictures of the interior and exterior.

We stayed here to go hiking. But the host was weird, and the place was—how to put it?—creepy. The host was bent on telling us ghost stories about another property he was building, and it frankly upset my wife. She said she couldn't get comfortable and felt like she was being watched. We left after the first night. He didn't have to refund our money but he did. I thought it was okay; my wife is sensitive to energies. But obviously we won't be going back.

Hannah felt a tingle of unease. Creepy? Felt like they were being watched?

She quickly quashed it. What was she going to do? In a sea

of positive reviews, and the freight train of her brother's desire, call attention to a years-old, poorly written review by a failed travel blogger about another property?

No. She wasn't going to do this.

Hannah, if she was being honest, *had* been looking for reasons to bail on this trip. But it was too late. In a few hours they'd be on their way, and she was going to make the best of it, use it to remind her husband what it was like to be the center of her attention.

She'd make sure, in Mako's words, that it was *epic* for both of them.

She closed her laptop and decided to get some sleep. First though, she looked in on Gigi who slept peacefully in her crib, dim night-light casting the room in a buttery yellow.

As she left Gigi's room, Hannah heard a buzzing.

It was coming from Bruce's office, where the door stood ajar.

His work phone.

She shouldn't; she knew that.

But she opened the door anyway and went inside.

4

LIZA

"My hot spot stopped working."

Mako had been either on his computer or on his phone nearly the entire drive from their house. They'd left before the sun came up and Liza, who loved to drive, had driven pretty much straight through to Sleepy Ridge, a seven-hour stretch.

The call Mako had been on just ended abruptly.

"Hello, hello? Jess, can you hear me? Shit."

Liza found a certain kind of peace behind the wheel, especially on the highway, where she felt at one with the road, the car. Her parents had always enjoyed road trips, had an old Jeep Wrangler. She and her brother saw most of the country bouncing around in the back of that thing. There hadn't been much money, so they'd camped. It had been nothing less than magical—those starry nights in the desert or in the forest, the sounds of nature all around—babbling creeks and hooting owls. She missed that time, when things were quiet. Married to a tech mogul, things were never quiet now—unless she retreated to her yoga studio, which she often did.

"Maybe that's a sign that it's time to stop working for a while," she said gently.

He put a hand on her leg. "I'm sorry," he said. "You drove the whole way listening to me bitch and moan."

She glanced over at him, casting him a quick smile then setting her eyes on the road. "I get it. This is a busy time for you," she said. "But look, we're almost there. And it's so beautiful. You brought us here. Try to enjoy it, okay?"

The trees towered over the isolated and winding road. The host had said that the navigation computer would stop working at a certain point and it had. He'd given her good verbal directions, and her father had taught her to find her way without the help of technology.

She always felt like she had a sense of where she was on the map, how to get where she was headed.

Mako tapped on her phone that was mounted on the dash. "Is this not working?"

"No," she said. "But I know the way."

He gave her a knowing smile. "You're using your magical yogi powers, communing with the universe."

"Not exactly. I talked to the host yesterday."

He gave an easy laugh.

His voice was soft. This was *her* Mako—not the man at the office, not the philanthropist, or even the man-baby he was with his dysfunctional family. Not the Mako of rumor and conjecture. The true man beneath all the other layers—kind, funny, thoughtful, romantic; this Mako was hers alone.

He moved his hand from her leg to the back of her neck. It was warm against her skin; she pressed into him, shot him a grin.

"What would I do without you?" he said, and for a moment he sounded sad. She felt a little flash of something—regret, apprehension. Like any couple, they'd had their issues.

"You'll never have to find out."

He would have to find out, of course. Someday. They'd all have to learn what it meant to lose everything. That was the way of it, though most people could scarcely acknowledge that truth.

But not today. Today, she was going to help her husband to find some serenity. At least for the weekend. She knew things weren't going well at work—that the new game wasn't performing the way they expected, and that there were other things keeping her husband up at night. She just wasn't sure exactly what, or how bad. She'd asked of course, but all she got were the typical Mako answers: "It's all good. Just some bumps in the road. We'll get it all handled."

She tried to stay out of his work, to be his safe place. She could get him to do yoga and to meditate some. But only sometimes. He was a live wire, giving off sparks. It was one of the things she had loved about him first, his raw energy and drive. If she was cool—river water over rocks—he was fire burning bright and hot. They balanced each other.

"Oh, wow," said Mako. "Holy cow."

They were rounding the final bend that Bracken had described and the house came into view over the trees. Finally they were in the circular drive. The pictures had not done the place justice—hardly a cabin. A towering wood and glass design dream, with a wraparound porch, three stories, surrounded by old growth trees—pine, maple, birch—landscaped with fecund azalea bushes bright and hot pink. She could see inside through the big windows the elegant and spacious interior—towering ceilings, leather and wood furniture.

Mako got out of the car as soon as she pulled it to a stop, let out a delighted whoop. This trip. Why was it so important to him? She knew him well enough to know there was always an agenda—either internal or external. He hadn't shared it with her.

She sat a moment, took a deep breath, and let the beauty of the place wash over her.

I am breathing in. I am breathing out.

She felt a twinge of nostalgia for the camping trips with her family—nothing like this of course. Luxury, which was Mako's number one concern for all travel, was not on the menu for her parents, both teachers. Tents and hot dogs cooked over the fire, her dad snoring too loud, and her brother kicking her as he tossed and turned in the neighboring sleeping bag. Her mother's slightly off-key but sweet singing as she made the coffee in the morning. It had been enough. More than enough.

Mako popped the trunk, grabbed some of the bags from the back, and headed up to the porch.

She waited a moment, liked to move slowly and mindfully so that everything didn't rush past. *I am breathing in. I am breathing out.*

Sitting there, watching Mako try to punch in the code on the door, that's when she felt it. A hard pain in her abdomen, followed by a mild nausea.

No.

Then the light around her seemed suddenly too bright, a throb beginning at the base of her neck. There, a little spate of floating white dots.

The IVF. It had brought back the migraines she used to get in college with a vengeance. She closed her eyes, took another deep breath and asked the pain to pass through her. It wouldn't. You couldn't, it seemed, meditate away a migraine. Maybe, she'd found, you could delay it a bit. But eventually it would come for her, fell her like a villain against whom she was utterly powerless. *What are you trying to teach me?* she'd asked the pain last time. *What can I learn from you?*

Be quiet, it had seemed to hiss back. *Just lie here until I'm done with you.*

Mako was cursing at the door, his voice carrying over the quiet. He was the smartest person she had ever known, and yet he had the hardest time with simple things. She sat another moment, settling into her breath. Finally, the pain and nausea passed. No, not *passed*. Receded. It was waiting.

Please. Not this weekend. Not now.

Her phone pinged on the dash. Okay. There was service after all. It was probably Hannah, saying they were on their way, or asking what she could do. Her sister-in-law who still, like all Mako's family, felt distant, not welcoming. Polite. The facsimile of warmth. But maybe it was Liza. Maybe it was *she* who was keeping Hannah at a distance. This weekend. She'd make more of an effort. It was more important now than ever that they grow closer.

But it wasn't Hannah.

It was a text from an unknown number; she felt her whole body stiffen.

You have something that belongs to me.

She stared at the screen. The words seemed to glow with malevolence.

"Liza! The code doesn't work."

Mako was looking at her from the porch like a disappointed little kid. He could run a company with a nearly billion-dollar valuation but he couldn't unlock the door to the vacation rental?

If you think you can run away from this—from me—you're wrong.
I'm right behind you.

Liza glanced out into the thick dark of the trees all around them. She quickly blocked the number and deleted the message. She wrapped her arms around her middle.

No.

What she had belonged to her and her alone.

"Liza!"

She opened the door, lifting the weight of her secrets and regrets, and climbed out of the car to go help her husband.

She'd push away the pain of her looming migraine, and maybe this weekend she'd share the big news with Mako. It was time, wasn't it?

That twinge again, this time more mild, less startling. It was normal. It happened when your body was changing, right? She centered her breathing, made herself solid, drew energy from the earth beneath her feet as she approached the house. The air was cool and the trees whispered. The trees, her father always used to say, they know all the secrets of the human heart. They have borne witness to all our follies, but they don't judge us. They just watch.

She hoped that was true. She hoped that she wouldn't be judged for the things she'd done.

From the trunk, she grabbed her bag of equipment and her yoga mat. She'd have to find some place to set up for her morning livestream yoga class. Then she joined her husband on the porch.

"Look," she said at the door. "It's still blinking. You have to give it a second."

She'd memorized the code, and when the keypad went dark again, she punched it in. The door unlocked easily and swung open. All she smelled was wood and flowers.

"I'm a dick," said Mako, pulling her in. "Sorry."

He kissed her deep and long. She wrapped her arms around him, took in the scent of him, relished the warmth and strength of his embrace. Then, a second later, he was sweeping her off her feet and she was laughing as he carried her over the threshold into the magical weekend they were planning.

5

HENRY

1997

Henry knew his mother was different from the other mothers. He just didn't know exactly what was different about her.

The other women gathered on the sidewalk in front of the school were chatting easily, peals of laughter rising up every so often. They were all pretty at various levels with shiny hair and healthy bodies—not all thin but fit, holding themselves with confidence. They wore jeans and colorful tops, or bright clothes they would wear to the gym after the kids had gone inside. They clutched to-go coffee cups, or water bottles, carried big totes. There was a kind of carefree lightness to them, or so it seemed.

Henry's mom was not like them. She was apart somehow, would not just slide easily into that group with a casual self-introduction and some friendly comment. *I'm Henry's mom. We're new, but we just love it here!*

He was apart, too, just like her.

"Have everything?" his mom, Alice, asked. Her hair was

mousy and pulled back tight at the base of her neck. Her glasses were large. She wore a skirt—a too-big denim thing with buttons down the middle, a cardigan though it was warm, a big leather satchel slung across her body. All wrong.

"Homework? Lunch?" she said when he didn't answer.

He nodded, feeling a little guilty because he wanted her to leave.

"Okay, then," she said with a dip of her chin. "Be a good, quiet boy."

He gave her another nod.

The other kids ran wild on the playground behind him. He, like her, would not just slide easily into the group. He was invisible, more or less, they both were. Somehow gray ghosts in the wildly colorful, brightly sunny, and warm going on hot Florida school day morning. Already there were waves of heat off the asphalt, the sun a burning ball in the sky. He didn't mind the heat, had inherited a dread of the cold from his mother.

Quiet. That was the most important thing to Alice. She startled easily, looked around them always, like someone might be following, watching. But no one ever was.

"What are you so afraid of?" he'd asked her once.

She'd looked at him, the way she did sometimes. Blankly at first, then thoughtful. "The world, Henry. I'm afraid of the whole world."

"Why?"

"Because it's full of monsters. I have to keep us safe."

What kind of monsters, he wondered. But he didn't ask. He didn't really want to know.

"Henry," she said, snapping him back.

"Yes," he said. "I will be. Good and quiet."

"Okay."

She seemed to want to say more, like *I love you* or *you're my special guy*. But she must have intuited that he didn't want that, pressed her mouth into a tight line. It was okay at night when she was tucking him in. But not here, not at school when the other kids were off and playing, moms forgotten for the day. He was aware of a desperation to be free of her—just for a while. He edged toward the school.

She moved away, too, getting it. "See you at three?"

"Okay."

She turned quickly and walked away.

In the group of moms she passed, one of the women raised a tentative hand in greeting. But Alice didn't seem to notice, kept her brisk pace. The woman, a green-eyed redhead with a full face and nice smile, looked a little embarrassed.

"She didn't see me," he heard her say.

"Shy, maybe?" said the slim brunette.

Not unkind or anything. When Henry looked after her, she was gone. Though he'd been eager for her to leave, he felt a brief, familiar flutter of panic. It was a complicated feeling. He desperately wanted her to go, and when she did he was afraid, always afraid that she might not come back.

He pushed the fear down, the way he'd learned to. Then he turned and walked purposely toward the playground where the other boys tore around with abandon. The girls stood in clutches, like the moms, chatting, giggling. One girl seemed to prefer the company of boys, playing soccer over on the far end. She was fast, agile, tough. He watched her for a while, her blond hair blazing, skin flushed.

There was no heaviness to them. They were not watchful, any of them. Not mindful, like him. It didn't seem that anyone had ever told them to be quiet. He marveled at this for a moment, standing by the fence.

When the bell rang, there was a great jostling rush to get inside and he was pushed along in the current of bodies. He was new here. The new kid—again. Not his first day, which was always the worst. But the first week.

He didn't fit. He knew that. His hair was wrong. His clothes were off. The boys wore Levi's and Chuck Taylors, polos, and tees. Not khakis, and pressed plaid shirts, stiff off-brand sneakers that his mom got for him. If he was going to "fit," he'd need to wear what the other kids were wearing. And even then he'd still be apart. He knew that. But less so.

What saved him from being bullied like some boys who didn't fit was his size and his natural athleticism. He could catch, throw, and run. He was strong. He could scale the rope in seconds, beat most of the others in a sprint. Gym was a proving ground where he'd already earned at least the respect of the other boys. He knew how it went. He was in eighth grade. This was his fourth—or was it his fifth?—school.

Math was first period and he took the seat he'd been assigned by the window, just behind the pretty girl who liked to hang out with the boys. Math he understood. There was a calming simplicity to it, a comfort in following clearly stated rules and getting things right. Numbers were the opposite of people. People were mysterious.

The boy beside him gave him a nod, which he returned.

The teacher stood up at the board. He couldn't help but notice her body, the way her blouse clung to her breasts, the shape of her calves beneath the hem of her skirt. The boy next to him gave him a knowing look, and Henry felt the heat come up to his cheeks. He looked down at his notebook and copied what she was writing on the board.

After a while, he looked out the window. He was surprised and embarrassed to see Alice standing across the street. She had both her hands around a coffee cup, leaning against the side of the building, nearly hidden in the shadows.

She was watching.

6

HANNAH

June 2018

She glanced over at her husband, who was staring at the road, hands at ten and two. He drove the way he did everything else—well, carefully, with precision. The space between them was charged; they'd had words before Lou arrived, and after they'd gotten into the car. Not the way she wanted to start off this vacation. It was her fault. She needed to apologize. But.

"I—" she started, touching her finger to the empty coffee cup in the center console. But the words died in her throat.

He drew and released a breath, shifted in his seat.

"I get it," he said, shooting her an apologetic glance.

"No," she said. "I mean. It was wrong. Really wrong. I'm sorry."

Last night while Bruce had been sleeping, after she'd checked on Gigi and heard his work phone buzzing in his office, she'd done something shameful. The pull of that buzzing phone was magnetic. She knew the window revealing at least part of the message would stay up on the home screen for a few minutes, so she quickly, without really even thinking, went into Bruce's office, sat at his desk and took the phone from the drawer.

There was a message from someone entered into his contacts as Angel: *R-61818200. If all goes as planned.*

A password, a serial number, some kind of code? She felt her face flush. Who was Angel? It didn't sound like a client name, and it wasn't one she'd heard him mention. But obviously, it was work related? Right? It's not like she stumbled on some sexting, or plans to meet. Why did she feel sick? She felt sick because she was spying on her husband.

"Hannah."

She had practically flown out of his chair and gone through the window. Her husband stood bare-chested in sweatpants, filling the doorway.

"*What* are you doing?" he asked mildly, almost amused.

She sat a moment, considered lying. "I, uh, heard your phone. And—"

"And."

"And—you've been acting so strangely. I—"

She couldn't read his expression, whether it was anger or disappointment. No there was something else there—a kind of careful stillness.

"Who's Angel?" she asked. "And please don't say a difficult client."

His brow knitted. "We can talk about this. But can you put my phone back in the drawer and leave my office, please?"

So calm, so level. She felt like a schoolgirl caught smoking out by the dumpsters. Her face burned and her heart was in her throat.

"Who is Angel?" she asked, still clutching the phone.

"Hannah. I can't tell you that, okay? You don't want me to say it's a client. And I can't tell you who it is or what I am doing for them. I'm sorry."

She put the phone back in the drawer and closed it. He moved aside to let her exit. She brushed past him and went to sit out by the pool with a glass of wine, her mind spinning and turning, creating scenarios, possibilities, imagining all the worst things she could think of. Eventually, having pulled on a T-shirt, he joined her.

"I thought we trusted each other," he said when he pulled up a chair.

The water of the Intracoastal glittered, silver on black. Across the canal there were other houses, an eclectic blend like all Florida waterfront neighbors of small ranch homes, big new McMansions, small condo buildings, bigger, newer ones dwarfing the older ones, stealing views.

"We do," she said. "But—something is not right with you."

There. She said it. That was the truth—whatever the reason. She knew her husband and that was how she felt. She wasn't some insecure, paranoid wife.

"Angel is a very difficult client. I cannot discuss it. I'm sorry. I wish I could. I'm just going to have to ask you to believe in me."

What if she told Cricket about this conversation? Her mother? No woman would accept that as an answer, right? Months from now if she found out he actually had been sleeping with someone else, she'd look back and think: *How could you have believed him?*

But he hadn't denied anything. Hadn't asked her to believe him. He asked her to believe *in him.* That was different. She looked at him; his face was earnest, dark eyes holding hers. Fine lines had started a debut around his mouth, his brow. He twisted his wedding band.

"Okay," she'd said.

He'd reached for her hand but she got up and walked away from him, went inside.

"Hannah," she'd heard him say as she slid the door closed.

In the morning—really just a few hours later—they'd bickered about what to bring. She was overpacked; he wanted to travel light. She'd picked up the wrong toothpaste. He hadn't gassed up the car on the way home last night and they'd have to stop. Gigi watched them from her high chair, confused, maybe picking up on their strained tone. She got fussy, started flinging oatmeal.

Lou arrived and they put on the happy family act. Hannah tried to make a quick exit, after kissing Lou and her baby. She tried not to cling, but Gigi got weepy as they moved toward the door.

Mamama. No syllables on earth could tug at her heart like those. Hannah almost canceled the whole thing then and there.

But Lou soothed and distracted like a pro. "Ooh! Gigi, what's this?"

When Lou and Gigi were happily engaged on the floor with Gigi's toys, Hannah and Bruce left quietly, got in the car, and drove off. As they pulled off their street, Hannah cried quietly in the passenger seat.

"It's okay," Bruce said. "Everything will be okay."

Now, miles between them and their daughter and last night, Hannah felt embarrassed.

"I'm truly sorry for looking at your phone, for sneaking into your office while you were sleeping. It was—horrible of me."

"I promise you," he said, reaching for her hand, looking over at her. This time she took it and squeezed. "There is no one in this world for me but you, Hannah. You and Gigi— you're *everything.*"

She felt the words move like electricity through her skin. Your body knew the truth, didn't it?

"I know," she said. "I know."

"I'll try to be more open with you when I can, okay?"

She nodded. But as she'd lain awake last night she'd decided that if they didn't have trust, they didn't have a marriage. She'd have to accept that he was faithful and good, until he was walking out the door with another woman. She wasn't going to be a snooping, accusing, and anxious wife. She'd never been that in her life. She wouldn't let baby brain, new mom anxiety, what-ever, turn her into a person she didn't want to be.

She glanced down at her phone.

"You're not still watching them," said Bruce, eyes back on the road, hands back on the wheel.

They'd passed the last town what seemed like hours ago and they were on some winding back road, trees all around. She noted the beauty, the peaceful silence of it. But barely. She only had one bar on her phone. Her connection was wavering. The video feed was glitchy and slow.

"They're having lunch. Gigi loves it when Lou cuts her cheese sandwich into little squares like that."

She watched guiltily on the security camera, Gigi in her chair at the table happily eating her sandwich, Lou slicing an apple at the counter. Lou knew about the cameras, of course—one in the great room, one in Gigi's room, one monitoring the outside front and another from the back. She probably didn't know that Hannah would be tuning into it obsessively over the long drive.

"Hannah," said Bruce with a patient smile.

She envied his calm, his ease. In all her years with him, she'd only seen him truly angry twice and never with her. For her, and for Gigi, he seemed to have endless patience with all their isms and quirks. Obviously, even with his wife snoop-ing in his office.

"You're a good mom, the best mom," he said.

How pathetic that she needed to hear that.

"Good moms don't leave their babies," she countered.

Bruce gave her a light eye roll. "In the care of a loving, com-petent grandparent? Yes, they do. All the time."

"Right. They do. Of course they do."

Reluctantly, Hannah clicked off the camera, stowed the phone in the door side pocket. She looked out the window. Trees towered, creating a canopy over the road, blocking the sun so totally that the headlights had flipped on.

"Wow," she said. "Middle of nowhere, huh?"

"Yeah," said Bruce. "It's nice. Except, I'm not sure we have a signal anymore."

He glanced at his phone, which was mounted on the dash with the maps app running. They were just a blue dot in a sea of green.

She looked at her own phone. No service now. She'd had it just moments ago.

"I think we're officially off the grid," he said.

She pushed back a little wave of panic. Mako *had sworn* there would be Wi-Fi at the house. He knew she didn't love leaving Gigi and wouldn't be comfortable out of contact with Lou. Mako himself would have to work some; no way he could—or would—go all weekend being disconnected. He wouldn't promise that just to lure her out there, just to get his way—this fantasy of an Instagram-able friends and family weekend for which he'd pushed so hard. Would he?

She forced herself to relax, to be present.

The road wound, and Bruce followed it. She rolled down the window to be greeted by a fresh-smelling coolness. Something in her loosened and relaxed. She inhaled deeply, looking into the spaces between the trees. She remembered how she liked the solitude and calm she found in nature, so different from their busy, chattering, town life. How she could hear herself think when things went quiet. She liked the sound of her own inner voice.

Bruce was calm; he always seemed to know the way to places. Even places that they had never been. They called it BPS, Bruce Positioning System. She took her husband's hand, leaned in to kiss him on the cheek. He was solid. The rock in her life.

"It's all fine," he said. "Liza said we might lose service, texted the directions. We're good."

And sure enough, after a while they saw a glow up ahead.

When they made the final turn, a huge home hulked at the end of the drive, the sky a vibrant blue punching into the deep green black of the trees behind it.

Mako had called it a "cabin." The pictures she'd seen on-line hadn't done it justice. Maybe it was a cabin—in that it was constructed from wood. But the photos on the site had made it seem woodsy, cozy.

"Wow," she said.

This was an *Architectural Digest* dream, expansive with tower-ing windows and vaulted roof. There was a huge wraparound porch, another big balcony on the level above, both furnished with plush seating. Elegant landscaping cast shadows on the circular drive as Bruce brought the car to a stop. Through the double-height glass front doors, she could see inside to the beau-tifully appointed living space. Was that a bear head mounted over the mantel, though?

"Wow," Bruce echoed. "Leave it to Mako."

Now *he* seemed tense. His shoulders were slightly hiked. Something about her brother and his ways. She knew that much. She put her hand on his shoulder and felt him relax be-neath her palm.

"Hannah." Bruce turned to her. And on his face, there was an expression she hadn't seen before. Something in her clenched. All her doubts and worries clamored for attention again.

"I—"

I'm having an affair.

I need a break.

I hate your family.

But then Mako was bursting out the front door, Liza behind him waving. Hannah felt an irresistible pull to them, started moving to get out, wanting space from whatever dark thing Bruce was going to reveal.

"What's wrong?" she whispered when he put his hand on her arm.

But that dark expression was gone. And it was just Bruce again, a half smile blooming on his lips. Lips she intended to kiss a lot this weekend. Because that's what they needed—more kissing, less talking, less worrying.

"Nothing," he said. "I'm just sorry—for making you worry. I'm sorry that I can't always tell you everything."

"It's okay," she said, and meant it. "I trust you."

"Can you believe this place?" Mako boomed, opening her door and offering a hand to pull her into his embrace. "What did I tell you?"

"It's amazing," she said, feeling his strength, his solidity. Her brother.

She looked around at deep evergreen contrasting the brightness of the cerulean sky, the stunning view of the purple mountains behind the house. The air was clean, filling her lungs. Suddenly, she felt a million miles away from their mundane day-to-day, from their problems, her worries.

If Gigi were with them, she could see herself staying in this peaceful place forever.

7

BRACKEN

Bracken took pleasure in sizing them up. He was good at that. Observing body language, and choice of clothing brands, tone of voice, types of cars. Apple watch? Fitbit? Dyed hair? How much makeup? From his place in the trees, he'd watched the Tesla drift up. Sleek and black, quiet but powerful like a shark. On the phone, the wife Liza had referred to her husband as Mako. *Like the shark*, she'd said. But his credit card said Michael. Telling.

They were early.

Bracken had been hiking the trails behind the house, making sure they were clear in case the guests decided to explore. His truck was parked a ways down the road at the trailhead. He stood back out of sight.

The man in the passenger side of the car got out first, looked around and let out a cry of delight. Tall, broad, wearing piped athletic pants, blue T-shirt, light gray hoodie and expensive running shoes—Nikes that Bracken happened to know cost over three hundred dollars since he himself had recently been shopping for running shoes. The guest had a thick head of inky black hair, pulled back in a loose ponytail, was handsome in a boyish way.

"Wow!" he said, voice booming. "Look at this place. It's AH-mazing."

Bracken felt a rush of pride. It *was* amazing. The pristine land, the house he'd built himself.

The slight woman in the driver's seat stayed behind a moment. She wore a tight ponytail, little or no makeup, hair a natural reddish brown as far as he could tell from a distance. He'd liked her right away when they'd talked yesterday. Her energy was quiet.

Her husband's energy not quiet.

"This place is fantastic," the man said again. "What do you think, babe?"

His voice bounced off the air and the trees. A big voice for the big man.

Babe. Bracken really hated that word for some reason. It was so—common. Anyone could see that the woman was anything but. Bracken definitely wouldn't call her *babe.* Maybe *love.* Maybe *darlin.*

But she was looking at her phone, her expression dark. People could not put those damn devices away. No matter how much agitation they caused. And she was supposedly a yoga teacher.

His guest looked around, up at the sky, toward the trees where Bracken stood hidden in the shadows. He should just walk out and introduce himself, but he didn't. He heard the other man draw in and release a long, slow breath. There was something on his face that Bracken didn't expect. A deep skein of worry. Not the arrogant blankness he'd expected. And something else. Was it fear? He seemed to inspect the trees, the road that led to the house. What was he looking for?

The trunk of the car opened as he approached it, revealing

that it was packed to the gills. Suitcases, backpacks, coolers, all high-end brands, items with high price tags but the same made-in-China crap like everything else.

Who would pay four hundred dollars for a cooler when sixty dollars would buy you something that worked just as well, was better designed, more practical? Very typical of a certain set. *Look at me! Look what I can buy!* He shouldn't complain. It was just that type of person who rented the house he'd built here on the twenty acres of land he owned. And his livelihood depended on them.

The guest grabbed a couple of suitcases and headed toward the house. Then he climbed the porch steps, put down the luggage, and looked at his phone. When he punched in the code on the lock and tried the door, it didn't open.

"What the fuck?" he said. Just a moment's delay and he was immediately angry. He walked back to the steps and called for his wife, looking like a helpless toddler. She didn't come right away. He sighed, called her again.

Finally, she got out of the car, dressed in expensive yoga gear. From the trunk, she took a bag and her yoga mat and then went to meet him on the porch.

He couldn't hear their voices from where he was standing. But Bracken noticed that the colors of their outfits coordinated. Did they plan that? Her pants dove gray, a lighter color than his gray zip-up hoodie, her tank top sky blue, his a deep royal. Bracken noticed that her exposed arms were lean, muscles defined.

Then the husband was picking her up like she weighed nothing at all and she was laughing as he carried her across the threshold. Bracken felt another rush of pride. He liked it when people were happy at his rental cabins. That was the whole point.

Bracken had let the grocery delivery person in earlier. A trunkful of organic this, vegan that, gluten-free, free-range, fair-trade, no-hormone high-priced items that he knew cost four or five times their store-brand counterparts.

The fridge and cupboards were packed; Bracken could stock the town food pantry for a couple of weeks with what his guests had bought for a long weekend. In fact, anything they left unopened would go there. He did that with all his rentals. People wasted so much food. They didn't know what it was like to go hungry.

Not a judgment.

Just an observation. He considered himself an observer of the very different ways people chose to spend their lives, their money.

He clicked on the phone app that activated the camera in the main room.

"What about the booze?" big man was saying. He opened and closed cupboards.

"I thought you wanted to detox," said his wife, looking at him. "Everyone else is bringing their choice of beverage or— intoxicant. Cricket's bringing gummies."

"I said I wanted to *relax*," he said, with a chuckle. "Not *detox*. Big difference."

"Hmm. I see."

She gave him an indulgent smile, like he was a loveable but misbehaved child. Could an adult woman truly love a man that she had to parent?

"I'll run into town," he said.

"Don't," she said, moving over to him. "Just call Hannah, have her pick up whatever you need."

"It's not going to take long." He kissed her quickly. It was clear that he would do as he pleased and there was fuck all she could do about it. "Was there anything else?"

"Looks like they forgot the kale," she said thoughtfully, peering into the fridge.

He lifted his hands in mock dismay. "Can't have that. God forbid we should go without *kale*."

"You like my smoothies," she offered with another sweet smile. Bracken liked her a lot.

Shark man kissed her on the top of the head. "I *love* your smoothies. And I love you. See you in a bit."

"Be careful," she said. "Don't take those blind turns too fast."

"Oh, wow—look at that. Bruce and Hannah are here," he said.

Yes. A sturdy black Volvo SUV pulled up, another young, well-heeled couple inside. A Volvo was in every way opposite from the Tesla—reliable, safe, understated. An expensive car, but not one that screamed conspicuous consumption. A car bought for its value, not for what it said about the owner.

And then it was all hugs and happy greetings. Bracken stood watching, a familiar twinge of longing, undercut by a little bit of anger. What was it like to be a part of a family, to be welcomed and embraced? He didn't know. He'd been deprived of that for whatever reason. The world was not a fair place and nothing—not looks, not wealth, not love—was evenly distributed. He knew that, of course he did. Why did it never stop hurting?

Inside there was more talk about who would go into town. Bruce offered. Hannah said that they'd brought plenty of alcohol—wine, vodka, gin. But Mako insisted. It was obvious to Bracken that the shark man had other things on his mind. And finally he was out the door.

Shark man was trying his phone before he backed out of the drive. Good luck getting service until he was closer to town. There was a router in the house, so they'd be able to use their phones on Wi-Fi but cellular service was spotty on the roads, some places dead altogether.

Most people were okay with it. It was why they came to this mountain town, to unplug, to connect with nature, to hike, to go quiet, remember what mattered, to silence all the chatter. Some people loved it, were nourished by the break. But some people, when the chatter was silenced, couldn't stand the sound of their own thoughts.

He was guessing that *Mako* was one of the latter. A shark man in a shark car. Stop swimming and die.

He turned his attention back to the camera app.

"Can I do anything?" Hannah asked, clearly wanting to help in some way.

"I think we're all set," said Liza. Was her tone a bit crisp? "Why don't you guys go check out your room? Upstairs on the left."

Interesting, they'd only just arrived but Liza already knew which room she wanted. The large master with the most spectacular views. The room she'd assigned to Hannah and Bruce was only slightly smaller, but just as well-appointed. The views were somewhat lesser. Still, it said something, didn't it? Established a hierarchy?

Bracken closed the app and waited until the car had been gone for a bit before he headed to the door to introduce himself, orient the guest, and let her know that he was close by if they needed anything during their stay.

He wanted to warn them about the hurricane that was moving up the coast and looked like it would make its way ashore around St. Simons Island. It should greatly diminish by the time it reached them. But still, a storm in this area could be dangerous, trees falling, roads washing out, rivers overflowing their banks and making roads impassable for a time. It was one of the reasons real estate was so cheap around here. The infrastructure just barely defied its natural surroundings.

But that was one of the things which drew Bracken there. He enjoyed the raw power and unpredictability of a natural environment. In a city, made by man, elaborate systems were needed to keep nature at bay. In New York City, pumps worked around the clock to keep water from swamping the whole island, swallowing it. What did they say? Just forty-eight hours without those pumps running and the entire subway system would be flooded, another twenty-four and the streets would be rivers. Here the streets were rivers in just hours, one lightning strike could cause a raging forest fire. Nature was always waiting to take itself back by any means necessary. There was something he liked about that, the violence of it, the truth.

But this afternoon, the sun was shining and the sky was clear. Birdsong was rich and melodious—the sweet whistle of the chickadee, the wildly cheerful chirp of the brown thrasher, the caw of the common crow. A pileated woodpecker knocked rhythmically somewhere above; Bracken looked up and saw the bobbing red head between the branches of a spruce.

He walked up the steps of the porch he'd restored with his own hands, and knocked at the thick-paned glass of the door he'd hung himself—what a bitch that had been. It had taken him and three of his crew to get it right.

When Liza came into view, he could tell immediately that she'd been crying, her eyes rimmed slightly red, her cheeks flushed. What had happened since her husband left? It had just been minutes.

In the glass, he saw his own reflection—the bulk of his frame, the thick beard, the worn jeans and Henley work shirt. He looked like a lumberjack, rough-and-ready. Maybe a bit unwashed, threatening? May said he scowled at people, made them uncomfortable with his heavy silences. He could see that the yoga girl was hesitant to open the door.

"Can I help you?" she said through the door.

"I'm Bracken, the host," he said. "Are you Liza? We spoke on the phone."

"Oh!" she said, brightening. She unlatched the door and opened it, stepping back. He walked inside.

"How's the house?" he asked. There was a scent in the air. Sage.

She put a hand to her heart. "Oh my goodness, it's just stunning. And thank you for letting the grocery delivery in, putting everything away. That was so kind, so helpful. And I know way above and beyond."

"My pleasure," he said. "Big crew this weekend?"

"Six of us," she said. She rubbed at her temples, like maybe she had a headache. "Should be fun."

He glanced around, expensive luggage at the bottom of the stairs leading to the upstairs master suite.

"Can I take that up for you?"

"Would you mind?" she asked. "My husband took off on some errands. And, as usual, we way overpacked."

He looked around for the other couple but they were not in sight.

"Of course."

People, almost without fail, overpacked. They thought they needed to cart all their stuff with them, everywhere they went. And they had *so much* stuff. Bracken counted himself as a minimalist. His own cabin, which he had also built, was half the size of this one. He limited himself to exactly fifty possessions and he was always looking to be rid of anything that could go.

She followed him up, taking the lighter bags.

He carried them to the master bedroom and left them inside the door. Through the closed door on the other side of the hall, he heard the voices of the other guests. The woman—Hannah—laughed delightedly.

"Oh, this is so lovely. Just stunning," Liza said to him.

He was proud of this room—the oak floors and picture windows, the fireplace. There was a large king bed, a desk looking out onto the stunning view of the mountains.

"It said on your website that you built all these homes yourself."

"With a crew," he said. "But yes, I was the general contractor and did a lot of the work myself—everything from laying foundations to painting walls."

She nodded, eyes searching his face for what he didn't know.

"That must be so satisfying," she said finally. She walked

into the bathroom to put a small bag there. Her body looked strong and lithe; she moved with grace.

"It is," he said.

It *was* satisfying to build something solid, to put in real effort and have a tangible result. So much effort in life yielded nothing.

Downstairs, he showed her around the kitchen, though he knew they had a chef coming in, where the vacuum was, showed her how to use the hot tub.

When he was done, they stood in the foyer.

"I guess the only other thing is just to be aware of the storm headed our way."

"I heard," she said with a frown.

"We do tend to lose phone service and power out here. There's a generator that will kick on. Should that happen, I'll swing by if I can. The roads get swamped and can be impassable for a time until the water recedes. What kind of car do you have?"

He knew, but he didn't want her to know he'd been watching.

"A Tesla," she said, a wrinkle in her brow. "It's a looker, but I'm not sure it's a match for swamped roads."

"Well, worse comes to worse, I'll come by in the truck as soon as it's possible to check on you all. So just stay put. I wouldn't want anyone getting stuck—or hurt."

She nodded thoughtfully, looked outside. His GMC pickup— a machine built for hauling, plowing, getting through—was parked at the trailhead down the road. She must be wondering where his vehicle was, but she didn't ask and he didn't offer an explanation.

"We'll do that if the weather turns, stay put. Thank you. For everything."

She held out a folded bill, but he waved her away. "Happy to help."

Tipping. People didn't mean it to be reductive. But it was.

He was the owner, not the help. What he did, he did because of a very personal code of hosting.

She slipped the money into the slim pocket of her leggings. He imagined that she'd forget it was there, maybe put it through the wash.

Sometimes, when people were chatty, he told them about the history of the land and the house that used to stand upon it. Some people were intrigued, but others were put off. So he'd stopped sharing the dark history of the place unless a person seemed like a ghost story around the campfire type.

Liza did not seem like that type of person. Liza seemed sensitive, tense, someone who took things seriously. She was rubbing at her temples again.

"This place," she said, as if reading his mind. "It has an energy."

He'd searched her online after she made the deposit and quickly discovered her Instagram, her YouTube. Yoga teacher and meditation instructor.

"Good or bad?" he asked with a smile.

She seemed to consider. "Unsettled," she said finally.

"I imagine after the fire is roaring and you've had a glass of wine, you'll all settle right in."

She nodded, folded her arms around her middle. "I'm sure you're right."

He handed her a card, even though he knew she had his number. Sometimes it was just easier to have a piece of paper lying around so that any of the guests could call.

"Call for any reason, anytime," he said. She took the card and gave him a smile.

"Thank you," she said. "We will but I'm sure everything will be perfect."

Nothing is ever perfect, he wanted to say. Wanting everything to be perfect is a recipe for misery. But he kept quiet. Her skin was so dewy, her body toned and lithe. He wondered what it would be like to hold her in his arms, to feel her lips on his.

He lost himself a moment to imagining, watching the way the sunlight danced on her hair, how she touched nervous fingers to her collarbone.

Was there something there? Would she move toward him?

He felt himself lingering, and the energy between them shifted. He wasn't ready to go, but she wrapped her arms around her middle and shifted away a bit. She glanced back at the staircase, then toward the door as if wondering how she would get away.

"Thank you again," she said briskly. A dismissal. And this time, he took the hint.

He gave her a little bow, and left.

He'd see more of her later.

8

CRICKET

"We're lost," Cricket said. She tried to quell the rise of anxiety. Honestly, it had started hours ago—okay maybe days ago—the anxiety. This trip. It probably wasn't a good idea. But like so many bad ideas, it seemed to take on an unstoppable momentum and here they were. On the way. "*Are* we lost?"

"It's literally impossible to be lost," Joshua said. He was smoothly confident. "The modern infrastructure will not allow it."

Weekend stubble, though it was only Thursday, a wrinkled but somehow still stylish blue gingham shirt, faded jeans, loafers. He was one of those men with his long, lean body, his floppy hair, heavily lidded eyes—he simply looked good all the time. When he just woke up, after his run, when he was taking out the trash. As if he'd fallen from the pages of an Abercrombie and Fitch catalogue and into her life. Cricket tried not to stare at him like a schoolgirl discovering boys for the first time.

"But the dot," she said, looking at her phone instead. "Our dot. It's just floating in—nothing."

She resisted the urge to tap the screen, shake them loose from the void. Joshua glanced away from the road and at her phone quickly, then pulled the car over into the shoulder, tires crunching on dirt and gravel.

All around them fecund, electric green. Silence. The towering trees cast the road in shadow, a dappled light barely shining through the canopy. She didn't know what kind of trees—pine, oak, maple, birch? Did it matter? Whatever normal kinds of woodsy trees.

Hannah would surely know. She'd know the trees and their medicinal properties, and which one would make the best firewood. She'd use one to build a shelter, splint a broken bone. Hannah was *outdoorsy*.

Cricket felt that her spiritual home might be Neiman Marcus.

She was far from the kind of place that made her feel comfortable—someplace gleaming and clean with lovely, expensive goods for sale. People were so into "nature," weren't they? Getting into it, back to it. Why? Nature just seemed spooky and unsafe to Cricket. There was that whole no-one-can-hear-you-screaming vibe. They hadn't seen another car for ages. Ages.

Joshua took the phone from her and stared. "Huh. We lost the signal."

They'd stopped in town a while ago, hoping to pick up some things—snacks, condoms, wine—even though she knew Mako would have enough expensive bottles to fill a cellar somewhere—some flowers for Liza and Hannah. She didn't want to arrive empty-handed.

But when they pulled through town, she'd been a little surprised. She'd expected something quaint and maybe a little tony, catering to the renter crowd. But a number of businesses were shuttered, the streets having the air of desertion. There had been a dingy diner, a sad general store, deserted hardware shop, a laundromat that just looked dirty.

The general store shelves seemed just barely stocked—peanut butter, some deflated loaves of white bread, candy. The highest-end item Cricket found hunting through the dusty offerings was a can of Planters cocktail peanuts. The store had plenty of beer, cigarettes, lottery tickets, and jerky, though. Joshua—always the paleo, hence those abs *good lord*—stocked up on some organic deer jerky.

The man at the counter leered at her, and regarded Joshua—who PS looked like a goddamn supermodel next to the toothless, unshaven man in the red cap and dirty shirt—with naked suspicion.

"Up for the weekend?" he'd asked as she approached with their paltry collection of items, including a box of condoms. The clerk picked up the tidy black box and held it high, looking at it too long. His nails were filthy, cuticles frayed.

"That's right," she said keeping her voice cool. Usually she was friendly, chatty. Cricket knew her gifts; she was a pretty, busty blonde, flirty and sweet when she wanted to be. But men like that? They needed to get the message fast: *Don't even think about fucking with me.*

She stared at him hard until he put the condoms down and started ringing up the other items. A fly buzzed in the window, knocking itself against the glass over and over. A rickety rack of magazines tilted, holding issues of *Gun World*, *Hunting & Fishing*, *Prepper's Household Journal*.

"Storm coming in. Big one."

She'd heard that on the radio but ignored it. Nature wouldn't dare mess with Mako's big getaway weekend. He'd wanted this—arranged it, harassed them all until they agreed, reminded them endlessly, paid for it. Some whim, some story he was telling himself about it, no doubt. Even mother nature wouldn't stand a chance against a Mako narrative.

"We'll manage."

"Roads get washed out," said the clerk, sucking at his teeth. "Might get stranded."

Oh my god. Shut up.

"Thanks for the warning, buddy," said Joshua stepping up behind her.

Buddy. Joshua used that word a lot. Sometimes *bro*, sometimes *brah*, depending on the situation, the person. It did seem to soften things with other men. The guy behind the counter gave a nod, backed up a bit as Joshua moved to collect their sack of things.

"Have a *nice* time up there," he'd said as they left, but it sounded nasty, like a warning. *Up where?* she wondered. They hadn't told him where they were staying.

"Have a good one, bro," said Josh affably, shooting her a look when they got outside. He sang a funny banjo riff and Cricket laughed as they got into his car.

But the encounter had left her with a creepy feeling, deepening her anxiety about the weekend with her best friend, her new love. Her *ex*. His *stunning* wife. Who's idea was this again?

Oh, right. Mako's.

"Huh," Joshua said now, still staring at the phone as if willing the signal to return. Finally, he glanced over at her with a crooked grin. "Yep. We're lost."

They both started to laugh. He laced his fingers through hers and leaned in for a kiss. It was sweet, and hot. Just like him. Oh my god. He was so, *so* hot—bedroom eyes, lean but muscular, and much taller than Cricket. Which was nice because she was tallish and sometimes she couldn't wear heels with the men she was dating. And she *really* enjoyed wearing heels. They made her legs look *awesome*.

"I can't think of anyone I'd rather be lost with," he said softly, hand drifting up her thigh.

Truthfully? She loved him.

She didn't want to. She hadn't said anything.

But he lit her up inside like no one else she'd ever known. Conversely, he made her feel calm, safe. If she'd been with Mako, or any of her more recent exes, in a scenario like this there would be yelling, frustration, high stress. *Why were they lost? Who's fault was it? Why was there no fucking service?*

But Joshua? No. She'd never seen him lose his temper, never heard a harsh word from him. He was light, easy, kind, nice to everyone. Loving, tender. An *amazing* fuck.

He leaned in closer, whispered playfully in her ear. "Am I less of a man to you now that you know I can't get us to our destination without a technological crutch?"

"No," she said quite seriously. "If anything, you're more of a man for not losing your shit when we're out in the middle of nowhere with no cell service and no way to find the cabin."

She thought about suggesting that they turn around.

"Hmm," he said, hand now under her skirt, roaming, insistent. She flashed on the creepy guy holding the box of condoms, pushed the thought from her head. She brought her lips to Joshua's neck, took in the scent of him. Her touch elicited a moan.

And then they were crawling over each other to get into the back seat where they used this lovely moment of lost isolation to have a quickie, his pants down around his tight ass, her skirt hiked up, panties shed.

Oh god.

Everything with him was so good.

Too good.

Definitely too good to be true, she thought as she experienced a seismic orgasm that left her weak and breathless beneath him, staring at the swaying green leaves above them. He came inside her; so much for the condoms still in their package. She loved it, even though it was a hundred different kinds of roulette. She was on the pill but she knew so many girls who got pregnant on the pill.

The trees swayed and sighed, as he breathed deeply, lying on top of her.

What was that thing? Forest bathing. The soothing power of nature. Yeah, maybe she could see it now, from this angle. For a moment, she got this floating feeling like she was one with the trees, their silence. That it was just her and Joshua and that they would stay just like this—sated, at peace. Every dark and shitty thing about modern life, every bad memory, or daily aggravation left behind for good. Her work in public relations which had become a joyless slog, his in technology which had him pulling all-nighters for this outage or that glitch. Maybe they could just leave it behind, come out to the woods, live off the land. People did that.

Yeah, right.

He buried his face in her neck as she closed her arms around his broad back. *I love you*, she thought but of course didn't say.

"You are an angel," he whispered. She was hardly that. She was so far from that. But she kissed his cheek, relishing the smell and taste of him.

Definitely too good to be true.

No, Hannah had said when Cricket had told her best friend about Joshua, about her fears that he was just too wonderful. *Don't do that. It's okay to be happy, to be in love. Enjoy it and stop waiting for something to be bad about it.*

Cricket didn't say, *But something bad always happens*. Because they both knew that was true, or often true, or could be true. Especially when you were a bad girl like Cricket was, or could be. It didn't need saying. And it wasn't helpful. It didn't *serve* them, as Liza would surely put it. Liza, who she liked as a person (even though she had married Mako, Cricket's first—everything—kiss, love, fuck), and whom she also followed on Instagram, *and* took her morning yoga class with via livestream on Thursday mornings. *Yoga with Liza. Everyday Zen.* Wellness and calm are within reach of everyone, no matter how imperfect. Cricket liked that idea. Hoped fervently that it was true.

Joshua climbed off her with a farewell kiss. The back seat was a little cramped for two tall people, and he awkwardly pulled up his jeans and backed out of the door, grinning at her in that way that she loved. Like he was a man who was fully satisfied by just the sight of her.

"Wow," he said from outside. "This is beautiful."

She shimmied into her discarded panties, pulled down her skirt and joined him. It *was* beautiful. The air smelled—green. Fresh and moist, clean and clear. She took it into her lungs.

There were a lot of things about this trip that might not be ideal, but now that they were here, or almost, it seemed like just what they needed. A moment to unplug, to be in "nature," and with each other—her friends, the man she *maybe* loved. Okay, she definitely loved him. *Maybe* he loved her, too. Maybe she was about to be the one with the ring on her finger, the wedding to plan, the sash that said "Bride" on the bridal party weekend. Hannah would be *her* maid of honor. *Mako* would be the one sulking in the corner, drinking too much.

She heard Joshua's phone buzz.

"You have service!" she said, stupidly thrilled.

He reached into his pocket and pulled out his phone. What he saw there made his face darken, brow furrow, eyes go a little dull.

"What's wrong?" she asked.

"Ugh," he said, glancing up at her. He suddenly looked stressed, eyebrows meeting in the middle. "Just work stuff. Figures we can't get service to find our way, but she can always find me."

She. His boss.

Something about the way he said it caused a little flutter of worry in her stomach. He was such an easygoing, lighthearted guy, but he really seemed to hate his IT job at a big cyber-security firm. Apparently, his boss was a bit of a tyrant. She was probably some not-hot-anymore middle-aged cougar who wanted Joshua under her thumb because she was secretly into him. But Cricket was just making that up.

Cricket didn't know much about his work because he didn't like talking about it. Which she loved because most of the men she'd dated talked about little else. But she knew he was an engineer, that he was responsible for the hardware, that he got called away at all hours when this or that went down with long rides out to a big data center in the middle of nowhere.

I'm basically a computer mechanic, he'd said. Did it seem like he was purposely vague about his work sometimes, changed the subject quickly when it came up? Maybe.

"Don't answer," she said. "You're on vacation."

He nodded, some of the brightness returning. "You're right. Yeah, I'll get back to her in the morning."

"Or not."

She wrapped her arms around his waist, glanced up at him. "We were going to unplug, right? Everybody is entitled to some actual vacation time. Time not thinking about work."

He nodded, smiling. "Right. You're right."

And then her mouth was on his, soft, gentle.

He pulled away, put a soft hand on her cheek.

"Cricket," he started, voice throaty. Oh my god. Was he going to say it? She definitely wasn't going to say it first. She held his gaze, trying to look encouraging. "I think—"

I think I love you.

It was *right there.*

But the honking of a horn broke the moment. She lost Joshua's gaze. Following his eyes, she turned to see a brand-new gleaming black Tesla coming to stop behind them in the shoulder of the road. The Model S, the most expensive, of course.

She'd just ridden in it last week actually. Mako had made sure to show off *all* its features.

"Look at you two lovebirds," said Mako climbing out.

As he approached, she noticed big purple circles under his eyes. But still he looked good to her, virile and vital. Cricket felt an unwelcome tug to him. Always did.

She looked in the car for Liza but the passenger seat was empty.

"Hey," she said, greeting him with a big hug. He felt strong, familiar, safe, like family. He *was* family; so was Hannah. They were the family she would have chosen, if she'd had a choice.

She used to fantasize when she and Mako were dating in high school about their wedding, how Hannah would be just like a real sister. She imagined Sophia and Leo treating her like a true daughter. Her own family was so—broken. She was the only child of unhappy people who'd had a nasty divorce, and still hated each other a decade later. Toggling between miserable homes, she'd wanted to be part of the Maroni clan so badly. And she was. Just not the way she expected.

"This must be Josh," said Mako releasing her after holding on just a millisecond less than she had. Big manly handshake, a shoulder clap from Mako. "The guy who's making our Cricket so happy."

Our Cricket. He always called her that. Possessive in a way that she relished.

"Ah," said Joshua with a pleased glance at Cricket. "I'm a lucky guy."

"It's Joshua, actually," said Cricket. She knew he didn't like Josh but was too nice to ever say so. Somewhere along the line she'd started speaking up for him.

"Joshua," Mako corrected himself.

Joshua raised a palm. "All good, man."

Mako pinned him with that stare he used to intimidate, size up, assert his place in the hierarchy. But Joshua only squared his shoulders, smile deepening. There was some kind of male standoff that Cricket didn't quite get and really couldn't care less about. But she was pretty sure Joshua won.

"You guys lost? Follow me. Service drops here. I only found the place because I mapped it out ahead of time," Mako said, moving back toward the Tesla. She picked up on the "I" not "we."

"Where's Liza?" asked Cricket. For a moment she felt a little malicious glee that she was not proud of. Trouble in paradise? Had he come without her?

"Back at the house," he said. "I just made a run into town

for some things the grocery delivery forgot. Bruce and Hannah just arrived."

He rubbed at his eyes with his thumb and forefinger, which Cricket knew from bitter personal experience was a tell for when he was lying. But she couldn't care less about that either. Because Mako was not her problem. He was Liza's.

"You guys," said Mako, before shutting the car door. "This place is *epic*. You're gonna die."

9

HANNAH

"Let me know if there's anything, Liza," said Hannah, wanting to be useful in some way. Mako had dashed off into town. Bruce was unloading the car. She felt that usual awkwardness, like there was a sheet of glass between them. She could only get so close.

Liza just shook her head again, gave her a warm smile.

"We're all good," Liza said easily. "Just relax and enjoy. That's what the whole weekend is about."

Hannah wanted to say something more. The truth was that Liza looked horrible, pale and gray around the eyes. Fragile.

"Are you okay?" Hannah ventured. "You look—"

"Terrible, I know," she said. "I've had this headache come on. Really bad."

Hannah reached for her, feeling a motherly urge to comfort her, to tend to her. Liza took the hand Hannah reached out and gave it a little squeeze; her fingers felt cold.

"Migraine?"

Liza nodded, looked embarrassed as if she hadn't wanted to admit that she wasn't well. "I think I might have to lie down until dinner. I'm so sorry."

"Don't be," said Hannah. "What can I do? Have Mako grab some medicine while he's in town? Do you have anything for it?"

"I do, but it will wipe me out."

Hannah didn't know much about migraines but she knew when they came on, there wasn't a whole lot you could do about it.

"Please let me know if I can help."

They stood in the dreamy, aspirational kitchen with its gleaming double-sized Sub-Zero fridge, and restaurant-quality Wolf range, expansive quartz countertops, stainless steel sink. Along the backsplash was a gigantic display of knives on a magnetic strip, shimmering, razor-sharp blades, a cleaver. Chef's tools. Hannah's eyes kept returning to them. They glinted in the light.

"I will," Liza said, offering a wan smile.

Through the big front window, Hannah saw Bruce unloading the car.

"So," Liza said, changing the subject. "What do we know about Cricket's new boyfriend?"

Hannah shrugged. "Almost nothing. She's smitten though. I know that much."

"Really? Nothing?"

"All I know is that she seems happy, like truly happy. Not giddy or overexcited. Just—in a good place with it. With him."

Liza's smile deepened. "That's good. That's *great*."

She glanced back outside. "They should be here soon. And we'll see for ourselves."

Liza's smile dimmed as she brought her forefingers to her temples. "I'm going to take a shower and then lie down, try to rally. See you at dinner?"

Hannah almost brought up the blog she'd read, but then held her tongue. Why introduce negativity? She gave Liza's hand a final squeeze, then moved away.

Poor Liza. At the best of times, she always seemed so shimmery and barely there, overpowered by Mako and the volume of his being. Now it seemed like she could just disappear altogether.

"Just shout if you need me," said Hannah moving toward the stairs. What did the kids call it these days? Sweaty tryhard? When you bent over backward to get someone to like you?

But Liza had taken her phone from her pocket and was looking at the screen, didn't seem to hear.

Hannah climbed the floating staircase, passed some framed black-and-white images of wildlife—a stag on a ridge, a black bear with her cubs, a mountain lion staring at his reflection in a puddle—then stepped onto the carpet runner over the hardwood floors.

Everything was pristine, walls seemed freshly painted, not a hint of dust or grime. Most vacation rentals had the air of being overused. Not this place.

Over the railing, she looked down on the great room. The vaulted ceiling towered, a huge wrought iron chandelier hanging from its height. There was some kind of strange sculpture hanging near the dining room table—it looked like an animal skull surrounded by bleached wood. She'd have to get a closer look when she went back downstairs.

There was a long table outside the door to Bruce and Hannah's room, grained wood, varnished, atop it were three carved white statues of deer—a stag, a doe, and a fawn. She picked up the tiniest one; it was smooth and cool to the touch, surprisingly heavy. She looked at it more closely and saw that it was porous, oddly grained. Not stone or wood.

Bone, she realized suddenly. It was bone. She put it down quickly, almost toppling the other two.

Bruce came up behind her, carrying their bags, startling her.

"You good?" he asked with a smile. She was easily startled; it was a known thing between them.

"These are made from bone."

He looked at the statues as he passed. "Huh. Weird."

"Do people do that? Make things from bone?"

He shrugged. "I guess?"

Hannah decided to drop the topic but she had the urge to wash her hands.

Downstairs she heard the doorbell ring. Her heart leapt, thinking that it might be Cricket already. But when she looked over the landing, she saw Liza hesitating at the entrance. Finally, Liza opened the door and let a large outdoorsy-looking man inside.

Their voices were soft and Hannah couldn't hear what they were saying. When he stepped into view, she recognized him as the man who built the houses, the host.

Liza looked tiny next to him, and he seemed to be standing too close to her. Should she go down?

"Wow," said Bruce from inside the room, distracting Hannah from Liza.

She stepped over the threshold and drew in a breath.

A huge four-poster bed piled high with plush pillows, fireplace, a cozy sitting area looking out onto a private balcony, colorful area rugs, more wildlife photographs and thankfully no mounted animal heads. The wood floors shined as she walked over them to the spacious bathroom—a steam shower, a soaking tub, stacks of fat white towels. If it were up to her they wouldn't leave the room for the next seventy-two hours except to eat. In the air, the slightest mingling of sage and lemon.

Hannah felt her body relax. Okay. This might be just what the doctor ordered, after all. Maybe there *was* a method to Mako's madness.

Bruce closed the door then sat himself on the plush sofa for a moment, then got up to open the sliding door that led out to a big deck.

She went out on the balcony to join her husband, took in the cool of the air, the rustle of leaves. The afternoon light was starting to wane; the mountains were purple in the distance.

"This is—something," Bruce said.

"Leave it to Mako," she said. "Nothing but the best."

She felt rather than saw Bruce frowning.

He had a hard time relaxing in general, his mind always turning—she knew that. His work was complicated, consuming—yes, lots of difficult clients. He was more comfortable with code than he was with most people. She accepted that about him; a weekend surrounded by people was not something he'd have chosen. Even if he hadn't caught her snooping; even if they hadn't been arguing.

"Look, I get it. You're not having an affair," she whispered, not sure what could be heard from the deck below them. "So what is it then? Talk to me and let me help, okay?"

He motioned for her to come back inside and she followed. Bruce flipped on the switch that turned on the fireplace and it flamed to life. He sat on the sofa and she melted in beside him, feeling his arms close around her. He released a deep breath.

"Doesn't this just seem like—too much?" he said.

"How so?"

"I mean he pressed for this, for months, insisted on paying for everything. We're out here in the middle of nowhere. There's an *itinerary* on the bed."

Mako. Yeah, he was a bit much, larger than life, big ideas, big appetites, grand gestures. That was his way. "He's just trying to show his gratitude."

But it was more than that, even she knew it. He was running some kind of an agenda. What was it? It might be internal. It might be something he wanted from them. No way to know until the big reveal.

"Family is never perfect," she said. "But he loves us."

She felt him nod. Then,

"Hannah, I don't think I can work for your brother anymore."

She looked up at him. His face was drawn, still. There was a heaviness to his tone.

"Okay," she said. "Why not?"

He glanced away, rubbed at his temples with a thumb and forefinger. "There are things going on at Red World that I—can't live with."

His words landed oddly, making a strange kind of sense, but frightening her at the same time.

"What kind of things?" she asked, feeling her throat constrict a bit.

She'd worked at Red World, too. There were always trolls and ugly rumors about Mako, about the company. But power, success, always attracted hatred and jealousy, right? That's what Mako always said. And there was just something about her brother. Even at school, there had been rumors and lies circulating about him—that he'd cheated on an exam. Other things. Hannah felt a clench in her middle.

"What kind of things, Bruce?" she repeated when he didn't answer.

"Oh my GAWD! Look at this place!" Cricket's voice carried up from downstairs. "Hannah! Hannah! Where are you?"

They locked eyes. He looked so—sad.

"Coming!" called Hannah. But she kept her gaze on her husband. Bruce kept watching her for a moment, then looked down at the floor.

"I'm sorry. I shouldn't—just forget I said anything, okay?" he said, voice taut. "This isn't the place to discuss it."

She wanted to push him, but she knew it was true, that whatever it was, they needed to talk about it later when they were alone. She couldn't hear what Bruce had to say and then go downstairs and face her brother, pretend that everything was all right.

She could see the strain on him, that whatever it was, it was big.

"Whatever it is," she said. "It's okay. We'll figure it out. I love you."

He seemed about to say something else.

But when she turned her head up to him, he kissed her instead, slow, loving. If she sometimes missed the ease of their early couple-hood, she knew there was something deeper between them now. Their love, their friendship had grown. And now there was Gigi, the little life their love had made, connecting them always. No matter what.

Then Cricket was calling again, and Mako's voice was booming. Her brother had obviously returned, as well.

"Hey, you lovebirds. Come on down."

Then she did what she always did, had always been able to do. She pushed it all away. Whatever it was that was bothering Bruce about Red World, her own worries, fears and doubts. All that was for another time. For now, they were here and they'd enjoy this moment, get whatever pleasure they could. Face whatever came next when they'd returned home.

Hand in hand, they headed downstairs.

10

HANNAH

And then she was in the embrace of her childhood friend who still smelled of lemons and very faintly of marijuana. Cricket was slumber parties, and manicures, martini night, and days at the beach. She was the person who knew everything—everything—about Hannah. And vice versa.

"You look *so beautiful*," Cricket said.

Which was a lie; Hannah knew she looked as tired and worn down as any toddler mom, but she loved her friend for her unfailing kindness.

Cricket looked rested, gorgeous as ever with her flawless skin, and shining hair—as if she'd just *come* from a vacation, a shower, a spa treatment. She wore a slim denim shirt dress that clung to her curves. "You're the gorgeous one," she said. "Always have been."

They'd become friends when Cricket and Mako were dating, back in high school. Cricket had ditched Mako—or had he ditched her, who could remember?—but kept Hannah. Now, as adults, they were all friends.

Cricket pulled her in again, and whispered, "I think I'm in love."

Her friend's smile was beaming, and Hannah looked around for Cricket's new beau. But then Mako was hugging Hannah.

"This is going to be such an awesome weekend. I'm so glad you guys are here. I thought you might bail. I know you didn't want to leave Gigi."

She reflexively reached for her phone at the mention of her daughter's name. But remembered it was still in the car. She'd have to go out for it.

"There's Wi-Fi, right?"

"Of course," he said. "I mean, it's a little wonky. But of course."

She didn't have time to ask him what *wonky* meant, because Cricket was dragging her around the cabin-slash-ridiculous-mansion, gawking at the expansive great room with double-height vaulted ceilings, and floor-to-ceiling windows, fresh flowers in towering vases. Outside, the sun was setting, painting the sky orange, purple, pink. The view of acres and acres of trees, the blue shadows of distant mountains, watercolor sky was stunning.

And yep that *was* a bear head mounted over the mantel. Why did people think that was okay, to kill something and stick its head on your wall? The glassy eyes seemed to stare at her, accusing. The review she'd read online came back to her. *My wife felt like she was being watched.*

There was a tall, slim dark-haired man standing outside by the sliding glass doors, watching another man at the grill who Hannah assumed was the hired chef by his white coat and *toque blanche.* When had the chef arrived? She didn't think they'd been up there for long.

The slim man spoke, but the chef seemed not to be listening, his face still and pale, lit by the flames from the grill. Finally, the other man nodded and headed inside. The chef watched him walk away, an expression on his face that Hannah couldn't read. She found herself staring a moment, until the chef met her eyes, gave her a quick nod. Hannah looked away, embarrassed to be caught looking at him, though she couldn't say why.

"Hannah," said Cricket with a flourish of her hand. "This is Joshua. Honey, this my forever best friend, Hannah."

When Joshua offered her a warm smile, Hannah felt something drop in her stomach. Without meaning to, she backed up a step. He was—so familiar. Those heavily lashed dark eyes, the high cheekbones, the stiffness of his carriage.

"Wait," she said. "Have we met?"

He looked around, shaking his head, offering a confused smile.

"No," he said. "I don't think so."

Whatever Cricket saw on Hannah's face made her beaming smile fade a little.

"Do you guys know each other?"

Joshua took Hannah's hand, gave it a firm but gentle shake. "No," he said. "I remember all the beautiful women I meet."

"Oh," said Cricket, with a mock-serious lift of her eyebrows. "Do you?"

"Until I met you, of course," he charmed, turning to her. "Now they've all faded away. Ghosts of the past."

Hannah grappled for it. But no. When he turned back to her, stepped further into the light, she realized she'd been mistaken. Maybe she was just tired, hungry. She'd had a horrible night's sleep, and barely anything to eat all day and it was getting late. No. The more she looked at him, she didn't know him at all.

"No," said Hannah. "Just a for moment—you looked so familiar."

"I might just have one of those faces," he said.

"I'm sorry." She offered an apologetic laugh at herself. "It's lovely to meet you."

Joshua's smile was warm, friendly, forgiving.

"I've heard so many wonderful things about you, Hannah. Cricket says you're more like her sister than her friend."

He gave Cricket a sweet kiss on the forehead. There was something so lovingly intimate about it that Hannah felt herself blush. Her friend looked well and truly happy. Which was good, wonderful, great. She deserved that. They all did, right? They all deserved to be happy and relaxed for a while.

A young blond woman, with sharp, defined features and searing blue eyes, dressed in a crisp black oxford and slim pants, offered Hannah a drink on a cocktail napkin. These strangers must have arrived when Bruce and Hannah were upstairs settling in and talking. She hadn't heard the bell, or even heard the host leave.

Bruce's words rang back for a moment. *Things I can't live with.* Hannah pushed it away.

"Vodka soda," the young server said, her voice low. Hannah noticed her nails were trimmed and short, her hands tiny. There was a delicate tattoo of a black spider on her right hand. Her face was dewy and full—so young—early twenties at the most.

"Oh, hello," said Hannah, taking it from her. "Thanks so much."

"Chef Jeff and Ingrid will be helping us out tonight," said Mako, coming up from behind. "Chef is the best in the area, according to our host."

Of course he is, thought Hannah.

Leave it to Mako to have a staff for dinner. It did change things a bit. What could have been homey, now felt like they were at a restaurant, a hotel. Which whatever, fine—at least she and Liza wouldn't wind up doing the dishes.

"Where's Liza?" asked Cricket.

"Migraine," said Mako with a sympathetic wrinkle of his eyes. "It came on just after we arrived. She's lying down."

Hannah mentioned that Liza was hoping to rally for dinner.

"I doubt it," Mako said.

She and Cricket exchanged a *WTF* look. By the way—migraines? Since when did Liza get those?

"Which means—" Mako went on, falsely bright. "We can eat the meat off the bones of the ribs Chef Jeff is cooking up without feeling like barbarians."

"Carnivores unite!" said Cricket, a little too gleefully.

"Poor Liza," said Hannah, but no one heard her; they were heading toward the seating around the outdoor fireplace that blazed and crackled. She'd go up to check on her sister-in-law before dinner if Liza didn't come down.

"What can we get for the big man?" said Mako.

Hannah looked around for Bruce but he was gone.

"Bourbon straight for Bruce," she said, certain that's what he'd want.

Mako looked at Ingrid. "Do you mind, Ingrid?"

"Of course."

She, too, wore that same stiff expression—there was no warmth or chattiness. Maybe that's what passed for professionalism. Hannah looked for warmth in people, though, a way to connect. She felt uncomfortable when she couldn't find it. Maybe she'd ask about the tattoo later. People loved questions about themselves.

Ingrid moved to the kitchen area, which was open to the great room.

That row of giant knives gleamed on the backsplash. It seemed like such an odd display, dangerous, menacing. Unsafe. Who would need so many different types of knives? What if there were children in the rental party?

Hannah also noted a battalion of liquor bottles—Grey Goose, Blanton's, Bombay Blue Sapphire, five bottles at least of red, more white. This was in addition to the alcohol she and Bruce had brought, which was not on display. Not up to Mako's standards, she guessed. How much did they plan to drink?

Hannah drifted into the dining area to get a closer look at

the sculpture. As she drew closer, she felt goose bumps come up on her flesh.

Yes, it *was* a skull but not an animal. It was unmistakably human. She found herself transfixed by the dark eyeholes, moved in closer.

What surrounded it was not bleached wood but more bones. She was no expert but she could make out ribs, pieces of vertebrae, hip bones, collarbones, shards and fragments, sharp and ragged. Hannah released a little gasp, then backed up and found herself knocking into Chef Jeff.

"Interesting piece, isn't it?" he said.

Hannah felt at a loss for words. "Is that real? Are those— *human* bones?"

He smiled coolly, holding a big pair of grilling tongs. His apron was smeared with something dark. It looked like—blood. His gaze was steely. Hannah felt her stomach churn a bit.

"Yes," he confirmed. "Those are human bones. This piece is created by a local artist, a friend of the host's. Are you familiar with the concept of *memento mori?*"

Hannah shook her head, wishing she could just return to the group but not wanting to be rude.

"From the Latin," he went on. *"Remember that you must die."*

The words, his tone sent a little chill through her.

"Um, okay. Wow," said Hannah.

"It sounds grim," Chef Jeff went on. "But really it's a reminder that every moment is precious, and that nothing matters as much as you think it does. Because death is certain, its time uncertain."

"Oh," said Hannah, feeling uninformed and uncomfortable. She looked around again for Bruce, hoping for a rescue from this conversation. But she didn't see him.

"Most people don't like to think about death. But the more you do, the happier you'll be that you're alive."

That did make a kind of sense.

"Where did he get the bones?" asked Hannah.

Chef Jeff gave a sudden, deep belly laugh, startling her. "I have no idea. Grave robbing maybe?"

"Oh," said Hannah again as Chef Jeff returned to the kitchen still chuckling.

She looked at the sculpture once more and felt a deep shudder move through her. *Remember that you must die.*

Creepy, she decided. This place was beautiful, but creepy as fuck.

Cricket's laughter drew her attention away from the bones. Her friend and Joshua sat close together on the couch, whispering.

She was surprised to feel something like jealousy. Lately she'd found herself envious of couples who seemed to have nothing on their mind except each other—when Bruce seemed always to be thinking about work, or *whatever*, and Hannah's thoughts centered on Gigi or her paranoid imaginings.

She missed the ease of that phase of life—before marriage, house, and children. Only sometimes. Her job at Red World had been manic, but fun. Lots of parties, travel, managing big personalities—which was something at which she excelled through a lifetime of training. It wasn't what she ever planned to do—she had been a business major at USF, graduated at the top of her class.

It had just been easy when Mako offered her a job after graduation.

But she'd happily given it up at Bruce's behest when she was eight months pregnant. *Stay home with the baby for a while. Figure out your next act. You don't want to work for your brother forever.*

But she hadn't figured that part out yet, that next phase. Maybe it was Gigi. Just being a mom for now. What was wrong with that?

Hannah moved to the front porch and found Bruce outside. He was putting his phone in his pocket, then getting another bag from the car. Who had he been talking to? She didn't even want to ask.

She walked out to him, gave him a kiss instead of an inter-rogation.

"I just forgot my laptop, love," he said. "Let's go in."

It reminded her that she had to get her phone.

"I'm just going to give Lou and Gigi a quick call."

"Give them my love," he said, heading toward the door.

It wasn't disconnected. But the statement carried the very male assumption that everything was fine unless you heard otherwise, that a simple expression of love was enough. Again, an ease she wasn't sure she'd experienced since before Gigi was born. Why was it so different for him? He cared. But he wasn't hooked into Gigi's well-being in the same way.

Hannah was grateful to find a strong signal when before it had been poor. Wonky, Mako had said.

She checked the time. 7:00 p.m., story time. She dialed Lou.

"Mama," said Gigi, when Lou put her on the phone. "Nighty night?"

It might not have been intelligible to anyone else, but Han-nah spoke fluent Gigi.

"Yes, bunny," she said. "Having fun with Lulu?"

"Yes. Story now," said Gigi, sounding sleepy. "Lulu reads."

"Sleep well, sweet baby," she said. "I'll call you in the morn-ing."

"Sleep sweet, Mama."

Hannah's heart hurt a little.

"We're all good here," said Lou coming back on. "You guys got there safe and sound?"

"Yes," she said. "All good here. Did you track us?"

"I did," said Lou. "Did you watch us on the camera?"

"I did."

"Well, thank goodness for technology," Lou said with a chuckle. "Back in my day there was none of that. You just had to trust that everything was all right and that you'd only hear if the news was bad. Simpler times."

Better or worse? Hannah couldn't say.

"You two relax and have fun. Remember that one of the best things you can do for your daughter is take care of each other."

Truth.

Hannah heard Gigi chirping happily in the background as Lou ended the call. She stood a moment, breathed, took in the cool night air. She looked back at the house, to see Mako with his arm around Bruce, Cricket laughing.

She was about to go join them when a movement in the trees caught her attention, the rustling of leaves, a shifting of branches. She turned on her phone flashlight and shined the light.

Nothing there. No glowing eyes in the dark.

She thought of the bear head mounted over the mantel, the sculpture of bones, and backed toward the open door. When she turned to jog up the porch steps, she felt a tingle on the back of her neck.

A final turn around revealed that there was nothing—no one—there.

11

HENRY

1997

The girl who liked to play with the boys, who was faster, smarter, and more competitive than any boy he had ever met, was named Piper. She turned around in her seat to look at him, gave him a smile that somehow reminded him that she'd left him in her dust during the hundred-yard dash in PE yesterday. It was the same look she'd given him then. It excited him, made him smile, too, though most guys would be mad to be beaten by a girl at anything.

He liked it—her speed, her confidence.

She reached her arm behind her, and he took the note she dangled.

Loser, it read.

Dork, he wrote back. He put the piece of paper in her waiting palm, heard her giggle when she read it.

He was helping her with math and a few other subjects. She wasn't a great student, always looking out the window, waiting to be let back outside to run and play. She was smart, though, when she wanted to concentrate.

"Something you'd like to share, Piper?" asked Ms. Banks from the front of the room. She wasn't mean enough to make them share their note.

"No, Ms. Banks," said Piper. "Sorry."

Later they'd meet in the library where they'd study for a while until his mom came. Piper walked home alone. Her house wasn't far.

"Okay, guys," said Ms. Banks. "Pop quiz."

Everyone, except for Henry, let out a collective moan. Piper put her head down on her desk. She was barely clinging to a C.

Ms. Banks gave him his paper and he got to work.

He was starting to like it here, as much as he could like it anywhere. Which made him anxious. Because he remembered that other times he'd started to like places, they were suddenly packing up whatever apartment his mother had rented and leaving, often in the middle of the night, always without notice. Alice never gave a reason, just that it was time. Sometimes she'd seem angry, or anxious. He'd never challenged her.

He'd just come home from school one day and then wouldn't go back the next. He'd never really had a friend before, someone who might miss him, wonder what happened to him.

He finished his test before anyone else and just sat for a while, staring at Piper's wild golden mane, her head bent in concentration.

The day outside was brutally hot and humid, the sun blared, heat waving off the playground. The tall palm trees swayed lightly. His mom had been complaining about the heat—a lot. He wondered if that was a sign that they'd be moving soon. He liked it hot, when the air was heavy, and you could feel the sun on your skin. They weren't far from the ocean; he could walk there and did. Something about the shorebirds calling, and the lapping waves, sand beneath his toes was soothing. It reminded him of—something. A memory just out of reach, a feeling that he'd like to have again but couldn't quite touch. There were faces attached to the memory—a man, a child. But they were amorphous and strange, like faces in a dream.

The bell rang and he waited by Piper's desk.

"How'd you do?"

"Maybe okay?" she said, wrinkling her nose at him.

"I'm sure you did fine." He wasn't, even though she knew the material. She was an outdoor creature, meant to run and play, not be penned inside regurgitating information she'd likely never use again.

"If I didn't my mom's not going to let me play soccer. I have to make Cs."

"You will."

"Dork," she said, nudging him.

"Loser."

They shared a bag of Doritos under the table in the library where you weren't supposed to have snacks. He helped her with her biology homework. She told him that he was turning his right foot out when he ran, slowing his time.

At three they walked out and she headed home.

"See you," she said, giving him a wave. She was certain of that. That he'd be there tomorrow and so would she.

"Yeah," he said. "See ya."

"Where's your mom?" she said, glancing back. "She's usually waiting."

He shrugged, trying for nonchalance. "She'll be here."

He watched Piper until she disappeared around the corner.

He waited fifteen minutes. Twenty. Watching up and down the street. He could hear the football coach's whistle blowing way off from the field behind the school. The air was thick with humidity, causing him to sweat beneath his backpack.

It was spring, the bright days already long and growing longer. He knew the way home. It wouldn't take him much time to walk, though he hadn't done it alone before.

At his other school, the teachers had waited to see everyone off. But they didn't do that here in middle school. He could just walk home. But what if she came here and didn't find him? She'd freak out. What if he waited and waited and she didn't come?

His stomach felt queasy. A couple of times she hadn't picked him up from other schools. Once she'd been late at work; he'd had to wait with a teacher who didn't seem too happy about it. Once a nice mom who felt bad for him gave him a lift. He found his mom sleeping on the couch.

"Oh my goodness!" she said when she saw him. "I dozed off!"

She didn't apologize and acted like it was nothing. It didn't feel like nothing to him.

But he was older now, almost fourteen.

Finally, he left the school and made his way home.

He'd have to pass the mall with the gun shop and the strip club, where there was always a suspicious gathering of men hanging around. Sometimes they called at his mom as they walked by.

"Just ignore them," she'd say, tugging on his arm. "Men are pigs."

He knew his mom wasn't pretty. That her nose was long, and her face marked with some faint acne scars. Even when she wore makeup, it didn't seem to quite take. Her hair, when she loosed it from its ponytail, was limp and flat. But she'd had a few boyfriends. Men who were there for a time, then not. He barely remembered any of them.

That day, the men in the mall ignored him, didn't even seem to notice him at all.

Their apartment building sat beside a green lake with a rusty fountain in the middle of it. The building was painted bright white and the hallways were exposed to the elements, like an old motel. He climbed up the stairs. He had a key and let himself inside, dropped his heavy backpack, relishing the cool of the interior.

"Mom?"

He walked through the living room to her room, which was empty. Then to his, also empty. Everything was plain and neat and orderly, beds made, kitchen clean. In the kitchen, he made some microwave macaroni and cheese, then ate it in front of the television, which he would not be able to do if his mom was home.

He watched *SpongeBob*, which was silly, childish but always funny.

He fell asleep on the couch with a knot in his stomach and an ache behind his eyes. When he woke up the dim light of dusk colored the room gray. There was a dryness to his throat, a humming in his ears.

"Mom?"

She wasn't home.

Who could he call? He couldn't think of anyone. There was no one—no grandparents, aunts, or uncles. Should he call the police? What would he say? *My mom. She didn't come home.*

Henry didn't know his father. For a long time, when he'd asked, she simply said, "You don't have one."

But after health class and sixth grade biology, he'd insisted on answers. *There has to be a father. Scientifically.*

"Look," she told him then, cheeks reddening. "I went to a sperm bank. I wanted a child, not a husband."

"Who is he?" Henry asked, grappling with that bit of information. *A sperm bank?*

"I have no idea and those records are sealed. Whoever donated his sperm, he didn't want to be known. He probably just did it for the money."

Henry had been aware of a feeling that would only grow and expand. A kind of shame. A kind of otherness. That there was something deeply and truly deficient within him. That feeling would only grow as he got older.

"It's okay," she said gently, maybe reading the horror on his face. "Some people have a mom and dad, a big family. Some people might have two dads, or two moms, or just a dad. You just have me. We only have each other. That's it."

Alice was a big proponent of the idea that you get what you get and don't get upset. Henry pushed down that ugly, hollow feeling, but from that day forward, he was always aware of it.

Henry didn't know where Alice worked. They hadn't been here long and the subject hadn't come up. In other places, she'd had a number of jobs—once a waitress, then a grocery store clerk. Once she'd cared for an elderly woman named Faith. Alice had worked at a bookstore, a clothing store. But where now? Another question without an answer.

At school, there were career days where parents came in to talk about their important jobs—doctor, lawyer, fireman. Some parents came to show skills—like cooking, painting, or crochet. Others came in to talk about their religion. His mom never did things like that. But they always had what they needed, a place to live, food, clothes, video games, books. She never talked about money. He never thought about it.

That he knew too little about his mother, about where she could be, about who she came from, dawned on him for the first time. She, too, must have had a mother and a father. They were dead. That's all he knew about them. *They were rotten, the both of them. Good riddance.*

The sky was almost fully dark when he left the apartment again, key in one pocket, the twenty from his birthday card in the other. He walked back to school. The world seemed changed, store signs glowing, road busy with cars, a blur of red and white lights. But when he got to the school it was dark, deserted. Even the field lights were out, no games being played that night. The school was a hulking black shadow in the near dark; above, cumulous clouds towered, big as mountains. The air was sticky and hot.

He knew the way to Piper's from school. She'd invited him one afternoon and her mom had made them gooey grilled cheese sandwiches. They'd had a swim in her pool. Her family kept horses on their expansive property. She'd taken him to the small barn down a path from her house. He remembered the smell of manure which somehow wasn't that unpleasant; he loved the way the mare had nuzzled him.

At her house, he rang the bell and Piper's mom came to the door. She was full-bodied and smiley, nails done and face flushed.

"Oh," she said. "Henry! Are you here to help Piper with her homework?"

He shook his head, wasn't sure what to say and didn't trust his voice anyway.

Her face darkened with concern and she opened the door wider. "Honey, what's wrong? Come on in."

Later, when the police came, they asked all the questions that he couldn't answer. Where did she work? Was there other family? A boyfriend, friends? Where had they lived before? He could tell by the way they looked at him that he should know these things. That it was weird that he didn't.

The police took him back to the apartment; he rode in the back of the squad car and under other circumstances that might have been cool. But he felt rigid and brittle, like he might shatter into pieces. Piper's mom followed behind them in her own car.

But when they got there, Alice still wasn't home. Henry let the two policemen in, they walked around, footfalls heavy, radios chattering, looking in closets and behind shower curtains.

Piper's mom stood with him, a hand on his shoulder.

"You'll stay with us tonight, Henry. Get your things and we'll leave a note for your mom. I'm sure she'll call when she gets in. Must be a good explanation."

The two officers exchanged a look. While Henry gathered his things, he heard them talking to Piper's mom. *If she doesn't come back by tomorrow, call this number.*

More than anything he remembered that the air was heavy with things the grown-ups didn't want to say in front of him.

That heaviness settled on his shoulders; he carried it out when Piper's mom took him back to their safe, pretty house where bad things didn't happen, and photographs everywhere showed smiling faces.

When a detective came to Piper's house that night, Henry was roused from sleep in the guest room bed.

"Honey," said Piper's mom. The hallway light shined in bright through the open door. Her hand was warm and gentle on his arm. For a second, he thought she was Alice.

"Mom?"

"No, honey," she said softly. "Come on downstairs."

Her voice quavered, and her usually smiling face was grim. He followed her down the hallway lined with all those family pictures, a stone in his gut.

He felt small and shaky in the room of adults. The detective was older with salt-and-pepper hair, deep wrinkles. He had a hard set to his jaw, a deep furrow in his brow, wore a look of dread underlaid with a layer of compassion.

"I'm afraid I have hard news."

Later, when Henry was asked to identify Alice's body, he imagined that on her still, gray face he saw the same expression.

12

HANNAH

June 2018

Mako sat at the head of the table, of course, with Hannah and Bruce to his right, Cricket and Joshua to his left. The king and his subjects, the table laden with baskets of bread, a meat and cheese board, bottles of wine—Mako and Liza's favorite Caymus Cabernet, Cricket's favorite Cakebread Chardonnay—the silverware gleaming, water glasses shimmering. Candlelight. Jazz from speakers.

Liza sat at the opposite end of the table, dressed in a simple black shift, her hair loose and shining. She chatted easily with Joshua. She'd rallied as promised, but she still looked unwell—a little gray around the eyes, her usual high color dulled. But she seemed to be holding up.

"Now a toast."

Here we go, thought Hannah. The Mako show.

"Everyone at this table is special to me," he began. "Hannah, you're the best sister a guy could ever have. Bruce, I don't consider you an in-law. You're my brother, and one of the smartest people I know."

Bruce raised a glass stiffly, glanced at Hannah. Hannah put a hand on his leg.

"Cricket, you're a part of this family, have been forever. And Joshua, you make Cricket happy so that makes you part of our family, too."

"Best friends forever," said Cricket, beaming at Mako and Hannah.

"And Liza—simply put, you're the love of my life. I can't imagine who I would be without you."

Liza smiled, then looked down at the table shyly.

Hannah felt lifted out, watching them all from above. Her husband's admissions echoed around her head. Her sister-in-law looked like she was about to topple over. Joshua was watching Mako with a kind of amused wonder. Bruce just looked blank. Only Cricket seemed happy, at ease. Even Mako seemed—off. There was an uncharacteristic darkness in his tone.

"Life's not always easy, right?" he said. "Running a company definitely has its ups and downs."

Bruce squeezed her hand under the table and she turned to look at him. He gave her a flat smile. What kind of things could her husband not live with? Maybe she should have pressed him. Maybe it couldn't wait.

"But one of the great things about success is sharing it with the people you love. On behalf of us both, welcome to a peaceful weekend of good food, time in nature, and the love of family and friends. Chef Jeff has prepared a feast. Cheers! Let's eat!"

He raised his glass and everyone followed suit.

"Cheers!" they all said in unison, Cricket laughing.

Just as they lifted their utensils, the lights flickered and went out. They all sat in darkness a second, Hannah's eyes adjusting, everyone cast in shadow and moonlight.

"Oh, no," she said.

But as quickly as they went off, they came back up again,

the appliances in the kitchen beeping and ringing. There was a collective sigh of relief.

"Must be the ghosts," said Chef Jeff, appearing by the table.

He'd slipped from the dim of the kitchen, his tall, broad form looming. He'd removed his hat to reveal a blond buzz cut. She wondered if he was about to deliver another lecture about remembering death. As if a mother ever had to be reminded of that. Maybe it was just men who needed to acknowledge how fragile, how temporary, how unsafe life was.

"Ah, yes," said Mako, face grim. "The cabin is haunted, right?"

Hannah flashed on the blog she'd read. What had it said? A dark history to one of the properties.

"That's right," said Chef Jeff with that tight unsmiling smile he seemed to have perfected. Hannah was starting to hate him a little.

He put down a huge platter of meat—ribs, steaks, chicken breasts. Then he returned with sides—macaroni and cheese creamy and gooey, Brussels sprouts crisply browned, potatoes, salad. The silent young woman assisted. Hannah watched that spider tattoo as she filled everyone's water glasses from the pitcher.

Hannah's stomach was rumbling, and she really did not want to hear about ghosts.

"A decade ago—more," said Chef Jeff. "A man murdered his family on this property."

Liza made a surprised gasp, put her hand to her heart.

Hannah wouldn't have thought it was possible for her sister-in-law to look more unwell. But she literally grew grayer, paler before Hannah's eyes, a light sheen of sweat on her brow. The woman needed to be in bed. She needed care and rest.

Hannah was about to speak up, but Chef Jeff obliviously went on.

"Now people say they see the wife wandering through the

woods, looking for her children. And some people think they've seen the little girl wading in the lake."

Chef Jeff seemed proud of himself, like he thought this was entertaining.

Mako let go of a booming laugh. "Don't look so freaked-out, Hannah," he said. "Chef's just messing with us."

"I don't believe in ghosts," said Chef Jeff. That same odd *un*smile stayed plastered. It was practiced and icy. Not nice at all. "Do *you*?"

Hannah felt like he was talking directly to her.

"Of course not," she said, sounding prim and defensive even to her own ears. "Is that true, though, that a family was murdered here?"

Chef Jeff shrugged. "Maybe. It's a rumor I've heard from some of the locals. For years, no one would buy this property because of that story."

No one spoke, all eyes on the chef. "Anyway," he said with a small bow. "Enjoy your feast."

"Of course it's not true," said Bruce, putting an arm around her. He cast an annoyed frown toward the chef.

Hannah and Cricket exchanged an uneasy look across the table.

The meat platter which had at first seemed so appetizing, looked greasy and overdone. Hannah had her back to the bone sculpture, but she could feel those hollow eyes on her neck.

"To our hosts," said Joshua, lifting his glass. He was clearly trying to clear the negativity of murder and ghosts, which Hannah put as a mark in his favor. "Thank you for this wonderful invitation and for welcoming me into your clan. I'm truly honored to be here."

Hannah imagined how they must look from the outside. Happy, privileged, enjoying life. They were all that, weren't they?

Mako gave him a kingly nod. "Okay," he said. "*Now*—let's eat!"

As Hannah started serving Bruce some potatoes, Liza rose quickly, her chair scraping back against the floor.

"I'm sorry," she said. "I have to lie down."

She slipped away from the table and was gone.

Mako rose to go after her. "Excuse me. She hasn't been feeling well."

Murder, ghost stories, mounted skulls, her husband's secrets. The ailing hostess. Her daughter far away for the first time. The things she had been pondering and puzzling about herself but had been buried deep and were a dark riptide, threatening to pull her under.

She pushed her swirl of thoughts away, and took a long sip of her wine. An awkward silence fell over the remaining guests.

Even Cricket had stopped smiling.

Everyone who remained at the table started to eat in silence.

13

TRINA

It's nice here. The house, the trees. The perfect getaway really, just like it said online. There are so many windows, it's like a doll's house. From where I stand, I can see inside clearly. The happy gathering of family and friends around the big table, a feast prepared.

They smile and laugh, served by the tall chef and his assistant. The served and the servers. I try to imagine myself sitting among them, maybe beside Hannah. I can't. Story of my life.

I am the puzzle piece you think will fit—but doesn't. People always try to guess my nationality. They might ask: Are you Italian? Or I might get: *Habla español?*

The truth is, until recently, it was a mystery, even to me.

My mother is French and Turkish, raised in Paris; I always knew that much. But her parents died young and she always thought of herself as an American, since she moved to New York City in her twenties to become an artist, met the love of her life, Scott, when they were both living in the East Village. My mom, Giselle, became a US citizen after she married, finally settling into life as a grade school art teacher before having me. She grapples now for her French, even her accent faded.

My father—well he was a biological wildcard, even to my mother.

My *dad*, Scott, the man who raised me and who I have always thought of as my father, had a vasectomy at an early age. The child of abuse, he decided before he ever met my mother that he never wanted kids. When he changed his mind after they married, the reversal didn't work. So my mother got pregnant via a sperm donor. Anonymous. Records sealed.

Like everything about the world, they gave it to me straight. I don't remember *not* knowing that about myself, or thinking it was strange. My mother always said things like: *Love comes into our lives in all sorts of mysterious ways.* Or: *Any man can be a father, but it takes a special one to be a daddy.* How I came to them was the unique texture of the fabric of our particular family.

Maybe if Scott hadn't died, I never would have even been curious about my donor father. Because my *dad*? He was enough, more than enough. A big loving bear of a man—full of stories and belly laughs. The smell of Old Spice can conjure him, his big hugs, the scratch of his stubble.

I always think of it as sadness that killed him, a deep incurable unhappiness that he carried with him, a note I heard beneath every laugh, a riptide pulling at every happy moment. This thing he'd carried since childhood, a voice in his head, a shadow in his periphery. It caused him to drink too much to quiet it, to drive too fast to outrun it.

He fought it for us, I promise you, my mother always said. *But it was too much for him.*

I was fifteen when he crashed his Indian—the motorcycle he'd restored, worked on tirelessly, polished and babied. We'd drive to swap meets—seeking this obscure part or that. Big, crowded places, dusty and hot, people selling, buying, passionate about old machines. He was happy on those days. I know he was—I remember that smile, the crinkle around his eyes.

But it wasn't enough.

We weren't enough.

I wasn't enough.

Maybe it was because I wasn't *really* his, that's why I wasn't enough to keep him around. If I'd been his biological daughter, something more powerful would have kept him bound to this world. I offered this theory to my mother only once. She wept.

He loved you. More than anything. Her fading French accent lilted, her dark eyes gleamed. She told me I didn't understand depression, how it was a con and a thief of joy. How it lured people away, making them believe that the world was better off without them.

She was right. I didn't understand it then. I do now.

He did it for us. He thought he was doing it for us. The insurance payout.

He was gone and we were set for life. That's what he thought was important. Money.

And we would have given it all back for one more day with the man who was my father in every way that mattered.

I am thinking about Dad now as I watch the chef put big piles of meat before the diners. I don't know why, except that I am always thinking about him, really. I wonder what he would have had to say about this enterprise of mine.

"Dad," I say out loud. "I've done bad things."

Sometimes when the world is topsy-turvy, bad things are good things.

That's what I imagine he'd say. But probably he'd say what Mom says. *I'm worried about you, kitten. Come home.*

My parents. They're good people. They loved me, did their best. I mean, my mom and my dad.

Now my biological father, well, that's another story. We don't have to get into that right now.

My dad taught me how to play chess. He was a good player,

had competed in college. There were some trophies on a shelf in the living room.

"Chess is a dance. Your moves influence your opponent's move. When you understand the board, the player, you can anticipate what others will do. Some of the time."

I've found that to be true in life, as well.

They're all here now. They don't know it, but my moves have influenced theirs.

Before, I stood in the trees and listened to Hannah talk on the phone. I could hear her soft voice, the tinny voices on the line. *Sleep sweet, Mama.*

Her little girl. I feel a pang. Doubt, regret. Of course, I feel them. I'm human after all.

As if he's connected to me, can feel my energy across time and space, I receive a text:

I saw the security footage from that building in Miami. I know what you've been doing. It needs to stop.

I don't bother answering him.

I haven't since the last time we were together. But I can't bring myself to block him, either. I like knowing he's out there. A good guy in a bad world. I shove my phone in my pocket.

Before Hannah headed inside, she stopped on the porch and turned around, as if she could sense me watching. All mothers are a little bit psychic, aren't they? Now I watch her at the table between her husband and her brother. She doesn't look happy or at ease. She looks worried—a furrow in her brow belying her smile.

From where I stand, hidden, watching them through the glass, they are the picture of the perfect family. Instagramable. But I know better. What people show the world is rarely the whole truth, especially these days when everything must be curated and cropped, filtered and brightened. Real life is messy and complicated. Ugly.

The week after my dad died, I found his journal. I went through his things while my mom was out. The motorcycle crash was ruled an accident—a wet road, a turn taken too fast.

But everyone who loved him—we knew. The sadness; it took him. He had to make it look like an accident if we were going to get the insurance money. There was no motorcycle clause in his policy; he'd made sure of it.

His notebook was tucked between the mattress and the box spring on his side of the bed. My mother probably didn't even know it was there. Every page was full—edge-to-edge—with drawings and poetry. Sad faces with exhausted eyes, line drawings of barren woods, empty rooms, broken windows.

His last entry:

There's just too much darkness.

I'm drowning.

A sketch of a tired, stubbled, big man drinking in through his open maw a flood of ink coming from the sky.

I kept it. I carry it with me, even now. It's the only piece of him I have.

I went through the motions after that—finished high school, went to a small private college in upstate New York, graduated with a degree in computer engineering, learned to code. I did all the things a person is supposed to do.

But I had a darkness in me, too.

It wasn't until I took that Origins test that I understood why.

14

BRACKEN

Bracken pulled his truck up the long drive to his other rental property, this one far more modest than the one he called Elegant Overlook on his website, the one the shark man and his crew had inhabited.

This smaller one with just two bedrooms and a loft, great room, big porch looking out on a lovely but lesser view than Elegant Overlook, he marketed it as a couples or creative retreat. He called it Luxurious Stillness. *Finish your novel. Reconnect with your spouse. Or just be, watching the hummingbirds and the sunset in peace and solitude.*

The white Toyota that May, his one-person cleaning crew, drove was parked out front, hatch open to reveal buckets and supplies, a vacuum cleaner, a box of rags. It was late, the sun already below the horizon, the last vestiges of light clinging to the sky.

He walked inside and smelled the mingle of lemon and vinegar. All organic cleaning products (except in the bathrooms where only the hard stuff could combat mold), finest linens, thickest towels and plenty of them, artisanal soaps, shampoos and conditioners sourced from a local company. The kitchen could be stocked if his guests requested, chefs hired, daily maid service, in-house massage visits, what have you. Often the folks who rented Overlook wanted those things. But those who rented Stillness usually wanted to be left alone.

He could hear May singing, as she usually did while she cleaned. She had a nice voice, smoky and perfectly pitched. She'd have her earbuds in and be deep in her work. He scared the bejesus out of her at least three times a week, though really she should be expecting him. She just lost herself. That was one of the many things he liked about her.

He stood and regarded the view, a final buttery yellow light fading from the horizon line and the glowing green of the leaves, the silvery blue of the mountain shadows. In the kitchen, he looked around. Garbage had been emptied, surfaces were gleaming, paper towels refilled.

"Tidy couple," said May coming up behind him. His turn to be startled. "Everything left as they found it. They even stripped the beds."

He turned to regard her. Her fine brown hair, muscular arms, collarbone taut against tanned skin. She smiled, revealing straight white teeth.

"That's nice," he said. When she turned to head back toward the kitchen area, he admired the valentine shape of her ass, the fullness of her thighs.

He already knew that the couple had stripped the bed.

He'd watched them.

He'd watched them cook last night. Make love on the porch in front of the fire. He'd watched the wife in the shower, her body soft but pretty, youthful and full. She'd hummed, contentedly soaping herself, eyes blank and peaceful. He'd watched them sleep, curled around each other.

Earlier, he'd watched Liza shower. Leaning her delicate body against the tiles, she wept. He'd wanted to race up there and comfort her, fix whatever had been broken to make her cry so inconsolably. But that was a boundary he couldn't cross. When she was done, she'd vomited in the toilet. Carefully wiped it down when she was done.

He'd been thinking of her ever since. Her fragility. Her vulnerability. The boundary between them. What would it take to cross over that? To hold her? To *have* her?

They belonged to him while they were in his houses, didn't they? He never tired of people and all their different ways. Their voices and gestures, their conversations, the way they were with each other, what they did when they thought no one was watching. He kept their secrets, though. He kept his distance. Usually.

"They left you a six-pack of craft beer in the fridge. From Tall Elk Brewery in town," May said. "With a sweet thank-you note."

That was a bit of surprise. People didn't usually offer thanks or leave gifts. Never in the big house. Entitlement. That's what he saw in most of his guests. They'd paid and expected to be served, maybe rightly so.

Privilege. A word that suddenly inspired jealousy, resentment, rage. Some people were born with it—that beautiful ease, that aura of never worrying about making it, surviving. Some stood on the other side of the glass, watching. Even if tireless effort or extraordinary achievement opened the door to that shining universe, it always felt like a mirage. People born to privilege just didn't know there was anything else. People born without it knew what awaited if the destroyer came to call. And the destroyer was always waiting, wasn't he?

"Want one?" he asked. He took two from the fridge and held one up to her.

"Yeah," she said. "I'm just about done. Can't drink on the job, you know. My boss is a real dick."

She gave him a wink.

He nodded solemnly. "I'd heard that."

He walked out to the porch and sat down on the couch, the two beers sweating in their bottles on the table. After a while, May came and sat in the rocker beside him. The warm evening air hummed with the sound of insects, punctuated by the trills of birds in the trees. The light wind whispered in the trees.

He took a deep drag of the cold beer, and May did the same. She had a thoughtful gaze on him.

"Come for dinner tonight?" she asked. Her eyes were hazel, almost amber. And he liked the way she looked at him. They'd slept together three times. She had a young daughter, Leilani, a precocious ten-year-old who was half-time with May, and half-time with May's ex, Leilani's dad. It was an amicable arrangement, most of the time. Leilani was a sweet kid with a little bit of a learning issue.

"With Leilani?" he asked. It was fine if Leilani was around. But it was better if she wasn't.

"Leilani's with her dad tonight." She looked at him, bit on her lip a little.

It was easy with May. He could be himself; she didn't seem to have any expectations of him or want him to be any one certain way. He didn't do well with people usually—found them confusing, their cues difficult to understand. But he was okay with May.

"Sure. What time?"

"Eight? I have a chili in the Crock-Pot, made some corn-bread early this morning."

She was a good cook; he'd been astounded by that. He'd never known anyone who could cook well.

"I'll bring the wine." Though he rarely drank he had a pantry full of bottles left behind by guests who had brought way too much. They wouldn't take it at the food pantry, but he wound up giving the bottles as gifts so that they wouldn't go to waste.

She nodded, finished off her beer. "Oh," she said, standing. "I found this. I'm not sure what it is? It was in the master shower."

She pulled something from her pocket and handed it to him. He pretended to inspect it. "Huh."

"No idea what it is," she said again. "But maybe they'll call for it?"

"Yeah," he said. "Strange."

"See you later," she said, tossing back an inviting smile and he felt something stir inside him, a tug, a longing.

He recalled the feel of her, the taste of her. He doubted they'd do much eating. As he made love to her, maybe he'd be thinking of Liza.

When she was inside, he looked at the item in his hand. It was the tiny lens encased in black plastic from one of his pinhole cameras. It must have fallen from the showerhead. Shit.

He looked back at May, who was gathering her things inside. If she knew what she'd found, it didn't show. She caught him looking and gave him a wave, and then she was gone.

What would she think of him if she knew what he did? How much time he spent watching the people he rented his cabins to? What did it make him? A stalker? A Peeping Tom?

The gloaming settled and the night was a silvery blue. He sat for a while, letting the stillness wash over him. After a bit, he took out his phone and opened the camera app. His big group at Overlook was just sitting down to dinner.

15

LIZA

Her head. It was a million jackhammers. A blinding light that wouldn't stop shining. A siren that wouldn't go quiet. Until recently, she hadn't had a migraine since she'd started practicing yoga and meditation seriously. Not until the IVF, this push for a baby, to start a family. It was something Mako wanted very badly. Apparently everyone did IVF these days—a new norm. Not okay to just try for a while and let it happen naturally. Of course, they *had been* trying for over a year. Too long, according to Mako. They needed help.

And they got it. Just not the way either of them thought.

She lay very still, knowing that any sudden movement now would result in waves of pain, a terrible bout of nausea. She'd tried to will it all away.

She could still smell the smoke from the grill, the meat. It turned her stomach; she covered her nose with the bedsheets. She never complained about it, even forced herself to eat a bit of meat or fish on occasion because she knew it made Mako happy, but the smell of charred flesh revolted her. The weird chef, his terrible stories. Did anyone else notice that sculpture made from bones? It was all—just awful.

Downstairs they were all laughing and shouting, the volume coming up slowly as the evening wound on.

They were loud people—Mako and Cricket. Hannah and Bruce less so.

The hot tub was right below the master bedroom window. How long would it be before they were all in there? Probably getting high?

She should try to rally again.

This looked bad. She was the hostess after all.

But the pain, the nausea. It kept her rooted and still, wanting to be a part of the fun but stuck in the darkness. Though, of course, she was never really a part of it. Not with those three. Everyone else was on the outside of that group, even Bruce. But it was fine, really. They had all that history. And Liza knew she held herself apart a little, even if in her heart she didn't want to.

She'd planned to do a special morning class from the deck with the stunning view and the sun rising. But she doubted she'd been in any shape to do that. Maybe Hannah would step in as a guest instructor; she had a beautiful practice.

Liza tried to rouse, to push herself to a seated position, but the pain made the room spin and she wound up back where she started.

Earlier, when Mako followed her up from the table, he'd lain beside her for a while, holding a cold compress to her head.

"I hate seeing you like this," he'd whispered.

"I'm sorry."

"No," he said softly. "*I'm* sorry. What can I do?"

"Just go enjoy yourself," she'd assured him. "This will pass. I'll be fine by morning. Once the meds kick in."

She hadn't taken them. She couldn't, but she couldn't tell him why. Not yet.

She'd looked over at him and he'd been watching her with that intense searching stare he had, as if he could see right through all her layers, straight to her core. It had turned her into a puddle of herself the night they met, and never failed to move her even years later. But there was something else there lately—a sadness, a heaviness.

"Are *you* okay?"

"Yeah." He took her hand and pressed his lips against it, averting his eyes.

"What is it?"

He hadn't been himself. Not for a while. *Does he know?* she wondered. *On some level does he know?* Or did he find something on her phone, her computer. She was careful. But the digital realm was his natural habitat. He knew all its back alleys and secret doorways.

"Remember those tests?"

"Tests?" There was the battery of tests they both took for the fertility doctor. Mako had recently had a full physical where the doctor got on him about his weight, his cholesterol. She felt her heart stutter. Was something wrong with him?

"The DNA kits we got from Secret Santa."

"Oh," she said. "Right."

She'd thrown hers away only for Mako to later reveal that he'd fished it out of the trash. He'd wanted her to do it; but she'd refused. She didn't want some random company to have that much access to her genetic information. Who knew how it could be used in the future—by the government, by insurance companies, by corporations trying to sell this or that? If there was something dark coded into her DNA, she'd find out about it soon enough. She wasn't going to go looking for trouble. But Mako had spit in the vial and sent it in.

"Did you get your results?"

Statistically speaking, she understood from the research she did after Mako insisted on sending in his kit, you'd find out something surprising. Something that made you question who you are. And whether that was a good thing, or a bad thing you couldn't know until it was too late.

He still held her hand, didn't meet her eyes. She waited for him to answer and when he didn't she pressed.

"What did it *say*, Mickey?" Sometimes she called him that, in their most intimate moments. He hated it when his family called him that, but he liked it from Liza.

He shook his head. "It was weird. I've been doing some research."

"What kind of research?"

Her head was pounding, but the pain suddenly took a back seat to her worry for him. He'd asked for the full suite of information from family history, medical data, other potential relatives out there looking for connections.

"It's just that, you know, how my dad is from Italy—like his whole lineage is pure Italian."

"Right…"

"According to this test, I'm not Italian. Like, not at all. Zero percent."

"Oh," she said, relieved. "It could be a mistake, right?"

"Yeah," he said. "That's what I thought at first. But this is not the first time I've taken one of these. I took one a couple of years ago when a buddy of my mine was investing big in this technology. It was a different company, the science was still evolving, so when the results were not what I expected I didn't really think anything of it."

"Did you talk to your parents?"

He laughed. "I tried after the first time. But—you know Mom—it didn't really go that well. They acted like I was trying to hurt them or something. I just dropped it. She said something weird—" He did his best Sophia impression, complete with fluttering eyelids and a hand at his throat. "'Family is not about biology, Michael, it's about actions.'"

"Okay," said Liza.

"That was a while ago," he said. "I kind of forgot about it.

Or buried it, or whatever. And then the Origins test at Christmas opened up the issue for me again."

She put a hand on the worried furrows in his brow. His head felt warm to the touch.

"What about Hannah's results?"

"I haven't asked," he rolled on his back and looked up at the ceiling. "I don't even know if she did it. I guess I don't really want to know. I thought maybe we'd have time to talk this weekend."

That was classic Mako—ignore, deflect, bury until you couldn't.

"Do you think that's true?" he asked. "That family is about actions, not just about biology."

She considered it. "I think it's true in a way. I mean, if you think about it, all family is about choice. You choose who you love; you choose to have children from that love. You choose to be a good parent, take care of your children. You *could* be biologically related but not really a family. You can be family—like spouses—but not be biologically related."

He nodded, seemed about to say something else, when Cricket's laughter rang up from downstairs.

"I should get back to the table."

He shifted away, but she reached for him, pulling him back. "Mako."

The darkness had left him. He was just Mako again, bright and looking for a good time. "It's probably nothing. I shouldn't have brought this up now. We'll talk it all through later."

"Are you *sure*?"

"Totally," he said, kissing her head. "You just try to feel better."

"Okay," she said. She was just relieved it wasn't something like he had the genetic coding for some disease or disorder. Lots of people were wrong about their heritage, weren't they? And how reliable even were these tests?

Then he was gone; she heard him thundering down the stairs. And she was alone in the dark, with the pain in her head that was getting worse instead of better.

Now she heard him laughing downstairs.

He'd get drunk and forget all about her. That was his way. He could only focus on what was in front of him; it drew all of him. All of his attention, all of his energy. It was like he slipped into a trance when he was coding, when he was partying, when he was doing whatever it was he was doing. And the world around him disappeared completely. When you were in the high beam of his vision, there was nothing else. When you were not, you didn't even exist. Or so it seemed. She envied him that focus.

It's not focus, her lesser self whispered. *It's selfishness. He doesn't think or care about anything that's not feeding his ego in that moment.*

Footsteps on the stairs, slow and measured, the wood creaking.

Occasionally, he surprised her, remembering a date she was sure he'd forgotten. An act of consideration or kindness she didn't expect. Coming home early with takeout for a movie night, or sweeping her away on a romantic weekend.

Yes. That small voice again. *Occasionally, he steps out of himself and remembers he has a wife. A wife who had her second miscarriage three months ago. A wife who is having a migraine for the first time in a decade.*

A wife who has made a horrible mistake she deeply regrets. Sort of.

The pain. It pulsated behind her eyes. When she closed them she saw a field of too-bright stars, one that swirled like a galaxy.

Those footsteps were moving down the hall toward the door.

It was probably Hannah, coming to check on her. She wished they were closer. But Hannah seemed to hold her at arm's length—always kind, always polite, just never crossing that line to real friendship. Or maybe it was Liza. Maybe Liza held Hannah away because—well, because maybe she didn't know how to be close to women. That was the truth, wasn't it? Her mother was gone; she didn't have any sisters. The few women she'd thought were true friends had turned out not to be.

It was quiet again. She heard Mako laughing again downstairs, voice booming through the floorboards. Whatever had been bothering him earlier forgotten, or locked away. She thought she heard Hannah, too. But maybe that was Cricket. Maybe there hadn't been anyone on the stairs, after all.

She closed her eyes again, focused on her breath, allowed the tension to leave her shoulders, her forehead. The edges of the migraine were starting to soften. Maybe she'd be fine by morning.

Liza almost didn't even hear it at first as the door to the room softly creaked open. When she opened her eyes, there was the shadow of a figure there.

"Hi?" she said, squinting through the darkness, through the pain. "Who's there?"

Was she dreaming? Sometimes her headaches played tricks— vivid dreams and strange imaginings.

When she opened her eyes, there wasn't anyone there but the door stood slightly ajar. It had been closed before, hadn't it?

Beside her, the phone buzzed. She reached for it.

The words in the bubble on the screen made her heart stop:

I'm here.

The number was unknown to her, no name attached. Different from the number of the text yesterday. She'd blocked that one.

Who is this? she typed, hands shaking. The pain in her head ratcheted tighter.

I'm here.

Where?

I'm in the guest cabin, north of the house.

What? Was that even fucking possible? She forced herself to stand, and moved unsteadily toward the window. The guest cottage. She'd told the host that they probably wouldn't even need to use it. He'd pointed it out to her when he'd carried the luggage upstairs for her. She looked at the window through the darkness.

There.

A light was glowing in the window. Oh my god. Her whole body was shaking now.

I'm going to call the police.

No. You're not. You have something that belongs to me. You're going to come out here and talk to me, Liza.

She felt a lash of anger, a boldness. She didn't deserve this. Not for one mistake. What *she had* did not belong to him. It belonged to *her*.

Nausea was a roil in her gut, rising up her throat.

Or what? she texted.

The dots pulsed; she watched, eyes aching, laughter carrying up from downstairs. She stared at the screen. That's when she felt it, the now too-familiar pain in her abdomen. It was like a mean, angry finger poking into her mercilessly.

No. No!

She doubled over with it when the phone started pinging and pinging, message after message.

Or I'm going to
blow
your
house
DOWN
Bitch.

16

HENRY

1997

"Well here it is," said Miss Gail.

She placed a plump hand on Henry's arm and gave a little squeeze.

The room was big and sunny with two twin beds pushed up against opposite walls. Each side of the room was furnished with a bedside table, a desk and chair, a dresser as well. The right side of the room was clearly already inhabited, walls covered with posters of anime characters, and some photographs. It was tidy, though, bed made, books stacked in a neat pile on the desk. A stuffed bear was tucked into the covers, tattered head on the pillow.

"It's not The Plaza," she said, looking at him. She had big kind eyes, magnified by thick glasses, a crooked smile. "But I promise you that you'll be safe and cared for here, Henry. Which maybe doesn't seem like much after all you've lost. But there we are, okay?"

He nodded. He hadn't spoken much since he'd identified Alice's body. He found that words died in his throat, or got stolen by his breath which seemed too thin to carry their weight from his mouth. In fact, everything from that night forward was a bit of a blur—a million questions, embraces and pitying looks from strangers. *Isn't there any family, son, someone we can call?*

But there was no one. No one he'd ever met, or even heard of.

What about your father?

He didn't want to say what Alice had told him. That his father was a sperm donor. It seemed so—clinical. Like there was something so wrong with him, that he was somehow not *natural*, not *real*.

I never met him. My mother wasn't sure who he was.

One of the police officers spent a few days looking for Alice's family of origin. Henry stayed with Piper's family until the state found placement for him at Miss Gail's.

Finally, after a few days with Piper's family, in their big, tidy house, with Piper's kind, generous parents who cooked for him and did his laundry, and shuttled him back and forth to the police station, Miss Gail came for him.

You're always welcome here, Henry, said Piper's mom as they walked him out to Miss Gail's older but well-kept minivan. *Weekends, holidays, whenever.*

Piper hugged him hard, then ran away into the house.

He hoped he properly thanked them, but it was as if a strange fog had descended around him. He couldn't think straight. He couldn't feel anything at all.

"Get yourself a little settled," Miss Gail said now. "We have to go back to the police station after lunch. They still have questions—about your mom. I'm so sorry, honey."

He saw that she was teary, but he just nodded.

She took him into a soft embrace which he didn't mind but couldn't bring himself to return. When she left, he lay on the bed and stared at a large crack in the ceiling, his bag with his few belongings on the floor beside him. Then he looked out the window at the tall oak that stood in the yard. He felt that he was floating, untethered, belonging nowhere.

At the police station, the same man who'd come to tell him that his mother was dead was waiting for him with more questions he couldn't answer. The same questions.

Where were you born?

Where did you live before?

Do you remember any place your mother might have worked?

He dug into his memory, and yes, he remembered one place his mom had worked, a café in a town in upstate New York, Lucky's. A diner with really good fries and big creamy chocolate shakes.

"That's good," said the cop, Detective West. He had dark circles under his eyes, ran a thick hand through his salt-and-pepper hair.

"Because I have to tell you. You and your mom—"

He seemed not to know how to go on. Henry watched the older man's face, his furrowed brow. West took and released a deep breath.

"You're ghosts."

"Ghosts," Henry repeated.

Yes, that was right. They were barely there. Now Alice was gone altogether and he could feel himself fading.

"Your birth certificate and social security number," he said. "They belong to someone else. A kid who died before he was a year old."

The information landed but didn't make any sense. What did that mean?

"And your mom. Alice? We haven't found any identification at all. No driver's license, no social security card, no passport. Not in her purse, or at your house. The social security number she gave the school belongs to a woman in Tucson, another deceased party."

Henry and Alice *had* been in Tucson for a while. It came back to him vaguely. Alice worked for an elderly woman there, running errands, and doing housekeeping, shuttling her back and forth to the doctor. Faith. She'd smelled of lemons and was always baking for Henry. He remembered her kindness. They'd played checkers a lot. He told Detective West about it now, and the man scribbled notes.

"Do you have a last name for Faith?"

Henry shook his head. He realized in that moment that the world of a child was very small. It only consisted, at first, of what your mother told you was true, what was important. It was only later, when you went out into the world that you started to question what you'd been told. It was a terrible shock if you learned that the world was very different from the small sliver your mother had shared.

"She was afraid," Henry said. He hadn't intended to say it. But now that his mother had been killed, it seemed important.

The detective held him in a curious gaze. "Afraid of who, of what?"

"She said that there were people, bad people who would come for us, try to take me. We always had to keep moving."

Slats of light came in through the blinds, landed on West's messy desk, dust motes dancing in the brightness. There was the smell of burned coffee, a sandwich half-eaten on his desk. The detective's frown deepened.

"She never said who? Or why?"

Henry shook his head again. "But she was right, wasn't she? Someone came for her. Someone killed her."

He kept seeing Alice, lying still and gray, her face grim but peaceful. He tried to remember her smiling, but he couldn't.

"You don't have any idea who would want to hurt your mother, Henry? Can you remember ever seeing anyone lingering around your house, or school? Did she have a boyfriend somewhere, someone who hurt her?"

Henry thought back but there was no one he could name or even picture. Maybe there had been a man once, somewhere. Someone with a smiling face and big jaw, blue eyes. But it was like the blond woman he sometimes saw in his dreams, the one who sang a song—*you are my sunshine, my only sunshine*; a fantasy, not real.

"They came for her. But they didn't come for me."

Detective West looked at Henry, seemed again at a loss for words. "This is hard, son. The hardest thing. I'm sorry this is happening to you."

Things happen to you, Alice used to say. *You don't always choose those things. But you just make the best of it. You just keep moving.*

"She said there was a sperm donor," said Henry, again without planning to say it. It was like all the little pieces of himself and his life with his mother were trying to fit themselves together.

The detective cocked his head. "Come again?"

"My father," said Henry. "She told me once that he was sperm donor. That she didn't have any idea who he was."

"Do you think that's true?"

Henry shrugged. "I guess?"

"Did she say where the sperm bank was?"

"No."

"No," echoed West. "Of course not."

"I'm sorry."

The older man blew out a breath, rubbed at his wide neck. Henry noticed that there was a small stain on his tie, looked like ketchup.

"Nothing to be sorry for, son. I'm going to figure this out for you. Who you are, who your mom was, what happened to her. Okay?"

"Okay," said Henry. But Henry didn't believe him. Because Henry was a ghost, and he knew it.

"Is there anything else, Henry? Any other detail you can share about your mother that might help us?"

Henry shook his head. There were a million little details—that sometimes she stayed in the shower for more than an hour, that she liked old movies, that she tucked him in every night, read to him from the newspaper, always made sure he had a good breakfast, did his homework, had the things he needed. But that there was something—wrong. Something missing between them. He didn't have any words for that.

When he didn't say anything else, the detective handed him a card. "Sometimes things come back. Like that diner name. Those are the kind of things that might help me, okay?"

He promised the old detective, who he could see was trying hard to understand the puzzle in front of him, that he would think and call if anything else came back to him. He would.

Back at Miss Gail's, he found Piper sitting on the front steps waiting for him. Her house wasn't far. He'd go back to the same school, Miss Gail told him, when he was ready. He was ready. He'd go back on Monday. Alice would say: *No use sitting around feeling sorry for yourself.*

He went to sit next to Piper.

"How is it?"

She looked back at the big Victorian which was rundown a little but still managed to look well-kept and cheerful with big planters filled with flowering bushes, rockers with red cushions on the porch, checkered curtains, stained glass in the front door.

"Not bad."

She nodded, her hair shining in the afternoon sun. She rubbed at her nose which was covered, like her cheeks, with a wild smattering of freckles. Rangy, the fastest runner at school, bold, full of laughter, Piper was the prettiest girl he'd ever seen.

"You haven't cried," she said. "Not once. My mom said you hold it all inside. That you need to let it out—all that sadness. That it will make you sick if you don't."

He wanted to tell her that he didn't feel anything at all. Her mom was wrong. He wasn't holding anything in. There was nothing there. But he sensed that it might frighten her. It frightened him.

"I cried. Some," he lied.

She seemed satisfied with that.

"You're an orphan now." She said it easily, with a touch of wonder. A thing that was true and couldn't hurt because of its essential truth. She was a practical girl; he understood her. But *was* it true, if his father was out there somewhere? Maybe orphan just meant that no one cared more about you than they cared about anything else. That much was true now that Alice was gone.

"Yeah."

She held out her hand and she took it. "Don't worry. You'll always have me."

He wondered if *that* was true.

17

HANNAH

June 2018

Hannah was drinking too much. Two vodka sodas already, and the red wine Mako had served with dinner was going down fast, her glass almost empty. What was it? Liquor to wine, you'll be fine? She hoped that was true. She hadn't had this much to drink since Gigi had been born, and not for ages before. And had she seen on the *printed itinerary* left on their king bed that there was someone picking them up early for a hiking excursion? Had it said 7:00 a.m.?

She felt warm, her cheeks flushed. Bruce had knocked back a couple of bourbons and he was relaxed and easy, all the tensions he was carrying seemed to have vanished. She'd let herself surrender to her buzz, forget all the things that were worrying her.

When Mako returned to the table with assurances that Liza just needed some rest and would be fine in the morning, they'd settled into dinner—the ghost story, the creepy review, too, faded, were washed away in a tide of good food, drinks, and laughter.

The meal had actually been heavenly—the meat perfectly grilled, charred at the edges but moist inside. Every side was an explosion of flavor. And a surprise dessert was on its way, Chef clanging about the kitchen while his silent assistant cleared their plates. Hannah thanked her, but she didn't seem to hear.

Mako was loudly telling a story about buying the Tesla and how he needed the tax credit, and Cricket was hanging on his every word. *I made so much money last year,* he said as if it was a problem. Cricket literally had her chin in her hand, staring at him like a lovesick schoolgirl. Joshua, with a slight smile, and possessive arm around Cricket seemed less impressed.

Hannah had felt Joshua's eyes, once, twice, but ignored him. Now it was her turn to look at him for a second. His elegant high cheekbones, short shorn dark curls, his good posture, his slimness. He seemed tense, maybe his mind elsewhere, maybe picking up on the energy between Mako and Cricket.

Cricket might always be a little in love with Mako, Hannah thought. The thought came out of nowhere, surprising her. No, that wasn't true. Was it?

Joshua pulled his phone from his pocket, glancing at it with a frown.

"Excuse me a moment," he said, rising.

"Of course," Hannah said, giving him a smile which he returned before moving away quickly.

Cricket and Mako didn't even notice, Mako drunkenly going on—and on. Hannah had already heard this story. "And the guy was like: Wait. Dude, you're paying cash?"

Earlier in the month, Hannah's mother had intimated that Mako was having some issues with the business, that he'd asked their dad to invest more money. But that Sophia and Leo had declined, saying that they were "tapped out" when it came to giving Mako money. Still Mako talked ceaselessly about the things he had, what he was buying next. So, what was that all about?

Hannah felt Bruce's hand on her thigh and when she looked over at him, they locked eyes.

"Looks like the fire is dying outside," he said. "I'll go see to it."

"Let Chef get it," said Mako, not eager to lose another audience member. Was his tone a little sharp?

There was a moment where she looked back and forth between her husband and her brother, wondering at the balance of power. Then Bruce rose and left the table, and after a moment Hannah followed.

"Hannah, where are you going?" asked Mako.

But then he went back to his drunken rambling as she left the table and walked outside. She found Bruce bending before the dying fire. He used the poker to bring the embers up, then threw another log on. The flames leapt back to life.

"That's very manly," she told him. "If we were cave people, I'd have to reward you for keeping us alive through the night with your mad fire skills."

"Are you," he said, rising and pulling her close, "a little tipsy?" He buried his face in her neck and she started to laugh, ripples of pleasure, of desire moving through her.

"What if I am?" she said.

She'd surreptitiously checked the baby monitor app earlier and saw Gigi sleeping peacefully. She felt light and free. She didn't want to think about anything else. Wasn't that her biggest problem? She was always thinking.

"It's good," he whispered into her ear. "I am, too."

His lips found hers, and she ran her fingers through the silk of his hair. She was hot for her husband; she didn't know many women who were, especially after the babies started to come. For a lot of her friends, a deep-seated anger, a resentment set in about how much life had changed for them, and how little it had changed for their husbands. Hannah didn't feel like that. She loved him for taking care of them, for giving her the space to be fully present for Gigi.

"I saw a gazebo, down that path back there," he whispered. "Follow me."

He took her hand and tugged.

Was it rude? She glanced inside the big windows where Mako was *still* prattling on, and Cricket was adoring, and Joshua hadn't returned to the table.

"You're not on duty here," Bruce said. "You don't have to attend to them."

That was true. And, as she'd worried, Cricket was so wrapped up first in Joshua, now in Mako, that Hannah and Cricket barely exchanged a word. So really nothing to bring her back to the table. In fact, she'd been a little bored, sitting there watching the familiar dynamic play out.

She followed her hot husband into the dark, walking up a narrow path through the trees. It led to a clearing and there *was* a lovely little gazebo. Above them, the sky was a field of stars. The air was warm but not hot, not humid. Cicadas sang and when she looked out into the trees, she saw the languid blinking of fireflies.

"This is magical," she said. "When did you see it?"

But he didn't answer, just pulled her into the wood structure and kissed her—her lips, her neck, the dip of her collarbone—until she was weak with desire. There were wide cushioned benches along the long octagonal sides, and he lowered her down, his hands roaming her body, his breath in her ear.

She felt herself release, relax, the blessed drift of pleasure, of the alcohol buzzing through her veins. Gigi far away, safe in her bed, not even the sound of her breath on the monitor to connect Hannah to her mommy self.

"I love you," she whispered.

"You're everything," he answered, voice deep, almost a growl. "You and Gigi, you're my whole heart. Please always remember that."

It sounded odd, like an apology or a good-bye. But she was too lost in passion to ask what he meant by that.

He hiked up her skirt as she tugged down his jeans. Then he was hard and deep inside her, and she lost herself to him, to desire. They knew each other's bodies so well, but there was always discovery somehow. Here in this strange place, a forbidden escape from dinner, the stars twinkling violently. It was new. They were new. She wrapped her arms tight around him, pulled him in as close as she could.

She watched his muscular shoulders and the pools of his black eyes. Then rockets of pleasure and he pressed in deeper, moaning. Then they were just the breath and the night. Hannah closed her eyes, her body consumed with passion.

But as she climaxed she opened her eyes to look at Bruce. And that's when she saw a white form in the trees. It twisted and floated, light like the flowing folds of fabric, and then it was gone. She drew in a gasp, kept watching. But there was only darkness.

"Wow," Bruce said, leaning his weight against her. "Wow."

"I saw something," she whispered, sitting up.

Bruce followed her gaze into the darkness. "What?"

"It looked like—a ghost."

Bruce stroked her hair, gave her a chuckle. "You were just hallucinating from extreme pleasure."

"No," she said, still looking. "I mean—yes, it was *amazing*. But I saw something."

"Just the fireflies maybe?" he said, sensing her seriousness.

"Yeah, maybe."

She kept staring off into the night, watching for the glowing white she'd seen. Chef Jeff's words rang back:

Now people say they see the wife wandering through the woods, looking for her children. And some people think they've seen the little girl wading in the lake.

"It was that guy with his ridiculous ghost stories," Bruce said, echoing her thoughts.

"You're right," she said, wanting him to be. The idea of a mother wandering around looking for her dead children had been unsettling. Actually, heart-wrenching was more like it.

They heard voices then, and Bruce pulled up his jeans, grinning. Hannah sliding her skirt down, still watching. But there was only the darkness.

Voices again, closer. Were there only going to be stolen moments on this trip? But it was quiet again. She'd thought she heard her name but whoever was calling was headed away.

They were missing dessert.

"We should get back," she said. She kept looking into the trees. But now she wasn't even sure what she'd seen.

Bruce sat beside her. "Let's just take a minute and be."

He dropped an arm around her, and she rested against him breathing in the night air. Somewhere there was shrieking, now. Cricket. She got loud when she was drunk.

"That guy," said Bruce. "He was staring at you."

"Joshua? No," she said. "He's head over heels for Cricket."

She told him how when she'd first seen him, she thought she recognized him. It was still bothering her to be honest. But she was too tired to probe into the recesses of her memory further.

"One of your many conquests?"

"That must be it."

"No," said Bruce, nudging her with his shoulder. "He *was* though. In a weird way. Almost sad."

Bruce was a sensitive guy, nearly empathic. He always seemed to know what she was thinking, was very in tune with what Gigi needed which most fathers she knew were not.

"He *does* have a strange vibe," she admitted.

"Hannah!" Cricket.

"You guys better put your clothes on!" Mako. His voice was getting closer. *"We're going to find yooouuuu."*

"Oh no," said Bruce. "They found us."

"You thought they wouldn't?"

Mako came into view on the path, covering his eyes. "Are you guys decent?"

"Of course," said Hannah, tugging at her skirt. "We're old married people. We're not romping out in the gazebo like two teenagers."

"Anymore," added Bruce, earning a guffaw from Mako.

"You always were *such* a slut," put in Cricket, coming up behind Mako. She slipped in next to Hannah, and pulled her into a hug.

"That's my wife you're talking about," said Bruce, mock offended.

"And my sister," said Mako, with a hand to his heart. "But yeah—a total slut."

It was only funny because Hannah was the straight arrow, the rule follower, the eternal good girl. The designated driver—for life. She was fine with that. She didn't mind being the one to take care of the wild kids, the one who made sure that everyone else was safe.

"I took the cover off the hot tub," said Mako. "Let's have a soak."

"And a smoke," said Cricket, producing a joint from her pocket with a wicked grin. Cricket was a walking pharmacy—she always had weed, gummies, all manner of pills.

"Where's Joshua?" asked Hannah, looking down the dark path.

Cricket rolled her eyes. "He had some work to do. He might join us later. But he'll probably just turn in. He's a chronically early riser."

"For now, it's just us. The OGs," said Mako, pulling Cricket up and leading her back toward the house. "Let's chill."

"Private party?" asked Bruce when Cricket and Mako disappeared up the path. Bruce and Hannah followed behind the other two, hand in hand, listening to their laughter. A hot tub, a joint, significant others MIA. That was a recipe for Cricket and Mako to get into trouble. What was it with those two?

Hannah frowned, thinking of poor Liza, sick in bed with a migraine while they all partied on. "Not on my watch."

18

HENRY

Graduation day dawned gray and cool.

Miss Gail had bought him a suit and it was the first thing he saw when he opened his eyes that morning. The suit, navy blue, was hanging on the hook on the back of his door. His first thought was of Alice, though he didn't think about her as much as he used to. Something about the way the suit hung, the way Miss Gail had placed the red-and-navy-striped tie over the shoulder. He felt a knot in his stomach. Alice would have been happy, proud of him.

We don't always choose what happens to us. But we choose what we do with it.

That was true. His mother had been murdered. Her case gone cold, never solved. He'd essentially grown up at Miss Gail's, a small, safe group home. He hadn't chosen any of that. But he chose to stay in school, to take the comfort and the security Miss Gail offered, to do well and keep his grades up. And now he was graduating high school. In the fall, he'd go off to college, a full ride to MIT, the essay about his hardships certainly playing a factor.

Resilience. Miss Gail's favorite word. *Fall down seven, get up eight. That's it. Sometimes I suspect it's the thing that separates success from failure, maybe the only thing.*

A slight rap on the door.

"Are you awake, graduate?" Miss Gail asked, a singsong lilt to her voice.

"Yes," he answered. "I'll be right down."

He was the only one still staying with Miss Gail. Other boys had come and gone. Orphaned boys, or kids taken from abusive homes, sometimes returned to those homes after a while. Sometimes they ran off; some of them stealing from Miss Gail. Some boys came in the middle of the night. Henry had spent a lot of hours lying awake listening to one of the new arrivals weeping. Some of them got into trouble, were arrested for drugs or assault. Henry had been there through it all. He helped Miss Gail now—with the cooking, the chores, getting the new kids settled, serving as a role model when he could. But for a while, more than six months, it had just been the two of them.

Down in the foyer, Miss Gail fixed his tie, tried to pretend she wasn't crying. She was dressed in a blue shift, had her wild red hair tamed into a bun.

"I'm proud of you, son," she whispered, putting a warm, plump hand to his cheek. "Not everyone could do what you have done."

"I couldn't have done any of it without you," he said.

She waved him off, a flush coming to her cheeks. She moved toward the door and held it open. "Let's go get that diploma."

He waited a second, looked at her, the open door. He felt a flood of emotion, which he tamped down.

"Someday, I'm going to pay you back." It was all he could think to say.

She shook her head, eyes brimming. "You've already done that. A thousand times over. Just by being you."

Outside, the gray morning had turned brilliant.

By the time they got to the school the sky was a bright blue, sun shining. There were balloons tied to the outdoor stage, a big banner congratulating the graduates. Cars pulled up, parents and students, lots of smiles, shrieks of joy, tears. The air was electric with excitement, anticipation of the future.

He was only watching for one person; his heart leapt like it did every time she moved into his line of sight. Piper. A periwinkle dress that clung to her waist and flowed around her legs, hair swept up, a blush gloss on her lips. She was more woman than girl now. But he knew her knees were scraped beneath that pretty dress from her weekend soccer tournament.

"You look very handsome, Henry," said Piper's mother, Gretchen. She put a hand on his shoulder. "We're so, so proud of you."

"Thank you for everything you've done for me."

Piper's father, Paul, hung back a bit, aloof and bespectacled, slim. He'd never really warmed to Henry, though he was always cordial.

"Congratulations, Henry," he said. "MIT is a good fit for a mind like yours."

They shook hands. A mind like his. It seemed like a strange thing to say, but the other man was smiling, an arm around his daughter. Piper slipped away from her father to embrace Henry, and Henry locked eyes with the older man for just a moment. Finally, Piper's father looked away with a resigned nod.

Piper sat next to Henry with the rest of the graduates, took his hand in hers and they laced fingers listening to the principal's address about the road ahead, and learning to love change, and leading with your heart.

"Maybe you're not such a loser after all," she said quietly.

"You either."

It wasn't until he'd received his diploma and was posing for pictures with Piper and their friends, that he saw Detective West hanging back by the edge of the football field.

West checked in with Henry every few months, letting him know that even though the case was cold, West was still digging, still looking for answers. Henry didn't want to tell him that *he* had let Alice go, that he'd *had to* in order to move on. He'd had to accept that he might never know who his father was, who had killed Alice, who she had really been, even, in fact who *he was*.

Miss Gail and Detective West, through some herculean effort had managed to get him his own social security card. He remembered Miss Gail losing her temper at City Hall. "Well, I know he doesn't have a birth certificate, but he does exist! He's right here."

He used that social security number to get his driver's license. They were never able to find his actual birth certificate, though. Searching for answers was a black hole he'd almost let swallow him. When he saw West pulling up to the curb, or waiting for him after football practice, or like now, lingering on the edge of this graduation, he didn't feel hope, or even curiosity. It was cold dread.

Miss Gail was chatting with Piper's parents, and Henry walked over to see the old cop, something pressing into the middle of his chest.

"Big day," said West as Henry approached. "Good job, kid. You could have easily taken other, darker roads."

"I had help." He glanced back at Piper's parents and Miss Gail.

"Sure," he said. "But it was all you. Don't forget that."

Henry nodded. It was true that there was something inside him, a kind of iron will to just keep going, to do right, not to collapse into fear or sadness. Maybe he got it from Alice, her stoicism, how she always seemed to move forward, never back.

The wind picked up, blowing at the older man's jacket, flipping it open to reveal his big belly pressing against his button-down shirt, straining against the constraint of his belt. Overhead the clouds started moving fast. A hawk circled, looking for its kill.

"Did you come to watch graduation?" he asked, hoping that was it.

"Not just."

West hesitated a moment, then pulled an envelope from his lapel pocket. He looked down at the long white slip for a moment, holding it tight with both hands against the wind.

"I have a lead on your mother. Not on who killed her. But on her identity."

Joyful voices carried on the wind. Henry looked back at Piper and her parents, Miss Gail, the gathering of his and Piper's friends. Summer lay before them, a sun-kissed Florida promise. He had a good job at the local yacht club, thanks to Piper's mom. He and Piper would help with the kids' summer camp, work as lifeguards. There would be sailing on the Hobie Cat and lazy days at the beach, parties. Then in the fall, Henry would go to MIT. Piper, who'd managed to turn herself into a star student as well as a star athlete in high school, was going to NYU. It would be hard to be apart, but they'd make it work. They'd lost their virginity to each other, and he belonged to her. Her laughter, the turn of her soft neck, the pink of her lips, the smile in her eyes. There wouldn't be anyone else. Ever.

He looked back at Detective West and his envelope thick with information he wasn't sure he wanted.

"You have an aunt up north," said West. "Your mother's sister, someone who's been looking for her all these years. The technology just caught up."

Henry felt frozen. West went on:

"I put Alice's photo and information up on a new national missing persons database called NamUs and I got a match with a decades-old missing persons case from up north. Your aunt identified her from the photographs. All the information is here."

Your aunt.

Detective West held the envelope out to Henry.

"If you want it."

He didn't. He didn't want to know who he really was, who Alice had really been. He only wanted to know who he could become. The past was a swamp, a morass. If he walked in, what darkness, what monsters awaited? Would he sink into its murky bottom? Would he find his way out again?

Piper's laughter rang out. Her girlfriend Beck was shrieking about something. Henry felt drawn back to them.

And yet—it was primal, wasn't it? Something coded in the cells. The desire to know who you came from, where. Why you were the way you were.

He took the envelope, put it in the lapel pocket of his own suit jacket. Maybe he should ask questions. But his throat felt sandpaper dry, constricted. Detective West looked off into the trees edging the field.

"I haven't stopped looking for her killer, Henry. But I have to be honest. I don't have a single lead, not one solid clue. Of course, DNA technology is changing all the time. It's impacting cold cases, just like this—so who knows. I won't stop looking. I promise."

Why do you care so much? Henry wanted to ask. What kept this man holding on? Henry wanted to let go. If he could take a pill to forget Alice and his past completely, he would.

"Thank you," he said.

West gave him a sad smile. "Good luck, son."

The syllables felt weighted, always did, no matter who uttered them, as if the speaker knew too well all the pitfalls and hairpin turns on that seemingly bright road to the future.

"Thank you, Detective West," he said again.

"What did he want?" asked Piper when Henry returned to the group. There was that little notch she got between her eyes when she was worried. Her dress clung to the fullness of her breasts, at her narrow waist, the color lighting up her skin. She wore her hair up, and pretty wisps floated around her face. He pushed one behind her ear.

"Nothing. Just to wish me well."

"He gave you something."

"A gift." Maybe. Maybe not. An aunt, somewhere up north. Family.

Piper nodded uncertainly, but then her best friend, Beck, pulled Henry into a hug, and everyone was laughing, moving toward cars, ready to head to next events. There was a big party at Piper's tonight. And Henry had the feeling that life, real life, was about to begin. He let the feeling swell and carry him along, away from Detective West and his grim expressions.

It would be a long time before he opened that envelope.

19

BRACKEN

June 2018

May dozed beside him and he could feel the storm coming, something about the air, a sizzle, a kind of electricity. Today, the shops had been packed, people stocking up on bottled water, nonperishable food and supplies. He always marveled at this. He was a minimalist, but even *he* had a storeroom of supplies. In a place where the weather could be violent and unpredictable, where roads got washed out and you might be stranded, didn't it just make good sense to plan ahead and not be caught last-minute scrambling for the things you need?

The last storm that had come through here had the power down for days, roads impassable. He'd had one family stranded at Overlook for three extra nights. If not for his big truck, he wouldn't have been able to get to them, bring them supplies, let them charge their phones in his truck. They offered to pay him, but of course he didn't accept. That was against his personal code as a host. Help whenever possible, free of charge.

In return they left him the most glowing review he'd ever received: *Bracken, our host, was a true hero. Making it to us over impassable roads, bringing supplies and letting us stay on until we could get our car out, free of charge. I wish all people were like him. The world would be a better place. He took "superhost" to a whole new level.*

The woman, what was her name? Lara? She had a dragonfly tattoo on her hip. It was pretty, tasteful. In the shower she rubbed her soapy hand on it, like it was some kind of charm or worry stone.

"Stay tonight?" May whispered now as he tried to shift away from her. She lay a hand on his arm.

He turned and picked up her hand, kissed it. "I can't tonight."

"You *can*. If you want to." It wasn't like her to ask for more than he offered. Usually she didn't even stir when he left in the night. He'd never stayed until morning. With a kid in the house, it just wasn't right. Even when Leilani wasn't there, she was there—her toys, books, little girl all around.

"I'll stay a while longer," he said, settling back. Outside, the moon was high and full.

She moved in closer to him, and he dropped an arm around her.

"Okay," she said.

He toyed with it. The idea of staying here. Being here with May. But he couldn't, his other desires an itch he couldn't scratch. An appetite he couldn't sate. He waited until her breathing became steady, then he slipped from the bed.

In her small, tidy kitchen, he picked up his phone and clicked onto the camera app. Mako, Cricket, and Hannah were in the hot tub. Liza, it seemed, had turned in early, a motionless form in the master suite. Bruce sat at the desk in the second big bedroom, his face blue in the light from the screen.

Bracken saw Bruce bring the phone to his ear and he clicked on the audio.

"Yes," he said. "That's right. Okay."

He was grim and serious. People were so into their work,

thought it was so important. *Get outside*, he wanted to shout. *Enjoy your wife, the stars.*

But if there was one thing he learned it was that you could only help people so much, at a certain point they had to help themselves.

"I just need to be sure that no one gets hurt."

Woah. What was that now?

"My wife," he said. "This is going to be so hard on her."

Bruce nodded at whatever was being said on the other line. Bracken strained to hear, but it was muffled, a female voice maybe. "Yes, I know. You're right. It's time."

When Bruce hung up the phone, he dumped his head into his hand. Bracken watched him a moment. *What do you have going on, Bruce?*

Bracken clicked through the rest of the rooms.

Where was the other guy?

A quick check of the driveway camera showed that one of the cars was gone. They should have everything they needed, he thought with mild annoyance; no reason for an intoxicated run into town.

Joshua. The mystery man.

The other guests were all wide open and living online. It had taken under an hour for him to learn pretty much everything he wanted to know about them. Hannah, wife and mom; that was her center. Cricket, the single party girl with big aspirations. Mako, the tech mogul with the huge Twitter following. Liza, the yoga influencer, with a popular YouTube channel. Bruce kept a lower profile, just a ConnectIn account listing his professional accomplishments, résumé, glowing reviews from former employers, as well as from clients of his company. No personal social media at all for Bruce. He was all business.

Bracken knew where they each went to school, who their friends were, where they shopped. He knew what they did on the weekends. He knew what was important to each of them, because people telegraphed so much about themselves without even realizing it. (He'd even taken one of Liza's online yoga classes; it helped his back quite a bit.) Hannah: home, motherhood, family. Liza: mindfulness, the environment, wellness. Mako: fame, success, wealth. Cricket: beauty, enjoyment, partying but really looking for love. Bruce: work.

People told all in this confessional culture, showing one thing, and revealing so much more, maybe not even knowing about the kind of people out there, watching. Lucky for them, Bracken had their best interests at heart.

But Joshua Miller, there was nothing on him. In the rental application, Bracken required all the names of the guests staying at the house. And in the decade he'd been doing this, no one yet had balked at giving that information; it was a man's right, wasn't it, to know who was staying in his rental property?

But when he'd entered Joshua's name into his search engine, there was only a little information. Just his name and picture on a bare-bones website for some tech company. Joshua was the head of security for a place called Razor. But there was almost nothing about the company, what they did; it wasn't publicly traded, and there were no news items about it.

The site was very vague: systems consulting, some business-speak about helping companies to maximize the efficiency of their processes. What the hell did that mean? Joshua Miller had no social media. Or more accurately, there were so many Joshua Millers on social media that it was like a swamp of uninteresting people he'd have to wade through.

Bracken ran a simple background check on the name; he didn't have access to a social security number and he really couldn't ask for that. It would seem like an unusual request on an application for a rental. Maybe for the person paying, but not for each guest in the house, especially in this climate when people worried about identity theft. Which was funny—because they allowed themselves to be tracked by their phones, and broadcast every intimate detail of their lives online. But ask for those numbers and people got very careful.

Again, there were too many Joshua Millers and nothing leapt out when he scrolled through the items that came up on the online background check service for which he paid monthly. Not a crime to keep a low profile. Bracken had his bio on his vacation rental website, and that was the extent of his own online presence.

Where did you go, Joshua Miller? he wondered now.

And Bruce, Hannah's husband. He was a bit of mystery as well. No social media presence except as he appeared in Hannah's feed. Pieces of him—his arms holding the baby, a profile, smiling at the sunset, their hands clasped, rings glinting. There was a raft of wedding pictures, family shots at the baby's "spiritual, not religious" blessing ceremony. He owned his own company, a consulting firm that "develops tailored business systems," and "troubleshoots broken code." But the language on his site was esoteric, clearly designed for a certain group who knew about things like "debugging" and "stack trace." Bracken had him pegged as a standard nerd who found more to interest him on a screen than in the real world—like his beautiful wife in the hot tub downstairs.

Blink and you'll miss it. You'll miss everything, he wanted to tell Bruce. Whatever drama you have going on—another woman, some kind of business crisis—just let it go and be here now.

May turned in the bed; he heard her sigh, the mattress squeak, from the other room. He felt a tug back to her, but instead he pulled on his boots. Outside, the sky lightened briefly and a few seconds later he heard the distant rumble of thunder.

The storm was barreling toward the coast, picking up speed in the warm water. It might never make it this far. But even the outer bands of a hurricane could do damage. He had work to do before it hit—securing woodpiles, bringing in outdoor furniture, planters. He was the steward of the homes he owned, and the people who stayed there.

Might be time to pay his guests at Overlook a visit.

20

HANNAH

Don't do it, Hannah admonished herself. *Just let it go.*

She was still tipsy but less so. Fatigue was tugging at her—her horrible night's sleep, the long drive. But she knew Cricket would be waiting for her downstairs looking for some hot tub time.

She and Bruce had come up to the room to change into their swimsuits and of course Bruce had immediately opened his laptop to "check on a few things." He sat at the desk now, chin on hand, staring at something on the screen. She was about to remind him about his promise to unplug—or try to. Maybe she should press him about Mako. But instead she held her tongue. She was still glowing from their stolen moments.

Hannah slipped into her black one-piece and then grabbed one of the luxuriously plush robes that hung in the bathroom. It was heavenly, soft and smelling lightly of lavender detergent as she shouldered it on. She stood in front of the big mirror in the bathroom, brushed, then put up her hair, which looked full and soft.

"Just go downstairs and enjoy yourself," she whispered to her reflection. Hot tub. A joint.

Let it *all go*.

"What's that?" asked Bruce.

"Nothing," she said, stepping back into the bedroom. "You won't be long, will you?"

"No," he said, but he already had that distant tone, that blankness to his stare. "Not long."

But she could tell by the set of his jaw that Bruce was in the zone. Hours could pass, the whole place could burn down, and he wouldn't notice.

She took the phone from her pocket, hesitated. Finally, she couldn't help it. She sank down onto the sofa and opened the internet browser, typed in: family murdered Sleepy Ridge.

It was all right there, multiple articles about the Anderson family. More than thirty years ago, a local cop with a history of domestic violence killed his wife and two children, then set his house on fire before killing himself with a gunshot to the head.

She flipped through news stories, images of the family— so young looking, smiling and the very picture of "normal." Churchgoers, kids in Little League. Him, virile and dark, in his uniform. Her, delicate and fair. The children cherub-faced towheads. All beloved in the community, never a hint that anything was wrong between them.

An image of the girl in the arms of her mother brought tears to Hannah's eyes. How the young woman smiled, the child's head rested against her chest—it was so tender, so lovely. Hannah felt a hard ache for Gigi as she scrolled through article after article detailing the horror story. Hidden violence at home. A woman who tried to flee with her children. A brutal struggle ending with an entire family destroyed. She sat a moment, feeling her skin tingle. Right here on this property. She kept reading.

Finally, she got to something more recent—an article about the host, Bracken, and how he was restoring rundown old properties, bringing new life to the quiet town with his vacation rentals.

A knock at the door startled her, shuttling her back to the present where Bruce's fingers clicked across the keyboard. She wiped at tears she didn't even realize she'd been crying.

A soft voice at the door. "Han?"

She opened it to find Cricket standing there. She had her own phone clutched in her hand.

"Look at this," she said, pulling Hannah out into the hallway. She held up the phone to reveal one of the same articles Hannah had just been reading.

Hannah held up her phone to Cricket, who grabbed her arm, eyes going wide. "Isn't it just awful," she said. "Can you believe that happened *right here*?"

"I think I saw her," whispered Hannah.

"Who?"

Hannah pointed to the picture of the murdered mother. Her name was Amanda—friends called her Mandy. "When I was out in the gazebo. I saw this strange floating white light. Just like the chef said."

Cricket stared at her a moment. "Really?"

"Swear to god. It hovered for a moment, then disappeared into the trees."

She remembered it now. Just a trick of light maybe. But no. She'd seen something.

Cricket looked at her phone again, enlarged something on the screen then turned it back to Hannah. It was a drawing of the property, a map. Cricket pointed to a body of water. "Where they found the little girl's body. It's called Tearwater Lake. I think it's just down that path behind the gazebo."

Hannah looked back at Bruce who was still typing at his keyboard.

"Do you want to go find it?" asked Cricket, who Hannah noted was also in one of the plush robes.

Hannah thought of the dark of the woods, the heavy silence. She was more comfortable looking for ghosts on a smartphone screen.

"Where's Joshua?" she asked, hoping to deflect the request without declining it.

Cricket rolled her eyes. "Still working. Some emergency that won't wait. He could be a while."

Hannah looked back at her husband, still staring at his screen. What was it with these guys? Were they just hardworking men with important jobs? Or was it something else, a desire to check out, to separate? Maybe it was a little of both.

"And Mako?"

Something crossed Cricket's face—it looked like guilt, then sadness. "I think he went to check on Liza. He went into her room and hasn't come back out."

"In our bathrobes?"

Cricket shrugged. "Why not? Who's going to see us? We're in the middle of effing nowhere. Then—right in the hot tub."

It wasn't real to Cricket, what she'd read, Hannah could tell. It was a ghost story, something from the distant past. A romp into the woods after spirits was just a game to her, just another way to have fun, like stories around a campfire. But Hannah couldn't shake that image of Mandy holding her little girl. It was real—or had been. That love. That horrific murder.

Cricket reached into her pocket then held out her palm.

Two pink gummies rested there, fat and dusted with sugar. Oh, Hannah hadn't been high in ages. She hesitated.

Cricket lifted her palm higher, smiled her wicked smile. "Come on, Han. Live a little."

Hannah looked into the twinkling eyes of her best friend. The bad girl. The pretty one. The wild one. The one who frequently needed Hannah's rescue. The one who always seemed to have way more fun than Hannah.

A final glance back at her husband. He didn't even notice when she shut the door. "Why not?"

She grabbed one and popped it in her mouth. Cricket did the same, her grin widening.

"Let's go ghost hunting."

Fifteen minutes later as they made their way down the rocky path in robes and flip-flops, the pleasant effects of the gummy not yet taking hold, the errand seemed less fun and more irresponsible. Not to mention scary.

"I don't feel anything, do you?" asked Hannah. She hadn't been high since—when? She couldn't even remember. College maybe? Maybe she'd forgotten how it felt. Or maybe her mom brain wouldn't allow it. Like, it just wouldn't take or something.

"It takes a while," said Cricket, looping a strong arm through Hannah's. "It said in the article that Mandy was planning to leave him. Her parents—they were waiting for her and the kids."

Hannah had read the same, imagining those poor people waiting and waiting for their daughter, their grandchildren who never came home.

"The medical examiner deduced that he killed Mandy first," Hannah said. "Her husband strangled her. The little boy was found in his bed. But the little girl must have run. He chased her down to the lake."

"Maybe on this path," said Cricket, looking around them.

It was depraved, wasn't it? Like those people who listened to endless crime podcasts, sifting through the details of cold cases, all the different ways people can torture and kill each other. In the listening, in the examining, things seem like fiction, stories told to explain, to frighten, to excite. But these stories were real—a mother and her children had died in pain and terror, their deeply disturbed killer, a person charged with caring for them, then taking his own life. So much pain. There was so much pain in the world. Hannah clung to Cricket and the woods seemed dark. Hannah felt small.

"I don't think it's much farther."

Behind them, Hannah could see the porch lights glowing. Above them the stars wild and violent in the velveteen black of the sky. The Big Dipper. Ursa Minor. Orion's Belt. Mars glowed red. Venus blinked, always the brightest star in the sky.

One Christmas, her father gave her a huge telescope. Mickey and Sophia had no interest in the night sky. But Hannah and her father spent so many late evenings out on the porch with the big device, and piles of books. This was before all the apps that you could hold up to the sky now, that revealed all the galactic secrets. *Before*, you had to do your research. They spent hours searching, discovering, naming, watching for meteor showers or other astronomical events.

"We're so small, tiny," Leo said one night. It was late. Mickey was out, and Sophia was inside watching television. She had her dad all to herself. "We're ants. Not even."

He said it softly, with a kind of wonder. Hannah knew she was small. The youngest in the family, the quietest with the easiest personality. But not him. Not her dad. He was strength, security. He had all the answers, the bear hugs that banished monsters, piggyback rides forever. He was huge.

"You're not tiny, Dad."

He looked over at her, then pulled her into the crook of his arm, pressed her to him tight.

"It's okay," he said. "Look out there. All those points of light. Massive explosions, light-years away. That's where we all came from, all of us. There's stardust in our bones."

The telescope was at Hannah and Bruce's house now. She couldn't wait to share it with Gigi.

There. A shooting star. She made a wish. Her everyday wish. May all people be happy, safe, and free.

That's where we all came from, all of us.

The Origins test.

It was another hum in her subconscious.

Bruce had opted out. But Hannah had spit in the vial and sent it off—without too much of a thought. Just something to talk about with her family when the results came back. Maybe they'd find some long-lost relative, or some strain of the family they'd never otherwise have known. She did the full suite—ancestry, medical, and traits. She'd even ticked the box to allow any searching relatives to get in touch via the app. Why not?

It was a curiosity, nothing more. After all, she *knew* her family. She *knew* where she came from. On her mother's side, she had a big group of aunts and uncles, a passel of cousins all over the country. Her mother was of Scotch-Irish descent whose parents had come to the US in the thirties and settled in Brooklyn. Hannah's grandmother had been a seamstress, her grandfather a chauffeur. Eventually, the warm Florida weather called them south, and that's where Sophia was born and stayed. Hannah's father was Italian, both maternal and paternal grandparents from Naples. He was an only child, parents passed before he was fully grown. He lived with relatives before he joined the army. There were aunts and uncles, cousins who were less a part of Hannah and Mickey's life than Sophia's family. But she knew them—cards at Christmas, random visits, once a big family reunion at Disney.

Hannah *had been* curious. What would she learn about her ancestry, about herself? Who, if anyone, would reach out claiming this connection or that? She'd read that all humans share about 99 percent of the same DNA. That it was less than a 1 percent difference that makes you who you uniquely are, that connects you to the people you call family. There was something about that that she liked; this idea that all people, no matter what they thought or believed, were essentially the same.

But the results when they came were—confusing.

"Earth to Hannah."

She jumped, startled back to the moment. "What?"

"You have that look."

"What look?"

Cricket tapped her temple. "That *thinking too hard*, lost in your head look. Your brother does that, too. Just blanks out, goes on some kind of internal journey."

"Doesn't everyone do that?"

Cricket laughed, ahead of her on the path. "No, not everyone. For example, Joshua doesn't seem to do any deep thinking at all. That's what I love about him. He's about food and sex and good times."

Hannah gasped. "Did you just say the *L* word again?"

Cricket covered her mouth, looked with big eyes at Hannah. "Maybe?"

Something rustled in the bushes, something big. Both of them shrieked, their voices echoing in the silence. Glancing back the way they came, Hannah couldn't see the house at all anymore.

"What was *that*?"

It came again, and this time they took off running. Hannah lost a flip-flop but didn't go back for it. They ran up the path shrieking.

Then they were laughing. Yes, there it was, that lightness, that bubbling happiness she remembered from the days when she still partied. How it took her away from all those deep thoughts, her worries, whatever darkness in the world.

"Oh my god," breathed Cricket, slowing, breathless. "Was there something out there?"

"If there was," said Hannah. "We scared it away."

Around the next turn, they were at the lake, which was really more of a large pond, still and inky black, dappled with silver moonlight, tall trees all around whispering.

"Tearwater Lake," breathed Hannah, coming to its edge.

Hannah stared at its blackness, thinking about the little girl who died there. She couldn't help it. She started to cry.

"Hannah," whispered Cricket.

"I'm okay."

Cricket grabbed her arm. "No, Hannah. There's someone there. On the other side of the lake in the trees."

"What?"

"Look, there, right across."

Hannah stared, and then yes, she detected a shift in the black. As her eyes adjusted to the distance and the blackness, she saw it, a tall form standing among the trees. She could see the legs spread, arms akimbo.

A jolt of fear moved through her. "Oh my god."

"Someone's there," Cricket breathed. "Someone's—watching us."

"Hey," Hannah called. "Who's there? This is private property."

Was it? She didn't even know.

The form stood rooted like the trees around it, unmoving, impervious.

Hannah felt like the world stood still, as she watched the strange form across the lake. Who was that? *What* was it? Man? Woman? *Ghost?*

"Hey," she called again. Cricket tugged on her arm, and she took a few steps back, one bare foot cold against the earth. "Do you hear me?"

No answer, maybe the slightest shift of movement. Then as she watched the form seemed to leak back into the darkness like ink soaking into cloth.

"Hannah," Cricket was pulling her, harder now. "Hannah, let's get out of here."

Then they were running. Hannah stooped to grab her lost flip-flop on the way, looking back into the night where there was nothing.

21

HANNAH

Mako was already in the hot tub when they returned breathless to the deck.

"What the fuck?" He'd had his back against the edge, eyes closed but sat up to look them as they thundered up the stairs. "Where were you guys?"

"There's, there's someone out there. By the lake," said Cricket gasping, looking back the way they came.

Mako followed her glance but did not move from his relaxed slouch in the bubbling water. The scent of bromine wafted from the lit circle of blue water.

"Out where?" he asked, still peering into the darkness, unconcerned.

"By Tearwater Lake," gasped Hannah. "Where they found the body of that little girl."

Mako laughed, hardy and loud. "That guy was just fucking with you, Han."

"No," said Cricket. "It really happened. We Googled it."

"Oh, yeah," he said with a mock-scared widening of his eyes. "If it's on Google it *must* be true."

There was music coming from speakers somewhere, something low and jazzy. From where Hannah stood, the kitchen and the house looked empty. Chef Jeff and Ingrid had obviously cleaned up and headed out. She thought about the chef, his steely blue gaze, the bone sculpture, the assistant with the spider on her hand. What if it was one of them, still lingering, watching?

"There was someone out there," said Hannah.

"Wait," said Mako. He floated over closer to them, squinting at Cricket. "Are you guys *high*?"

Cricket, calmer now, smiled. "Maybe a little."

Mako held out a meaty palm. "Hand it over."

With a coquettish tilt of her head, Cricket produced a third gummy from her pocket, handed it to Mako who popped it, unhesitating, into his mouth.

"I think we need to call someone," said Hannah, still peering into the darkness.

"Who?" asked Mako, annoyingly chill.

"Uh, the *cops*," Hannah said, heart still thudding. "The *owner*."

"And say what?"

"That we think we saw someone on the property. That someone *was watching* us."

The rest of it tumbled out—the old review she'd read, how she'd felt someone was watching her when they first arrived.

Mako wore that certain look that she absolutely hated—a kind of knowing, male smirk. "Hannah, are you being serious right now?" he asked easily. "And should we also tell them that you are drunk, and high, to boot?"

She started to argue that she was neither drunk nor high, and then she realized she was both. Like very. The world felt vague and wobbly.

She and Cricket locked eyes. A beat passed before they started laughing—big, gulping belly laughs so hard that Hannah almost peed.

What had they seen out there? Anything? Something. Definitely something. But what?

"It could have been anyone—a neighbor maybe?" Cricket said.

"There are no other properties around here for miles."

"Or maybe it was just the trees. It *was* dark. We *are* fucked-up."

Maybe. Probably. Like the light she saw from the gazebo. Just stories sparking her imagination. She was prone to that, wasn't she?

"Maybe you're right," she admitted. She kept watching the path, the night, though. Something tingling, a sense of unease, of foreboding.

Cricket moved toward the house, the whole thing dropped as though it never happened.

"I'll be right back," she said. "I'm just going to see what's going on with my workaholic boyfriend."

Hannah observed Mako watching Cricket with something like petulance on his face. She ignored it as she dropped her robe and climbed into the tub. Oh, the water. It felt so good.

She glanced at the clock on the wall inside. It wasn't as late as she thought. Not yet midnight. It seemed so much later.

And was that thunder? She listened but it was hard to hear over the hot tub jets. She watched the sky for the telltale flash, but didn't see anything.

Florida people were always staring up at the sky, watching for those big thunderheads, waiting for the air to chill with the approach of a storm. As kids it was drilled into you; if you hear thunder, come inside. And as kids, they'd always pushed the edge of that warning, waiting for the next rumble, or to see a distant skein of lightning in the darkening sky before racing out of the pool or the ocean and inside to safety.

Now, as a mom, she was inside even at the most distant sound. But they weren't *in* Florida; they were deep in the woods in Georgia. Gigi was safe at home. And, Mako was right about one thing, she *was* pleasantly buzzing. She let the water bubble and soothe, wash everything else away.

"Where's the big guy?" asked Mako.

She rolled her eyes. "Where else? Working. He said he wouldn't be long. Must be something in the water. Can't get the men around here to take some time off."

"*I'm* here," said Mako. "Present and accounted for. Ready to protect the women from ghosts and shadowy figures on the property."

Mako leaned his head back, closed his eyes again. And Bruce's words rang back to Hannah. She tried to keep the guilt, the worry off her face. She didn't want to think about real things right now—ghosts and strangers in the woods were preferable to the real dynamics of family.

"He's a good guy, Hannah," said Mako. When she looked over at him, he was gazing at her. "You seem happy."

Hannah studied her brother's face, saw something she didn't recognize and didn't like. A sadness. This was the moment to ask him if he'd taken the test, what he'd found. They might not have another moment alone.

"How's Liza?" she asked instead.

She was eager for her sister-in-law to rejoin the group. Poor Liza had left the table so suddenly, looked so unwell. The migraine, Chef Jeff's story, the big platter of meat. It had clearly been too much for her; Hannah had seen the strain.

And Hannah did not love the energy between Cricket and Mako. It was always annoying. The Cricket and Mako show. But it was also that they were bad for each other. Had Liza picked up on that, too? She was so sensitive.

"Sound asleep," Mako answered. "She didn't even move when I came in to change, and I tried not to disturb her. Those meds are hardcore. She'll be okay in the morning."

Hannah remembered that Liza hadn't wanted to take the medication. But maybe she'd changed her mind, the pain finally winning out.

"I didn't know she got migraines."

"She hasn't had one in years. Since college she said."

"Everything okay?"

She expected a blustery blow-off: *Of course, of course, everything's perfect. Liza's perfect.* But instead his eyes glanced off to the side. Another Mako tell.

"There's been some stress. Work. And, you know, we've been *trying...*"

Hannah felt a little rush of joy. It was one of her dreams—a big bunch of kids, a couple more for her and Bruce, at least two from Liza and Mako. They'd raise their kids together happily, with lots of sleepovers, family nights and big vacations, matching Christmas pajamas.

"For a baby?"

The look on his face tamped down her excitement and it morphed to concern.

He nodded. "But—"

"Oh my gaawd! What a gorgeous night!" Cricket returned. Svelte, skin bronzed, in a white bikini.

Hannah felt suddenly self-conscious about her mom bathing suit, the simple black one-piece she'd ordered online.

Cricket had had her boobs done a couple of years ago to go from an A cup to a C. And, honestly? They looked spectacular, high, round, and firm. Since the pregnancy, Hannah's body had taken on a kind of softness. She'd breastfed Gigi for a full year. And Bruce had already wondered aloud if maybe it was time to start trying for another one. So, svelte was not in her immediate future. Or in her distant future. Or in her past for that matter.

Cricket ran and did Pilates or yoga at least four times a week. Hannah barely had time for a shower.

Mako's eyes roamed Cricket's body as she climbed gracefully into the tub. Hannah kicked him under the bubbles and he gave her a guilty shrug, like: *I'm only human.* Cricket was oblivious, or pretended to be.

Hannah cleared her throat, sank a little deeper into the bubbles. "Where's Joshua?"

"You know," she said, not looking at Hannah. "Looks like he went into town. The Wi-Fi is down apparently and there are problems at work. He left a note, said he looked for us. Must have been when we were out ghost hunting."

Okay. That was weird, right? Hannah flashed on that moment when they first met. That strange feeling of familiarity, the way he'd been watching Hannah at dinner. There was something off about him.

"He said he'll be back soon," Cricket went on.

"The Wi-Fi is down?" said Hannah. Bruce was logged in online upstairs, wasn't he?

"Yeah," said Mako, with a shrug. "But I have a decent cell signal. I was able to use my hot spot to get online, check email just now."

Hannah didn't say anything about Bruce. Either he'd lied about checking in at work, or he, too, was using his hot spot. Wouldn't Joshua have a hot spot to use, as well? Why would he need to go into town? Would anything even be open there?

But Hannah stayed quiet. She could tell by the pitch of her friend's voice, the furrow in her brow that she was annoyed about it, but trying to stay cool. Cricket wouldn't want to admit that Joshua's behavior was odd, especially in front of Mako.

"I don't know," Cricket said with a shrug and a sigh. "But if he'd rather be driving around looking for Wi-Fi than here in this amazing tub with me, what can I do?"

Hannah could say the same of Bruce.

She looked at her phone, which she'd placed on the edge of the tub. She had a couple of bars. She'd still be able to reach Lou and Gigi, and they her, if there was a cell signal. So it was fine.

"Why would the Wi-Fi go down?" she asked.

"Because we're in the sticks," said Mako. "And I heard there might be weather coming. I'm surprised we have service at all."

Hannah glanced at her phone again. Now there was one service bar.

"This place, though," said Cricket, changing the subject. "It's amazing. Thanks for this, Mako. It's so generous of you and Liza."

He waved her off. "Hey, do you remember that time when we got drunk at your parents' anniversary party—at the yacht club—and they found us making out in the state room of their boat?"

Cricket tilted her head back and laughed, throaty and deep. She pushed playfully at Mako.

"Oh my god, I was grounded for the rest of the summer."

And then the Cricket and Mako show was back on, their attraction to each other barely concealed, laughing over shared memories of their youth—memories which had become idealized, overblown over time and which rarely, and although she was almost always there, rarely included a mention of Hannah. Because she was the one covering up for them, cleaning up after them, comforting Cricket when Mako was a dick, holding Cricket's hair while she puked, or lying to their parents.

Hannah zoned out, letting them chatter on.

Mako took three beers from a cooler Hannah hadn't seen behind the tub, popped the lids and handed one to her and to Cricket. Hannah took a deep swig even though she'd had way too much already.

Hannah looked through the big glass doors into the sweeping great room.

Where was Bruce? She kept waiting to see him come down the stairs in the new trunks she bought for him.

"So let's hear more about Joshua," said Hannah.

But Cricket and Mako were laughing so hard about something that neither one of them heard her.

She looked out over the property and a glow coming from the trees caught her eye.

"What's that?"

Mako turned and looked. "Huh," he said. "That's odd."

"What is it?" asked Cricket.

"There's another cabin over that way," he said. "There shouldn't be anyone out there, though."

"When did that light go on?" asked Hannah.

"No idea," said Mako.

Just then, as they were all looking, the light went dark again.

22

LIZA

How had she gotten here? To this dark place?

Liza crept down the stairs, leaning heavily against the wainscoting. She was in so much pain. Her head, her abdomen. She didn't think there was any way she would be able to sneak out of the house.

Maybe it didn't matter anyway.

Her life was about to blow up and it was her fault. She'd always thought if she and Mako ever split, it would be because of him. His transgressions, his mistakes.

But no. It would be because of her, what she had done. She'd had an affair, had managed to get herself pregnant—maybe by another man. Now she was being punished. Brutally. This was another one of those moments where you could do something better, something smarter. And then didn't.

She remembered that day so clearly. Her biggest mistake. It was Christmastime; she'd been shopping for Mako and his family.

Inside the refrigerated air of the mall, an ambient remix of Elton John's "Tiny Dancer" greeted her. And she wandered through the departments, avoiding the baby clothes—no need to torture herself today even though she needed something for Gigi. She moved slowly through designer bags, picking out a lovely tote for Sophia (who would no doubt *not* like it since she didn't seem to like anything or anyone), some perfume for Hannah (who would be kind and grateful for any gesture, even the smallest). She found some beautiful ties for Leo, who would be absently pleased. What about Mako? There was literally nothing she could buy for him that he hadn't already bought for himself.

So she picked up some of his favorite underwear and socks, a cool pair of boots (which he'd probably return because he was so picky). It didn't really matter how things were received, only that she gave with love. That was the subject of the guided meditation she offered today on YouTube. *We give because we love, not because we fear. When we give with love, we can disconnect from how things are received. Only the act of pure giving is important.*

Some of her viewers didn't seem to get it. *But don't you give to please the people you love?* asked one woman who always had the most difficult questions.

It's lovely when people accept your gift with gratitude, but you can't control that. You can only control your intention.

Crickets. No likes. No responses.

She had to take her own advice then, which she often did—especially when it came to YouTube and social media comments. Talk about something you couldn't control; the whole catalogue of humanity was online, feeling entitled to their opinions and to their right to share. It could be brutal.

When she was done shopping, she found herself famished. There was a lovely organic café over by Tiffany, so she wound her way there. She could call Mako. His office wasn't far, but sometimes she'd rather be alone. She had some journaling to do, some thinking to do. And when Mako showed up, it was the Mako show. Not always, but definitely during the work-day. He'd bluster in, full of big ideas, or complaints, or ranting about this or that. He'd take up all her energy, without even meaning to.

The hostess seated her by a window, and she piled her bags on the empty booth seat across from her. She ordered the kale apple walnut salad with lemon vinaigrette, a large glass of ice water. She took out her journal, and sat a moment, centering. Taking in the aromas of the café, a brewed coffee, some fresh sage in a little glass jar on the table, the scent of baking bread somewhere. There was ambient music on low, soothing.

She saw him come in, ask for a table. He was tall and lean, walked with an elegant swagger as he followed the hostess. Liza recognized in him something that she liked about Mako, an easy confidence. He had dark skin, and wide shoulders; the limber, fit body of a practiced yogi, or a dancer. As he moved closer, she picked up the lightest scent of patchouli, noted the expensive cut of his jeans.

He caught her looking and gave her a smile. She felt herself blush stupidly, then opened her notebook. Those eyes. My, my. She was reminded of her mother who often admired handsome men, even if they were much younger than she was. When Liza admonished her, she'd say: *I'm an old married lady, but I'm not dead, Liza.* Which Liza always found funny.

She started writing, forgot about him, though he was seated one table over.

"I'm sorry to bother you."

She looked up and he had moved himself to the table closer to her. He had a nice energy, something gentle, easy. She was sensitive to energies. Some people made her want to wrap her arms around her middle, or shift back—like her mother-in-law. But something about him made her want to shift closer.

"Can I help you?"

He smiled, leaned a little closer. "Are you Liza? Yoga with Liza?"

She startled a little. She'd never been recognized anywhere

before, not by a stranger. Lots of people she knew took her yoga and meditation classes. But she'd never been approached by anyone who wasn't a friend, or a friend of a friend.

"I am," she said.

"I take your Monday online *Yin with Affirmations* class. It's fantastic."

"Oh," she said, closing her notebook. "That's wonderful. Thank you so much."

"It completely fixed my lower back pain—which I think was half physical, half psychological, you know." He offered a self-deprecating chuckle, rubbed at something over his right eyebrow.

She did know, gave him an affirming nod. "It usually is some combination of those things."

"Where did you study?"

They started talking then, about how she thought she wanted to be a doctor, but realized that she was also interested in world religions, how she discovered yoga and meditation at college. Studied at a famous school in Upstate New York, went to India to finish her teacher training. How he played football in college, never good enough to go further, but was now wracked with various injuries from his efforts. He didn't look like a football player, or someone struggling with injuries. She could usually tell where people hurt from the way they carried themselves— hiked shoulders, or a slight limp, overpronated foot. But there was something about him—his voice, the way he listened to her when she spoke, his gaze. It was hypnotic. Mako was always on his phone. If he wasn't, he was distracted by his own thoughts. Not that he didn't love her, that they didn't connect often enough. But it was new to feel like someone was hanging on her every word.

By the time their entrees came—he'd ordered the same kale salad—she'd invited him to sit with her.

That's how easy it was, how unexpected. Life happens.

"Do you teach any in-person classes?" he asked as he was paying the check. He insisted—*since I talked your ear off all through your lunch when you'd clearly intended to journal.* But hadn't she done most of the talking? He'd told her very little about himself, hadn't he?

She hesitated. Was it weird? But no, her schedule was posted on her website, public for everyone to see. She told him as much.

"I'll see you there," he said. And she felt her heart flutter a little. Silly.

It was only after she'd gone that she realized he'd never offered his name, and she'd never asked. But that was fine. Likely he wouldn't show up at class; she'd never see him again. That was best.

And even if he did. No big deal. He'd take her yoga class. And she was married. And that was the end of the story. Right? Right.

But no. It was just the beginning.

Now the pain in her stomach twisted cruelly. The one good thing that might have come of it was probably already lost.

At the bottom of the stairs, she stopped and listened, her breath ragged. It was quiet now.

Where were they all?

She heard Cricket's laughter ringing outside. The rumble of Mako's voice.

But the table was empty, napkins on dishes, silverware askew, wineglasses half-empty. They'd gone outside.

Another wave of pain; Liza leaned against the wall. Her vision was blurred, faded at the periphery.

Should she ask them for help? Should she call the police? Get Mako?

She could tell him that she was being stalked. It was true. But she couldn't face them. Mako's anger. Hannah's disapproval. Cricket's superior glee. Bruce's blank distance. And when the police came or Mako confronted her stalker? Brandon would tell Mako everything. About the affair, that Liza was pregnant, probably *by that affair*. Mako wouldn't be able to abide it, would he? If she was carrying the baby of another man? He'd never forgive her. No one could forgive that.

And as flawed and broken as Mako was, she couldn't stand to lose him.

No. She'd handle this herself. She'd give Brandon whatever he wanted—probably money—and he would go away. She'd sneak back inside and it would be like this had never happened.

She slipped down the rest of the stairs, through the foyer, then out the front door. He wanted something, obviously. Probably it was money. It wasn't her; she knew that much. After she'd ended it, he'd never reached out again. It was like he'd never existed at all. He faded away and she could barely remember what she'd liked about him.

Then, suddenly, after Liza had discovered she was pregnant, he seemed to *know*. Started texting again, turning up in her socials—liking her posts, and making cryptic comments in her feed.

You have something that belongs to me, he kept texting.

How could he know? She'd told no one. There was *no way* that he could have found out. Was he following her? Had he seen her buy the test? Or was he sifting through their garbage?

Her phone pinged: I'm waiting.

Liza let the cool of the night air wash over her, give her strength. She felt stronger, the pain in her head lessening just a fraction.

Be strong, she told herself. *Be solid.*

When she found the path on the side of the house, she followed a quaint little white sign that read: Guest Cabin.

And how in the world had he found her here? Gained access to this place? She ticked through all the details. It had been Trina, Mako's old assistant who had booked this place for them. Liza had never liked her, but she'd been good at her job. She was a disgruntled ex-employee now, one of many. Had Brandon somehow gotten to Trina maybe? Or had he somehow hacked into their computer? He worked with computers. You always heard how easy it was for people to install spyware on your devices.

More laughter echoed through the night, and Liza felt lifted out. Like she was operating on another plane from the rest of the world. If only she'd stayed on the straight and narrow path, this wouldn't be happening to her. They were in the light. She was in some netherworld of darkness and pain, fear.

But she was stronger than she looked.

In the pocket of her jacket, she gripped her small gun. A yogi with a gun! Can you imagine? It was Mako's. He kept it in a locked box on a shelf in the master closet by the safe—where they kept her nice jewelry, a big stash of cash, their supply of marijuana gummies. She'd taken it a month ago and had been carrying it everywhere with her since he started online stalking her. She figured it was only a matter of time before he turned up someplace, maybe tried to hurt her. She was a pacifist, of course. But she was no victim.

The cabin was dark, but the door stood ajar. She marshalled her resources, pushed back her pain, her fear, her sadness. She waited, looking back at the big house with longing.

Then she walked up the path, and pushed into the open door.

There was a shadowy form standing in the dim living area. "Liza."

Brandon. They'd had a white-hot affair starting after that first yoga class. Nearly five months, she'd seen him off and on, meeting at nice hotels, once at his place, once on the beach late at night. Then she'd ended it abruptly.

Mako, she knew, was often unfaithful. She didn't mind. Her love was expansive and total. She forgave this flaw of his as the flipside of his power, which was a major turn-on for her. Many powerful men were broken in this way, unable to stay faithful to the women who loved them.

So she hadn't felt that guilty when she'd embarked on her own fling.

Until she did.

Until she realized that she couldn't live with her own infidelity. She might endure Mako being unfaithful, but she couldn't abide that type of flaw in herself.

And then there was the matter of the positive pregnancy test. Who's child was it? She'd already miscarried twice; she hadn't even told Mako she was pregnant.

Now, she thought, grief-stricken, maybe she wasn't.

"What are you doing here?" she asked. "What do you want?"

But when the person stepped into the light, it wasn't Brandon at all.

It was Joshua. Cricket's new boyfriend.

She grappled with it, trying to make sense. What? Why was this happening?

"You look pale," he said, moving toward her. He seemed genuinely concerned.

"What do you want?" she asked, making her voice hard. "What are you doing?"

The room spun and wobbled. The pain came in great waves. Her head hurt so badly; it was a like a siren she couldn't silence. Maybe this was a nightmare? She'd wake up in the bed upstairs with Mako beside her. Please.

"We just want what everyone wants."

The voice came from behind her.

Liza spun to see a woman she recognized but couldn't place right away. Wait. Disparate pieces, ideas, tried to fit themselves together but didn't click.

Finally: Trina. Mako's old assistant.

Some of the pieces clicked then.

"*You,*" she said. "Where's Brandon?"

Trina laughed a little, and Liza remembered how fakely sweet she'd always been, how there had always been something dark behind her gaze.

"Your Brandon's long gone."

"I don't understand," Liza said, tears threatening. The texts, the online stalking. Who had it been? Then finally she got it.

Trina. It had been Trina all along. But why?

"You have something that *I* want, Liza. Brandon moved on long ago. He probably doesn't even remember your little fling."

Trina held up her phone to reveal the text chain Liza thought had been with Brandon.

"*What* do you want?" asked Liza, wrapping her arms around her middle. "Is this blackmail? Because whatever it is—you can have it. Just leave us alone."

Her hand rested on the gun. She wasn't even sure how to use it. Was there a safety, was it engaged? She knew she should take it out, at least. Point it. But she felt so weak, so sick. She quaked now with fear.

"Do you know what your husband is? The things he's done?" asked Trina.

Liza didn't answer. She *did* know Mako and all his many flaws. The rumors about him at Red World. The truth was that she didn't care who he was in the world outside, only who he was to her. She forgave him everything else.

"Why do you stay with him? All he does is cheat and lie," said Trina. "He's still sleeping with her, you know? Cricket."

A wave of pain and nausea almost doubled her over. She knew. Of course, she did.

"What did he do to you, Trina?" asked Liza. That's what this was, wasn't it? "How can we make it right?"

Trina shook her head. "Why are you protecting him? Why do women always enable and apologize, cover for monsters. You, Cricket, Hannah. Why?"

Liza didn't have time to answer. Finally, she found her strength and drew the gun. But Trina was on her, the gun knocked quickly from her hand, falling useless onto the floor. Joshua came up fast behind her. It all seemed floating, unreal—

his strength, the coldness in the other woman's eyes. What were they going to do with her?

When Joshua spoke, Liza heard fear in his voice.

"Wait," he said. "Don't, Trina. You promised."

Within the volume of her other pain, her terror, she almost didn't feel the knife in her abdomen, until she was screaming with it, and Joshua was putting a big, calloused hand over her mouth. The world started fading, pain a siren drowning out everything else.

They'd have heard her, wouldn't they? Someone would come to save her, the baby.

"No one's coming for you," Trina said, as if reading her mind. "I took your things. Left a note for Mako. He'll think you left him. That you are finally sick of his shit."

"No," she gasped.

Liza leaned hard against Joshua, her own weight too much for her legs.

"I'm sorry. I'm sorry," he said, his lips next to her ear.

She tasted his skin. And she was falling and falling. "I don't understand. What do you want from me?" Her own words sounded faint, distant.

There must be an answer. Trina had been stalking her, pretending to be Brandon. She knew about Liza's affair, her pregnancy. She'd lured Liza away from the group. She'd obviously been lingering in the periphery of their lives, watching, for months, longer. She'd booked this trip. Was it her plan all along, to get them out here and destroy them one by one? Was it just revenge against Mako? No, she wanted to hurt Liza, too. Take her baby. Kill her. Why?

She was insane. A destroyer.

The room darkened, or seemed to. The sounds around her grew fuzzier.

I'm so sorry, she told her baby. *I wasn't strong enough to protect you even now. I wouldn't have been a good mom if I couldn't even get you this far.*

Joshua lowered her gently to the ground.

Blood. There was so much blood. And the world around her was fading. She *was* sorry. For everything she'd done that led her to this moment. She wrapped her arms around her middle, curled up, let the darkness come for her.

"Why?" she whispered.

"I'm just trying to clean up the mess of this family," said Trina.

The last thing Liza heard was the other woman's derisive laughter.

23

TRINA

"Turn off the light."

Joshua stands rooted, staring at Liza's still form on the ground. He's gone pale, eyes glassy. "Y-y-you said it was only about him."

"This *is* about him." How is he not seeing that?

His face. It's a mask of accusation, of fear. I've seen that look before. I should have known that he'd unstitch. "You—*killed* her."

Like he's surprised that it came to this.

I glance over at Liza's lifeless body. "Maybe." Blood seeps silently, pools black.

I walk away from her, turn off the light, as he sinks onto the couch and dumps his head into his hands. "What have I done?"

No one likes to be confronted with the truth about what they will do when motivated by fear. But it's only human to act in our own self-interest. The slope is a slippery one, an abyss below. It gets away from you, that morality you cling to when things are going well. It's when the bottom falls out of your life that you really see who you are.

"What happens now?" he says, although I'm not sure he's talking to me.

"That depends."

He lifts questioning eyes to me, shakes his head.

Uncertainty. We don't care for it.

But I have come to understand—in my mindfulness and meditation practice—that there is nothing certain in life but death. We may labor under the delusion that we know what the day ahead of us holds, what the hour holds. But we don't. We may think that our death—our very certain death—is something distant and remote, an island we might never visit.

But for some of us, it's right here, waiting.

Just pay attention. You can feel its breath on your neck.

I am the agent of uncertainty.

He rises now, pulling himself to his full height. The sadness is gone, replaced by anger. Not good.

"Sit down," I say, summoning the voice of the lion tamer. I have intimate knowledge of all of his little isms, habits, appetites. All his secrets. I am good at that, peeling back the layers people hide behind, to find the beating heart inside. I try to imbue my words with that knowledge.

The truth. That's what ties him to me now, even though I can feel him edging away.

I take a breath and feel it fill my lungs. I can hear the distant rumble of thunder. There's a big storm coming.

My phone pings and it breaks the standoff between us. I press back a swell of annoyance as I read.

This has to stop.

I couldn't agree more. All of it has been so much harder than I imagined.

That's how it is when you strike upon an idea, something

huge, something you imagine will change your life and change the world. There's a fantasy element to that type of thinking. There has to be, otherwise we'd never embark on the big journeys.

But when you're in the thick of it, with so many mistakes behind you, and so many uncertainties again, there's an inevitable dark night of the soul where you're being swallowed by the morass of self-doubt.

And this one has so many layers, so many well-constructed masks, one sluicing off only to reveal another. Things have gotten complicated. And the truth is, I'm tired. I've lost my way. I almost answer that text, my finger hovering when it pings again.

Let me help you, okay?

Shit.

I *almost* answer: Come get me. I'm lost. I've lost my way.

But I don't, of course.

Sometime after my father died, I started cutting myself. I'm not even sure how it started. My sadness, my grief was a balloon inside me. It swelled and expanded sometimes until I felt like it was crushing me, suffocating me from within. I couldn't breathe.

In the bathroom, I found one of my dad's old razor blades and felt compelled to put its edge to the flesh on the inside of my thigh. The pain was a release, a trade. A visible cut that bled, thick and red, drew my rapt attention from my own inner misery to the outer wound. Physical pain is easier to bear than psychological pain, far easier. It's a wonderful distraction from the inner swamp of our thoughts. It took my mom a couple of months to notice. First a drop of blood on the bathroom floor, then on the inside of my jeans, then a confrontation.

After that tearful discovery, it was right to therapy for me. Which helped. Some.

"You can bring yourself out of your thoughts and into your

body anytime," said Dr. Rowen. "You don't need to self-harm to do it."

"How?"

"When you focus on your breath, the activity of the mind will lessen."

Initially it did sound like bullshit. But it turned out he was right. It was slower, too, more discipline required. Took some effort to learn how to do it.

"Count your breaths. Notice the presence of each object in your field. What do you smell, hear? Ground yourself in this place, this moment."

I still repeat that to myself now when the stress becomes too much. I remember his soothing voice, his kind eyes, the way he would touch the gold frames of his round spectacles. Like now. I look at the crooked posters, the rickety chairs, the foggy window. I draw a deep breath, release it.

It was Dr. Rowen who suggested an Origins test. He thought it would just give me some extra data on my heritage, something interesting. He wondered if a new knowledge of myself would help me deal with the grief of losing my dad.

The technology was still new back then. Today, millions upon millions of people have submitted their DNA to Origins and other companies like it. Chances are that, even if you haven't, someone you are related to has already done this. There's no way to know how the data being collected by private genealogy companies will be used in the future. It's the Wild West.

But back then, when I sat in Dr. Rowen's office, it was new. It was long before the Donor Sibling Registry or the Facebook DNA Detectives page, forensic genealogy, or any of it.

Of course, Dr. Rowen didn't imagine the road it would lead me to wander. He thought I was just a grieving girl in pain. He didn't know that I would discover poison in my DNA, or how it would inspire me.

Now Joshua and I lock eyes. There's a connection there,

something true and deep. Something powerful. He's hooked into me for all sorts of reasons, but that connection which reaches back through time is not the least of it.

He is about to say something. But then he stays silent, just glances haunted into the middle distance. Outside, a skein of lightning slices jagged and electric in the distance. There's a storm coming tonight. No one can make it rain, but I'm very good at knowing when the rain will come.

My phone pings again; I glance down at the message on my screen.

You don't have to do this.

That might be true. But it's far too late.

"I've been thinking," Joshua says.

"Don't think," I say. "It's not a good look for you."

I feel the heat of his gaze.

"What's the point of this?" he asks. "What's the endgame? How do we walk away from this?"

"Don't worry about that now," I answer.

It's a five-mile run into town where my car is waiting. That's how I've planned my exit. But my endgame may not include him, depending on how this goes. No need to get into that now.

"I mean," he says. "They're not bad people. They're not."

"You only think that because *you're* a bad person. Your perspective is skewed."

"Mine is?"

He hasn't pushed back like this before and it's bad timing. I pin him with my most menacing gaze and he looks away. But then instead of cowing, he moves toward me.

"I'm leaving," he says. "I'm getting out of here."

I almost feel sorry for him. He's not a good man, but he's not a truly bad one either. He's made big mistakes, and committed some petty crimes. But his heart, it's not irredeemable, not like some of the men I have known. Honestly, he's just bad enough to use for my purposes. Like most, he's been driven by fear of the things I know about him, and therefore malleable, easy to control.

Another tickle of self-doubt. Maybe he doesn't deserve this. Maybe no one does.

Is it weakness that motivates me to do nothing as he strides past? Or exhaustion? Or the texts connecting me to my better nature? I *do* have one, after all. He stops at the door.

"Come with me," he says. "Let's go. Remember what we talked about?"

I ignore him and bend down to pick up Liza's gun. It's cool and heavy in my hand.

I turn to face him, but I don't point it at him. Something passes between us, and then he disappears into the night. A few moments later I hear the rumble of an engine. He's gone.

24

HENRY

2006

Henry sat in his car, watching the house. His back ached, and he was aware of the low hum of anxiety. He shouldn't be here. This was a mistake.

The street was lined with towering oaks, the leaves swaying in the light summer breeze. Cicadas sang, their song rising and falling. Through the slightly open car window, the whole place smelled fresh. Clean. Wholesome. This was the kind of place people moved to raise families, safe, pretty. Idyllic. At least from the outside looking in.

It was one of those neighborhoods he'd always fantasized about when he was a kid. Basketball hoops in the driveways; bikes left askew on nicely tended lawns. He imagined that people who lived in neighborhoods like this decorated for Halloween with big jack-o'-lanterns and goofy, glittery skeletons hanging on doorways. At Christmastime, there'd be lit and trimmed trees in big bay windows, twinkling lights outside.

In summer, kids would play in the street—kickball, and flash-light tag. They'd ride bikes to each other's houses.

When he was living in this apartment or that with Alice, he would see neighborhoods like that on television or in the movies, wonder what it was like to have that sense of commu-nity, of home.

"Can we live someplace like that?" he'd asked one night.

He didn't remember what they'd been watching—some made-for-television movie where every home was decorated with bright colors, and every woman was pretty and well-coiffed.

"With all the normies?" she'd answered with a scoff. "You want to go to a block party where I make small talk with *housewives*?"

She leaned on the word with disdain. But what was so wrong, he wondered, with taking care of a family?

But Alice's disdain for that type of life was so palpable that he didn't bring it up again. But it was all he had ever wanted; just one of the many things he didn't get.

That's the good news about life, Miss Gail liked to tell him. *You get to create yourself when you're grown. No matter what circumstances you come from, no matter what darkness, you can write a new story for yourself and the family you make.*

Maybe he could give a place like this to his own kids. The thought gave him a pang of longing so severe he had to breathe his way through it.

"Are you sure you want to do this?" Piper had asked him this morning. "What about always moving forward, never look-ing back?"

"That's the thing," he said. "Maybe I can't move forward without looking back."

Piper rested a hand on her belly, gave him that look. She hadn't even started to show yet. "Ready or not, we're mov-ing forward."

They were too young to be married, too young to be having a baby. Everyone said so, especially Piper's parents. Especially Piper's dad, who never stopped giving Henry the side-eye.

Piper had finished her English degree at NYU, a hugely expensive education which her father complained prepared her to do absolutely nothing, especially with a baby on the way.

Henry was starting grad school in the fall, having graduated top of his class at MIT. He'd pursue a master's in computer engineering at Columbia University nights, while working at a startup cybersecurity company during the day.

"I want him to know who he is," Henry said, in their tiny Riverside walk-up. The windows had been open, sun streaming. The place wasn't huge; the neighborhood wasn't great. But it was theirs and they loved it.

"Or her."

"Or her," he agreed.

Piper moved over to him, took his hands and placed them on her middle. "He'll know, or she'll know, because of us. Because of who we are."

She was right. Of course, she was. But when he looked back into his past, it was as vast and as mysterious as it was when he looked up into the stars. The mind boggled at infinity. The infinite possibilities of where he'd come from, from whom. Who Alice had been. Those strange, buried memories that surfaced in dreams. Piper had grandparents, aunts and uncles, stories of where people came from, how they'd made their way through the world. She could give all of that to their baby, a history, origins. Henry had nothing but questions, a dark mystery to be solved.

He started to move out of the car, prepared to walk up the driveway lined with pretty perennials, knock on the red door. He was expected. But he sank back, heart thudding.

He gave himself another moment, thinking of his last talk with Detective West.

So many years later the detective still hadn't closed Alice's case.

The old cop was a year from retirement now, but still at it. He was nursing a theory about some guy who might have followed Henry and Alice from Tucson. Tom Watson, the son of Faith Watson, the woman for whom Alice had worked as a caregiver.

"Based on the information you gave me, and the new information I got from your aunt, when I was in Tucson on vacation, I was able to track down the family of Alice's old employer," said West.

Alice it seemed had stolen money from Ms. Watson; Tom, according to his sister, had suspected that Alice might have been responsible for the old woman's death—an error with her medication. Maybe an accident. Maybe not.

Henry had felt a twinge of guilt. West, a stranger to Alice was using his vacation time to hunt Alice's killer, while Henry had been doing everything he could to tamp down thoughts of her—burying himself in his studies, taking the train to see Piper on Friday nights, partying with her in the West Village all weekend, working nights in the school's bursar's office, digitizing records. Those years were good ones; he was so busy that he rarely thought about anything but what was right in front of him.

But Detective West hadn't forgotten.

"Faith Watson's daughter, Corinne, said that her brother, Tom, thought Alice tweaked the dosage on the old lady's meds, then cleared out her accounts. But Tom was a bit of shady character—some drugs, perpetually unemployed. Corinne didn't believe him, in fact, she'd suspected that Tom and Alice were involved."

"That sounds like a pretty big lead."

"Did you ever see her with a man in Tucson?"

Henry searched his memory. Maybe there was someone? A bearded man, smiling and holding a bouquet of wildflowers. There had been men, here and there. No one who'd made a lasting impression.

"Tom admitted to tracking Alice down, but said he never hurt her. Just asked for the money back. Said in exchange he wouldn't tell the police what she'd done."

"If he thought Alice killed his mother and took her money, why wouldn't he call the police?"

The old man cleared his throat. In the background, Henry

had heard the noises of the busy police station. He glanced at his watch, a gift from Piper's parents on graduation. He had the urge to cut the conversation short. He'd been running late for work, and honestly he hadn't wanted to talk about Alice.

"Good question. I wondered the same. But—there wasn't any real evidence. Just his suspicions. Honestly, it didn't seem like Tom cared that much about his mother or how she'd died. I think all he really cared about was the money."

"How much?"

"About five thousand."

"Did Alice have that? Did she give it to him?"

"He says no. As far as I found, your mother didn't have a bank account. Unless she had one under another name. She didn't even have a credit card. Maybe she had a stash of cash somewhere."

"There was always money for whatever," said Henry, remembering. "But I never found anything when we cleaned out the apartment."

"So maybe the person who killed Alice took that money."

Henry had turned the information around in his head, trying to fit this knowledge into the fractured pieces of his memory. It did make a kind of sense. They left places in the middle of the night. Alice always seemed to be in flight, looking over her shoulder. If she'd been taking money from people then fleeing, it made sense that she'd be worried someone would come after her.

So probably it was this guy Tom Watson. He'd killed her, taken whatever money she'd had. Or what if she ripped off other people in other places? Had someone finally caught up with her, just as she'd feared?

"It was this guy Tom Watson, right? It had to be."

Detective West made a noise that was kind of like a verbal shrug. "He didn't have any priors. No history of sexual assault or violence against women."

"What about the DNA evidence? You said the technology was improving all the time."

"Since Tom Watson was never arrested, there are no fingerprints or DNA records for him in the national databases."

Henry stayed quiet. Then, "I mean—could you ask him to give it now since you've found him."

Detective West grunted. "I did. And guess what? He said no."

"You can't force him?"

"I'd need a warrant, someone in his area to cooperate. But I don't have the physical evidence for that."

"So you don't have enough evidence to collect more evidence?"

"Something like that. I'm sorry, son." Detective West continued on into the silence. "Anyway, after I interviewed him and his sister, Tom Watson died last week. Heart attack."

It wasn't funny. But Henry almost laughed. In all those made-for-television movies he'd watched with Alice, all those unsolved mystery documentaries he watched with Piper, there was always something, no matter how small, no matter how many years later, that led to the truth. But the real truth was that many crimes went unsolved; so many questions were left unanswered. People did terrible things, then died unpunished. What if he, Henry, died one day, never knowing the truth of who he was? Would that mean he'd never really lived?

"I'm still looking, Henry."

"I know you are, Detective."

"What about your aunt. Did you ever connect with her?"

West asked him that every time. Henry usually made up some excuse for why he hadn't gotten in touch. The woman, Alice's sister, had sent him a few emails which he'd never answered. They were nice. *We're here for you*, she'd written. *We want you to be a part of our family.*

"Yeah," he'd lied. "We're in touch."

"Good. That's good," said West sounding relieved. "It's important to stay connected to family."

Was it though?

Or was that just something people said. He and Piper were *very* connected to Piper's family and it wasn't always easy, or pleasant. At their small backyard wedding, Piper's mom and dad had a big fight in the kitchen that carried out into the yard. Some distant relatives who Henry was meeting for the first time asked him pointedly: *Where are you from, son?* His dark skin, and mass of black curls communicated to them something suspicious about his heritage.

Racist fucks, Piper complained. *Don't worry. We don't see them much.*

Henry had a hard time understanding racism. People were just people, right? They might differ in the color of their skin, features, or cultures, but *under* the skin, they were all the same. He'd read that all humans shared 99 percent of the same DNA. That it was only like 1 percent that accounted for the superficial differences of appearance.

Miss Gail felt more like family than Alice ever had, and she was just some stranger who had taken him in, raised him as best she could. He loved her in a way he wasn't sure he had loved Alice.

All these thoughts churned as he sat listening to the wind in the trees. Finally, he saw the door to the house open and a woman stepped out onto the stoop and waved.

She looked a little like Alice, but fuller bodied, prettier. She had fluffy blond hair, and wore a flowered dress, simple flats.

He waved back. He couldn't just drive off now, which is what he had been considering doing before she came out of the door. That's what happened—thoughts of Detective West, and Alice, and Piper's family, and their baby, and who Henry had been or would be were like a hurricane in his head, a chaos of thoughts that spiraled until he couldn't hear or think anything else.

She approached as he crossed the quiet road to go meet her. At the sidewalk she put both her hands to her heart, and started to cry, then took him into a warm, tight embrace. He stood stiffly, awkwardly, letting her hold on—simultaneously touched and surprised, a little scared. He wasn't really a hugger. Finally, he closed his arms around her.

"I'm Henry," he said, though she clearly knew who he was.

She pulled back and looked at him, put a hand to each of his cheeks.

"I see her in you," she said, tears streaming. "Oh, I'm sorry. I'm a wreck. It's just that I've waited so long for any piece of her. I'm *so glad* you're here, Henry. Thank you for coming. I know nothing has been easy for you."

She took him by the hand and led him inside the house that was everything it promised from the outside—warm, filled with photos, tastefully decorated. She'd baked cookies, the scent still hanging in the air.

"I don't mean to overwhelm you," she said when they sat at the table. There were white tulips on the counter, dipping in a crystal vase. Everything was clean, surfaces shining.

He noticed the stack of photo albums then, other notebooks, some files. Detective West said that his aunt was an amateur genealogist, tracing the roots and branches of her family tree back into history. The idea of that, that there was all that data about her family, about *his* family, was as exciting as it was frightening.

"I want you to know, Henry, that we would have taken you after she passed. I would have raised you as my own. But Margaret—she didn't want us. Her family. She just, I don't know, always wanted to get away."

"Margaret."

"You knew her as Alice, that's what Detective West said. But that wasn't the name our parents gave her. She always loved that book—*Alice in Wonderland*. She went down the rabbit hole, didn't she?"

His aunt had started crying again. He wanted to comfort her but he didn't know how. He reached out an awkward hand and she took it.

"By the time Detective West and I connected, you were

grown, heading off to college. And you didn't answer my emails."

"I'm sorry," he said. "I just—I don't know why I didn't. I should have."

"It's okay," she said. Her smile was warm, understanding. "There's no rule book for dealing with a mess like this one, is there? We're all just trying to get through, aren't we?"

She got up and came back with a cup of tea and a plate of cookies.

"Detective West says that I had the birth certificate and social security number of a dead child. Do you know anything about that?"

She sat with a long exhale, rubbed at her eyes. "Margaret... we called her Maggie...got pregnant in her senior year of high school. It was a big deal. Our parents were devastated, you know. They wanted so much for her, for us. But they planned to help her raise the baby so that she could finish school."

She opened the first stack of photo albums, slid it between them. They flipped through the thick pages. A picture of Alice as a child—holding out the skirt of a yellow dress, smiling, coquettish. Then as an adolescent, lithe and striking, if not pretty, in the embrace of a younger girl, Henry's aunt. There was a family portrait, everyone stiff and smiling against a gray backdrop. Alice wore a blue dress, eyes sullen. Picture after picture of the girls—Christmas morning, Hawaiian vacation, riding on horseback, playing tennis. His aunt paused at each, sharing memories. *Oh, my, Maggie hated horses—everything about them. But Dad wanted us both to know how to ride. The fights!*

Our parents fought every Christmas. Dad was always on Mom for spending too much.

There was a picture of Alice, her hair cut short in a pixie cut, wearing a skintight striped dress. *Oh, the Pat Benatar look. My parents were furious that she cut her hair. But she did what she wanted. Always.*

Then, finally, the photograph of a baby wrapped in a blue

blanket. Not Henry. This child had strawberry blond hair, light eyes.

"Honestly, for a kid, it was kind of exciting, to have a nephew and a baby in the house. I was four years younger than Maggie."

She smiled at the memory, but the happy expression darkened. "But the baby, also named Henry, he died. SIDS."

She traced a hand over the picture of the infant.

"It just blew us to pieces. Maggie took off after that. We'd get a postcard from this town or that over the years. But I never saw her again."

She shook her head, was quiet a moment. Henry heard a clock ticking somewhere, a chime for the quarter hour. Then,

"Our parents passed—young for these times. My dad had a heart attack; all the men on his side of the family died young. My mother, well, she had a car accident. But if you ask me it was more that she'd just given up on life. She didn't really recover after the loss of Margaret, the baby, my dad. She had been depressed and drinking heavily the night she died."

They were just sentences. A flat recount of the decline of a family. But he could see the pain and loss in the older woman's face.

"I'm so sorry," he said. And he was. Sorry for her, for himself. It seemed like Alice had hurt a lot of people.

"Life," she said. "It beats you up, doesn't it?"

"Not everyone," he says. Some people seemed to live charmed lives, even if they didn't know it. Intact families, the privilege of heritage, an expectation of a certain kind of future, a safety net beneath them.

Her smile was kind. "Yes, everyone. Eventually."

Henry pointed to the baby photograph. "That's not me."

"No," she said, shaking her head. "It's not."

"Then who am I? Where did I come from? I think maybe I didn't really want to know. But my wife and I, we're having a baby."

Her face lit up. "How wonderful, Henry. That's such lovely news."

"So I guess suddenly it feels important to know more about my history."

His aunt nodded. Even with tiny lines, and a softness around the jaw she was still a pretty woman with shining, smiley eyes and creamy skin, delicate features, well-kept. There was the shade of Alice around the brow, something in her smile. She had none of Alice's darkness, her edge.

"Of course it does. Of course."

She patted the stack of albums, notebooks, and files. "I am a bit of an armchair genealogist," she said. "As for the past, it's all here—or a lot of it anyway. And with all the new technology, finding answers about you will be easier than ever before. If you want me to, I can help you. I can help you understand who you are. Maybe we can even find your father. Is that what you want, Henry?"

He was surprised by the rush of emotion, feelings he hadn't let himself have, a stunning desperation to belong somewhere, *to* someone.

"Yes," he managed, his voice cracking slightly. "I want that very much."

After lunch, he followed his Aunt Gemma up the staircase to the second floor.

"Step into my office, said the spider to the fly," she said with a chuckle as she swung open the double doors to a room filled with bookshelves, a big desk with two computer screens, a cozy couch facing a coffee table stacked with photo albums, notebooks, files.

She urged him to take a seat and he did, nearly sinking into the soft floral cushions.

"Our father started this project before Maggie and I were born. He could trace his heritage back to British landowners, though by the time his parents came to America they were tradespeople. His father was a tailor; his mother was a governess until they married.

"Our mother was descended from Russian Jews," she said. "It's a funny thing that the people who are privileged by history are also the beneficiaries of better record keeping. It took me years, two trips out to Utah where the Church of Jesus Christ of Latter-day Saints has the largest collection of records in the world, hours and hours online, to find the name of the town where I think my maternal grandmother was born. We had a trip planned to Russia, but then my husband passed."

"I'm sorry."

She paused a moment. "Thank you. He was a wonderful man and we had thirty good years together. I try to be in gratitude for that, not grief."

"Children?"

A flush came up on her cheeks, her eyes filling. She shook her head, seeming not to trust her voice.

His hand found hers again and she looked at him gratefully.

"That's my life's biggest sadness," she said. "We tried and tried. But…"

They sat a moment until she was ready to go on. And then she did. They sat talking, the sky going dim outside as she shared her research—telling him stories about distant relatives on both sides, things she'd gleaned from old letters, and news stories, birth and death certificates. She shared grainy photographs, and wrinkled copies of wedding announcements, handwritten ledgers from churches she and her husband had visited in the UK.

It was a journey into the distant past, brought alive by his aunt's meticulous research. And something in Henry settled, something that had been an endless restless question was answered. He did have a history, a family. He wasn't just floating in time, disconnected, a stranger even to himself. Maybe.

"I still have so many questions," said Henry.

"Yes."

"I mean, Miss Gail worked hard to get me my own social security number. But we never were able to track down my actual birth certificate. What if I'm not even Alice's child? What if she abducted me or something?"

It was just one of a myriad possibilities he'd turned over in his mind. Had she stolen him? Is that why they were always on the run? Those foggy memories he had, were those from his real family?

His aunt shook her head. "No," she said. "I see her in you, the shape of your eyes. You even have the chin cleft everyone on our father's side has. I feel it, Henry. I do."

He put his hand next to her arm. His skin was so much darker than hers. He gave her a meaningful look.

"That means *nothing*. We have to find your father to get the other pieces of your puzzle. And that's all it is. DNA. It's just one big puzzle, and we're each just tiny little pieces that all fit together somehow, somewhere."

He found himself smiling, which he didn't do often. Piper was always on him. *Lighten up, loser.* His wife was the one person who could always get him to crack a grin, until he met his aunt. He liked her energy, warm, practical, loving. She was right; he felt it, too, their deep connection.

"But how do we find that piece?"

She got up and went to her desk. When she came back, she held a glossy brochure. She handed it to him.

"Lucky for us, the technology in this field is growing by leaps and bounds," she said sitting back beside him. "A couple years ago we may never have had answers."

It was a sell piece, featuring pictures of people smiling around dinner tables, or holding hands, cradling babies, or beaming at older people on sunny paths, for a company called Origins. The *s* on the end was comprised of a DNA helix.

Every family has a story, it read in bold letters. *Let us help you tell yours.*

25

CRICKET

"So there *is* someone else on the property," said Hannah, voice a little shrill. She reached for her phone.

Mako put a hand on her arm. "It's probably just on a timer. Weed has *always* made you paranoid, Han. This is a known thing."

It *was* true, though Cricket wasn't going to side against Hannah with Mako. That violated the sister code. Hannah was Captain Safety—she was the don't run by the pool, come in from the rain, don't take a shower in a lightning storm type. She was the one you called when you needed advice, a rescue, or a recipe to make sourdough bread. But, yeah, when she was high—totally paranoid.

"If it comes on again, we'll call the host," said Cricket. Both Hannah and Mako nodded; Cricket was very pleased with her mediation of this crisis, rewarded herself with a deep swallow of beer. The world tilted.

They all kept looking in the direction of the light but it stayed dark—the bubbles bubbled, the THC coursed through her bloodstream. Even if there was someone out there, she was way too relaxed to do anything about it. From the looks of him, it would take someone running up the deck wielding a knife to get Mako to move. She knew that lidded stare, that half smile.

Why did she still want him *so badly*?

The pull to Mako was almost magnetic, physically drawing her closer.

He started talking about some trip to India to meet with his programmers, and how he got sick in the airport, and was stopped by security, his bags searched only to find a stash of turmeric he was hauling home for Liza. There was something too big about the story, something that rang false. And he sounded like a total dick telling it, the classic humble·brag— like this shitty thing happened, but only because I am this internationally traveling, super successful businessman. *I was still dry heaving when I got to the first-class cabin. The stewardess looked at me like I had leprosy, leaning back as she handed me my complimentary champagne.*

Still there was something enthralling about him, always had been. From the minute she first saw him in the hallways of the private school they all attended, his arm draped over another girl, his smile broad, confidence radiant, she was hooked.

He had been a junior; she a freshman, like Hannah. Cricket didn't like to think that she'd sought out Hannah's friendship just to get close to Mickey, as everyone knew him then. But that was partially the truth, even though the friendship that blossomed was real. Did it make their friendship less wonderful, less important because Cricket had essentially *used* Hannah to find her way to Mako? She didn't think so. Hannah had forgiven her long ago. Hadn't she?

Mickey hadn't been the jock football hero. He was the charming brainiac, the homecoming king, the student council president. He was the guy with the near perfect SAT scores.

He was the charismatic genius. His appeal was less physical than it was cerebral, energetic. Cricket lost her virginity to him on his senior prom night. He dumped her before he left for college. They'd fucked about a dozen times since then—midnight booty calls, and "catch-up" dinners that ended predictably back at her place, after breakups, after Liza's first miscarriage.

Hannah was not aware of these assignations—unless Mickey had told her. Cricket was fairly sure he would not have. Hannah wouldn't be happy to hear he was cheating on Liza. She wouldn't be happy that Cricket kept sleeping with a man who was obviously using her and had been since high school—even if that man was Hannah's own brother. Especially.

"So tell us more about Joshua," said Hannah from the other side of the tub.

Cricket realized that she was leaning into Mako ridiculously, chin on fist, like a schoolgirl with a crush. And that Hannah did not approve. Hannah had that look, that look that said, *I know you two. I know you better than anyone, better than you know yourselves.* And yet it still managed to be nonjudgmental. Like she was the beloved babysitter, and Mako and Cricket were the mischievous toddlers. Even if they were bad, Hannah would still make the grilled cheese sandwiches and read the bedtime story. Even the question was just a gentle nudge back toward Cricket's better nature.

Joshua. Yes. Cricket was *in love* with Joshua. Mako—well, he was like the habit you'd had to quit for your own good. Cigarettes. Or too much pot on the weekends. Carbs. You never stopped wanting it, even when you knew it was bad for you in twelve different ways. It was always something you forced yourself to push away.

She edged back from Mako, pushed herself up onto the side of the tub to cool down. Her skin steamed in the cold night air and somewhere an owl hooted, spooky and low. She took a swig from the beer he'd handed her. What she really needed was water, to sober up. To grow up. Yes, they both needed to grow up. And tonight was the night to start.

Hannah, she noticed, kept glancing over in the direction where they'd seen the light go on, then off. Must be on some kind of timer, they'd concluded. They were in the middle of nowhere. Who else would be out here? They'd have heard anyone approach.

"Yes," said Mako, his eyes raking her body. "Tell us about your mystery man. The one who seems to have *disappeared*."

He made an explosive motion with his fingers to punctuate the word.

"Well, we can start with him being *hella hot*," said Cricket. She and Hannah clinked beer bottles, while Mako blew out a mocking breath.

"And also so considerate, romantic—flowers, candlelight dinners, calling to talk before bed when we're not together."

"Love that," said Hannah, with a smile.

"He's smart," Cricket went on.

"Where does he work again?" asked Mako, looking bored.

"Razor?"

He shook his head, took a swallow of his beer, draining it. "Never heard of it."

It was a pretty big company. Most people in tech had heard of it, even if they weren't sure exactly what they did.

"Cybersecurity. Government contracts," she said. "We don't talk about work much. Some of his projects are classified."

"Hmm," said Mako. "Interesting. Well, as long as he makes you happy. That's what counts."

He looked away.

"He does," said Cricket.

She looked toward the door, then glanced at her phone which rested on the side of the hot tub. Where *was* he anyway? It was weird that he'd just taken off into the night, wasn't it? If she wasn't so buzzed she might be worried or annoyed. Instead she just felt woozy.

Mako heaved himself from the water, creating a tsunami over the sides. "I think it's time I went up to check on my wife."

He was doing that to punish her; she'd broken the spell between them, or Hannah had. And now he was playing the role of devoted husband.

"What about the light?"

"Forget about it, Han. It's nothing." His tone was a little sharp, a little bossy. He was like that.

Hannah gave her brother a look, but said nothing.

It was fine that he was going inside. It was good even. Mako and Cricket were bad together. He put on the good husband show sometimes after their random assignations. Cricket would get a text, meet him at bar, he'd be down about something or another. She'd talk him through it. He'd come back to her place. Afterward, he'd often leave with an attitude, as if she was the one to blame. *I have to get home to Liza,* he'd say, her name pronounced with a kind reverence, even though he'd just fucked Cricket raw. As if to say, I *fuck* you, but I *love* her. He'd hurt Cricket so many times; in ways even Hannah didn't know about. And she still came when he called. Why?

My brother, a sixteen-year-old Hannah had warned, always wise beyond her years, *he's not always a nice guy. Be careful.*

She hadn't been.

Her phone pinged.

Sorry! Read the text from Joshua. On my way back!

She felt the sting of shame for how she was acting with Mako, a wash of relief, and then vowed to drink less and not be alone with Mako, not at all, for the rest of the trip.

She was kicking that habit for good.

And no more gummies. Wow, were they ever strong.

"Crick?"

Cricket looked up from her phone and Mako was disappearing through the door leaving wet footprints on the wood behind him. Hannah was watching her.

"All good?"

"Joshua's on his way back."

"Oh, great." Hannah glanced up toward the second level where she and Bruce were staying in the only slightly less luxurious second bedroom. Cricket and Joshua had been given what was surely the room intended for guest children—in the basement. They'd pushed the two single beds together. *We're going to have some fun down here tonight,* said Joshua with a smile. The guy had no ego. Whatever message Mako was trying to send, Joshua had not received it.

"Bruce?"

"He'll be back down soon—maybe. He gets swallowed up in work."

"You okay with that?" asked Cricket.

They could not be as perfect as they seemed. No one was. They just seemed—easy with each other, accepting, loving, considerate. She watched at dinner as he'd filled her wineglass, she'd picked a piece of lint off his shirt. They were *together* in a way she'd never felt with anyone. Maybe it was the baby. That made them a family, not just a couple. There was this powerful bond that could not be broken. She envied it.

Hannah shrugged easily. "I knew who he was when I married him. A workaholic. A stoic. Solid. I never planned to change him."

Hannah shot another glance toward the lake, eyes traveling toward where they'd seen the light come on. Ever vigilant.

"Couldn't even if you tried. That's what they say, right?"

"That's the truth."

Hannah slid over to sit next to Cricket. "And you and Joshua?"

Cricket slid from the side, back into the tub, let the warm water heat her skin. "I mean it. I think I'm in love."

"Well, he's *definitely* in love with you," said Hannah with a big grin. "He hangs on your every word, gazes at you like you are princess, angel, goddess all wrapped into one."

"He does not," she said, nudged her friend with her shoulder. Did he?

"Oh, yes," said Hannah. "He does."

"Do you like him?"

There was only a flutter of hesitation. Cricket chose to ignore it. That moment when Hannah and Joshua had met was weird; it gave Cricket an unpleasant sense of unease, had raised goose bumps on her flesh. But they'd all chosen to blow it off. Just a weird mistake. Nothing.

"He seems kind, smart. He's funny. He makes you happy. What's not to like?"

When they were younger, Cricket had taken Hannah's friendship for granted. It was only now that they were older, now that she'd seen what friendship meant to other people, that she truly appreciated Hannah's brand of loyalty and unflagging support. She tried to be the same kind of friend to Hannah; she knew she fell short too often.

"And how's my girl?" asked Cricket.

"Gigi," said Hannah, eyes drifting to the phone. "She's an angel. Truly. Just a sweet little soul. We're blessed."

"Was it hard to leave her?"

"Awful. I'm checking the cam a hundred times a day."

"Oh, I would be, too," she said.

But probably that wasn't true. Probably she'd be one of those selfish mothers who couldn't wait to fob off the baby on a doting grandparent to run off to this thing or that. She suspected, though she hadn't shared this with Joshua, that she wasn't exactly mother material. He wanted a big family, lots of kids. He'd said this more than once. She usually just responded with some kind of warm noise like "aw" or one of her usual "I love that!" Then she'd kiss him and that usually ended whatever conversation they were having. Hannah was *born* to be a mother. Maybe that wasn't true for every woman. Surely it wasn't.

"But it's good for you and Bruce to have some time away. Some couple time."

"And Lou's so great."

"But."

"But—" said Hannah, brow wrinkling. "Just a feeling."

"You're a new mom, first time leaving her. Of course you're nervous. But it's fine. She's fine. This—ghosts and strangers in the woods aside—" she swept her arm to indicate the house, the trees, the stars. "This is good."

Hannah closed her eyes and leaned back. "Yes," she said. "It is. But what did we see out there, Crick?"

"Honestly? Probably nothing. We just scared ourselves silly like we used to do with the Ouija board."

"And the light at the cabin?"

"Just a timer?"

Hannah laughed, leaning her head back. "You're probably right."

Cricket didn't mind a little drama, a little intrigue, some safe scares like their ghost hunt. *Had* there been someone by the lake? She really wasn't sure. But Cricket didn't *want* anything to be *really* wrong. Joshua would come back soon. She didn't even want to think about him leaving to go to town— like *why*? It was weird, wasn't it? She knew the Wi-Fi wasn't down. And she knew there was something weird between him and his boss. But she could hardly throw any stones in that area, chronic cheater that she was. All that was for another time. He'd come back. They'd get high—higher—and then they'd all have fun tomorrow.

A flash of lightning lit the sky, but Hannah didn't see it because her eyes were closed. Cricket didn't say anything. Hannah would make them go inside. And Cricket was loving the bubbles, her buzz, the stars. She didn't want it to end yet.

"Was that thunder?" Hannah asked, eyes still closed. No way she could have heard that over the hum of the jets. Mom ears.

"I don't think so?" said Cricket. "Just relax."

"I think I felt a temperature drop," said Hannah. "There's a storm coming."

Cricket dropped her head on Hannah's shoulder; Hannah sighed. Cricket stared up into the starry, velvety sky above. It did look like a cloud cover was moving in, obscuring the sky. Cricket didn't say anything.

Mako pushed back through the sliding door.

Great. He's back.

But then, the look on his face gave Cricket a jangle of alarm.

"What is it?" asked Cricket. Hannah opened her eyes and sat up.

"Mickey? What's wrong?"

"Liza," he said. He clutched a piece of paper in his hand, looked down at it in wondering despair. "She—uh. She's gone."

26

HANNAH

The trees around them sang with insects and frogs. Fireflies blinked a languid, slow brightness in the black.

"What do you *mean*? Gone?"

Hannah climbed out of the tub, grabbed one of the towels on the big pile and wrapped it around herself. The air was cold on her skin; her brother looked pale. He sank onto the big couch by the fireplace.

"I mean—" he said, looking up at her. "She left this note."

"What does it say?" Hannah moved over to sit beside him, and he handed it to her. She dried off her hands and took it. Cricket sat in the chair across from them. Hannah read it out loud.

"I'm sorry to do this.

I just need some space from you right now.

You know it's a long time coming. Stay here this weekend. Don't call.
I do love you.
Liza"

"Did you fight?" asked Hannah.

The handwriting looked odd—scrawling and rushed. Hannah knew that Liza had beautiful penmanship—from all the lovely cards and notes she'd sent over the years. Hannah had in fact admired it, how elegant and looping it was. But maybe when you were upset enough to leave your husband, you weren't worried about how you formed your letters.

"No," he said, drawing the syllable out. "She was sick with a headache. We talked a little before and after she left the table. But she said she was just going to rest so that she could be well in the morning."

"What does she mean? A long time coming?" asked Cricket. She'd wrapped up in a towel, too. She sat shivering a little, a worried wrinkle in her brow.

"I have no idea," Mako said, dumping his head into his hands. "I mean. No marriage is perfect, right? We've had our issues."

This was news to Hannah. She and Bruce had their *issues*— the things you argue about as a couple. He left his laundry on the bathroom floor instead of putting it in the basket; she dropped spent tea bags in the sink instead of putting them in the trash. She used his razor. Bruce was a workaholic. Hannah fussed over the baby too much. More recently her paranoia and snooping. But neither one of them were going to take off in the middle of the night, were they?

"What kind of issues?" She knew she sounded shrill, a little like Sophia.

"I don't *know*, Hannah," Mako said, voice sullen, not looking at her. "Things. Stuff. I don't *know*."

"Let's call her," said Hannah. "This is crazy."

"She said not to call."

"That's bullshit." Hannah got up to grab her phone from the picnic table, and pressed Liza's contact. It went straight to voicemail.

Sorry I missed you. Leave a message. Namaste.

Both Cricket and Mako were watching her, looking young, stricken. Why did Cricket look so guilty?

"Hey, Liza, it's Hannah. Look, I'm not sure what's going on. But can you call back so we can talk? Please?"

Bruce pushed out through the sliding door.

"What's up?" he asked, looking at Mako, then up to Hannah and Cricket. Cricket offered a recap.

"Okay," said Bruce, his usual even, measured self. "Wow. Did you guys fight?"

Mako shook his head miserably, and Hannah could see that he was close to tears.

"It just doesn't seem like her, does it?" Hannah asked. "To take off."

It was true that Hannah and Liza weren't close, but Liza had been with Mako for more than five years. It was safe to say that Hannah *knew* her sister-in-law. Liza was patient, unfailingly kind, polite, thoughtful. This kind of behavior was definitely out of character.

Unless.

From the upstairs window, had Liza maybe seen Cricket and Mako flirting, or something more, when Hannah and Bruce left them alone for their own little assignation?

The pieces didn't fit together. And Mako didn't seem right. A light sheen of sweat glistened on his brow. What the fuck was going on?

Hannah walked into the towering great room. Inside, on the kitchen island, pieces of chocolate cake sat sliced on dessert plates—their forgotten dessert. The surfaces were gleaming and clean.

When had the awful Chef Jeff and his unpleasant assistant

left? Had they seen Liza leaving? Those two were like ghosts, slipping in when Hannah wasn't looking, drifting out without a word.

Hannah climbed the stairs, shivering in the air-conditioning. At the end of the long upstairs hallway, she entered the master bedroom suite.

She heard the others follow her inside, Bruce talking low.

A huge four-poster bed dominated the room, and for a moment it looked like there was a sleeping form on the left side. She walked over to find pillows placed lengthwise beneath the sheets.

"I thought it was her," said Mako coming up behind her. "When I came up to change. I didn't disturb her, wanted to let her sleep. But it's like she stacked the pillows that way to fool me."

Mako's suitcase was on the ground, contents spilling sloppily probably from his digging around for swim trunks.

"Her stuff is gone," said Mako, looking around. "Her suitcase, her tote with all her camera equipment for her yoga class, her laptop. She packed up and left."

"That makes no sense. We would have seen her go, wouldn't we?"

Maybe not, when they'd all been outside.

"Did she take the car?" Bruce wanted to know.

"I didn't check," said Mako, helpless, miserable.

Hannah walked into the bathroom, noticing right away Liza's toiletries bag—makeup, lotions, a pill bottle spilled across the counter. If she'd taken her other stuff, this had been forgotten. That wasn't Liza, either. She was meticulously neat; Hannah had always envied their kitchen where surfaces gleamed and everything was an object—the finest knives, the outrageously expensive coffee maker, the handmade acacia wood cutting boards. All the stemware, dishes, plates like polished sentries behind glass doors. Liza's bathroom at home was no different; it was a department store showroom of high-quality organic products, plush white towels rolled on teak shelves, shining tile. Liza *curated*. She liked things a certain way.

Hannah left the toiletries bag as it was, turned back to the room. Things look tussled, like Liza had left in hurry. That's when Hannah noticed that the bedside lamp was tilted to one side, shade askew as if it had been knocked over, tipped again against the wall.

"Why would she have done this?" asked Cricket.

Mako said nothing, just stood in the doorway, looking stunned. Hannah would expect him to be raging; that was his default setting when things happened that he didn't want. His picture-perfect weekend was ruined. Usually he'd be yelling and ranting. Calling everyone they knew to try to figure out where Liza might be. But instead, he looked ill—pastier than he had been downstairs, leaning heavily against the doorjamb. What wasn't he telling them? She found herself staring at her brother. His eyes darted to hers and then away.

Bruce walked into the room and approached the bed, pulled back the covers where the pillows had been stacked.

"Hey," he said, taking a step back. "Is that blood?"

"What the fuck?" said Cricket, moving in. Hannah came up behind her.

Three big stains of red blossomed like roses on the pure white sheets.

"Oh my god," said Hannah. She couldn't bring herself to turn around and look at her brother. But both Cricket and Bruce did.

Hannah was surprised at the rush of emotion—anger, fear. She moved closer and saw that the stains were still wet, had transferred onto the top sheet as well.

This moment, this feeling.

It brought her back to an ugly place she'd been with her brother before. She felt the cold finger of dread trail down her spine.

This was all wrong.

"So she packed up all her things and left without any of us noticing?" Hannah said. "But she forgot her toiletries bag. She left you this letter—which doesn't even look like her handwriting?"

"What are you saying?" asked Mako.

"I'm not *saying* anything. I'm *asking*. Does that seem like Liza to you?"

Mako looked at her blankly. "No—not really."

"So—what?" asked Cricket. "Do you think something happened to her? Like someone *took her*?"

"Woah," said Bruce. He did not like drama, or Cricket's desire to create it. "Let's not overreact."

"That chef was a creeper," said Cricket. "His horrible stories. The blood on his apron. And they just kind of snuck out, didn't they?"

"And I saw the host earlier," said Hannah, feeling a dark tingle of fear. "He seemed really off, too. Like he was standing too close to her."

"What?" said Mako, alarmed. "When was this?"

"When you went into town."

"And we saw someone out by the lake," said Cricket, grabbing onto Hannah.

Bruce looked inquiringly at Hannah who filled him in. "We couldn't be sure. We took some gummies."

Hannah's buzz was long gone. This secluded cabin, which had seemed so serene, now just felt like a house of horrors.

A bright flash of lightning lit the room, casting them all in harsh white. It was followed by a boom of thunder so concussive that it rattled the house, Cricket issuing a frightened shriek.

Then everything went dark.

27

CRICKET

What the actual fuck?

Seriously?

Cricket groped in the dark for the doorjamb while her eyes adjusted. Another flash of lightning cast the room in harsh white. Hannah was by the bathroom, hand on her heart. Bruce was by the bed, watching out the window. For a second, everyone seemed frozen and pale as statues.

She braced herself. Another huge crash of thunder seemed to rattle the house. Something had definitely been hit. Rain started to tap on the windows.

"Crick? You okay?" Mako came up beside her, put a hand on her arm. She felt her body tense, and shifted away.

"I'm okay," she said. "I think there are flashlights in the bedside tables. There were some in ours downstairs. There was a note, too. Said the power went out often in storms, but usually came back on quickly."

Her eyes were adjusting to the dark and she saw Bruce move over to the bedside table, retrieve a flashlight and turn it on. He pointed it on the bed. The blood there looked black, three large, ugly stains that would never come out of the white sheets, which had probably soaked all the way down to the mattress.

"What happened here?" she asked of no one, her breath catching.

She looked to Hannah, who had still said nothing. She could tell by the still, stoic look on Hannah's face that her friend was freaking out, deeply. When Cricket lost it she usually freaked out on the outside—yelling, hysterics; Hannah kept it in. This was a known thing between them. Hannah was cool when the shit hit the fan. She might break down later, after things had settled. But in the moment, she was dead calm.

"Someone should call Liza again," Hannah said, voice level.

"Or the police," said Bruce.

"Woah." Mako. "The police? Why the fuck would we do that? She *left*."

He was still clinging to that letter, held it out in front of him now. Cricket remembered something that she always, *always* forgot about Mako. He was a liar. A really good one. Creative and easy with it. He'd lied to her so many times, about so many things big and small, sometimes about things that she had witnessed or heard herself, knowing better. And somehow she almost always believed him. Some people were just like that, weren't they? They were so magnetic, so hypnotic that you didn't ever realize or care that you were being duped. Or was it that they had a knack for finding the people who would believe them?

"Left *bleeding*? What if something's wrong with her?" said Hannah. "What if she's sick? Or hurt? Or what if someone else is here?"

That's when Mako released a sob. They all turned to look at him, Bruce hitting him with the flashlight beam like a spotlight.

"She didn't tell me," he said, a tear trailing down his face. "But I think she was pregnant. I found the test in our bathroom last week."

The rain knocked at the window, the wind picking up with a moan. Almost as one, their gazes drifted from Mako to the blood stains on the sheet.

"Why wouldn't she tell you if she was pregnant?" asked Hannah. Her tone was icy.

"I don't *know*, Hannah. Maybe, maybe she was *afraid*," he said. "We've been doing the IVF. She's miscarried—twice. It's been really...*fucked* for us."

There was a stunned silence, punctuated by Mako's sobs. Another flash of lightning, the ensuing thunder more subdued. Not a crack but a rumble.

This was not news to Cricket, though it clearly was to Hannah.

Truth be told, Cricket and Mako had met at a hotel bar just a couple of weeks ago. After a couple drinks, he told her he had a room and she'd gone up with him. He'd wept telling her about Liza's second miscarriage. She'd comforted him. Then he'd fucked her from behind, and left while she was still sleeping. She'd felt used, cheap, promised herself that was the last time, even though she knew she'd meet him again if he called.

"Why didn't I know about this?" asked Hannah finally. "About the miscarriages?"

"She didn't want anyone to know." Mako wiped at his eyes. Cricket had seen him cry a couple of times over the years. Usually when he was caught in a lie. "You know how she is. She's private."

"Okay," said Bruce. He raised his palms, had a natural air of calm authority. When Hannah had first introduced them, Cricket thought he was a bit dull, nothing special. Over the years, she'd come to see the appeal of that. A steady, reliable man who didn't cheat and lie. What a novelty.

"Let's go downstairs and call the host," Bruce went on levelly.

"Mako, you try to reach Liza. Then we'll regroup and decide what to do next. Nobody needs to panic. Everyone is okay."

Except Liza, thought Cricket.

All that blood.

Cricket watched as Bruce moved over to Hannah and put a protective arm around her, ushered her toward the door and down the hallway.

We should get out of here, Cricket heard Hannah whisper. *I want to go.*

Cricket moved to the other bedside table and found a second flashlight. The beam flickered, went dark, then came back on again. Great. A glitchy flashlight in a storm. Fucking perfect.

She turned the beam on Mako, and something about the way he looked made her stomach lurch.

"What did you do, Mako?" The words escaped her mouth before she could stop them.

His expression went cold. "Nothing, Cricket. I didn't do a fucking thing to her."

She flashed on a night with him years ago, the strength of his grip, the weight of his body.

Stop, Mako. I don't want this.

I've never known anyone who wants it as much as you do, Crick.

But that night was long ago, as much her fault as his, right? For being there? For leading him on? She brushed past him now, following Bruce and Hannah downstairs. And meanwhile, *where the fuck* was Josh? How long ago had he said he was on his way. Was he okay? Driving in this storm?

A dark thought occurred. Was Liza with Josh? No, no. That wasn't possible.

When she got downstairs, Hannah and Bruce were bent over the meticulous detailed instruction binder, pages and pages, looking for the host number.

"Got it," said Hannah. "Call anytime, day or night, with anything you need."

"I have one bar," said Bruce. "The cell service here is crap. The power is out so the Wi-Fi is down."

He picked up his phone and dialed the number they'd found. Cricket moved over to Hannah and her friend wrapped her up in her arms.

"Are you okay?" Cricket asked.

"I mean," said Hannah. "I don't know. This is really— weird."

"Don't leave me here," Cricket whispered.

Hannah stroked Cricket's hair. "If we go, you come, too."

Bruce sounded like he was leaving a message. "The lights are out here. Can you call the electric company and find out when power will be restored? If they don't come back on soon, we'll probably need to leave."

Lightning lit the view outside, the trees black line drawings, punching against white. Cricket felt thunder in the floorboards. The rain seemed to be subsiding, though. Then the sweep of headlights across the back wall.

Cricket ran to the door to see Joshua's car pulling up, the rear windshield cracked, the trunk dented. Joshua got out unsteadily. Was that a gash over his right eye, a line of blood trailing down the side of his face? Oh wow, was he hurt?

She rushed out to him through the rain; he took her in his arms, leaned against her and she led him out of the rain to the porch.

"Oh my god," she said. "What happened? You're hurt. Oh *my god.*"

Cricket reached up to wipe away the blood with her sleeve. Hannah and Bruce came to stand on the porch from the front door.

"A tree came down in the last big bolt of lightning," he said. He was pale, hands shaking. "It was so loud, like an explosion. Then there was this deafening crack and a huge tree just fell. It hit the trunk and now it's blocking the road."

"What happened to your head?" He reached up to touch the wound, winced and pulled his hand away.

"I must have hit it on the steering wheel or something."

"The airbags didn't deploy?" asked Bruce looking between Joshua and the car.

Joshua's face was drained of color, eyes confused. "I—I don't know. No, I guess not."

"The road's completely blocked?" asked Hannah, voice tight.

"Yeah," he said. "There's a huge tree across the whole thing. It's going to take some major equipment to move it. And some of the other roads were already full of water."

"You could have been killed, man," said Bruce, looking at the car. "You got really lucky."

"Oh my god," said Cricket again, clinging to Josh.

"I shouldn't have gone out like that," he said to Cricket. "I'm sorry. I should have told my boss to handle things herself. I—it was so stupid. I've made a lot of mistakes."

He seemed really upset, color wan. She held him tight, and his arms closed around her. She felt him kiss her head, and she started to cry a little but not so that anyone would see.

"We're having a crisis of our own here," said Bruce. "The power's out. And Liza is gone."

"Gone?" asked Joshua. She felt his body tense. "How?"

That's when Cricket noticed that Mako's Tesla was still in the drive. If Liza had left, how had she gone? On foot? Did she call an Uber? Liza had made all the arrangements for the house, hadn't she? Maybe she'd been planning this all along. It *was* a good moment to leave Mako, if that's what she wanted. In front of everyone, he couldn't resort to the usual tactics he used to manipulate women.

But the blood.

"Let's get inside, take a look at that cut," said Bruce.

Back in the living room Mako was standing in the kitchen, staring at his cell phone. They could hear a faint ringing coming from the call Mako seemed to be making. Cricket still clung to Joshua and he was leaning on her heavily. She moved him over to the couch where he sank down hard. How bad was that head injury?

"Let me get some ice," she said, heading to the kitchen area. Maybe there was a first aid kit, too. She looked to Hannah for help. She was good at things like this—Camp Fire Girl, lifeguard, trained in CPR, at least when they were kids. But instead Hannah stood frozen, was looking at her brother with a deep frown. Mako was looking at his phone.

"What are you *doing*?" Hannah asked Mako, voice sharp.

He looked up at her quickly, then back at the screen. "I'm calling Liza and tracking her on Find My Friends."

"Where is she?"

"Shhh. Service is shit."

The moment swelled and expanded, all of them waiting. But finally they heard the call engage with voicemail, Liza's voice faint.

Sorry I missed you. Leave a message. Namaste.

He ended the call. "Fuck."

"*Mako.* Where does it say she is?" Hannah asked again.

Mako turned the phone so that they could all see. A blue dot blinked in a sea of green. Mako's dot was right beside it.

"It says she's right here," he said, looking between each of them. "Somewhere on this property."

PART TWO

family of strangers

"Beware that, when fighting monsters,
you yourself do not become a monster."
—Friedrich Nietzsche

28

HANNAH

"What do you mean?" Hannah asked her brother, grabbing for the phone. He had that helpless, overwhelmed look that he got when things were not going his way. He was a man-baby.

He held up the screen again, its glow casting their faces in white. "Her phone is *here*, somewhere on the property."

Hannah stared, mind grappling for understanding. Was this some kind of joke or prank?

"That makes no sense."

"None of this makes *any sense*, Han," he said.

The rain came down hard, a million fingers drumming loudly on the roof, pouring down the windows in sheets. They'd left the hot tub cover open and Hannah watched as it overflowed, pouring onto the deck. A lightning flash, a rumble—maybe further apart a little, less intensely loud. It gave her hope that the storm was passing.

Cricket was tending to Joshua who sat over on the couch.

She'd cleaned the cut on his head with paper towels and dish soap, obviously more concerned about him than she was about Liza. Cricket had dug around for a first aid kit but hadn't found one. Joshua did not look well, wobbly and—scared. Yes, that was it. He looked scared.

Mako did not look well either, pale and sweating.

Bruce's phone rang and he picked it up, putting it on speaker.

"Hey, it's Bracken, your host. Everyone okay?"

Bruce gave him the abridged version—one of their party had left in the storm, the lights were out, Josh's accident and the news that a tree was down, closing them in. He didn't mention the blood in the bed, the marital strife. He wouldn't. If Mako was quick to anger, Bruce was slow to react. Measured and calm. Thank God.

Because panic was a winged bird in Hannah's chest. She should have known not to leave Gigi. She'd had a sense that this was a mistake. As usual, she hadn't listened to her own instincts. Why did she never learn that lesson? Now what? Liza was missing. Joshua was clearly hurt and they were all trapped.

"There's a generator up there." Bracken's voice sounded tinny and distant, the connection poor. "It should have kicked on when the power went out."

"Well, it didn't," said Mako. "Obviously. I run a business. I can't be out of contact like this."

God, he really sounded like an entitled asshole. Hannah didn't like the way Bruce was looking at Mako, annoyed to the point of being disgusted. She realized that her husband looked at her brother like that a lot. She found—especially right now— that she couldn't blame him.

"Okay," said Bracken. "I hear you. You're stranded without power and that's upsetting."

Mako moved closer to the phone, pointing an angry finger at the screen, nostrils flaring.

"Don't *manage* me, dude," he said, voice sizzling. "What are you going to *do about it*?"

"He can't control the weather, Mickey," said Hannah.

Mako cast her a miserable look, then sank onto the sofa, deflated.

"Look," said Bracken. His voice had grown harder. "The bad news is that the weather is going to get worse before it gets better. I'll try to find someone to help me move that tree, but we'll have to wait for a break in the storm."

Hannah and Cricket looked at each other.

We're stuck here, Hannah thought. *We're trapped.* Cricket's eyes went wide as if she was reading Hannah's thoughts.

Mako spoke up again. "Tell your guys whoever is willing to go out in the storm *right now* to move that tree, I'll give them a thousand dollars."

"Mako," said Hannah. How fucked was that?

There was a pause on the phone that expanded. Hannah could hear the other man breathing, but he stayed silent.

Was he not going to help them? Hannah thought about all of the reviews that said he went above and beyond. But they were all on the curated site. There were no reviews on any of the other major booking apps. Were they off the grid, at this stranger's mercy? Had that been him by the lake? If so, was he on the property somewhere? Her eyes fell on the bone sculpture over the dining room table. *Remember that you must die.*

"You sound upset. Is this an emergency?" said Bracken. "Is there something else going on?"

What was that supposed to mean? Hannah walked to the sliding glass back door and looked out into the darkness.

"I'm not sure I'd say there was an emergency exactly," said Bruce, looking at Hannah uncertainly.

Was there an emergency? Where was Liza? What was all that blood on the bed? And what about Joshua? She glanced over at him. He had his head back now, an ice pack Cricket had found in the freezer over his head. He'd insisted that he was fine. But how bad was that injury? They were stuck in this isolated house, couldn't leave if they needed to. What if he actually needed medical attention? What if Lou called with an urgent issue? They wouldn't be able to get home. Her chest tightened.

Breathe, she told herself. Just breathe. She was about to speak, but then Bruce did.

"But my wife and I have a small child at home, and since things have gone a bit sideways here we'd like to get back sooner rather than later."

"My wife is *missing*," said Mako. "Is that not an emergency, Bruce?"

"And Joshua *is* hurt," Cricket chimed in.

"Wait," said the tinny voice on the line. "Someone's *missing*? Someone's hurt?"

"Well," answered Bruce. "One of our party decided to leave. There seems to be some confusion about where she might be. And one of our group, as I mentioned, was on the road when the tree came down. He had a minor accident and has a cut on his head."

Did it sound like he was underplaying it all? Why would he do that? Her husband didn't like drama, but...

"Seriously," said Joshua. "I'm totally fine."

Another pause. "Okay," said Bracken drawing out the syllable. "Do we need to call the police? An ambulance?"

It couldn't be, but it almost sounded like he was being sarcastic, taunting.

"What the hell good is that going to do?" said Mako. "No one can get to us anyway, right? Just move that goddamn tree so we can get out of here."

Hannah found herself staring at her brother now, waves of anxiety pulsing through her; she *hated* it when he got this way.

She remembered another night standing in a darkened room with him, that same look of anger and fear etched into his face. It was their parents' bedroom that time, Sophia and Leo away for the weekend, Mako and Hannah left alone to take care of the house, each other. They were supposedly old enough—

Hannah sixteen, Mako eighteen and headed off for college in a few weeks.

She remembered the girl in Hannah's parents' bed, naked, so skinny she looked like a child, sick from drinking too much, her vomit on the floor. She had been curled up and weeping. Downstairs the music from a party that had gone out of control pulsed through the floor.

Blood. There was blood on the sheets that night, too.

What did you do, Mickey?

She wanted it. She said she did.

She shook away the memory. Ancient history.

"Okay," said the host, sounding tight and annoyed. "I'll see what I can do."

"You do that," said Mickey, voice heavy with sarcasm.

Another pause, then the beeps that announced the end of the call.

"You're such a dick," said Hannah with a lash of anger that surprised even her. "Could you have been any ruder?"

"Ha, *I'm a dick*?" said Mako. "That guy was useless. Do you know what I paid for this place?"

She felt a familiar rise of annoyance at her brother, for his selfishness, for his entitlement, for how he always had to remind everyone around him what he had and how much he'd paid for it like an insecure little boy. That's why Bruce had wanted to pay their way; he didn't want the cost of the place lorded over them in a million different ways. It was also, she knew, part of the reason that Bruce was so eager to leave the place they were renting from Mako. Mako would only take a fraction of what it was worth month to month. But it came up over and over, casually, in jest. *You guys are practically living rent-free, haha*, he might joke at dinner with their parents. *I really need to charge more for this place*, he said every time he came to visit.

"Mickey, just stop," she said.

"What?" he asked shrilly. "What the fuck did I do?"

She turned away from him, caught Bruce's expression again.

The disdain she saw there, before he was aware that she was looking at him, it surprised her. Wow, did he actually hate Mako? Some things clicked into place, how hard he'd been working to get off Mako's project, how enthusiastic he was about the new house, how he hadn't really wanted to come here at all and she knew it. He was trying to get out from under Mako's thumb. That was what he couldn't live with. It was Mako.

I'm sorry, she found herself wanting to say. She and Bruce locked eyes; it was all there. They knew each other so well. How had she not seen this layer before? Because she was blind when it came to her brother, willfully blind. Always had been. She wanted so badly for them all to be close, for that fantasy she had about their future to be true.

She was just like Mako that way, how he'd forced them all here for some Instagram-able friends and family moment, just another thing to feed his ego.

Something about the storm, and Liza missing, and Joshua hurt, their all being trapped—things seemed clear. Too clear. *God*, she thought. *Poor Bruce.*

Mako got up quickly from his slouch, as if he'd reached some internal decision, and moved for the back door, pulled it open.

The wind rushed in howling; the rain roared, thunder distant.

"What are you doing?" Hannah shouted.

"Mako!" said Cricket, leaning away from Joshua.

"I'm going out to find my wife. That guesthouse down the path. That light we saw, remember? Maybe that's where she went. She didn't take the car. She certainly didn't *walk* down the road in this storm, carrying all her stuff."

"Mako," Hannah said. "Wait."

But then he was gone, slamming the door hard behind him.

"Oh my god," Hannah breathed, as he disappeared down the steps.

"I'll go with him," said Bruce. He grabbed the jacket he'd left on a hook by the door, and moved over to her.

"No," she said, grabbing a hold of her husband's arm. "Just let him go. What if there's someone out there?"

"Look, we're fine." Bruce kissed her head, moved toward the glass sliders. "Gigi's fine with my mom. So, no worries there. Liza and Mako are just having a fight, obviously. Whatever you saw, who knows, right? You said yourself that your perception was altered. This storm will pass, they'll clear the road and we'll go home."

The way he said it, it all sounded so simple, so light. Maybe he was right and she was overreacting.

"But we saw someone." All her buzz, that pleasant loopy feeling was gone. She may have been a little high, but she knew what she saw.

"I'll be careful. Let me go after your brother."

"Okay," she said following. She kissed him on the mouth.

"Bruce," she whispered. "I'm sorry. For everything."

He put a warm hand to her cheek and smiled.

"You never have to apologize to me."

"Bruce—"

"I'll be right back."

Then he was gone, too, into the storm which seemed to pick up volume after he left. She could see the tops of the trees thrashing and waving, wild dancers against the night sky.

Cricket was sitting on the couch with Joshua, holding the ice pack to his head.

"Worst vacation ever," said Cricket, voice a little wobbly.

So, Cricket and Mako's on-again, off-again thing that Hannah pretended not to know about but did. Both of them had promised that it was over for good, but clearly it wasn't. She wondered again if Mako and Cricket had been up to something and Liza had caught them. How many times had Mako cheated on Liza with Cricket? And others? Had they stopped when Cricket started seeing Joshua?

She flashed again on the blood stains on the white sheets, felt the cold finger of dread down her spine.

"What?" said Cricket. "Why are you looking at me like that?"

"Like what?"

"Like this is *my* fault."

Hannah sank into one of the plush oversized chairs, rested her head in one hand.

Her head ached, pain throbbing behind her eyes as she looked up at her old friend. Cricket wasn't just her friend, or Mako's, over the years she'd become part of the family. She kept in touch with Sophia independently of them, even had a yearly tradition of stopping by with gifts to leave under the tree for Christmas morning. She was the sister Hannah would have chosen, if you could choose such things. But like Mako, Cricket had a wild streak, a *selfish* streak. She couldn't always be counted on to do the right thing.

"Do you remember Libby?" asked Hannah.

Cricket's eyes darted to Joshua, then back to Hannah. "Why would you bring that up now?"

"Who's Libby?" asked Joshua, sounding a little groggy. Her first aid and lifeguard training kicked in. You were supposed to keep people with head injuries awake, right? Looking at Joshua more closely now, she wondered if they did have an actual emergency. Mako hadn't even seemed to notice that Joshua was hurt. Because, truly, he didn't care about anyone but himself.

"She's a girl we used to know, a hundred years ago," Cricket said quickly.

"She accused Mako of raping her," Hannah said.

Cricket's eyes went wide, as if she couldn't believe Hannah would say it out loud. But it was public knowledge, out there for anyone who wanted to do a Google search.

"She *lied*," said Cricket. "Everybody knows she was a slut. She was trying to ruin his life because he rejected her."

That was not the whole truth and Cricket knew it. Hannah would have thought her friend was above slut shaming; she'd have thought every educated woman was. Libby. The name had rung back to her many times over the years. Every time she felt a complicated wash of anger and shame.

"But that was before you could ruin someone's life that way," said Hannah. "In fact, that was back when if you accused someone of raping you, it ruined *your* life."

"Did he? Rape her?" asked Joshua. He seemed more alert now. And Hannah felt a rush of guilt, of protectiveness for her brother.

Hannah lifted her shoulders, shook her head. "No," she said. "I don't know."

"Anyway," said Cricket. "It was a hundred years ago, when we were kids."

When we were kids. They hadn't been kids really, but young adults. But yeah, better to leave the past where it belonged.

Hannah got up and found another flashlight in the kitchen.

"Can I check your eyes?" she said, walking over to Joshua. "To see if they dilate?"

He nodded. She shined the light on his face, and there it was again, that powerful feeling of recognition, of knowing him. His pupils grew tiny in the light, then expanded again when the beam was less direct.

"That's good, right?" said Cricket.

"I think so," said Hannah. "Any nausea, sleepiness, ringing in the ears?"

"I mean I don't feel great. But no none of that. I think I'm okay."

She inspected the cut. It looked was deep, gaping like a mouth. He needed stitches. She'd dig through her purse for some Band-Aids and try to butterfly it, at least.

She moved away from him, keeping her eyes on him. Cricket had her fingers laced through his. "I'll get some more ice," she said, rising.

"Did you lose consciousness at all?" asked Hannah. "Do you remember the accident?"

"I didn't lose consciousness, I don't think."

"Tell me what happened exactly."

"I was driving back from town, maybe a little too fast. I felt bad for leaving and I wanted to get back to Cricket. The roads were wet, already flooding in some places and I was worried about swamping the engine. It was storming pretty badly."

He touched gingerly at the cut on his forehead. "Uh, I think—there was something on the road; it disappeared into the trees. At first I thought it was a person, there was like a flash of white. But maybe it was a deer. I veered to miss it. Then there was this huge bolt of lightning and the tree fell."

"Wait," said Hannah. "You saw someone on the road?"

That flash of white Hannah had seen came back to her. It sent a strange tingle through her, raising goose bumps.

Joshua frowned uncertainly. "I'm not sure. It was probably a deer."

Or whoever it was by the lake? Or whoever had turned on the light in the cabin? What was going on here?

"No one would be out walking on the road in this storm," said Cricket. "You're right. It was probably a deer."

"Could it have been Liza?" asked Hannah. She imagined her hurt, tiny sister-in-law walking up a deserted road in the storm. What could have inspired her to do that?

Then she thought again about the ghosts Chef Jeff had so creepily mentioned. The mother wandering the woods looking for her children.

Stop. Stop it.

Hannah walked back over to the window, peering out into the storm. The other structure on the property. She remembered it from exploring the link Liza had sent, a cabin on the other side of the gazebo—perfect for the teenagers or the in-laws, something like that. Like a whole other house with a kitchenette, smaller but as nicely appointed as this one with a sleep loft. Or so it looked from the photographs.

Maybe Liza had struck out, then turned around to come back, realizing she wasn't going to get far, that it was dangerous. That would explain the light they saw. The timing worked, right?

"Would Liza have done that?" asked Cricket, reading Hannah's mind as usual. Her friend came up behind her, stared out into the night beside her. "Just go to the other cabin?"

"Maybe? If the storm was bad and she needed to get away, but couldn't. Didn't want to deal with Mako or with us."

Hannah turned to her friend. Josh had his eyes closed on the couch.

She whispered. "Did she see you two? What were you up to when Bruce and I snuck off?"

Cricket widened her eyes again—she'd perfected the look of innocence—and gaped her jaw, shooting a quick glance at Josh. When she spoke her voice was softer than Hannah's.

"Nothing! Do you really think I'd do that? Here?"

The truth was, Hannah suspected that Cricket would do anything Mako wanted her to do. That's how it was. How it had always been. Cricket, despite her party girl persona, was a smart woman. But when it came to Mako, she was as clueless as it gets. He led. She followed. Liza was the first woman to exert any control over her brother; that was one of the things Hannah liked most about her. *She makes me want to be a better man*, Mako had confided to Hannah on his wedding day. Hannah had hoped that she would.

Too bad it didn't seem to be working out that way.

Cricket looked hurt; her eyes filled. "*What* do you think of me, Han?"

"I'm sorry," she said, pulling her friend into an embrace. "I'm just asking. You guys have—a history." A past. Possibly a present. But no future. Cricket should know that.

She felt Cricket nod. "We didn't do anything."

Hannah had heard this before.

Joshua was snoring on the couch now. Should she let him sleep? Or wake him up. She had no idea. The truth was that most of her lifeguard training was a distant memory like everything before Gigi was a distant memory. She should take an online refresher course—in her spare time. And she had way too much on her mind. Mainly, getting out of here and home to Lou and Gigi. Reflexively, she checked the app on her phone, Cricket still leaning against her.

She imagined Gigi was a cherub floating on a cloud, arms up, beanie hat, onesie, chubby legs bowed. If she listened she could hear the baby breath. But there was no service. The app announced that Hannah was offline.

"She's okay, Han. This will all be okay."

Hannah wasn't used to being comforted by anyone but Bruce. Usually, she was the one doing the comforting for other people in her life.

"I know," she said softly. Even though she didn't.

Just then the rain picked up, and the wind toppled one of the outdoor chairs, skidded it against the sliding door with a crash. Cricket jumped and Josh woke up with a start.

"What's happening?" he said.

Hannah went to the door. When a skein of lightning lit the sky, she drew in a gasp. There she saw it again, that stranger, a form, slim, black, moving fast down the path in the direction of the gazebo.

A crack of thunder. Darkness again.

"What is it?" asked Cricket.

She cupped her hands around her eyes and peered into the darkness. There—another shift of shadows.

"Oh my god," she said, looking at her friend. "There really is someone else out there."

29

TRINA

Until recently, did you ever stop to wonder what makes you who you are? I doubt it. People like you almost never do. You just *are*. Born to privilege, overpraised by well-meaning parents, raised on an oral history about your past, your family history, that you never even think to question. It's as if you sprang from the head of Zeus in full armor. All you are is your appetites, your desires, the hurricane of your endless thoughts, opinions, ideas about yourself. What came before you, who made you, what link you might be in the chain of humanity interests you not at all.

Now I watch as you and Bruce trek down the wet path. I'm right behind you, not twenty feet away. But you—you're the predator, not the prey. You don't even think to look back for anyone who might be on your trail. The two of you tromp, not speaking, rain glistening on your backs. The air smells of leaves and humidity. The falling rain, the wind in the leaves is a sound barrier and I am just a shadow.

Some of us are seekers. Broken links. We're always trying to figure out how and where we fit.

"So is your family local?"

You asked me this our first night working late. You sat at your desk, and I was on your couch surrounded by applications. I was helping you look for some new testers. What a job. Kids who sit in a dark room and play the games you build all day, looking for glitches and bugs, offering feedback. I was holding the application of a kid finishing his junior year at USF, looking for a summer internship at Red World. *I'm a gamer,* he writes in his letter. *My YouTube channel has 10K followers.* This is how we define ourselves now, our worth determined by how many people like, follow, engage.

"Actually, I don't really have any family," I answered.

"Everyone has family," you said absently, staring at your screen, your face washed in that ugly blue light. It made you look sickly with shadows for eyes and a hard line for a mouth.

"No," I said. "Not really. I mean—biologically, yes. But in actuality, some people are on their own. I'm an orphan."

You looked at me, cocked your head.

"My dad—" I went on. "I have no idea who he is. My mom—she was troubled and died in an accident when I was a kid. Got a job, paid my way through school and, well, here I am."

All lies, half-truths, almost real, not quite what happened. But close enough. The essence close enough to reality that it rings true.

"That sucks." I heard real empathy in your voice, and for a minute I almost liked you.

I shrugged, not into feeling sorry for myself. "It is what it is. I have a half brother. But we don't talk much."

The truth is that we're all essentially alone. The lucky ones have a crew to share the load from birth to death. But in the end, we go as we came—a single entity, just passing through. But that's not a thing people like to hear. The story of being surrounded and supported and loved, being a part of something, the whole, almost sacred notion that family is everything is sold hard, and bought completely.

"Family isn't easy either," you said into the silence.

"No," I said. "I'm sure that's true. What about this guy?"

I handed over the application from the USF computer science major, and you regarded it, flipping through the letter and the résumé. "Yeah, yeah. Drop him an email. YouTubers are good; free exposure."

"And this one." You handed over another application, which I stuck in my pile of kids to reach out to the next day.

Outside the sky was growing dark, towering cumulous clouds impossible white, gray, blue mountains in the sky and the orange sun painting them pink, sinking into the black horizon line. The day had been a scorcher, a blistering 95 that with the humidity felt like 110. Sometimes it seems like Florida is trying to kill its residents, doesn't it? It wants us to go away so that it can reclaim its swampy self, be left alone to its darkness—alligators, snakes, and roaches free from pavement and walls of condo buildings, and wildlife corridors butting up against superhighways.

When I looked back at you, you were staring at me. Which made my skin crawl. I had been working there a little under a month and starting to wonder if the things I thought I knew about you were true. I hadn't seen anything illegal, or picked up on anything unethical. People in the office seemed happy; you kept your eyes and hands to yourself, were respectful. The things I'd put together about you were whispers, vague accusations, rumors—an idea gleaned from piecing together articles, an accusation from your teen years, and bits from Reddit chats, company reviews on job boards.

Red World is a toxic workplace.

My boss wanted me to cook data for the investors.

M can't keep his hands off the young interns. One of them said he drugged her at a tech conference.

Some men came in late; they looked like thugs. I think the company is borrowing money from bad people.

I heard RW could go under in a year. Everyone is going to lose their jobs unless the new game saves the company.

But people lied and made things up; the internet was full of trolls and saboteurs, cancelers and disgruntled people looking for revenge, bots, competitors trying to subvert and undermine.

I was starting to wonder if I may have been wrong about you. I wasn't.

Now I stand back, slip into the trees as you and Bruce come to the cabin.

"It doesn't look like there's anyone in there," says Bruce, his voice deep. He glances behind him, but I'm sure he can't see me as I've ducked into the trees.

"The power's out." You knock on the door, hard. "Liza! Liza! Are you in there? Tell me what's going on."

When you try the knob, you find the cabin open. As you both disappear inside, I head back to the main house. The sound of your wailing catches up to me as I run through the darkness; it's animalistic and desperate. My nerve endings vibrate in response; I could almost feel bad.

If I could feel anything at all.

You have to incapacitate the women first. Because women are the fighters. They will go claw and teeth to protect their families.

Liza barely put up a fight. Next Cricket; then Hannah. Your little love slaves, the women who enable and hold you up, who come when you call, who help you cover up your crimes. Bruce should be easy enough to manage, a computer geek who has probably never even been in a fistfight.

And he's got some secrets of his own.

And then it's down to us.

Just you and me, little pig.

I'm the big bad wolf come to blow your house down.

30

HENRY

2010

Did you even get out of bed today?

What do you care?

I care, loser. I still care.

The apartment was a wreck, had been since Piper left. He'd slowly let it devolve. He hadn't done the dishes in a week; they piled up in the sink, emanating a slight odor of rot. There were take-out containers littering surfaces in the living room. And, no, he hadn't gotten out of bed today. It was past noon, and he was still lying there in the darkened room, listening to the city rumble and boom, honk and shout outside. Which was fine, because it was Saturday. He *did* still manage to make it to his job. There were bills to pay. But mainly because he was able to lose himself there, disappear into the work.

His thumbs danced across the screen: Come home. Please. Did he sound desperate? He didn't care. He *was* desperate.

I can't. I love you. But we can't be together. Not like this.

It was the miscarriage that did them in. The heartbreak of it, the depression that followed. His was so total that he could not comfort her. She was far enough along that the whole thing had started to feel real. Like there was a real person coming, a life that their love had created.

And then there wasn't.

That baby, it was their future, the thing that tied Henry to Piper, to the world, the little person that would make them a true family, linked by blood, by biology. He'd wanted that so badly; he hadn't even realized how much until it had been wrested from him. To lose that felt like a punishment for a crime he hadn't committed.

But that wasn't the only thing that caused Piper to leave.

Another text when he didn't answer: Anyway. I didn't leave you. You left me.

That's not true.

A truck rumbled over the big plate in the avenue outside their window, issuing a loud clang. He heard the neighbor's dog yipping through the floorboards in response.

But it *was* true in a way. The moment his aunt had opened the portal into his past, he'd disappeared. Where he came from, a thing he'd tried not to dwell on for most of his life became his obsession.

What are you doing today?

He didn't answer, just stared at the words on his screen. As if I have to ask, she texted when he didn't respond.

★ ★ ★

February had been Alice's most hated month. He still thought of her that way even though his aunt Gemma always referred to her as Maggie. She hated the desolation of the second month of the year, cold and gray, the holidays a distant memory, spring just a dream. That's why they were always heading south he guessed, to escape February. And this was exactly the kind of day she hated, a gray ceiling for a sky, the air bitterly cold.

He hustled up Avenue A with winter leaking into his cuffs and down the collar of his too-thin jacket, hunched his shoulders in against the stiff wind that blew desiccated leaves and paper garbage up the sidewalk past his feet.

Finally, he saw the sign for his destination up ahead: Ian's Pub, an Alphabet City dive like so many others. He didn't even have to go inside to know what he would see when he arrived. An old railroad flat, concrete floors, a bar running along one side, high tops or tattered couches up the other. Some buff, tattooed, and bearded guy slinging the drinks. Maybe a pool table toward the back.

He ducked inside and was surprised that it was much nicer than he expected with black-and-white tile floors, leather banquettes edging one side, a polished wood bar lining the other. There was a gleaming jukebox, Frank Sinatra crooning through Bluetooth speakers mounted in the corners of the ceiling. Fly me to the moon.

It was only three in the afternoon and the bar was empty except for the woman sitting all the way in the back, alone.

The warmth of the indoor air was a relief, but Henry was still shivering. It wasn't the first such meeting he'd had. He had sworn to himself that if it was as soul crushing as the other two, it would be his last. Some people, he had determined, were just destined to be alone in this world. And it was very possible that he was one of them.

"Cat?" he said, approaching the table.

"Henry?" Her smile. Her eyes. There was a zap of electricity, familiarity. He knew her—his cells knew her.

She slipped out of the booth quickly and before he could stop her or move away, she tackled him with a big hug and held on tight. He was stunned for a second, as he had been when Gemma had done almost the exact same thing, then he closed his arms around her stiffly, enduring her embrace just to be kind. *Alice never liked affection either,* Gemma had told him gently. *She bristled when other people touched her.*

The only touch in his life that hadn't made him uncomfortable was Piper's. He craved her touch. His whole body ached with missing her. She wouldn't even talk to him right now. Text only.

When Cat pulled away she took off her thick-rimmed black glasses and wiped at her eyes.

"I'm sorry," she said with an embarrassed laugh. "You must think I'm a freak."

"No," he said. "No. It's—all of this. It's strange, emotional."

"Yeah."

She put her glasses back on, then slipped into her seat and he slid in across from her. The bartender came over and Henry ordered a hot tea with a side of bourbon—to warm him up and calm his jangled nerves.

There was a stuffed canvas sack beside her, filled with notebooks and folders. This was common to people like them. Seekers. People wanting to find lost pieces of themselves, their pasts. Gemma called them Soul Miners, people hunting for what makes them who they are.

Sometimes I think none of it matters, his aunt had tiredly admitted to him recently when they were knee-deep in the story of a great-uncle on her father's side, reading a letter she'd found in the attic of a cousin. It was a stilted love poem to a woman named Sylvia, not his wife. *Sometimes I think we're all just like cut flowers in a vase. That what came before or what will come after doesn't mean anything at all. We have our time here and that's it.*

But that didn't seem right to Henry, there were all these stories—people living, loving, dreaming, working, hoping, falling in love, making babies, dying—and all those stories linked through time to other stories. His story was just a chapter in a book that would be written forever. It didn't make any sense unless you read the chapters that came before, did it?

"So how many meetings like this have you had?" asked Cat. He tried not to stare at the shiny black locks of her hair, at the narrowness of her face, the shine to her eyes, lighter than his. Henry's eyes were so brown they looked black, but there was something about the shape of Cat's that reminded him of what he saw in the mirror.

He knew that she was five years younger than he was, that she was some kind of wunderkind programmer, with advanced computer engineering degrees from Harvard, that she lived in the Village. They determined that they'd probably been at a few of the same conferences over the years.

"A couple," he said, answering her question.

"Who?"

She reached over and took out a folder, on top was a printout of the report he knew you received from Origins, listing percentages of ethnic heritage. Just a glance across the table revealed what he already knew.

When Henry's results had arrived, he and Gemma had printed it out and pored over it. As they suspected, 47 percent of Henry's heritage came from Great Britain, which included Scotland, and Ireland. Gemma was almost 100 percent from that region, with some "lower confidence" results tracing to Scandinavia, Eastern Europe, Italy, and Greece. The rest of Henry's results had been from the Iberian Peninsula which consisted primarily of Spain and Portugal, and Caucasus, the region that contained parts of Southern Russia, Georgia, Armenia, Turkey, among other countries. As they poured over his results, he found himself gazing at his reflection in the china cabinet across from Gemma's dining room table. The room was rarely used for dining, unless it was takeout they shared late at night when they'd "gone down the rabbit hole" as Gemma called it. The room instead was dominated by books, boxes, a second computer—all overflow from her office upstairs.

His dark skin, his thick black hair. The shape of his eyes; it made sense. Actual genetic sense. He told Gemma as much.

"That's cool, isn't it?" she said. "To know. To understand."

There in the results that listed relatives was Gemma, and a smattering of other people they had in common who had opted to be contacted by newly discovered relatives. But there was also a long list of other people with no connection to Gemma.

"Oh my goodness," said Gemma, scrolling through.

"What?"

"These people—a couple of them. They're a twenty-five percent match."

"What does that mean?"

She looked at him, mouth agape. "It means that they're very close relatives, like aunts, uncles, or *half siblings*. Most of these people are very young."

He stared at the thumbnails over his aunt's shoulder. Some of them looked a little like the face he saw in the mirror. Some not at all. Half siblings.

"The sperm donor," they both said in unison.

The people he was looking at likely all had the same donor father.

"I met Ted in Pennsylvania," he told Cat now.

"He's a dick," said Cat, taking a sip from her drink. "Like, honestly, I think he tried to hit on me. I was like dude, seriously? You're my half brother."

"Wow," said Henry. "Yeah, we had a beer. We weren't on the same wavelength."

"Yeah," she said. "Because you're not a perv."

"I talked to Clarice in Atlanta on the phone."

Cat rolled her eyes. "I guess it's true what they say. You can't choose your family."

Clarice had been reluctant to talk at first and finally agreed to a call. Apparently she'd just recently learned that she'd been conceived by sperm donor and her curiosity about her true origins was tentative at best. But she'd done the DNA kit, and ticked the box that allowed others to connect with her.

"I wish my mother had never told me," Clarice had confided. "I wish I'd died not knowing."

You can't choose your family. But that wasn't true was it? Family was nothing but a series of choices—who to love, how to conceive, to keep your child or give him up, to lie or tell the truth. If he'd learned anything from his romp into genealogy it was that.

He'd hung up with the recalcitrant Clarice feeling more alone than ever. Apparently, she was the most disappointed that she no longer qualified for her membership in the Daughters of the American Revolution.

"You watch all those videos of tearful meetings between half siblings and you think it's going to be like that. But really it's just like online dating. Some people are cool. But a lot are just assholes. You're looking for a connection but it's not there."

"I'm sorry," said Henry.

The bartender brought his tea and bourbon, and he wrapped his hands around the ceramic mug, hoping to leech off some of its heat.

"Are you an asshole, Henry?"

He took the bourbon in one shot. The heat slicked down his throat and offered its pleasant tingle. "Maybe."

Cat laughed at that, and then so did he. Then they were *really* laughing and he felt something true, deep. A connection with the person sitting across from him. It wasn't just DNA; it was chemistry. Like Gemma always said, you have it or you don't. Alice never felt like she belonged in her family of origin, always referred to herself as the black sheep. Switched at birth, she liked to think. But no. According to Henry's results, he was related to Gemma. So it followed that Alice had been born into her genetically true family. She'd just rejected them completely. She chose.

"I've been at this awhile," said Cat. "I've found out some things. Strange things. Are you interested?"

Was he? He'd promised Piper that he'd let it go. That he'd come back to the present tense with her. That he'd put the miscarriage behind them, try for another baby and move into the life he'd planned with her, the one they'd planned together. A simple life, with jobs they loved, children who grew up knowing who they were. He had Gemma now, a bit of family he could offer, at least some knowledge of his heritage. There was a house Piper loved near her parents in Florida; she wanted to make an offer. If he was willing to move there with her, they'd start again. A fresh slate, a life that started now, not way back when on other continents with strangers who only offered a tiny bit of genetic material to the mix.

She waved for the bartender, and when he came to the table, they each ordered another drink.

"Yeah," he said. "I'm interested."

"I know who he is. Maybe."

His throat went dry, stomach tight.

"He. You mean—our father."

Henry and Gemma had not been able to break into that particular box.

The half siblings who wanted to be found had taken the Origins test and visited the Donor Sibling Registry; they were looking for connections. There was a Facebook page, DNA Detectives, where Henry had lurked in the shadows as some of his half siblings shared notes, all searching for their shared donor father through the other common relatives listed on their reports.

But their father remained a shadowy figure for all of them. A donor who had contributed to a sperm bank, one who at the time had been guaranteed anonymity. And though those laws had changed and were changing all the time, no one had been able to find out anything about him.

"Back then, donors were promised complete anonymity," wrote one half brother William, who'd declined an in-person meeting or even a phone call. "They never expected anyone to come looking. Maybe it's better that way. I love the people who raised me. I have a good life. Might just leave well enough alone."

Well, good for you, bro.

Cat opened one of the files in front of her. "On DNA Detectives, one of our half siblings—Bethany in Connecticut—had this woman pop up in her relatives group as a twenty-five percent match. I have her, too. Do you?"

She turned the page out toward him. There was no thumbnail photo just an androgynous white figure on a gray frame. Marta Bennett. The name rang a bell.

"I think so. Yeah, maybe." He didn't carry his files around with him.

"It looks like she's a close relative but she's much older. So maybe an aunt?"

"Our father's sister?"

"Maybe," said Cat. "She took the Origins test, checked the box to be connected. But she hasn't answered anyone's messages on the site. A couple of people have tried in the past to reach out to her, sent friend requests on Facebook. But she didn't respond."

"Maybe she changed her mind about wanting to connect. Maybe she was surprised by what she found."

That happened a lot, he'd gleaned from his research. Some people wish they'd never sent in the kit. They thought they were one thing, then discovered they were something else altogether. What they learned about themselves and their family they couldn't unlearn.

"Well, I did some digging around and I found a Marta Bennet living up in the Bronx, in Riverdale. I went up there."

He found this surprising. The woman sitting across from him, this found sister, had silken dark hair much like his, the same searing intensity to her gaze that Piper always commented on in Henry. *Dial it back, honey. You make people nervous.* The same high cheekbones, long nose. Cat's features were puzzle pieces that fit with his; it was comforting in a strange way, to be of a piece with another person. But there was something about her that unsettled Henry. A boldness, a kind of edgy determination.

"You did? You went to see her?"

"Yeah," said Cat. She took off her glasses and rubbed at her eyes. "I basically stalked her. Waited around her apartment building, looking for a woman who maybe looked a little like me."

The bartender came and brought another round, a fresh tea, another bourbon, a vodka soda for Cat though they hadn't ordered.

"On the house," he said, giving Cat a smile. The bartender was, as Henry predicted, thickly muscled, bearded, with full sleeves of tattoos. A type.

"Thanks, Max," she said. "You're the best."

"Regular here?" asked Henry after the other man was back behind the bar.

"Max and I are—friends. I met him actually at a Donor Sibling conference."

"He's not—?"

"Related to us? No," she said. "But his father was a sperm donor. They've met; not a love connection. Sometimes the biology is there but the chemistry isn't, right? Anyway, there are a lot of us, looking for answers."

He was getting that. Maybe when it came to family, there were more questions than answers for some people. Maybe some people had to live with that.

"So, you were stalking Marta. Did you connect?"

Cat took a breath, shook her head.

"She wouldn't talk to me. I approached her when she was coming home from work one night. I introduced myself politely, asked if she would have a coffee with me, answer some questions."

"But she refused?"

Something flashed across Cat's face—anger, frustration. But it passed quickly and left the shape of sadness around her eyes.

"She more than refused. She looked—*terrified*. She said she made a horrible mistake, that she never should have taken the test. And if I knew what was good for me I would stop looking for my father."

Henry tried to imagine it. A gray street in the Bronx, Cat approaching a stranger on the sidewalk, blocking her way home. He wouldn't have done that; wouldn't have had the nerve.

"Huh," said Henry. "What does that mean?"

Cat shrugged, looked down at her glass. He thought she wasn't going to answer. But then, "She said something like 'Your father. He's a bad man and you don't want to know him. Whatever piece of him is inside you—exorcise it.'"

"Exercise?"

"Like *exorcise*—as in demons. She pushed past me but I followed her to her front door. I'm not embarrassed to say that I begged her to tell me more, even just his name. But she went inside and said if I came back she'd call the police."

Cat stopped a second, took off her glasses again and wiped angrily at her eyes. He waited. Didn't press. "So I hung around awhile," she went on. "It was cold, about to snow. I thought maybe she'd see me waiting, feel sorry for me, come back out. But it got later, colder, and finally I left."

"Okay, wow," said Henry, not knowing what else to say.

"The next day, her Facebook account had been deleted. And she was no longer available for messaging on the Origins site."

The sadness was gone from Cat's face, a kind of closed-off hardness was left in its place.

"Maybe I could try to reach out," Henry suggested.

Cat shook her head, looked down at her drink. "No."

"Or my aunt Gemma, my mother's sister. She has a way with people. They talk to her." Gemma did; there was a warmth, a kind nonjudgment that encouraged people to open themselves to her. If anyone could get this woman to talk it was his aunt. He was about to press, but Cat raised a slender palm.

"Marta Bennet," Cat started then stopped, took a long swallow of her drink. "She—um—she died."

"Wait, what? How?"

"It appears she killed herself, like she jumped off the top of her building a couple days after I went to talk to her. Police said it might have been an accident."

Henry didn't know what to say, so he just looked down at his hands. He felt his heart beating in his throat.

"And she's not the only one," Cat went on.

Henry frowned at her. "Okay."

"Five of our half siblings have died over the last five years. They started looking for answers about their origins, and at some point after that, they were gone."

She pulled out a file from her sack, opened it and turned it around. It was thick with printouts from the internet. A couple died in a suspicious house fire. A young actor overdosed. Another dead by accidental strangulation—autoerotic asphyxia. Others. He recognized each name from the Origins results, from the Donor Sibling Registry.

Henry slicked back the second bourbon. But instead of calming him, it made him feel sick.

"So what does this mean?"

"It means that these folks started looking for answers and now they're gone. All of these deaths are considered suspicious by the police. No evidence. No leads. The one thing they all have in common is that they took an Origins test and found out that their father was a sperm donor."

"Our father."

"That's right."

Henry's stomach churned. He found himself rising and walking quickly to the bathroom. Once in the stall, he threw up copiously in the toilet. When he was done, he sat on the cold tile floor that was surprisingly and mercifully clean, and put his head on his knees. He wasn't sure how much time passed. But during its span, he decided right then and there that he was done. Done with Origins, done with searching for siblings, for connections.

The door opened and Max walked in. His bulk filled the doorway. "You okay, man?"

Max offered a hand, but Henry waved him off.

"Yeah," said Henry rising, embarrassed. He flushed the toilet but his vomit had splattered on the seats, the stall walls. "Yeah, I'm good. Thanks. Sorry for the mess. Let me help clean it up."

The other man smiled, a patient turning up of the corners of his mouth. "Happens all the time. No worries."

Henry walked out to return to Cat, to tell her he had to go. But when he got back to the booth, she was gone. She'd scribbled her number on a napkin. *Sorry I upset you. Call me if you want to talk.*

He took the napkin, shoved it in his pocket, but he had no intention of ever calling her. He was going to call in sick to work Monday, get on the next plane to Tampa, and beg Piper to take him back. He was going to walk away from his genealogical quest for the past and into the future with the only person he'd ever really loved. The mystery of his father, his dead half siblings? He'd leave it behind, another untold story in his past, one that mattered not at all.

31

CRICKET

June 2018

"Stay here," said Hannah. She'd put on a rain jacket, and had the flashlight in hand.

"What?" said Cricket, taking hold of Hannah's arm. "No way. You're not going out there. I mean—*why?* What are you going to do?"

But she recognized the look on her old friend's face, a kind of set determination. She'd seen it before, many times.

It was the I'm-going-to-fix-this look.

Hannah had worn it the night she'd had to sneak out, essentially stealing her parents' car, to pick Mako and Cricket up from a rave they weren't supposed to be at. She'd worn it when Mako dumped Cricket after prom—*I'm leaving in a few months, Cricket. I care about you, but it's not going to work*—and Hannah bailed on her own prom date to comfort her. She'd worn it the night they drove Libby away from the house, the girl weeping in the back seat.

"Bruce and Mako are out there," Hannah said. "I'm going to check the circuit box and the generator and see if there's something visibly wrong. Then I'm following that path to the cabin and get them to come back here. It'll be fine. Storm seems to be letting up."

"But there's someone out there."

"And I need to let them know that."

"*Call* them."

Hannah rolled her eyes. "You don't think I tried that?"

"I'll go with you," said Cricket. "Safety in numbers."

Hannah hesitated, then offered a worried frown and they both glanced over at Joshua.

"You should stay with Joshua. He doesn't look good."

But it wasn't just that? Her friend knew, of course, that Cricket was no good in a crisis. It *would* be faster if she went alone, even Cricket could admit that.

"What should I do?" Cricket, it had to be said, wasn't really a *caregiver* either.

"Just—keep him awake. And maybe keep trying to get a call to go through. I think Joshua needs some medical attention. If you get a signal, call 911. We do have an emergency. We need help."

Joshua seemed dazed, head in hand. They'd woken him up but they were having a hard time keeping him awake. *That wasn't good, was it?* He'd bled through the cloth she had wrapped around the bag of ice. There was a lot of blood on his shirt, too. So much blood from a cut on his head. She really *didn't* want to leave him alone. She also didn't want Hannah heading out into the dark.

"Let's call the host again first," Cricket suggested. "Then you can go."

Maybe if she stalled, the guys would come back.

"There's no service, Crick. I tried."

Hannah was already moving through the sliding door. The rain had slowed to a drizzle, whispering through the open door. That probably meant that the power would be on soon, maybe the road cleared quickly and they could get out of here, right? Cricket needed to leave, get away from Mako and the noxious affect he had on her life. Joshua needed to go to urgent care at least.

"Lock the door behind me," said Hannah.

"Why?"

"There's a stranger on this property. Who knows who it is or what's going on?"

She tried for a smile but it didn't take. "Okay, Captain Safety."

Hannah's forever nickname—don't run on the pool deck; don't go to the bathroom alone; never go back to someone's hotel room. That last one; Cricket wished she'd taken it. That was the last time she'd had occasion to see that expression on Hannah's face. A midnight call to her old friend brought Hannah out in the night to a downtown hotel to collect a weeping, sick-drunk Cricket.

I fucked up, Hannah.

Oh, Crick.

What did people without a Hannah do? Who cleaned up their messes and fixed their problems, who talked to them when they were depressed, came to get them when they'd screwed up?

"Be careful," she told Hannah.

As the words left her, she felt a sudden rush of panic, a strong sense that they should stay together. Wasn't this like the biggest horror movie "don't"?

Don't split up.

She was about to say so, but Hannah slid the door closed, and Cricket locked it, watching as Hannah disappeared down the deck stairs.

A rumble of thunder sounded distant but ominous.

Hannah knew best, of course. She was a wife, a mother, all the things that made you a real woman, right? Cricket still felt like a girl, a kid, just barely an adult at all. When did a person start to feel like a grown-up, in charge of her life, brave. What was that word she kept hearing? Self-efficacy, the ability to succeed, to solve problems. She didn't have enough of that.

She did as Hannah asked, went for the phone and tried to call 911. But the call failed. She tried again. Another time.

Just those frustrating beeps that meant there was no service.

"Come on," she said. "Please."

"There's no service, Cricket. Just—stop."

When she turned around Joshua was on his feet.

"Oh," she said surprised. "You good?"

He stood by the couch, looking tall and strong. He'd put the ice pack down. The wound, now that it was clean, didn't look so bad. And Joshua? He didn't look dazed and out of it—at all.

In fact, he wore an expression that Cricket hadn't seen before. There was a hardness to his face, a strange coldness to his gaze. She looked over toward the sliding door, hoping to see Hannah or the guys coming back. But there was just the darkness.

How long had Hannah been gone? Not even fifteen minutes. The guys not much longer.

Her throat went a little dry. What if something had happened to them? What if they weren't coming back?

"What's up?" she asked, fear gripping her. "What's wrong?"

She started moving toward him but something made her stop. Instinctively, she reached for her phone. It was up on the kitchen island; she grabbed it and dialed the number again. Just those beeps. Goddamn it. She fucking *hated* nature. The woods totally sucked.

"Cricket," Joshua said, now moving slowly toward her. "I have some things I need to tell you. I haven't been completely honest with you."

She squinted at him, tried for a smile as she backed up a step, another. In the kitchen she knew was a magnetic strip with big knives. She'd noticed it, thinking when she had a real house with a real kitchen someday, she'd have something just like that.

"Ookaay," she said, still inching back as he inched closer. "Why so serious? Are you feeling all right?"

"Just have a seat, okay? We need to talk."

"Joshua," she said. "You're scaring me."

She saw something flash across his face, sadness, regret. But then it was gone.

"Have you ever done something that you deeply regret?" he asked.

She laughed a little. "Lots of things."

"Do you know what it's like when you do a bad thing, and then you have to do other bad things to keep that secret?"

Like when you sleep with your best friend's brother, cheating on his wife, your boyfriend, then you have to lie. Or end the pregnancy that results from your affair, and keep that secret forever—from him, from your best friend, from yourself? Yes, she knew all about regrets, secrets, and lies.

"Do you think it's possible to get close to someone for a dark reason, but then fall in love anyway? And wish you could go back and start again?"

She felt tears well to her eyes. "What are you saying, Joshua?"

His gaze drifted behind her, and she turned to see another form standing on the deck, tall, hooded. Not Hannah. Not anyone she knew. A cold dump of fear hit her belly. The person at the edge of the lake.

"What's happening?" she asked, not liking how girlish, how afraid her voice sounded. "Who is that?"

When she turned back to Joshua, he was standing right beside her. He put a hand on her shoulder, a finger to her lips.

He was a stranger suddenly, someone powerful and threatening.

The form outside knocked insistently on the glass.

"What's happening?" she asked again. Everything was *so* not what she thought, what she expected, that it was the only thing she could think to say.

"Shh," he said. "Just stay quiet, okay? Don't scream. Don't make a scene. And we'll get through this."

His words made no sense. Get through what? Who was this guy? How had she never seen the darkness in him, the coldness? It was all he was now, like a switch had flipped. A frightening stranger. She tried to remember the man who'd made love to her in the car just hours ago. He seemed like a fantasy.

His grip on her shoulder was hard, painful. She tried to wrest away from him, but he wouldn't let her and he was impossibly strong, bringing his hand to her other arm. He pulled her closer to him, hard.

She wanted to plead with him to bring the Joshua she knew back. The one who made her smile and feel safe. What happened to him?

She'd been right, hadn't she?

She had known in her deepest heart that he was too good to be true.

"Just do what I say now and no one else is going to get hurt. Okay, Cricket?"

"Why would anyone get hurt?" Confusion wrapped around fear, muddled her thinking. "What do you mean no one *else*?"

Josh reached past her and unlocked the door, letting the worsening weather and the other stranger inside.

32

BRACKEN

The rain beat on the roof of his truck as he powered down the dark, winding roads. The storm had come on harder and sooner than he'd expected.

Bracken had been on his way to Overlook when he'd gotten the call from the angry guests. Angry or scared? Hard to tell the difference sometimes. When people were afraid, sometimes it made them rude, or unthinking, or both.

Power out.

Someone missing.

Someone hurt.

No electricity meant that the cameras weren't working, couldn't send their signal through the router. There was no way for him to visually check in on the group. He was cut off from them and he didn't like it.

And what had happened to the generator? He'd just inspected it himself. It had been in perfect working order earlier in the week. Was there someone else up there?

He had a strange sense that darkness had come to Overlook. Again.

His big truck made light work of the swamped roads. There were some smaller trees down and branches littered the blacktop, but the pickup rolled over those as if they were twigs. Gusts of wind buffeted the sides of the truck.

When he got closer to Overlook, up ahead he saw the tree down. A young oak, charred and splintered, twisted across both lanes, lay in the beam of his headlights as he approached. He brought the truck to a stop, wheels whispering in the water.

Bracken had placed a couple of calls to guys he knew were game to come out in any weather to deal with problems. You needed a rough-and-ready team when you ran rentals in an isolated area. But his calls had all gone to voicemail, which might mean that people were hunkered down or that cell signals were bad tonight.

He regarded the tree. He wasn't going to even bother getting out of the truck. It was too big to move alone. He'd need a plow, a bigger vehicle. He'd have to get help.

He only knew one person with a truck and a plow big enough to move that tree.

He sat a moment, thinking, listening to the rain beat on the roof of his car, watching it sheet down his windshield.

He thought about going back to May where he'd left her sleeping. How many years had he spent watching people, their lives and dramas unfolding before him? All the while, failing to live his own life.

He was about to turn around when he saw a large form disappear into the trees. Deer.

He kept watching. Where there was one, there were more. Not a breath later, a large buck and a smaller doe passed through the beam of his headlights. They both stopped to stare in his direction, eyes glowing, tawny fur shining in the wet, before bounding out of sight.

He sat, thinking about the people in the house. The pretty

yogi. The party girl. The stay-at-home mom. The tech mogul. The computer wonk. The mystery man. All players on his stage. What had they gotten themselves into?

He'd help them. That was his role as their host, wasn't it? The code he'd established.

The road to Old Bob's was swamped but he made it up the winding, isolated drive. Lights glowed inside the tiny cabin. Nights like this it was a good thing to be off the grid, making your own power. He saw Old Bob's truck sitting under the covered garage, plow already attached. He must have anticipated road clearing.

The door swung open and Bob's big form filled the frame. Bob wasn't that old, just prematurely gray. And Bracken was pretty sure his name wasn't Bob. He'd come to town a few years ago, kept to himself. Bracken knew he was a vet; had seen combat in the Middle East. He was a widower, rumor had it. He had the flat stare of a soldier, and the build of a heavyweight fighter, a head of slate hair worn long to his shoulders. He reliably did the work he was hired to do, and barely said a word.

Now Bob stepped out onto the porch holding a rifle.

Bracken climbed out of the driver's seat and approached; the rain had turned to drizzle.

"Hey, Bob," he said, climbing the steps.

"Bracken," he said, lowering the gun to his side. "What brings you out?"

"Power's out at Overlook," he said. "I have a tree down and can't get to my guests."

"Don't you have a generator up there?"

"It didn't kick on. Not sure why."

Bob frowned. The truth was that no one local liked going up to Overlook. Bracken had trouble with builders, tradesmen, groundskeepers. Even May didn't like to be there alone, brought someone with her if she could find the help, claiming it was too big to clean alone quickly. But Bob wasn't the type to spook.

Even though it was ancient history now, a family had been

murdered up there. A disturbed man had murdered his family. The Realtor had told him about it—because she had to by law. The property had sat empty for nearly twenty years when he bought the acres for a song. He'd razed the small house that had gone to seed, cleared the building site, and set out to build the house that he'd intended to live in. He wasn't afraid of ghosts.

Over the years, stories of a woman in white walking through the trees wailing for her children had circulated. In the nineties a group of teenagers said they saw a little girl wading in the creek. They told police that they chased after her but she disappeared. No evidence of a girl was found; no one had been reported missing. But the truth was the body of the Anderson girl had been found far from the house, as though she'd wandered off after she'd been shot and died by the creek.

Bracken had never seen anything of the sort, no woman in white, no wading child. As far as he was concerned dead was dead. And the world was full of terrible tragedies. Was there an inch of ground anywhere untouched by darkness of some kind?

He thought about what the yoga girl had said, about the place feeling unsettled.

It was true that there were more problems at Overlook than he had at his other places—some guests reported strange noises in the night. Raccoons, most likely. The power went out a bit too often, hence the generator. Now the generator, brand-new and recently inspected by Bracken himself, not coming on. There were roof leaks, the occasional plumbing problem. The banal challenges of home ownership. Not haunting.

"Can we wait until the storm passes?" asked Bob, more worried about the weather, Bracken was sure, than afraid to go up to Overlook.

"Seems like there's a bit of a break now," Bracken pressed.

Bob looked up at the sky. It was clear enough for a patch of starlight. "Not for long."

"The guest is offering a big bonus if we can get the road

cleared tonight. Seems like there might be something going on up there."

It was hard to motivate Bob with money. He was a man who needed little. But he regarded Bracken seriously. Finally, he issued a grunt and went inside. When he came back out, he wore a rain poncho with a hood, thick boots.

"I'll follow you out there," he said.

"Appreciate it," said Bracken and headed back to the truck.

He turned and headed back toward the tree. Finally the head-lights of the other man's truck appeared on the road behind him.

33

HANNAH

She headed down the slippery path, one hand trailing trees using them for balance in the slick mud, the flashlight gripped in the other. The beam bounced and the rain was just a slight drizzle.

Even as a kid, she'd loved the woods—camping with her dad, Camp Fire Girls outings where they learned to build a shelter, make a fire, find their direction. That smell of burning wood and marshmallows, the stillness, the stars. Bruce was not into camping. But she still craved that quiet, that separation from the modern world and all its noise and chatter.

But tonight it was so dark, all the lights in the house out, the moon and stars disappeared behind cloud cover. And she was intent only on getting them back home; any fantasy she had about communion with nature and disconnection from the modern world was blown to pieces. Connection to her daughter was the only thing she wanted now.

She looked in the direction where Bruce and Mako had disappeared, hoping to see them return, or to hear their voices. But no. The wind, the rain on the leaves, the distant rumble of thunder. The world felt big, and the woods a maw, an open mouth waiting.

Stop it. Pull yourself together.

There was no garage, just covered parking. The lower level was built into the natural slope of the property. The basement was finished with a comfortable bedroom and a game room.

So the electrical box and the generator had to be on the far side of the house. She moved down the slope on which the house was built, edging by the deck, feet slipping beneath her. But she kept her balance.

A fire pit surrounded by chairs sat empty waiting for light and laughter, s'mores, hot drinks. The weekend wasn't going to go like that, Mako's vision for it shattered.

No matter what happened next—power restored, road cleared, Liza and Mako making up, a good explanation for everything—they were out of here as soon as possible. She kept flashing on the look on Bruce's face, his disdain, his—anger. Yes, it was anger. How had she not seen it before? And why had he never talked to her about his feelings?

Something moved in the trees and Hannah froze.

"Bruce?"

She flashed her beam around, catching wet green leaves and dark empty spaces. Had she even seen a form moving through the trees before? It seemed like a dream now. How quickly you could doubt your own eyes.

Another shuffle, something small—just an animal. A bunny or a squirrel, right?

Hannah was no girly-girl. She was tough; she was handy. Her mother had taught her how to change a tire, replace a circuit, unclog a drain.

There's no waiting around for Prince Charming, Sophia always said. *He ain't coming. Even if he looks like a hero at first, he'll still turn out to be more little boy than man.*

Hannah cast the flashlight beam into the woods again, around her in a wide circle, heart thumping. Nothing. She was alone.

When you're going through hell, keep going, another Sophia-ism. Her mom was a piece of work but she was right about a lot of things.

A few more steps and she was around the house.

There.

A slim covered structure attached to the siding that had to contain the electrical circuits, and a big metal box that must be the generator. She didn't think it was going to be as easy as flipping a switch, but it never hurt to check, right? Bruce, computer geek, was famous for saying: Is the power on? Is it plugged in? Have you tried turning it off and on again? Sometimes the simplest solutions were the right ones.

She moved quickly, feet looking for purchase, wet, flashlight beam guiding her way.

The scene revealed itself in pieces.

The door to the electrical box was ajar. On the ground, deep footprints in the muck. Maybe Mako and Bruce had checked it before heading into the night. But the prints seemed smaller than Hannah's—Bruce was a size thirteen and Mako was a size eleven—and there was only one set.

Again, she made a sweep with her beam in a circle around her. Her throat felt constricted, breath shallow. Maybe she should go back to the house.

No. She was here. She had to see if she could fix the power.

But when she opened the door, she saw that the main switch had been flipped and the wire to the box had been cut, severed sharp and clean.

The electricity had not gone out in the storm. Someone had cut the power.

"What the fuck?" she whispered.

A quick inspection of the generator revealed that it was out of fuel, the gauge pointing to empty. Getting closer, she caught the unmistakable odor of gasoline. So, someone had cut the power, drained the fuel from the generator, plunging the house into darkness?

Why?

Would Liza have done it, to ruin the weekend?

No. Hannah knew her sister-in-law to be kind, respectful, unfailingly polite and considerate.

But, truly, how well did they really know each other? There was that uncrossable distance between them. And in the fog of war, enraged at Mako for who knows what, maybe Liza would be capable of sabotaging the weekend for all. Or, and this thought came unbidden—maybe it was Mako. To cover up whatever it was that had happened to Liza.

She found herself thinking of Libby again. She thought about the girl more often than she wanted to. It was a secret wound, a buried regret that surfaced in dreams during times of stress, could be brought back by the odor of beer, or certain songs.

"No," she said out loud to no one. "That's ridiculous."

She stood a moment staring at the generator. There was literally nothing to be done. An electrician would be needed to fix that box. Maybe they could siphon some gas from one of the cars? She'd need help to do that—a tube, some kind of container to carry the gas.

The rain started to come down again.

No, the only smart thing was to get her husband and get home to their child. Whatever was going on, she had to get to that other cabin, to Mako and Bruce, and hopefully Liza.

But when she turned around to head that way, there was a slim form standing in the trees, just out of reach of her beam. Hannah felt like she'd been Tasered with fear, backed up toward the house.

"Who's there?" she called.

But the form stayed silent and still, watching.

"Hey!" said Hannah, mustering her lifeguard voice, deep and authoritative. "Who are you?"

She moved closer, pointing the beam of light ahead of her like it was a sword.

But when she approached, there was nothing there. Just the dark and the trees. Her imagination. A trick of the night. One of the ghosts who roamed the property.

Relief flooded her body, making her legs feel weak. Ghosts were preferable to intruders.

And that was officially the last fucking straw.

Hannah was through with this place—ghosts and strange forms in the dark, storms and power outages. She and Bruce were leaving. She was going to find her husband, and they were out of here. Downed tree blocking the road? They'd move it themselves. Didn't mothers have all kinds of superstrength when they were separated from their babies?

This weekend. She had known it was a mistake. Her place was with Gigi and Bruce. She was going to start putting them both first, always. They'd move out of Mako's house; Bruce could stop working for her brother. They were their own family now.

Hannah almost didn't feel the blow to the back of the head.

She just felt her head jerk unexplainably, then a radiating pain down her neck. She dropped to her knees, bringing a hand to her skull and pulling it back to find it black with blood. Confusion. Fear. Pain.

She fell to her knees into the muck, the night spinning.

Oh god. What happened? The edges of her vision started to blur as she fell sideways into the mud. She looked up and thought she saw the moon.

But it was a woman she didn't recognize. She towered over Hannah, face pale and impassive, surrounded by a black hood.

"Sleep sweet, Mama," said the stranger.

Gigi, thought Hannah.

Then the world disappeared.

34

HENRY

2016

If he hadn't read the paper that morning, which sometimes he didn't, he might never have been the wiser. They'd had a long, long night; Piper was sleeping in after feeding their baby, Luke, three times in the wee hours—growth spurt.

And now Henry was on duty with the little man who in spite of keeping them up all night was bright and chipper and *super* into his oatmeal. The whole solid food thing was new—and it was everywhere—on Luke's chubby cheeks, between his fingers, on the floor, on the high chair tray.

"Buddy," said Henry. "You getting any of that in your mouth?"

Luke bounced happily, doughy legs kicking. "Ma. Ma."

"Mommy's sleeping. Let's let her rest for a little while."

Henry didn't have to be in the office until ten; Piper could have another hour. Luke wielded his purple plastic spoon like a sword.

"Ah," said Luke, which Henry took as an agreement. "Haha!"
A big gob of oatmeal went flying.

He wiped some from Luke's mouth and felt the wild rush of love he often felt when looking at his son. The absolute awed devotion he'd felt the moment Luke had emerged—miraculously, impossibly—from Piper and into the delivery room. The bloody, squalling emergence of this perfect creature who was made from the love he had for his wife—it just blew him away. People had babies all the time. Why did no one ever talk about what a wild, over-the-top miracle the whole thing was?

He put Luke on the floor mat for tummy time and proceeded to read to him from the newspaper—sports, the weather, international news, the business section. He still liked the print edition, though it was probably easier to read it on his phone or iPad.

"Stocks are at an all-time high, little man. Good thing we already have the 529 going."

Luke picked up his stuffed elephant and stuck it in his mouth, slobbering copiously, watching Henry intently. His curly dark hair was Henry's. His eyes were Piper's.

Henry reached out with a handy burp cloth to wipe at Luke's mouth.

Henry didn't know how to be a father. He had no role model. Wouldn't have thought there was any such thing as a "father's instinct" but Piper said he was a natural. And truly he just loved being with his child. He had the feeling that maybe 90 percent of it was just happily being there, doing your best. *He doesn't need anything but us*, Piper had promised. *All we have to do is keep him safe, love him, and do our best to make him a good human being, one that makes the world better, not worse.*

The item was on the third page: Tech Entrepreneur Murdered in his South Beach Penthouse.

He might have glanced over it if not for the smiling face staring back at him, one that looked eerily familiar. He read on to himself about how the young man, just a year younger than

Henry, was attacked so violently in his home that he was nearly decapitated. Surveillance footage was still being reviewed. Police had no suspects at the writing of the article.

He stared. The guy, with his dark hair and big eyes, slim build—they could be brothers. Henry's heart started to thump.

"You let me sleep." Piper padded in, bleary-eyed, and got down on the floor in front of the baby.

"You needed it," Henry said, looking up at her. He folded the paper up.

"My little wild man," she said to the baby. Luke smiled maniacally, kicked his legs. Wow, did babies ever love their mommas. Luke and Piper were inseparable. "You were partying all night."

Luke grinned wildly, issued a shriek of joy, like he was the funniest guy in the world.

"Won't you be late?" she said, sitting up and leaning in to Henry for a kiss.

"I'm going to head out now. I have to go to the data center to do updates anyway, not the office so I have some flexibility. Thought I'd let you catch up on a little sleep."

He took the paper and she didn't notice. Poor Piper wasn't operating on all cylinders, totally in love, sleep deprived, and on full-time with Luke all day. He often came home to find her as he left her—hair up, wearing the same thing, a little dazed. He found it cute, her devotion, how she was all in with this new role. He'd relieve her in the evening so that she could work out, or take a shower, or just go for a walk. They'd eat as a family, put the baby down early, have a little couple time. There was an ease and a peace to their life that he cherished.

"I think we'll go to Mom's today," she said. "She's dying to show off Luke to her friends."

"Good idea," he said. "I'll probably be late."

"So maybe Luke and I will spend the night there?"

He didn't love that but yeah, that was good. It would give

him a little time to dig into what he'd just found. Not that he should.

"Sure."

"You can come, too," she said.

"That's okay. I'll use the time to catch up on some stuff."

"Don't work too hard, loser."

She kissed him long and deep. Even disheveled, a little pale, fatigued, she was still the most beautiful woman he'd ever seen. Their life was good. He had a solid, high-paying job; they had Piper's parents close so there was help with Luke. Piper missed teaching, but she wasn't ready to leave the baby. Their house was comfortable and stylish. Maybe other people wanted more. But he just wanted this. It was enough.

"You okay?" she asked with a cock of her head.

"Yeah," he said. "I'm good."

"So go bring home the bacon."

He waited until he'd left their cul-de-sac before calling a number he hadn't used in a while. All these years the number was still the same.

The old cop, retired now and not living too far from Henry, answered on the first ring.

"West."

"Henry Parker."

"Henry, wow. Great to hear from you."

"How's retirement treating you?"

"Eh, you know. I hung up a shingle. I'm not the golfing, cruise to the Bahamas, wine on the beach at sunset type turns out. Much to my wife's dismay."

Henry smiled. That tracked.

"I was wondering—have time for a beer and a burger?"

"Sure. When?"

"Tonight."

There was silence, the shuffling of papers.

"What's going on?"

"You know, I'm not sure."

They set a time and place, and Henry headed to work, thinking about the murder in Miami, his half sister Cat with whom he had developed a complicated relationship, and the dark worries he'd pushed away until he couldn't.

The Palm Pavilion was a beachfront restaurant famous for its grouper sandwich and live music at sunset. The pretty blue and white building sat on the end of a boardwalk looking out languidly at the Gulf of Mexico and the sugar white sands of Clearwater Beach. It was the perfect sunset spot if you could take the late afternoon heat. Diners were cooled by umbrellas and lightly misting fans in the hotter months. Tonight was on the temperate side, the blanket of humidity that would fall in a few weeks still blissfully absent.

Henry waited at a table in the far corner of the deck, taking in the salt air, the laughing gulls. It was a quiet Tuesday night, and the singer-slash-guitar player was favoring Neil Young and David Bowie covers instead of the usual Jimmy Buffett. Henry turned his sweating margarita glass, watching the door. He'd spent the day researching the things he had on his mind, and he was glad for the warm wash of the tequila.

Henry and Cat shared eighteen half siblings that he knew of. Seven of them were dead. Eight if you counted the Miami tech entrepreneur, though he couldn't be sure about that yet.

He'd spent the day playing amateur detective, cross-referencing between the Origins site and the Donor Sibling Registry. He hadn't been on either in ages, having given up the quest for finding more family connections.

Henry had accomplished nearly nothing at work as he dug into each of their lives by searching the internet, visiting social media pages, tracking their friends, reading obituaries. He'd gone down the rabbit hole, as Gemma liked to call it. His head was full of images of the people who were related to him by a stranger's sperm. Their lives, their loves, their wants and dreams.

So many different types of people, all from the same man. A man who was still a mystery to Henry.

After a while, the detective walked through the door, looking tanned and svelte in a pair of khaki shorts, Hawaiian shirt, and Top-Siders, the Florida retiree uniform. His hair was snow-white now and he sported a wide mustache, neatly trimmed.

West spotted Henry and headed his way. When he took his seat, he ordered a beer from the blonde, hard-body, pink lip glossed waitress and looked out at the fading sunset. She brought back the bottle quickly, a tasty local ale from 3 Daughters Brewing.

"It's always a sight, isn't it?" said West. "Every sunset a different color show, a different mood, kind of a reflection of whatever you have going on any given day."

Henry looked out at the pink sky, the dark blue water, the orange orb moving inexorably toward the horizon line. He didn't have a ton of time for sunsets, in fact, he found the tourist fascination with the whole thing a little tiresome. *Yeah, people, the sun* sets. *Every. Night.*

"I didn't have you pegged as a poet."

A smile, a long draft of his beer. "Old age turns us all into poets. Or assholes. One or the other."

Henry laughed at that. His father-in-law was getting old, too. He was no poet.

Henry took the morning's newspaper article from his pocket and shifted it over to West, who picked it up, slipped a pair of readers from his shirt pocket and read.

"What's this now?"

"So, a couple years ago I connected with my aunt Gemma, Alice's sister. Remember?"

"Of course, nice lady. We're in touch."

"Yeah," he said. "She helped me figure some things out. She's into genealogy, our family's history. She got me the Origins test."

"I remember. As I recall it didn't get you any closer to your father."

"That's right. But through a Facebook page, and the Donor Sibling Registry, I connected with some of my half siblings, other kids fathered by the same anonymous donor."

He told the detective about Cat, about their conversation, how they kept in touch via email, the occasional call. He told West about the woman Cat had found up in the Bronx, Marta Bennet, how she'd died.

Then, he shifted a file out of the backpack he had at his feet. The manila folder contained articles about the donor siblings who had died. Eight, including the Miami entrepreneur, if he was indeed a donor sibling. He hadn't turned up on Henry's Origins page, and he wasn't hooked up with the Donor Sibling Registry—which he only would if he'd taken a test, or been digging into his own ancestry. But the resemblance he bore to Henry—and to Cat—was striking.

West flipped through the articles, twisted at his mustache.

"What are you thinking?" asked West.

Henry shook his head, looked out at the beach. The bell rang and people cheered. The sun had dipped below the horizon. Supposedly when conditions were right, a green flash of light was sometimes visible right after the sun went down. Two optical phenomena combined—a mirage and the dispersion of sunlight. Henry had never seen it.

"It's odd, right?" asked Henry. "All these people dead—suicide, murder, accident."

"Statistically, it's troubling, yes."

The waitress came and took their order—Famous Palm Burgers and Island Fries for them both. If Piper had been there, he'd have ordered the grouper sandwich; she'd have gotten The Sunset Salad with salmon.

"And this guy," he picked up the article from that morning's paper. "He's one of your half siblings?"

"I'm not sure. I hadn't been on Origins or Donor Sibling Registry in a while. I logged back on today. I didn't see him."

The detective cocked his head at Henry. "Why did you stop logging on?"

"I went through the motions, met up with a couple of people. It was just—weird. I realized that it's not just about blood, it's about chemistry, too. And I wasn't feeling it with anyone."

Henry took a swig of his beer. He hadn't really talked about this before. But he went on,

"So I decided that I needed to be here now. I have a son, a wife. We're building something. The past—my past—Alice. It's dark. It hurts. I have Gemma now. She's a part of our life. We have Piper's family. Not perfect, of course. But it's enough."

West considered him with a slow nod, looked down at the file.

"But here we are."

Henry drained his beer as West flipped through the pages in the folder. Yes, here they were. He wanted to forget everything to do with his past, and yet—he dreamed about Cat, found himself Facebook stalking their half brother Dave in San Francisco, Todd in Georgia, Mira in Portland. Now this. *Good old Dad* got around—or at least his sperm did.

"Did you reach out to the half sister you're in touch with. Cat?"

Henry shook his head. That was the other thing. His calls with her were getting weirder and weirder. Last time they talked, she hinted that she was getting closer to *understanding who our father is.* He pretended he had to go, promised to call back. But he never did. The truth was that she was a little scary. Intense. Sometimes angry, edgy. *I guess it's easy to walk away from this when you have a family.*

"No," he said. She was the natural person to ask about the tech entrepreneur. Something stopped him from calling her. "She's... I don't know. She's pretty obsessed with this stuff. Maybe she's unstable."

This earned a squint from West. "Unstable how?"

He told the older man about how she called at all hours, sometimes rambling, sometimes morose, sometimes elated when she'd made a new connection.

"I don't want to get her activated. She has some wild theories."

"Such as?"

"She thinks there's some kind of curse. Or, not really a curse but like something bad coded into our DNA."

"Okay. Like what?" West looked down at the file, picked up the top article. Drew, who committed suicide. "Like depression?"

West handed him the paper. Drew didn't bear much resemblance to Henry or Cat. He was slim, blond with dark eyes. Even though he was smiling in the school photo, he looked sad and ghostly.

"Yeah," said Henry. "Like something that makes you vulnerable. Like you're prone to depression, so you drink too much. Because you drink too much, you get into a fatal car accident."

West shrugged. "There are lots of things we don't understand about genetics. But I have to believe that our choices mean more than our biology."

Henry needed to believe that, too. Especially now that he was a father.

"I can make some calls if you want," West said finally. "Talk to the investigating officers, see what they have to say."

Henry felt a weight on his shoulders shift. Maybe that's what he wanted, to share this with someone. He didn't have the resources or the time to connect the dots between his dead half siblings.

But he couldn't quite let go of it either.

"That would be great," he said. "You don't think—"

"What?"

"That she's right. That there's some inherited darkness."

West leaned back, looked out at the beach, took a swallow of his beer.

"I think we don't control what we get from our parents, and we don't always choose what happens to us. But look at you, Henry. You could have gone a different way—but here you are, successful, married, with a baby, a nice home."

It was Piper who saved him. He knew that. She loved him and that made him want to be a better person, the kind she deserved. He said as much.

"You chose the light. We choose, Henry. That's what I believe. Leave this with me. I'll do some digging and you forget about it, okay? If I think there's something bigger here, I'll come back to you."

Henry considered it, then lifted his nearly empty glass, clicked it to West's bottle. "Deal."

Somehow over the years they had become friends.

A gull called, and a coast guard helicopter passed low overhead making everything rumble.

"It's funny you called. I was about to reach out to Gemma."

"Oh?"

"There's this group. People who are using modern DNA testing to find answers to long-cold cases. They are taking crime scene DNA samples and submitting them to companies like Origins, looking for connections that lead them to identifying the sample even if there's nothing in criminal databases. They're not-for-profit, volunteers and retired law enforcement folks trying to find answers to old cases. They're interested in Alice's murder."

Henry took this in as the waitress brought their food on colorful plastic plates. A group at the bar was watching a game; they issued a collective moan at a missed play. The singer was onto "The Man Who Sold the World," sounding more like Kurt Cobain than Bowie, gravelly and sad.

"Gemma will be all over that," said Henry. "She's never

given up on justice for Alice. But the evidence points to Tom Watson, right. And he's dead."

He didn't mean it to sound flat, uncaring. Piper was concerned about the distance he seemed to have from Alice, what happened to her, suspected that he hadn't dealt with it and had pushed for therapy prior to Luke's birth. These days she could only think about the baby, so Henry was off the hook for the moment.

"Closure is always healing," said West. "To have answers or something close."

Henry had spent a lot of time thinking about Alice, discussing her case with Piper. Occam's razor theory stated that in explaining a thing, no more assumptions should be made than are necessary. In other words, the simplest answer was probably the most likely. Alice stole money from her deceased employer. Tom came after it. He killed Alice, took the money, dumped her body. That was the story Henry told himself. It was a dark one; but at least it was an answer that made some kind of sense. Alice had always worried that someone was coming after them. That was probably why. She was guilty of theft, maybe worse.

"If the DNA sample we have stored from the crime scene brings up relatives of Tom Watson's, we'll be more certain of our theory," West went on.

"You never gave up on her," said Henry. "Thank you for that."

"It's one of those things, you know," he said. "Sometimes you can't let go. Something keeps you coming back."

Henry could relate.

They ate a while in silence, the burger juicy and good, the fries hot and crispy. Henry shared pictures of Luke. West had a million shots of his many grandkids.

"This is what matters," said West. "What we give to these little people. They're the present and the future."

"More poetry," said Henry with a smile.

"Just the truth, son," he said. "Just the truth."

35

CRICKET

The woman who Joshua let inside pulled back her hood to reveal long dark hair, and a face which was—not beautiful, but striking. Water dripped off her, making puddles on the wood floor as she moved inside. She brought a scent with her, something outdoorsy, the faint smell of smoke, or was it gasoline?

"I thought you left," the stranger said to Joshua. "You made a run for it."

"A tree is down," he said. "The road is blocked."

"So you didn't come back to save your girlfriend?" she said. "You're just trapped here like the rest of them."

"This was never how it was supposed to go."

"Oh my god," yelled Cricket. "Who is this? What are you talking about?"

"I never wanted to hurt you," said Joshua, addressing himself to Cricket. "That's what I want you to remember."

The nice Joshua was back, looking at her with big, sympathetic eyes.

She hated it when guys said that. What a shitty thing to say—like somehow it made them better people for breaking your heart when it wasn't their intention in the first place.

"What does that even mean?" she managed as she felt her heart shatter, its pieces fluttering into her belly.

The other woman stood staring at Cricket, her expression unreadable—like Cricket was a puzzle she couldn't solve. Cricket knew her—from where? Her confused brain grappled for it. Somewhere...

"Who are you?" Cricket asked. "What is this? What *is* happening?"

"Shut up," the woman said coolly. "Sit down and shut up."

Okay. Not okay. Cricket felt her brokenhearted, little-girl self, take a back seat to her woman-up, don't-fuck-with-me self.

"Seriously?" she said, stepping closer to the stranger. "Who *the fuck* do you think you are?"

The other woman moved so fast and struck her so hard that Cricket stumbled and tripped over the coffee table, falling and hitting her head against the side of the couch.

The world tilted, and stars swam before her eyes. She lay on the floor, stunned, pain radiating from her jaw down her neck. She'd never, in her life, been hit—by anyone. Her parents had never even spanked her. Her whole system reeled from the shock, from the pain. She felt herself curl up into a ball, the wood floor gritty and dusty.

The woman came at her again, yanking the coffee table out of the way with the squeal of wood on wood. Joshua moved to get between them.

"Heyheyhey! What the fuck?" He blocked the other woman's path. "You said she wouldn't get hurt."

"No," said the woman, standing and jutting her chin out at Joshua. He was a full head taller but it was clear that he was afraid of her. He lifted his palms and backed up as she advanced. "*You* said she wouldn't get hurt and *I* didn't correct you."

He bowed his head. "Just—stop. Let me help her up. You don't need to do this."

"How the fuck would you know what I need to do?"

They spoke like intimates, like people who knew each other too well. Cricket tried to piece it together, but everything was just a horrible jumble of every single thing gone wrong. What could this possibly be about?

"Here." Josh bent down to Cricket. She let him help her onto the couch, confused, in pain.

"What's happening?" she whispered in his ear when he was close. It was the old Joshua, the one she'd been falling in love with. He looked so worried, so loving.

Cricket felt like a little kid, hurt and afraid. She wasn't a fighter like Hannah; she wasn't really a tough girl, though she could talk tough when she needed to. Hannah was the one who got suspended for beating up a girl who was bullying Cricket, while Cricket stood on the edge of the sports court and cried. She was embarrassed then and now, too, but she started to cry. It was the kind of ugly crying that wouldn't stop, sloppy, sobby. Her face hurt—a lot. Oh god, she was going to be sick. She leaned over and vomited on the floor.

"Oh, Christ," said the other woman.

"Shh," said Joshua, pushing the hair back from her eyes, resting a hand on her head. "I'm sorry."

She looked down to see that blood was gushing onto her white cover-up. She swallowed hard, tried to stop crying but couldn't. She willed herself not to puke again. *Make yourself solid*, Hannah had said leaning with her over a hundred toilets.

"You said this wasn't about her," said Josh, looking back to the other woman. "That it was about him."

He grabbed the ice pack that she'd been holding to *his* head just minutes ago. She'd been tending to him but he seemed fine now—had it been an act?

"It's about *all of them*," she said. "You must see it. How they mollycoddle him, enable him. He's a monster and they're like his—his—his—*handmaidens*."

She was sour, angry. Cricket knew the type, the wronged woman who got bitter and then lost touch with reality a little.

Obviously, this was one of Mako's women scorned. They were legion.

She might have had an actual grievance at one point—he harassed her at work, used her, fired her when she didn't give him what he wanted. There was all sorts of chatter about Red World and about Mako on the chat boards, what a pig he was. No one had ever stepped up to file charges though. And like so many men in power, he just found his way to keep doing what he did. This was the post-#MeToo era. Nothing had changed. Guys just got way better at hiding, more accomplished in their gaslighting, lying, and covering up.

Anyway, whatever the initial wrong was, her anger had turned her into something ugly. Cricket had no idea what the woman was talking about, but she could tell that whatever it was, there was something even uglier, even deeper beneath it. Like the bully on the playground who's abused at home. Hurt people hurt people.

"What do you want?" she asked through her sobs. "Look. If it's money. We have it. Mako has it."

The other woman looked at Cricket like she was something she wanted to scrape off her shoe. "That is literally what every single person says. Like it's the only thing that motivates people."

The other woman shook her head in naked disgust.

"Then what?" Cricket asked. She was bolder with Joshua beside her. He wasn't going to let the woman hurt her again, was he? "You obviously want *something*."

The other woman ignored her, turned her attention to Joshua. "Just tie her up and put her somewhere. We'll deal with her later."

She felt Joshua stiffen, and she looked up to see him staring at the stranger with something like hatred on his face.

"The other one's out cold by the generator on the side of the house," she said into the tense silence. "When you've secured this idiot, go get her, too."

Tie her up? What? Who's out cold by the generator? Hannah? Oh god.

"Look," said Joshua, rising. "This isn't about him anymore. Killing him. Destroying him and his life and the people who enable him. Is it? This is about you. I think this has gone too far."

"*This* hasn't even started," said the other woman, looking back and forth between them both.

Joshua moved toward her, and she moved in closer, poked him hard in the chest, looking up.

"Don't forget," she said. "If anything happens to me, *everybody* hears about *everything*. Are we clear?"

Joshua deflated, lifting his palms in surrender.

"Just follow the plan," said the woman. She gave him a dark look, and then she moved out into the night again.

Cricket was alone with Joshua, who stood there, staring after the stranger.

"Oh, shit," he said. "This is so fucked."

"Joshua," she sobbed. "What *is happening*? Who is *that woman*?" She felt stunned, powerless, her head pounding.

"She's," he started, then shook his head. "She's my sister. My half sister."

Cricket shook her head, trying to let the information sink in.

Maybe she was hallucinating? It kind of seemed like that—everything topsy-turvy and nonsensical, Hannah's here, then gone. Mako running out into the rain after his wife. The ghost of Libby. A strange woman in the night.

Joshua's *half sister*? Had he mentioned having a sister?

As she sat puzzling over the pieces, Joshua still standing by the glass door, seemingly paralyzed, that's when she remembered the other woman. Her voice, cold and officious. On the phone at Mako's office.

Trina, his assistant, the one who quit suddenly. The one Cricket suspected Mako might be fucking, while he was fucking Cricket and married to Liza.

Okay, that made sense. So this was a revenge thing. Mako had fucked her over in some way. She had come to take her revenge on Mako.

"No, she's not your sister," she said, sitting up. "She's Mako's assistant. Or she was."

"Right," said Joshua, rubbing at his face in distress. "*And* she's my sister. Well, my half sister. It's complicated. Oh, wow, I've really fucked up, Cricket. I'm so sorry."

He moved back over to her quickly and got to his knees before her. She grappled with this new knowledge. Wait. So did that mean—?

"The night we met in that club? It wasn't a chance encounter? You were—what? Working with her? Looking for a way to get closer to Mako?"

He closed his eyes a minute. "It started as one thing. Her thing. I had to go along with it. But then it all changed, Cricket. Believe that. Please. I didn't know that I was going to fall—"

"Stop," she said. "Don't say it."

"I'm so sorry," he said again, taking her hands in his. He looked at her like she'd hoped he would when he was about to propose—earnest, loving.

God, she was so pathetic. She could still taste blood in the back of her throat, realized that their whole relationship was a plot to get to Mako, and still she was thinking about him proposing. Anyway, better to let him think they were okay.

"Look," she said gently. "Let's just get the others and get out of here."

She stood and the world spun. He rose to support her.

"I—I can't," he said. "She knows too much about me. I *have* to help her."

"What does she know about you? Explain this to me, Joshua. Make me understand you."

The rain started pouring down again, drumming against the roof and windows, and all she could think was that Mako, Bruce, and Hannah were out there with that woman.

What *did* Trina want? What was she going to do to all of them?

She felt something solidify inside her. She had to call up her inner Hannah. She couldn't just stand in here crying, bleeding, talking to Joshua—who was what? A liar? Had come here with some dark motive? Associated with the scary woman who just beat the shit out of her?

"She knows things about me," Joshua said. "I've done wrong and she knows it all. If I don't help her, I could go to jail. You don't want that, right, Crick?"

Was he really looking for sympathy from her? Understanding?

She backed away from him and moved toward the kitchen, locking eyes with Joshua.

"Cricket," he said, lifting his palms again in that passive gesture of surrender. "What are you doing?"

She put the island between them, and moved over toward the oven. The row of knives hung on a magnetic board. They both stood stock-still, a standoff, the kitchen island between them.

How fast could she reach for one of those knives?

How fast could he get to her?

A breath. Another one.

Then, she moved quickly, grabbing the biggest one.

It had a heavy wood handle and a gleaming blade.

He came up behind her and she spun, holding the knife in front of her. Could she use it? Plunge that blade into his beautiful flesh?

Yeah. Yeah she could.

"Back up," she said, summoning her power voice. "Get away from me."

"Woah, calm down," he said, taking a couple of steps back, "I'm not going to hurt you. I can get us out of this. We can walk away tonight."

"Get the fuck away from me," she said, voice wobbling. "I loved you. I *thought* I loved you."

"Cricket, please." His voice was low and soothing, but he kept inching toward her. "I love you, too."

"Oh my god. Shut up."

The sad thing was, it was exactly what she wanted to hear, what she'd wanted to say. *I love you.* Not with a knife in her hand, bleeding profusely from the face. She was so dizzy, confused. She was going to be sick, bile mingling with the blood she'd swallowed.

"She said you tried to leave," said Cricket, the other woman's words ringing back at her. "You already tried to run, but had to come back because of the tree."

"I came back for you. You know that."

She knew that he was lying. If the tree hadn't come down, he'd be long gone, wouldn't he?

"Where did you go when you disappeared?" she asked. Then another dark possibility dawned. Liza hadn't left Mako. Joshua and the other woman had—done something to her. "Where's Liza?"

He was crying now. "I never wanted to hurt anyone."

Mako cried, too, when he was caught, when he was backed into a corner. A certain type of man—the user, the manipulator, the sociopath—dissolved into tears as a last resort. Why did she always wind up with that type of man? If she survived this night, she was going to bring it up in therapy. But for now, she had to get tough.

"I have to—help Mako and Hannah." Her voice sounded too soft, weak. She had to rest her weight against the counter.

"Look," said Joshua, still soothing. "Put the knife down and let's just get out of here. I'll explain everything to you, everything. I'll make this right."

It was because she wanted love too badly. That's why she made so many of the wrong choices. She just wanted to love and to be loved. She just didn't know what love looked like, real love like the kind Hannah and Bruce had.

"Let's go, Cricket. Put the knife down, and let's get out of here."

She almost did it. Because, truly, that's the kind of girl she was. She'd do anything for love, anything for a guy. It was Hannah's age-old complaint about her, that Cricket threw everything over, even Hannah, for men, including Mako. She'd betrayed herself, Hannah, Liza, others over and over for him, for other even less worthy guys. But no, not this time. She was not going to let Hannah get hurt while she ran off with this guy who clearly had *major* issues.

"Back away from me," she yelled, pointing the knife at him. It was big, glinting dark, heavy in her hand. It looked to have a razor-sharp edge.

He backed up, staring at the knife. She edged toward the door.

God, her *head*. It was pounding from the blows she'd taken, from the fall.

"Cricket," he said, just as the rain started to fall even harder, and thunder rumbled in the distance. "Don't go out there. She's dangerous. Please, let's just go."

He held a hand out to her. His face—all the coldness she'd seen before had melted and he was the man she wanted him to be again. She wanted him to comfort her, hold her tight and tell her this was all a huge mistake.

Almost, she almost did it.

Put the knife down and left Mako and Hannah behind. She wanted to.

But what would *Hannah* do? That's what she always asked herself when she was in a bind. This time, she didn't have to think. Hannah would rush out after her and Mako, like she'd done a hundred times, and save them all.

When Cricket got to the door, she slid it open and stepped out into the night. The rain was coming down in sheets, soaking her. But as soon as she was outside, she turned and ran into the night.

"Hannah!" she yelled. A flash of lightning answered, followed by the wind picking up and a deafening clap of thunder.

"Hannah, where are you?"

36

HANNAH

Summer 2001

Oh my god, we are in so much trouble. The whole house—her parents' house—smelled like weed and spilled beer; someone had knocked over the bear statue that her dad had bought in Alaska and it lay on the living room floor, decapitated. He loved that thing. Hannah bit back tears as she moved through the rooms—which didn't even seem like her home, lights dim, full of strangers.

"Everybody needs to leave," Hannah shouted over the blaring of music, Eminem asking the real Slim Shady to please stand up. But nobody heard or paid attention if they did.

"I'm serious," she shouted louder, sounding whiny and shrill. "I'm calling the police."

"Chill, bitch," someone said, and whoever heard him laughed.

Hannah looked around for who but couldn't determine in the crowd of losers and stoners who might have spoken.

People were gathered in the foyer, many of whom she'd never seen before—where had they come from? Other high schools? A couple was making out in the downstairs powder room. The boy had his hand up her shirt; the girl was working on the boy's fly. The boy's neck was flushed red; the girl's pink bra strap had slipped down her shoulder. They hadn't even bothered to close the door. God—*seriously?* Hannah had never even been kissed.

Hannah pushed her way up through the kids hanging out on the stairs to find Mickey, who she was going to *absolutely kill.* How could he do this?

She'd left Cricket drunk and weeping in the basement. Her friend had watched Mickey kissing another girl, when he and Cricket had just broken up days earlier.

How could he do this to me?

So there was *that* drama to deal with. And somehow, when the plan was to have "a few friends over," now the house was full of high schoolers drinking from kegs in the backyard. There was a gathering of punk wannabes sitting on her mother's dining room table, cheerleader and jock types making themselves at home on the sectional. Oh my god. How are we going to clean this place up? Hannah felt sick. She would not cry. She would fix this, another Mickey mess.

Upstairs it was quieter, the hallway lights out. She heard voices from behind closed doors, but luckily her bedroom was empty. She reached inside and pressed the little button lock, then pulled it closed. She'd worry about how to open it later. In the meantime at least no one would be getting it on in her virginal bedroom.

She pushed into her brother's room to find a group of people sitting on his bed, in his bean bag chair, playing video games.

"Get out," she said flatly. "The police are coming."

"Oh, shit," said one kid who she recognized from school. He was tall with a large nose, floppy hair. The rest she'd seen around, as well, in the hallways, in the cafeteria—the spotty redhead graduated last year and now worked at the local con-

venience store. The one with the shaved head was on the re-
medial track in her grade. The other two were strangers—both
slovenly and looking like they were up to no good with heavy
brows and ripped jeans.

"I think I hear the sirens," she said, cupping a hand to ear.

They all cut and run. She heard them thundering down the
stairs, yelling about the cops. It sounded like that got people
moving—voices raised, doors opened and closed. She heard
more voices out on the lawn and went to the window to see a
line of people moving out the front door. Car engines started
up.

Okay, that was good.

Another noise down the hall caught her attention. It sounded
like someone crying.

Hannah moved down the long hallway toward her parents'
bedroom door which was shut.

"Get away from me! Don't touch me!" A girl's shriek followed by a wail so miserable that Hannah burst in through the
door without knocking.

The scene revealed itself in pieces. A skinny girl, naked in
the fetal position on her parents' bed. Blood on the sheets, a lot
of it. Her brother standing naked over the girl, arms akimbo.

He jumped, rushed to cover himself with a pillow, when
Hannah walked in.

"What the fuck, Mickey," she said. *"What the fuck?"*

"Do you not *knock*?" yelled Mickey.

"He—he—he raped me," the girl managed to push out between sobs.

Mickey looked at Hannah wild, desperate, lifted his hands
in a gesture of surrender. The pillow dropped and she averted
her eyes. "No, no, no. She wanted it. She came on to *me*."

Then Cricket was there, screaming at Mickey. The girl vomited on the carpet, retching and sobbing. And Hannah felt the
world spin—the house, her parents, this girl in their bed, her
brother. And then *she* was shrieking.

Shutupshutupshutup!

Mickey and Cricket fell silent, stared at Hannah with mouths gaping.

The girl in the bed—Libby. It was Libby from school. A senior like Mickey who smoked back by the dumpsters with the hipsters. She was part of the artist/theater kids clique with asymmetrical hair tinged pink, dressed in black all the time. She always looked so cool, so put together to Hannah. She was a girl with a thing—like she knew what she wanted to do, wanted to be. Her art was always in the student shows; Hannah heard she was going to the Cooper Union in New York City, a famous art school.

Now she looked as slim and helpless as a child. She *was* a child.

Hannah went to her. Cricket and Mickey started arguing more quietly, voices angry. *We broke up, Cricket. I don't owe you anything.*

They took it out into the hallway.

"He raped me," Libby whispered to Hannah. "I was a virgin."

That explained the blood—but so much? "I have my period," she said when Hannah helped her to sit. "I told him no, over and over. He was so—strong."

She was very, very drunk, slurring her words, her gaze unfocused, eyes swollen shut from crying.

"I'm going to take you home, okay?" said Hannah, pushing her hair back.

"He hurt me. He just took what he wanted. It was like I wasn't even there."

The girl was so disconsolate, sobbing, words coming jagged.

"I'm—so sorry," said Hannah. "It's okay now. You're okay."

Mickey. Was he capable of raping a girl? Hurting her? Deep in her heart, she knew the answer. He'd done other bad things, dark things. Even Cricket had said that he was cruel sometimes, nasty, hurtful when he didn't get his own way, that he was sexually aggressive. That was the phrase she used.

"I want to call the police," said Libby.

There was a moment—a breath, where she almost said, *Okay, of course. Let's do that.*

But it passed, and she couldn't bring herself to support that. Mickey was her brother. Things were bad enough. The house was trashed. Maybe the police had already been called. Their house was set apart from the other houses, not on top of each other like they were in subdivisions. They were on a full three acres, but maybe one of the neighbors had heard the music or seen all the cars. Their closest neighbors, the Newmans, knew that Sophia and Leo were away.

We trust you guys. We know you'll take of the house and each other, her father had said.

Of course, Dad. Don't worry, had been her honest answer.

Her mother would rage—that she could handle. But her Dad would be so disappointed in her, in them, and that she *couldn't* handle. They had to get this whole mess cleaned up like it never happened. They had twenty-four hours before Sophia and Leo got back. She had to fix this. She was going to fix it.

"Let me take you home," said Hannah.

Libby's head lolled. How much had she had to drink? Hannah shepherded Libby into her parents' walk-in shower, where she helped the girl wash up, getting herself soaked in the process. Hannah watched as blood swirled the drain, then washed away. Then she helped Libby into her skimpy black dress, her shoes. The girl was so out of it, definitely not a good judge of what had happened between her and Mickey, right?

"I'm going to need help," she said to Cricket, who sat in the chair over by the window. She had her head down in her hands, crying softly.

Mickey, naturally, was nowhere to be seen. Just like him to take off and leave her to clean up this mess.

"Cricket," said Hannah, her voice sharp as a whip crack. "Help me get her home."

Cricket nodded, looking up, mascara running down her cheeks. She got up and they flanked Libby and helped her down the stairs.

The house had quieted down. There were just a few people in the kitchen as they came down, practically carrying Libby between them.

"She is *wasted*," someone said with a derisive laugh.

Mickey was in the hallway, fresh beer in hand, watching as they took Libby out the front door. He was dressed in fresh clothes, looked relaxed and happy, just another party, another Saturday night for Mickey. He and Hannah locked eyes. His face. She had never forgotten it—a lidded look of apathy, almost a dark glee. It sent a little pulse through Hannah.

He did it, she thought. *He raped her.*

But then the look was gone, and it was just Mickey sheepish and embarrassed. He wouldn't. He couldn't.

At the sight of him Libby started shrieking. "You raped me! You bastard!"

But people were drunk, and the music still blasted, and as Hannah and Cricket dragged her out into the night, no one acknowledged her or even looked in their direction for very long.

"Shh, shh, Libby," said Hannah. "You're okay. You're just really drunk, okay?"

In the car, the girl just passed out cold across the back seat. Hannah covered her with a sweatshirt from the trunk—one of Mickey's. They drove her home.

"He's a monster," said Cricket. "How could he do this to me?"

Hannah blew out a breath. "To *you*?"

Cricket gave her an incredulous stare. "You *don't* believe her. She was *all over* him. She's wanted him *for years*."

They drove in silence, the radio off, Libby breathing heavily in the back, the car winding through the dark rural roads. Just around a bend, a doe ran out into the street, pausing in the beam of Hannah's headlights as she put on the breaks. She honked her horn, and the doe bounded out of sight. She drove more slowly. They did not need to have a car accident right now.

"You always cover for him," said Cricket. She was resting her head against the window, looking like a sad clown with the mascara rivers and her hair wild.

"That's not true."

"He told me about Boots."

Their mother's cat. The cat had been ancient, no one even knew how old. Boots was mean, only liked Sophia. He bit and hissed and smelled horrible.

"Boots ran away."

"He didn't. Mickey told me what happened."

Hannah gripped the wheel, stayed silent.

"He killed it, right?" said Cricket when Hannah didn't say anything.

"It was an accident."

She didn't like to think about that, how she found Mickey in the garage with his friends, blood on his hands. And that smile, that same lidded look of dark glee. *What? It was a science experiment. Now we know. Cats do not have nine lives.* It was better if Mom thought the cat ran away. Hannah had almost convinced herself of that.

"It wasn't an accident," said Cricket. "You know it wasn't."

Finally, they pulled in front of Libby's house and brought the car to a stop in the short driveway. Hannah half helped, half dragged Libby from the back seat. The house was dark and quiet, the porch light burning. Hannah knew where she lived because she used to go to Camp Fire Girl meetings there; Mrs. Cruz, Libby's mom had been the group leader.

"Help me," said Hannah, breaking Cricket from her fog of self-pity.

Cricket came and helped Hannah drag Libby up the walkway.

"Stop," said Libby in a hoarse whisper. "Let me go."

"You're almost home," soothed Hannah.

They were sweating from the effort in the spring evening when they got to the front door, which they found unlocked. Together they struggled to get her inside, knocking loudly against a console table, tripping heavily over a runner. Finally, they lay her down on the couch. As they were doing that, a light came on and Libby's mom came down, even roused from sleep she looked pretty, put together in a floral robe, thick hair nearly perfect. Mrs. Cruz taught ballet at a studio in town.

"What's going on?" she asked, flipping on the living room lights.

"I'm sorry, Mrs. Cruz," said Hannah. "We were at a party. I think Libby had too much to drink."

"What?" she said, putting her hand to her chest. "Libby doesn't *drink*. She's sixteen."

Hannah nodded. "She did tonight. Maybe that explains why it hit her so hard."

Mrs. Cruz moved over to her daughter, kneeling down beside her. "Libby? Libby honey."

"Mom," Libby said, and started to cry. Mrs. Cruz took her daughter into her arms.

"She got sick," Hannah said. She was only half aware that in putting Libby in the shower, she was washing away evidence of Mickey. "We cleaned her up and brought her home."

Mrs. Cruz turned angry eyes on Hannah. "Whose party was this? Were there adults present? I thought she was at her friend Beth's studying."

"We have to go, Mrs. Cruz," said Cricket, pulling Hannah out the door. "We're past curfew to bring Libby home. I hope she feels better."

Libby drew her mother's attention by throwing up again, and Mrs. Cruz turned back to her daughter. Cricket and Hannah ran for the car, got in and drove off quickly.

They drove in silence, Hannah's mind spinning. Mickey, Libby, Boots, the house, the party, how screwed they were.

"I hate him," said Cricket softly. "I was a virgin when we met. He was my first."

"I know," said Hannah. "I'm sorry."

Second time I've heard that tonight, she thought but didn't say.

She wanted to tell Cricket other things about her brother, things she'd carried since they were little, things she'd seen. But she couldn't. It was all locked up in a box labeled Do Not Tell. *Your number one job as siblings is to always protect and take care of each other. One day your father and I will be gone and you'll be everything to each other.* Her mother had said that a hundred, a million times.

"Why do you do it?" asked Cricket. "Why do you cover up for him all the time?"

"He's my brother," she said.

"Blood is thicker than water?"

"What does that even mean?" Hannah said, thinking of the blood all over her parents' bed.

"It means that no matter what he does, you'll always side with him, like tonight. Clean up after him, cover for him."

The roads were quiet, dark. It was late, after midnight. The headlights cut the night as they wound up her street.

"You said yourself that she was hitting on him. We don't know what happened," said Hannah.

She felt Cricket's eyes, the weight of her silence. The truth was that they both knew what Mickey was capable of. They both knew that Libby wasn't lying. Neither one of them said another word.

Back at the house, everyone had left, including Mickey. Hannah and Cricket stood in the foyer and surveyed the damage. Every surface was littered with empties, garbage, cups used as ashtrays. The floor was sticky beneath Hannah's feet. In the bathroom, Hannah found a used condom floating in the toilet.

"Oh. Wow," said Cricket.

They exchanged a look and silently got to work cleaning up. By 3:00 a.m., the house was back to a somewhat recognizable state. There was a stain on the carpet that Hannah treated and hoped she would be able to eradicate in the morning. There was the broken bear. Something had exploded in the microwave. Hannah wasn't even sure what; it was pink and viscous.

Eventually, Cricket passed out on the living room couch. The sheets from Hannah's parents' bed were in the wash, the scent of bleach filling the laundry room. Hannah picked the lock on her bedroom door with a bobby pin she found in her parents' bathroom, and fell onto her bed still in her clothes, falling immediately to sleep. Maybe an hour later, she was awakened again by voices.

When she went to the top of the stairs to see what was happening, she saw Cricket and Mickey making out in the foyer. How could she? Hannah thought. After what they just saw? Libby crying in the back seat. Why was Cricket so under Mickey's spell? Why for that matter had Hannah cleaned up his mess?

Hannah watched them for a moment, Cricket's arms around Mickey's neck, Mickey pressing her against the wall. She turned and went back to her room, filled with a strange mingling of anger and longing.

37

HANNAH

June 2018

Mud, rain, pain.

Hannah woke on the ground, mouth full of dirt, rain coming down hard. The smell of gasoline. A flash of lightning, a distant rumble of thunder. Her head throbbed, pain radiating down her neck, her back, her arm. Hannah drew a ragged breath, stayed still.

Blissful unconsciousness called her back. It was a lake, a deep black lake, that she could sink into and all the pain would go away. The weight of the water pulled her under, and she slipped back into the depths.

Don't you dare just lie there and give up, Hannah Gale. Sophia. *I raised you to be stronger.*

But I'm so tired, Mom. I just want to sleep.

Sleep sweet, Mama.

That little voice, so innocent, so in love with her mama. That was the voice that had Hannah clawing back up through the depths of unconsciousness. Her eyes flew open to be greeted by the lightning and the rain.

"Gigi." She pushed herself up to sitting. "I'm coming."

A voice.

Hannah! Hannah where are you?

What the fuck had just happened? Who had hit her? What had hit her? A fallen branch? Had she been struck by lightning?

She tried to stand, hands slipping in the mud, the taste of dirt and blood in her mouth. She put tentative fingers to the huge, painful knot on her head.

Pieces came back: The electrical box—main line cut; the generator—out of fuel; tree down—and road blocked. Liza was missing. They were trapped.

Hannah!

"Cricket!" she called out, summoning her voice, her strength. "I'm here."

When Cricket came around the side of the house, her face was a mask of fear. She dropped down beside Hannah into the mud.

"Oh my god, is that blood?" Cricket asked, putting a hand to Hannah's head.

Cricket was bleeding, too, from her nose. It ran down the front of her cover-up which was otherwise transparent, soaked through. The rain was coming down around them.

"Are you hurt?" asked Hannah, letting her friend pull her to standing. Her head.

Oh god, the world was spinning.

Words, nonsensical—*a strange woman, Joshua in on it, he said she's dangerous*—came tumbling out of Cricket's mouth. In her hand, Hannah finally noticed, Cricket clutched a huge kitchen knife.

"Woah, woah, wait," said Hannah, putting both hands on her friend's shoulders. "Breathe."

They locked eyes. Cricket drew in and released a breath. Rivulets of rain trailed her face, dripped off her hair.

"There's a woman here on the property," Cricket said. "Joshua's half sister. She was also Mako's assistant at Red World. Trina? Do you remember her?"

Hannah did remember her, never liked her, assumed Mako was fucking her because she was just his type. But he went through assistants like they were disposable utensils at a company picnic. He used them up and they quit, or he fired them. So she didn't bother getting attached to or annoyed by any of them. But—*what*?

"Trina. She quit before Christmas."

"She's here," said Cricket. They were both so wet that it had stopped being an issue. The rain was loud against the leaves, the roof, the ground. "She's got some axe to grind."

"Joshua is her *half brother*?" asked Hannah.

Cricket, wet, bloody, looked like a horror movie version of herself. "That's what he said."

Hannah shook her head, her mind grappling with all of this information—none of which made any sense.

Maybe I'm still unconscious, she considered, the world still tilting unpleasantly, nausea coming in waves. *I could be dreaming. I'll wake up next to my husband at home down the hall from my daughter. And this is not happening. Right, good. Let's go with that.*

But no. The rain, coming down harder, was swamping the ground, traveled down the slope beneath their feet in a river of mud.

"What does that mean?" Hannah asked. "What does she want?"

How did the pieces fit together? Liza missing, power outage, Bruce and Mako out looking for her, Hannah hit as she tried to fix the power. Trina, Mako's old assistant on the property with dark intentions.

Then Hannah noticed in the beam of her flashlight, which lay on the ground casting its light up, that Cricket's nose was swollen and purpled. "She did this to you? Tell me what happened?"

Cricket recounted the whole scene for Hannah. When she was done, she held up the knife. "I took this and came after you. We have to find Mako and Bruce and get out of here. On foot if necessary."

"Give that to me," Hannah said, like Cricket was a child, and took the knife from her.

Hannah told her about the electrical and the generator, how someone had hit her from behind. Who had hit her? Trina? Why had Hannah been hit and left there in the mud? Maybe just to incapacitate her. So that Trina could do what?

Cricket seemed dazed, like she wasn't taking in information.

"She said we were his enablers," said Cricket, holding on to Hannah's arm and looking out into the darkness. "That we were his handmaidens."

Again, Hannah thought about Libby. In fact, she thought about Libby a lot—more than she ever said. Libby who accused Mickey of raping her that night. She went to the police with the claim. No one at school believed her; she became a kind of joke. There was no physical evidence to support her claims—maybe because of the shower. Libby didn't finish out the school year. She sank into depression, never made it to Cooper Union. A few years later, when Hannah was in college, Libby killed herself by getting drunk and driving her car into a tree not far from the house where Hannah grew up.

That just shows how fucked up she was, Mako said when Hannah called to tell him. *She was a mess.*

Hannah shook it off. Ancient history. They had more immediate problems than mistakes they'd made as teenagers.

"Okay, look," said Hannah, still holding the knife and retrieving the flashlight. "Let's just go to the other cabin. Bruce and Mako will be there, maybe Liza. We'll figure out what to do."

Cricket looked out into the dark. "She's out there. Joshua said she's dangerous. And the road is blocked."

"Says Joshua," said Hannah. "Who is obviously a liar and a bad, bad guy."

Cricket gave a quick nod. "I loved him."

"I know," said Hannah, feeling a rush of sympathy. "This—whatever it is—is fucked."

Hannah flashed her light around. They were alone. Maybe Trina had hit her and then been surprised by Cricket. Maybe she was still out there waiting, just outside the beam. Who was she really? And why was she fucking with Hannah's family?

Her head cleared, and a familiar deep focus set in, the kind that came on in crisis. She had her purpose: find her husband, get back to their daughter.

"Whoever she is," said Hannah. "She can't take all of us."

38

HENRY

2017

Luke was fussy, and Piper's dad got up from the table to walk him around so that Piper could finish eating her meal and chat with her mother.

Henry followed the older man out of the dining room of the private club. It was family night, a Wednesday evening tradition that they'd observed with Piper's family since moving back to Florida. They exited through the grand foyer, and walked together through the gate to the beach boardwalk.

The air was humid, the sky overcast, towering cumulous clouds blocking the still-blaring early evening sun. Luke always calmed outside. Henry and Piper never parked him in front of a screen the way they'd seen so many parents do. If they were out and he got squirrelly, they walked him. If it got really bad, they left. End of story.

"Oh," Luke said, sticking out one doughy arm, pointing at

the pelicans that drifted elegant and swift as fighter planes just inches off the water. "Pelicans."

"Smart boy," said Piper's dad.

Piper's parents doted on Luke the way they doted on Piper—totally besotted, neither one of them could do any wrong. Since they'd moved down, and Luke was born, Piper's dad had even seemed to warm toward Henry a bit.

"Like his mother," said Henry.

Henry and his father-in-law didn't talk much, but the relationship was respectful, each acknowledging Piper's love for the other and behaving accordingly.

The beach was empty, far from the area's busy public beaches, butting up against the state nature preserve. Up here on North Beach was the club, a smattering of insanely big houses, and little else. There was a peace and a quietude that Henry cherished.

They chatted—about Henry's work, about how Paul was adjusting to retirement, Luke's obvious intelligence and stunning beauty. *Just like our Piper—and you, of course, Henry.*

"It's nice of you," said Paul after a long silence. "To have dinner with us every Wednesday."

It was kind of an out of the blue thing to say. They'd just been talking about the Tampa Bay Lightning.

Do I have a choice? he thought but didn't say. When it came to Piper's parents, Henry didn't feel like he had that much to say about it. Especially since he didn't have any family of his own. Just Gemma who they saw at Easter usually, and when she came down to visit. Miss Gail was still a part of their lives. Henry helped at her group home when he could, had mentored some of the boys in her care.

"It's our pleasure," Henry said.

It wasn't bad, really. The club was beautiful, and the food was delicious. Paul and Gretchen were good people, kind and generous. He just always had the slight sense of being on the outside looking in. But maybe that was just him; Gretchen especially worked hard to make him feel included, appreciated.

"I never thought you were the right man for Piper," said Paul. Luke was pulling at the older man's glasses.

Okay. Wow. No surprise there. But not sure it needed to be said out loud, right?

"But I was wrong," he went on. "You're a devoted husband. A loving father. You had a rough hand dealt and still you succeeded in your life. That's—pretty amazing."

Henry felt himself choking up a little, looked away. Paul gently wrestled his glasses back from Luke who yelled in protest.

"Easy there, buddy. Give PopPop back his glasses," said Henry softly.

Luke chilled. He was easy. An easy kid, happy most of the time, and not prone to melt down unless he was tired or hungry. And he probably *was* ready for bed. Wednesday nights were late for him.

"I just felt that needed saying," said Paul when Henry didn't know how to respond. "If not now, when? Right?"

"You've been good to me," said Henry finally, struggling through the awkwardness. "I'm not sure I would have survived if not for your family. You're right. She did deserve better. But here we are."

"No, son," said Paul, looking away. "There's nothing *better* than strong, loyal, and loving. You're all those things. And we'll always be here for you all. That's what family does."

Family.

"Thank you, sir."

Luke started to fuss again, weakly, but definitely building. The corners of his mouth were pulled down into a comical frown and he rubbed at his eyes.

"It's past his bedtime," said Henry.

"Best be going."

Piper and Gretchen looking like versions of each other in colors that coordinated—Piper in a navy shift dress, Gretchen in a periwinkle sweater set—were already exiting, the valet bringing the cars around. Just as Henry was buckling Luke into the car seat, his phone buzzed. He looked down to see a text that made his stomach bottom out.

Call me. We need to talk.

Cat.

Because West had encouraged Henry to keep up his connection to Cat, keep her talking, he waited until Luke was down and Piper was in the shower, then went out to the pool deck to call her.

He walked over the pavers, down to the gate that led to their dock. Their small boat sat on a lift; they hadn't touched it since Luke had been born and were thinking about selling—which he'd been told was the way of boats. Love them, then feel guilty about not using them, then sell.

Through the sliding doors, their great room and kitchen were visible. Across the Intracoastal, similar smallish houses, and some giant ones lined up along the seawall, interior lights glowing, palm trees lit by landscape lighting. He stood a moment, listening to the water lapping against the dock, the hull of his neighbor's much bigger boat. A halyard clanged in the breeze, and he drew the salt air into his lungs.

Before he dialed, he thought about his father-in-law and what his words had meant. More than Henry would have thought. All the time he'd spent looking for family, and now here he was, a part of one, helping to grow it. Maybe family is more than where you come from, maybe it's also where you're going, what you build with the choices you make.

"Henry," she said when she picked up. "Call off your dog."

"My dog?"

"West, the private detective you have asking questions."

Henry hadn't talked to West in a while. The last he heard, he hadn't come up with much. Most of the cases were closed, deaths declared natural, accidental, or the result of suicide. The tech guy in Fort Lauderdale was deep in debt with the wrong kind of people; his murder was a presumed organized crime hit. West had been digging around, talking to investigating officers, chatting with a landlord here, a neighbor there. So far, he hadn't come up with anything solid to connect the deaths to Cat.

You know, Henry, there are high-risk people and low-risk people.

What does that mean?

So, take your Piper for example. A nice girl from a good family. She buckles her seat belt, doesn't drink and drive, is careful with herself and her life. Low risk.

Okay.

Then there's someone like—

Like me.

Okay, yeah. Your mother is murdered. You don't know your father. You get sent into the system. You manage to find your way, to turn yourself from high risk to low risk. Another person in the aftermath of such a loss develops an addiction, PTSD, or depression. High-risk behaviors could result.

So you're saying my half siblings might be those kind of people.

It's a loose theory. None of them were making particularly good choices.

So not genetics. Circumstances.

Or a little of both.

"He's not my dog," said Henry. "He's just a friend. I didn't hire him if that's what you mean."

It was interesting that she knew about West. Not interesting. Worrisome. How? What did that mean?

"Look," she said. "Can you meet?"

From where he stood, he could see inside the house. Piper was in the kitchen making her nightly cup of peppermint tea, hair up, sweats on. She came to the glass door and peered out. He knew he couldn't be seen from where he stood; he lifted a hand anyway. It wasn't a secret. She knew about Cat, that he still talked to her from time to time. She didn't interfere, but it was one of those things—like the Thursday night poker game his colleagues organized, or his buddy Tim's yearly Cigar-B-Q which were debauched evenings of red meat, good bourbons, and fine cigars. Every once in a while was okay; but anything that veered into the unhealthy, the dangerous, and Piper would speak up. Like West said, she was a low-risk person. Likely she was the reason Henry was, too. There was no suggestion that Cat be invited for dinner. She was not on the Christmas card list.

"We're talking now," he said. "What's up?"

"There are things I want to talk about but not on the phone."

"Okay."

"I found him, Henry. I know who he is."

Henry didn't say anything. He felt a hard tug to her, a strong connection. He cared about her even though he was starting to think she might be not just a little unstable as he'd said to West, but actually diagnosable. Henry had suggested that she let all of it go, build a life, stop digging into the past. But it was clear that she couldn't do that.

"Who is he, Cat?"

"Meet me."

"Are you in Florida?"

"I am," she said, and it gave him a little chill. "Not too far from you, Henry."

Piper had planted herself on the sectional, flipped on the television. She looked small and vulnerable on the big couch, under the plush blanket. He felt a swell of protectiveness—for Piper, for Luke, for their life.

Cat—she was dangerous.

"Let's talk one last time," she said. "After that, I'll leave you alone, okay? I know that's what you want. You're a good guy, Henry. One of the few."

"Okay," he said. "Where and when?"

He half lied to Piper the next day, told her that he was meeting West after work. Those forensic detectives, he said, had turned up some new information on his mother's murder.

"Have him here," she'd suggested on the phone. "I'll cook."

"I'd rather not," he said. "I want to keep the past and the present separate. You know?"

It wasn't fair to say that, using her words against her. She sighed, unable to argue with her own logic.

"Okay," she said, sounding worried. "Do you want me to come? My mom can take Luke."

"No, don't do that," he said on the phone, lowering his voice.

He was climbing the ranks fast in the cybersecurity firm where he worked in Tampa; he'd been promoted twice since he started three years ago. But he still sat in a cube when he was in the office.

Around him the office was bright, windows looking out onto Tampa Bay and the glittering waters. The office hummed with conversation, ringing phones, pinging emails. Usually, he was in the data center among the rows and rows of servers and wires, the hum of electricity, the dark and refrigerated space. But today there were meetings. He was happier with machines than people. His degree was in computer engineering; computers made logical sense. People were confusing. This had never stopped being true for him.

"I'll tell you everything, I promise."

"Henry," Piper said. "*What's* going on?"

He'd been distracted since his call with Cat, restless last night, not sleeping well in general. Piper had noticed, kept pressing him to talk. He hadn't told her about the Miami murder, or that West had been casting around for more information on the deaths of his other half siblings. Henry had mentioned that he'd talked to Cat, but not that they'd planned to meet.

"It's time I came clean, honey," he said, lowering his voice to whisper. "I'm having an affair. With Dawn."

Dawn was the grandmotherly lady who ran the office.

"Very funny. Seriously."

"No," he said. "This stuff—with my mother—it's just. I don't want it in our life. Our life now, which we've built together. But at the same time I need closure, I guess. It feels dark, poisonous."

This was true without it being the whole truth.

"It's just the past, Henry. It can't hurt us."

He wished *that* were true. "You're right."

Another sigh, a pause. Then, "You don't have to do things alone."

"I'll invite West for dinner next week." Henry hoped that this was concession enough. "If there's anything important we'll discuss it together, okay?"

He heard Luke fussing. He was her little mini-me. If she was upset, Luke always reflected that.

"Hey, little man," he said.

"Da! Da!"

"Okay," Piper said, resigned and turning her attention to Luke. "Do what you have to do."

"I'll tell Dawn you said hi."

"Loser."

Now he waited in the dark. The Sunshine Skyway Bridge towered, its twin sails lit yellow and white against the night riven with stars. A sliver of moon hung in the sky.

He'd parked on the south fishing pier, the site of the original bridge torn down after a 1980 disaster where a freighter crashed into the support structure. The bridge collapsed, plunging cars into the bay, an area tragedy that people still talked about.

The sun had set and a few fishermen still stood at the pier edges, but mainly he was alone, the water glittering around him.

"Maybe she won't show," said West, his voice tinny over the car speaker.

Cat was almost an hour late.

Henry had turned off the tracking on his phone. Piper would check his location sooner or later and he didn't want to have to explain why he was at the fishing pier instead of Frenchy's where he'd told her he was meeting West. At some point, she'd notice that his location services were off, but those kind of glitches were more explainable.

"I'll give her a few more minutes," said Henry.

"You care about her," said West. He was parked in the dark behind Henry. He couldn't see the older man's vehicle.

"I understand her, I guess," said Henry. "She seems lost to me. Looking for things in the wrong places, in the wrong way."

"What if she's a killer?"

"Then it's a good thing you're right behind me."

"You're not afraid of her."

"No," he said. "We have a chemistry."

"Hmm," said West skeptically. "How are you doing with that other piece?"

The forensic detectives West had told him about had *in fact* made a connection.

Using the DNA stored from Alice's crime scene, they were able to make a match with some of Tom Watson's cousins through one of the at-home DNA testing services. These found cousins had been forthcoming that Tom was a bad guy, in trouble on and off most of his life, a petty thief, and often violent against women—though he was never arrested or charged for any crimes.

It seemed more likely than ever that he was Alice's killer.

"I'm still processing," said Henry. He still needed to talk everything through with Piper. Everything.

"Fair enough," he said. "Technology, right? It's all still like sci-fi to me, some of this stuff."

Yeah, but it was ancient, too. DNA was the language God used to program human beings. It was a source code—a list of commands to be compiled into an executable program. There was the hand you were dealt and what you did with it that defined your life.

A pair of headlights approached and a black BMW drifted into the space in front of him. It sat a moment idling, then went dark.

Cat climbed out. She was tall and slim in dark jeans, and tight T-shirt, light leather jacket as she approached Henry's car. He keyed down the volume on the phone.

"Take a walk?" she said when he rolled down the window.

He looked down the long expanse of the pier. A road to nowhere, ending in the big waters where Tampa Bay let out into the Gulf of Mexico. He looked over at the bridge. Over three hundred people had committed suicide from the Sunshine Skyway.

"A long walk off a short pier?" he said.

She smiled but it was sad. He slipped his phone into his pocket, climbed out of the car and they started to walk, a stiff, humid breeze whipped at them, pushing her hair around wild like snakes on the head of Medusa. She tamed it with an elastic, dug her hands into her pockets.

When they'd passed the last fisherman, she came to a stop, leaned against the concrete railing.

"The last time we got together I upset you," she said after some awkward moments passed.

He saw himself in her face, in the long nose, and the dark, deep-set eyes, in the angle of her mouth. His sister, half sister. What did it mean?

Alice was my sister, Gemma had said recently, when they talked about the new DNA discovery. *But she was a stranger, too. Al-*

ways to herself, always closed off from us. Left as soon as she could and never came back.

"It wasn't just you," he said now to Cat. "I was upset about a lot of things. Piper had left me. I just felt like I had to make a decision—between the past and the present."

She nodded slowly. "And can they be separated?"

"I think so," he said. "Maybe."

She reached into her pocket and pulled out an old photograph—square and creased, faded. Henry slipped his glasses from his jacket pocket, and took the photo from her.

A slim man in a black suit smoked a cigarette, his dark hair slicked back. He leaned against some kind of stone ledge, a city behind him, palm trees dark in the gray background. His eyes were lidded, smile wan. The resemblance was uncanny; Henry could be looking at a picture of himself. The date stamp read November 1980, four years before Henry was born.

"Is this him?"

"Yes."

"Where did you get the picture?"

"From his sister. She lives in Miami. She popped up a while ago in my relative group. We had lunch."

"Love connection?"

"Not exactly," she said. "But she had information about him that she was willing to share. In fact, unlike Marta, she was aching to get it off her chest. Henry, he was a bad man."

"Bad how?"

"Do you remember the Miami Slayer?"

Henry shook his head.

"In Miami in the '80s someone was breaking into the homes of single woman, waiting for them to return, then raping, torturing, and killing them. There were seven women in total between the year of 1982 and 1990 when the perpetrator was finally caught."

Henry didn't say anything. He wondered how much West could hear, if he was still on the line listening; he'd never ended the call, hoped it had transferred to the phone from the Bluetooth.

The photo in his hand took on a different energy, a kind of darkness emanating from it.

"Our father, Roy Alfaro was tried and convicted, sentenced to death," said Cat, her voice strained. "He died in a prison yard fight a few years later in the Union Correctional Institution waiting for execution. The same prison that held Ted Bundy."

The information landed like a punch to the gut. Henry felt physically ill, like he had in the bar. He drew in a breath, released it, willed himself to be solid.

"All those years as a young man, hanging around Miami, raping and killing, he was donating his sperm."

The world was spinning. "Are you sure about this?"

"I'm pretty sure, yeah," she said. "It's what his sister told me. And my research confirms it. There's no DNA evidence stored for him, the technology back then wasn't what it is today. So we can't one hundred percent confirm paternity. But his sister was a twenty-five percent match for me. So…"

The nausea passed and it was replaced by a flood of anger.

"Are you happy, Cat? You never gave up, you dug around and finally figured it out."

His voice rang out in the night. She looked down at her feet.

"Let me ask you," he went on. "How does this serve us? What *good* does it do us?"

She looked up at him with a frown. "It's the truth."

"The truth is overrated."

"You would rather live your life not knowing where you came from?"

"Actually, yes," he said. "I'd rather not have known this, Cat. It's toxic. It's poison."

He was embarrassed when angry tears trailed down his face. He thought of Piper, of Luke, of the things his father-in-law had said. He swiped at his face, turned to the water. It churned, black and deep. He should just fall into it, let it wash him away.

"I'm sorry," said Cat. She put a tentative hand on his shoulder. "Maybe you're right. Just forget it. You're a good guy, Henry. Whatever dark thing lived in his DNA, it hasn't touched you."

That feeling, the one he'd had since he was a kid, how he wasn't enough, that there was something deeply wrong with him. It was a tsunami inside him, rushing, swamping, raging.

"Genetics," Cat went on when Henry stayed quiet. "As much as they know, they *don't know* even more. A gene for violence doesn't mean you'll be violent. A gene for cancer doesn't mean you're destined get sick. It's *complicated*."

"Cat," he said, lowering his voice to a whisper. "Is it you? Are you behind the deaths of our half siblings, of Marta Bennet? That guy in Fort Lauderdale."

She leaned on the concrete railing, pushing in close to him. He didn't shift away from her. In fact, he wanted to take her into his arms and hold her, comfort her. He loved her because they were connected. More than that. He just loved her, even though she was broken.

"A few of us are okay, you know?" she said. "Like you. You're living an honest, hardworking life. You're contributing something, loving people, taking care of your family."

Low risk, that's what West called it. You don't drive drunk. You buckle your seat belt. You don't lie to people or steal from them. You don't hurt anyone. You donate to charity, volunteer for a cause.

"Some of us are not," she continued.

A big freighter drifted toward the bridge, a marine horn sounding, announcing its arrival to port.

"Some people," she said, shaking her head. She let go of a little laugh. "Let's put it this way. It's just better for everyone if they're removed from the gene pool."

Her voice had taken on an angry edge. Henry stared at the hard lines of her profile, her words sinking in.

"That's eugenics, Cat," he said.

She shrugged slowly. "I prefer to think of it as Darwinism."

"Darwinism is *organic*. It's natural selection." She didn't turn to look at him, just kept her eyes on the churning water. "Eugenics is something else. It's someone making a decision, usually a very bad one, about who should procreate or not. It's the stuff of Nazis and mad scientists trying to create a superrace. It's state-sanctioned sterilization of the poor, the mentally ill, the criminal. It's dark, Cat. It's *wrong*."

She turned her gaze up at the sky. He didn't think she was going to answer him.

Then, "Sometimes nature doesn't know what's good for it. It needs a little help. There are a couple of us who feel this way, Henry. A couple of our half siblings."

He stared at the hard lines of her profile, the determined set of her jaw. He could hardly believe what he was hearing.

"So—what?" he asked finally. "You're trying to figure out which of his children are monsters? And then you're—*killing* them?"

She shook her head. "I never said that."

"Look," he said turning to her. He took her by the shoulders and stared right into her eyes. They were black pools, cold and swirling. "You can drop this, whatever it is you're doing. Just walk away. Start right here, right now. Be a part of our family, build a life of your own. You're smart. You're beautiful. It's all right in front of you."

She smiled, put a hand to his cheek. For a moment, her face softened.

"See, Henry? You *are* one of the good ones. We won't see each other again, okay? You're free. You know the truth about our father, but it doesn't matter. You've made your choices and they're the right ones. Enjoy your life."

She leaned in and kissed him softly on the cheek. He reached for her hand, but her fingers slipped through his. Henry watched as she walked away, got in her car, and drove off.

He broke down right there on the pier, years of pain and sadness finally reaching a brutal crescendo. He wept great heaving sobs for Alice, his strange, unhappy mother, for the dark inheritance of his psychotic father, for his wife who deserved better, for his son who had to carry forward his ugly legacy.

For Cat, his sister, who'd let it all turn her into a monster.

After a while, West came up behind him, put a hand on his back. Henry pulled himself together, quieted. The night and the water and the salt air swirled around him.

"Let's get you home, son," said West. "Time to go home."

39

HANNAH

June 2018

They made their way down the path, holding hands and pressing into each other, like Hansel and Gretel in the haunted woods. The rain tapped against the leaves, sluicing down the path in front of them. A distant flash of lightning, then thunder again low and faraway. The scent of wet forest debris filled Hannah's sinuses. It was an aroma she used to find oddly comforting.

She held the knife, feeling the weight of it. Cricket had the flashlight, the beam bouncing on the path in front of them. They passed the gazebo where Hannah and Bruce had had their stolen moments a few hours earlier and it seemed like a week had passed.

"Do you think this is because of Libby?" asked Cricket, her voice small. "Like it's payback?"

"Why would it have anything to do with her?" asked Hannah. She was shivering, from cold, from fear.

Cricket's eyes were wide, her skin so pale it almost looked blue. Her pretty blond hair hung in heavy wet ringlets. They kept slipping in the wet, holding on to each other for support.

"I mean maybe Trina is connected to her somehow? Like this is revenge for what we did?"

"We didn't *do* anything," said Hannah firmly. But it wasn't true. They'd effectively—if not exactly—covered for Mickey. They'd encouraged Libby to wash, took her home. They'd sided with Mickey, even though on some level, even then, both of them knew—or suspected—that Mickey wasn't always an honest guy. It was a thing that she'd carried with her, had never forgotten.

"If anybody *did* anything, it was Mickey," she said. That was true, too. "Why should we be taking the blame for his actions?"

"Because we *helped*," said Cricket, her voice coming up an octave. "Maybe she's right—we're his handmaidens."

"No," said Hannah, clinging to her friend. "We still don't know the truth of what happened."

"Don't we?" asked Cricket. This was a complete reversal from their earlier conversation. Cricket was always the denier when it came to what happened to Libby. But Hannah wasn't going to look at this right now. She couldn't. They had to stay strong, solid, if they were going to fight. And they were.

Cricket tried to pull her to a stop, but Hannah didn't let her, kept her friend moving. The cabin; it had to be around the bend.

"Let's do this later," said Hannah. "But remember—whatever Mickey did, *he* did, not us. Women are always taking the blame for the bad deeds of men. And, you know what? That's bullshit."

The cabin appeared around the turn, a simple log structure with a small porch, and painted green door. Quaint, inviting. But windows dark; the door stood ajar.

They both stopped, Cricket spinning the flashlight around,

shining it into the glistening trees. There was a rustling, something small skittering away from the light.

"Bruce!" Hannah called.

But there was no answer, and the door gaped open leaking darkness. Every nerve ending in her body told her to go in the opposite direction. But if her brother and husband were in there, if they were hurt, she had to go after them. There was no other choice.

Cricket held the flashlight like a sword, banishing the darkness in front of them. They climbed the creaking steps up to the porch and went inside.

40

CRICKET

It was hard to take in the moment.

Mako was on the ground holding a frighteningly still Liza. She seemed so slight and long, like a skein of silk in his thick arms. Bruce stood over them, looking down, his face a mask of concern. When he saw them come through the door, he rushed over to Hannah, holding her back, taking her into his arms.

"What are you doing here? I told you to wait at the house," he said. "Oh my god, what happened? Are you bleeding?"

Cricket felt frozen at the door, unable to move in, unable to turn away. She wanted to run, suddenly, away from here, away from this place. But her legs felt rooted. There was nowhere else to go with Joshua and Trina out there somewhere.

"Oh, baby, nononono," Mako moaned. "Don't leave me, please."

He rocked back and forth slowly, head down. The first feeling of which Cricket was aware was jealousy. Mako, who she'd loved all her adult life, had never loved her liked that. God, that was pathetic wasn't it? At a moment like this. But she felt tears start to flood.

Hannah pushed from Bruce's arms to Mako and Liza, kneeling to ground. "Is she—?"

She put a hand to her sister-in-law's ghostly white throat, sighed with relief. "She's still alive. There's a pulse."

"There's so much blood," said Mako. He was covered with it; Liza's clothes were black with it. His eyes were glassy, face slack. Shock.

"What happened to her? Who did this?" asked Hannah, voice high with panic. "Where is the blood coming from?"

"She's been stabbed I think?" said Mako, more of a question than an answer. "Someone stabbed her? Why? What did she ever do to anyone?"

Hannah had dropped the knife to the floor beside them. She picked it up now and used it to cut open Liza's top.

"Cricket," Hannah said. "Help me."

Cricket was startled into action, moved to help as Hannah tore away the fabric, revealing a big gaping wound in Liza's abdomen between her navel and her rib cage. It pulsed with her heartbeat, oozing black blood. Cricket fought the urge to vomit, to flee, to get away. *Stay solid. Stay strong*, she told herself, *for Hannah.*

Hannah was stoic and grim as she shed her coat, then took off her own shirt to press it against Liza's wound.

"There's—no time," said Hannah, pushing Mako away. "We have to stop this bleeding right now, and get her to a hospital. I need more cloths. Someone find towels in the bathroom."

"How?" said Mako, looking helpless. "*How* do we stop it?"

"We apply pressure, keep changing out the cloths. And someone has to go move that tree and get an ambulance here. Fast."

Hannah, always in charge. She gave Bruce the abridged version of everything that had happened, while Cricket tried to leech off some of her power, her energy. She found the small bathroom off the open-plan space, and brought back the basket of hand towels from the teak shelf under the sink. Hannah changed it out right away, her shirt already dark with blood from the wound.

"Who are they really? Joshua and Trina? What do they want?" asked Bruce.

"I have *no idea*," said Hannah.

Cricket couldn't keep her eyes off Liza, who looked so tiny and unearthly, like she was drifting away. Cricket felt sick with self-loathing and regret. For Libby, for Liza, for all the ways she'd betrayed herself and others for Mickey. They were all so quiet, Hannah working on Liza, Bruce staring at the open door. He kept trying his phone, searching for a signal.

Outside the rain kept pounding. A crack of thunder seemed to break some spell.

"Okay," said Bruce. "We're going to take the car and find where the tree is down, get a signal and call the police. Hannah and Cricket, get to the car. Mako and I will carry Liza."

"It's a really bad idea to move her," said Hannah, looking up at her husband.

"We are leaving because we can't stay here waiting for whoever did that to come back," said Bruce, level and firm. "Now. Let's go."

Hannah nodded at the logic, glanced down at Liza. She changed the towel out again and rose, moved over to Cricket, pulled her toward the door.

They stopped in their tracks as Trina filled the door frame, the gun in her hand glinted in the flashlight beam.

Joshua came up behind her, standing a full head taller. They walked inside and closed the door.

"No one is going anywhere, of course," said Trina. "Sorry. Not Sorry."

Bruce came up and stood in front of Hannah and Cricket, while Mako stayed weeping on the floor, still with Liza's head in his lap. When he looked up and saw her, his whole face went slack with shock.

"You?"

"Yes, me, Mako," she said coolly. "It's going to take more than a payoff to get rid of your problems this time."

"You did this?" Mickey said, his voice taut with anger. "*You* did this to her?"

"No, brother," said Trina easily. "*You* did."

41

BRACKEN

He watched from the cab of his truck as Bob made short work of the tree, pushing it to the side of the road with the plow. Bracken observed the rain, the wild dance of the leaves, the night lightening and going dark again.

The other man pulled up beside him and Bracken rolled down his window. Rain tapped at his face, the interior of the car.

"Follow you up? Make sure you don't run into any more obstacles?" asked Old Bob.

The other man's skin was darkly tanned; he had fine lines around his eyes. Tonight, his long gray hair was pulled back. It wasn't like him to offer more than had been asked; but Bracken was grateful for the help. There was some kind of electricity in the air and not just the storm.

"No," he said. "I've got it from here. I'll pay you out, no matter whether the guest makes good on his offer."

Bob offered the rare smile, one that Bracken couldn't quite read, as if the guy had a secret. "Just happy to help."

Bracken engaged the engine and made his way slowly up the twisting road, careful to watch the sides of the road for deer which might leap out to their death without warning. The road was swamped, and great plumes of water washed up as he made his way. There were branches and other debris in the road, but the wheels of his truck rolled right over. In a couple of hours if there was much more rain, the roads would be impassable until the water receded.

Usually, he'd see the glow of Overlook up ahead, the loft window, the landscape lighting. But tonight there was nothing. He'd checked his app; some of the cameras were hardwired— the one in the living room, in the guest cabin—the rest battery operated. But, of course, the router was down so none of the cameras, even if they were still working, could broadcast their signal to the router.

That generator was brand-new and he'd inspected it himself. There was no reason for it not to have come on. Unless. Unless someone had messed with it.

What was going on up there? Something. Anything.

In his years watching, he'd seen the whole rainbow of humanity.

He'd watched a man abuse his wife; a mother slap her daughter. He'd heard people say ugly, terrible things to each other— *I never loved you; I wish you were dead.* Likewise, he'd witnessed great tenderness, affection, listened to belly laughs, and people in the throes of passion. A great mosaic of human experience playing out before him on his smart phone or computer screen. Life, relationships, how people were entwined, enmeshed, how they loved each other, hurt each other, needed or discarded each other. His own inner life was isolated and still. No family, few friends. He'd always felt alone, even as a child, apart. Watching was his way of connecting with the world. Even with May, for whom he felt a great deal of tenderness, he observed her, his feelings for her, for her daughter Leilani.

The phone rang and he pressed the button on the wheel to answer.

"Hey," said May. "Why'd you run off?"

"Problems at the Overlook," he said. "I didn't want to wake you."

"Couldn't wait until tomorrow? The weather's bad."

"Power's out, generator's down. The guests are in distress."

"Did you check the cameras?" she asked. The question shocked him a bit. She knew about the cameras. He didn't say anything.

"It's okay," she said. "Bracken, it's okay. I know why you do it."

He couldn't find words, washed in shame.

"There's a place for you here, with us," she said after a moment of silence. "I want you to know that. You don't have to stay on the outside, looking in. You can be home with us. Leilani and I—we care about you."

"That's—nice, May. Thank you."

"Nice?" she said. He heard a smile in her voice. She was a person who didn't judge; you could just be you with May. She was beautiful and smart, hardworking, slow to anger, a great cook, a passionate, thoughtful lover. She was real.

"It's—um—good," he said, throat constricted. He thought about hanging up, he felt so awkward, so tense. But he surprised himself by answering honestly. "I want that. I do."

"Okay," she said easily. "So when you're done up there, come home to me."

He made a noise, a kind of assenting grunt. Thankfully she hung up so that he didn't have to answer further. In the dark of the cab, his heart raced, shame heated his face. He thought that the cameras were his secret, his only way of connecting to, of understanding the confounding world of people. But she knew. She knew and she hadn't judged him.

Something that had been constricted inside him loosened. His mother had died young. His dad was a hardworking man who didn't have much time or patience for a kid. He'd been there, though—at school, at games. A silent, stoic presence that Bracken could never quite figure out. Even now, his dad was an old man living in a memory care facility the next town over. Bracken went to see him twice a week, spent an hour or two telling him things about the houses, about the people he saw on the cameras. His dad just stared, blank, empty, whatever he felt or thought about how his life had passed, about Bracken, locked up tight. *Who are you?* Bracken often wound up thinking in the inevitable silence that fell when Bracken stopped talking. *Did you get what you wanted out of life?* But he never asked that, and his dad couldn't have answered anyway.

He thought about his dad, about May, about his guests as the house came into sight.

Even though everything was dark and quiet, there was the air of trouble about it. The cars were all parked; one of them, a black Infinity, was damaged in the back, trunk munched. The Tesla and the Volvo sat in the drive.

Bracken parked and sat a moment, observing—the stillness, the night.

Then he headed for the electrical box and generator, not even bothering to knock on the door. He was surprised that no one had come out, as amped up as they all were about the power out, the road blocked.

He saw it right away, that the main circuit had been cut. He smelled the faint odor of gasoline. On the ground, there was a collection of boot prints. There in the beam of his flashlight on the side of the house, the bloody impression of a hand.

What the hell was going on here?

He headed down the path toward the house.

42

HENRY

June 2018

The beautiful house was dark and Henry was seized with doubt suddenly. It probably wasn't a good idea to walk up and ring the bell at nearly midnight.

He still had Detective West in his head. They had spoken again, the day after Henry and Cat's encounter on the fishing pier. He'd been processing all the dark and terrible things she'd told him, the things she'd said. He'd told Piper everything, just as he promised.

She wasn't afraid, didn't recoil from him as he'd feared.

"You have to let it go," she'd said simply. "We don't choose our origins. We choose our present. And you have to separate yourself from her darkness, from your father's. It's just the past. It can't hurt us. I won't let it."

Piper was raw power, all love. He still remembered her on the soccer field—how she was faster than any boy, smarter, stronger in her tiny way. Now as his wife and Luke's mother, she was an engine, a battery, the energy that kept them all moving forward together. She was pregnant again, another child on the way. Their family was growing.

Luke was an angelic child, calm and happy. There was no darkness in him. Henry knew that for a fact. Because whatever darkness Henry brought to the mix, Piper's light was stronger.

"You stay with us," she said. "Leave everything else behind."

Piper was right. But Henry couldn't stop thinking about Cat.

"It's her, Henry," Detective West had told him. "I have the footage. My pal in Miami shared the security tapes of the condo building. It shows her entering the building with him, and leaving a couple of hours later alone. They have not been able to identify her yet. But we know who she is and I have to tell them. It's obstruction of justice if we don't."

"Give me a day to find her," said Henry. "Let me convince her to turn herself in."

Detective West had been quiet for a moment on the phone. "I'm not sure that's a good idea."

"She's my sister."

"Not really, you know," said West, not unkindly. "I mean, you share biology. But honestly, that's it, right? Your family, your true family—that's Piper and Luke. You owe *them* your life. You have to protect yourself and stay safe, so that you can take care of them."

That was true. Undeniably. But it wasn't the whole truth.

"I want to help her." It sounded weak, and that wasn't the whole truth, either.

"She might be beyond that."

Still Henry had convinced West to give him twenty-four hours, and then the next call he made was to his aunt Gemma, the best detective he knew.

Together, they combed through Henry's various pages—his Origins and Ancestry accounts, the DNA Detectives Facebook pages, the Donor Sibling Registry. They found some more half siblings, people who had only recently been added. Henry started cross-referencing names with news searches, looking for people linked to crimes and wrongdoing. It didn't take long to figure out, given their last conversation, who she might be targeting.

This has to stop, he'd texted her. Please, let me help you.

Stay in your lane, Henry.

You're better than this, Cat.

I'm not. I'm really not.

What's your endgame?

I'm going to root out what I can...

And then?

And then, when I get too tired, I'm going to write a fittingly dramatic end to this ugly story of mine.

The rest of his texts went unanswered after that.

Now he sat in front of the dark house, wondering if he was doing the right thing. He had no idea where Cat was, but he knew that the person who lived in this house was related to her. Because he was related to Henry, added just six months ago, another almost familiar face on his list of Origins matches.

From a Google search, he'd learned that this person had been accused of a crime as a young man. A young woman accused him of rape. But he'd gotten away with it, if he had been guilty. And later that girl committed suicide.

The name turned up again on some of the online forums about tech jobs. These posts contained veiled comments about his corruption, his lack of ethics, his appetites. Stay away, one person warned, from the company, from the man.

He touched me.

He threatened me.

He came on to me, but when I went to Human Resources, I was fired.

He was just Cat's type, seemingly embodying all the worst of their father's DNA.

And this was his house, a grand waterfront home, all white stucco and blue glass, towering palms glowing in the elaborate landscaping, a huge gleaming Sea Ray sitting in the dock out back. The house was valued at nearly two million on Homes. com; the boat, new, cost close to half a million. Other things Henry and Gemma had found online during their deep dive into records: he was late on his mortgage; he hadn't paid his taxes last year.

Finally, Henry steeled himself and climbed out of the car into the humid night air. The croaking of frogs, the clinking of halyards.

He walked up the impeccably manicured path to the front door, motion sensor lights coming on as he moved.

But when he rang the bell, no one answered. He stood, waited. Thought about leaving. What was he going to say to the guy when he opened the door?

Hey, I think our half sister is going to try to kill you.

I'm Henry, by the way, nice to meet you. Did you know our donor father was a serial rapist and killer who died in prison? Messed up, right?

Oh my god. He should never have come.

But he rang the bell again; and saw a light come on inside.

He peered in the glass door and watched as an older woman with wild gray-and-black hair, a robe over pink pajamas, and thick glasses, shuffled down the stairs finally, looking sleepy and confused.

She clutched a cell phone in her hand. Henry felt buzzy with nerves; took a step back from the door to show her he meant no harm.

She flipped on the light and regarded him through the thick glass.

"Can I help you?" she asked, frowning.

"I'm sorry to come so late. But I'm looking for the owner of this house—Michael?"

The old woman shook her head. "No," she said. "My son and daughter-in-law live here."

Did he have the wrong house? He checked the address on his phone.

No, this was it.

"Michael," started Henry. He hadn't thought this through. "I have reason to believe he might be in danger."

The old woman pulled her robe tighter around her, seemed to size him up.

Did he look like a good guy? Hard to say—a strange man on your doorstep in the middle of the night was never a good thing, right? She wasn't going to swing the door open for him and welcome him inside, listen to his bizarre tale.

"What kind of danger?" she asked.

"It's a—long story," he said. "But I really need to find and talk to him. It's urgent. I wouldn't have come here like this if not."

He felt the other woman size him up. Whatever she saw softened her, but she didn't move closer to the door.

"Michael," she said. "That's my daughter-in-law's brother—they call him Mako now."

Her daughter-in-law. Another half sibling? Someone else in Cat's sights?

"Right, Mako," he said. "He owns a big gaming company. Red World is their most successful game."

"They're away. All of them, together." She looked worried now. "Hannah and Bruce rent this place from him."

Henry's heart sank. "Away where?"

"I'm sorry," said the woman, shaking her head. He could see

on the screen of her cell phone that she'd already punched in 911 but hadn't hit Send. "Who are you? What do you want?"

Even that was too long a story to tell here. He tried though and it all came out in a tumble, starting with his name and devolving into a ramble about his mother, his aunt, his genealogy journey, Cat. The woman watched him, eyes widening, still clutching her phone.

"It sounds unbelievable," he said when he was done. "I know that. But I'm telling you the truth."

"I'll call them," she said after a moment. "How's that?"

"Okay, yeah," he said. "That's good."

He nodded and watched as she dialed. It was so hot even in the dark, the humidity raising sweat on his brow. His clothes felt sticky, sweat soaking the back of his shirt.

After a moment, the other woman spoke. "Hannah, it's Lou. Everything's okay here but can you call when you get a chance? It's not urgent; Gigi and I are fine but it does seem important."

The older woman looked at the phone with a frown, then turned the frown on him. "It went straight to voicemail. You don't know my daughter-in-law; that's not right."

They were still on opposite sides of the door.

"I'll tell you where they are," she said. "But I'm also going to call the local police up there."

That was fair. He could only protect Cat for so long. He wasn't just there to help her. He wanted to keep her from harming anyone else. That was the reason, the real reason, he'd left his family on this errand, one Piper had not sanctioned and would be very angry to learn about. She thought he was at the data center, called in on an emergency. He'd lied to her and she would probably find out. And there would be hell to pay. But. He needed to do this. Not just for Cat. But also for himself. For Luke. For their baby on the way. He needed to be a good man, to do the right thing. If he could stop one bad act, maybe that balanced the scales, proved that his DNA was not the thing that made him, that his actions were. He'd tried to explain that to West.

I'm not sure that's the way it works, son, he'd said. *But I hear you. Twenty-four hours. That's it.*

"Okay," Henry said now.

"Wait here."

The older woman moved off into the darkness of the house and Henry waited on the porch listing to the whisper of fronds and the sound of water lapping against hulls. The moon was high and full, painting the sky silvery.

When she came back, she looked even more concerned.

"The police say that there's a big storm up there. That power and cell signals are down, roads impassable. But they'll try to get someone to them."

"I'll get up there," he said. "I promise."

She looked at him uncertainly, then seemed to reach some internal decision to trust him—but not enough to open the door.

"What's your number?" she said. "I'll text you the address."

He gave it to her and when her message came through, he texted her back with his full name and home address, so that she could trust him, so that she could reach him.

She didn't say anything as he walked away, just looked at him worriedly. Somewhere he heard a child crying and the woman went up the stairs.

In the car, he plugged the address into his GPS. It was a long drive, so he gunned it out of the quiet neighborhood, praying that he wasn't too late.

43

HANNAH

Time seemed to slow and Hannah focused on her breathing.

The room expanded, and everyone collected in the darkened room seemed like players on a stage. She felt above and removed, shock and disbelief pulling the moment long, making it strange. Stranger than it already was.

Trina and Josh stood at the door; the tall woman was holding a gun. Joshua looked frightened and unsure, shifting from foot to foot, eyes darting back and forth between Trina and Cricket.

Bruce had placed his body between Hannah, Cricket, and the intruders. Outside the storm raged, lightning casting the wet world in a white glow every few minutes, thunder answering.

Hannah clutched the knife.

Mako knelt on the floor, a motionless Liza in his arms.

Liza—was she dying before their eyes? All that blood, was it too late? She'd slowed the bleeding, and Liza's pulse was stronger. But maybe they wouldn't be able to save her.

Hannah felt her heart in her chest, her throat had turned to sandpaper with fear.

One question only in her mind now: How are we going to get out of here and back to our daughter?

She thought of her little baby peacefully sleeping. *Please*, she prayed. *Please, God.*

Hannah felt her mind clear, her focus turn to a laser. She had always been good at that, boiling the moment down to its essence. What needed to be done.

This woman.

She wanted something.

What was it? Probably money and that was easy enough. But no, she could see the anger on the other woman's face, her hatred. She knew the look—a woman who had been wronged and was out of choices on how to get even. All women knew that look—when you'd been hurt, dismissed, had something taken from you, but were powerless to bring any justice. Stronger forces knocked you over, made you feel small and helpless. In that space, maybe you did a wrong thing to make yourself feel stronger. That was it, right? Mako had harassed her, or worse. When she complained, he fired her. Hannah could fix this.

"Trina," she said, keeping her voice level and soft. "Why are you here? What did my brother do to you?"

Because that's what it was, right? Another one of Mickey's messes. Had he wronged her? Raped her? Hurt her?

"You were supposed to tie them up," Trina said, obviously talking to Joshua but looking at Hannah. The other woman's eyes were dark and cool. They were *Mickey's* eyes.

In fact, how had she not noticed it before—all the times she'd seen the other woman at Red World, company picnics, parties.

Trina looked *a lot* like Mickey. And so did Josh. The cylinders locked into place.

That was it.

"Brother," she said. Trina looked at her and smiled.

That was why she thought she knew Josh when they first

met, because he looked so much like her own brother. Some kind of cognitive dissonance had kept her from making the connections.

Then something truly ugly started to dawn. The Origins test. Holy fuck.

Were they all related? Joshua, Trina, Mako? She grappled with the moment. But she couldn't make sense of it.

"I'm sorry," said Joshua from behind Trina.

He looked miserable, was staring at Cricket with the energy of a beaten dog.

Hannah identified him as a weak link; maybe he'd side with them if things got ugly. Uglier.

Hannah lifted her palms and used her reasonable voice—the one she used when her mother was upset, when Cricket was having a meltdown, even with Mako when he was worked up about something.

"Look, Trina, whatever Mako did to you, we can deal with it, okay," said Hannah. "But Liza? She's hurt. And whatever this is she isn't part of it. So let us get her some help. Please."

"She's part of it, of course she is. Another weak, enabling woman. And, she was carrying his child, another bad seed."

Hannah shook her head, trying to grasp her meaning. "I don't understand. You wanted to *hurt* an unborn baby."

Trina looked suddenly sad. "I never wanted to hurt *anyone*. But we're apples—fallen from the same poisonous tree. I'm actually trying to *help*. To clean up this mess."

A single tear trailed down the other woman's face.

"Okay," Hannah said. "Then let me help you, Trina. Let me help you find a way out of this."

"It wasn't *my* baby," said Mako, still weeping. "Or maybe it wasn't."

"What do you *mean*?" asked Hannah.

"Liza had an affair—which she ended. She didn't think I knew. But I did. I just couldn't lose her. She's the only good thing in my life."

Hannah didn't have words, felt like the ground was shifting beneath her feet. They were all so flawed, weren't they? So many layers and mistakes, bad judgments, failures.

Trina stared at Mako, her face twisted in anger and disgust. "You're pathetic," she said.

But Mako didn't seem to hear. He just looked back to Liza, put a tender hand to her face.

"Tie them up," Trina said, glancing back quickly to Joshua but keeping the gun pointed at Hannah, Cricket, and Bruce who all stood frozen in place.

Hannah searched for the flash of humanity she'd seen but Trina's face was made from marble. Cold and still, unmoved. She didn't care, Hannah realized, about any of them, about anything except whatever agenda she might be running. "Do it now."

Josh shifted, still with his eyes on Cricket. "I left the bag back at the house."

"Men. They are fucking useless," Trina hissed. "Take the zip ties in my pocket."

Of course she had zip ties in her pocket.

Josh moved slowly, reluctantly, toward her pocket when Bruce took a big step forward. Hannah gripped his arm and Trina raised the gun, backing up into Josh.

"Just don't, Bruce," she said, sounding tired. "You're not part of this. I know you've worked to do the right thing here."

Bruce looked back at Hannah. What did that mean?

"And I don't want to kill you but I will. I promise you." Hannah didn't doubt her. There was something unhinged beneath the cool exterior, something broken.

"Not part of what?" Hannah ventured.

But Trina didn't even seem to register her, as if Hannah didn't exist.

Joshua did as he was told, removing a long plastic bag from Trina's pocket.

Hannah calculated—distance, strength. That gun. How good was Trina's aim? How fast could she fire it?

Cricket wept quietly beside her.

Trina pointed the gun at Bruce again. "You help him get Cricket and Hannah secure. Keep them out of the way and you all walk out of here. Okay, Bruce? You're the straight arrow here, right? The good guy."

Hannah still had a grip on her husband's arm. She couldn't see his face but she could imagine his expression—cool, almost blank, reading the situation, calculating, just like Hannah. Did he believe Trina? That if he tied them up, she'd let them all go?

Hannah did not.

This woman was going to kill them all, wasn't she?

She made the decision right there. This wasn't going to end without a fight. She heard Cricket weeping behind her, holding tight to her arm.

Time seemed to slow and stretch, outside the storm tossing the trees and wind moaning through the cabin.

Joshua moved toward them with the zip ties, his passage halting. His eyes hadn't left Cricket, who sobbed now, "Joshua, please don't do this. Whatever she has on you, whatever the reason you're with her, we'll get through it. I'll help you. We'll find a way. Please."

Joshua seemed to hesitate, looked at Trina.

"Joshua, do you want to go to jail?" Trina asked. "Because if we don't finish this and get out of here, that's where you're going. Do you think this little tramp will wait for you?"

Josh seemed to find some inner resolve and moved toward them.

"Sorry," said Bruce, his voice dark, squaring his shoulders. He cleared his throat and Hannah heard his voice shake. "This is—not going to happen."

"Just tell us why you're here, Trina, what you want," said Hannah, this time louder.

Hannah heard Libby's teenage voice, sobbing. *He raped me.*

"Put the knife down," said Trina. "Kick it over here."

Everyone was frozen, the rain pounding on the roof, the windows.

"Do it!" Trina shrieked. "Or I'm going to kill your fucking husband, and your stupid friend, and your raping, embezzling, money-laundering brother."

Hannah looked at her brother, all the rumors about him and Red World.

"None of that is true," said Mako, looking at Hannah. But she saw that look, the same look he gave her the night she caught him with Libby. It wasn't guilt or shame. It was self-knowledge.

"And that's not even all of it," said Trina.

What else? Hannah wondered. What else was he capable of?

"You *know*, Hannah. Look at you. You know what he is."

She and the other woman locked eyes. In that moment, there was a whole universe of understanding—about Mako, about men, about the world.

"Don't you ever get tired of cleaning up after him?"

Trina kept the gun trained on Hannah. And Hannah could see Trina, too—how far gone she was, what she would be willing to do.

Hannah dropped the knife and kicked it toward Trina. It spun over the wood floor, blade glinting. Hannah felt that tension, the one she used to feel on the diving block, before the whistle blew and her body would fly through the air, slice into the water, and she would start to swim with all her strength. She edged forward, knowing that Bruce could feel her. She gave his hand a hard squeeze and he pressed back. They were a team; they both understood what had to happen next. They had to fight. For Gigi.

Josh moved forward and Bruce lifted a hand. His voice sounded like a growl when he spoke. "Stay away from us."

The lightning flashed, and Hannah saw the great jagged streak of electricity through the window. When the giant crack of thunder sounded, shuddering the whole cabin, Hannah flew, rushing Trina, crashing her body into the other woman.

It didn't matter who Trina was, or what she wanted, just that Hannah and Bruce got home to Gigi.

As Hannah made hard contact, bone on bone, flesh on flesh, the gun fired—her ears ringing, filling her senses with the smell of cordite. Hannah heard the gun clatter to the floor as they both hit the ground hard. Hannah landed on top of the taller woman, her weight pushing all the air from Trina in a great rush.

Then it was mayhem, with Bruce rushing Joshua as Hannah thought he would, and Cricket screaming. Mako was bent over Liza, holding her and looking on like he was helpless, eyes glassy.

"Mako," she yelled. "Do something!"

But he didn't seem to hear her.

The knife. The gun. Where were they?

Hannah could see them both—just out of reach in opposite directions.

The other woman struggled, and Hannah punched her hard in the face. The pain radiated up her arm, skin on her knuckles splitting, burning. She hit the other woman again. Then, Hannah, still on top of Trina, pinning the other woman with her weight, reached over her for the gun.

Just as she almost got it, the other woman grabbed for her, and then Trina was on top, pinning Hannah to the ground, the gun skittering away from Hannah's grasp. Hannah writhed free to scramble for the knife, with Trina right on top of her, a hard knee in her back.

"Just stop," Trina said through gritted teeth. "Let me end him."

Hannah watched Bruce land a solid punch to Joshua's jaw, just as Trina grabbed Hannah's hair to keep her from getting closer to the knife.

"Cricket," Hannah screamed, as Trina brought another painful knee into her ribs. "Get the gun."

Bruce and Joshua were on the ground now, rolling and punching. Hannah felt herself losing strength. She reached, stretched painfully, for the gleaming knife.

Just one more inch.

Trina was on top of her again, grabbing at her arm.

Hannah felt herself weaken, air being pushed from her lungs. She realized then that she was bleeding, blood gushing from her arm. The pulse of adrenaline kept the pain at bay.

But the room was starting to fade.

No, she thought. *Gigi*.

Another lightning flash.

Another deafening crack of thunder.

Then two shots rang out. And the world seemed to come to a stuttering stop.

44

BRACKEN

The Elegant Overlook is empty. He's been through all the rooms. Their belongings remain, but the guests are nowhere to be found. Some uneaten desserts line the bar; there are towels scattered around the deck, soaking wet in the rain. There are signs of a struggle inside, a lamp knocked over, furniture moved oddly. By the door is a satchel containing ropes, shovels, a hammer, a hunting knife. Some plastic tarps.

Bracken listens to the silence of the night.

But then he hears it, a deep rumble. Something else, a roar from the air.

Then the front foyer floods with light and the rumble is not from thunder but the arrival of five black SUVs.

As they pull to a stop in the circular drive, armed personnel clad in black with big FBI vests exit and fan out.

Bracken feels a drop of dread. Is this about him? His cameras?

He stands speechless, watching, waiting. Will they take him to jail? What about May? What will she think of him now?

Bracken watches as the Feds fan out around the property, moving like wraiths, swallowed by the night as they disappear down the path to the guest cabin. They seem to know where they're going. How?

He stays frozen, listening.

Bracken thought he knew his guests. But maybe you never really know anyone. Not from their online presence. It only went so deep, and people had so many layers.

He thought about May who was waiting for him, laid bare, offering everything and asking very little.

There were loud voices, shouting. He heard the blades of a helicopter above. In the distance, the whine of sirens.

And then he was alone in the Overlook.

Bracken stood, breathing heavily. Relief washing through him. He had no intention of getting involved in the mess his guests had made.

Bracken set about dismantling his surveillance equipment. He didn't need to watch anymore. He'd seen enough. Now, maybe, it was time to live.

45

HANNAH

The silence in the room expanded; the wind howled outside. That wailing. Were there sirens? Or was that just her ears ringing? The moment seemed frozen, as if time had slowed and warped.

Hannah looked over to see Bruce sitting on top of Joshua, the other man bloodied and dazed. Another glance revealed Cricket holding the gun, arms outstretched, face a mask of shock and horror.

Pieces of the Tilt-A-Whirl moment came together. Hannah felt the breath in her lungs, electricity on her skin.

Cricket released a sob but kept the gun pointed in front of her. "Did I hit anything? Hannah, say something."

Trina's weight was heavy, unmoving on top of Hannah. Hannah rolled out from beneath her and the other woman fell hard to the ground. Hannah scrambled to get away. But when she looked at Trina, the other woman's face was a mask of blood. An open black wound gaped in the side of her head. Trina's dark eyes stared, as empty and seemingly bottomless as Tearwater Lake. Hannah felt a shock move through her—terror, regret, nausea. She was dead. Trina was dead.

Cricket dropped the gun, hands flying to her mouth. After a long moment, she started to wail, falling to her knees.

"I killed her," she managed between sobs. "I killed her."

Hannah felt nothing, numb, shock moving through her like flu. She and Bruce locked eyes. There was so much there—love, fear, relief. Something else.

Outside, Hannah heard voices, footfalls. Or was it just the storm?

Mako had never moved from where he held Liza. He slumped over her.

When Bruce climbed off Joshua, Joshua crawled to Trina's dead and bloodied body. He, too, started to wail, issuing a great keening sound of grief. He reached for her, pulling her to him. Hannah wouldn't have expected to see so much tenderness there.

"Cat," he sobbed. "Catrina."

She heard the pitch of his sadness, his loss. She felt it in her bones. But all she could think about was Gigi, her little girl and getting back to her.

Remember that you must die.

But not today. Today, she was going home to her child.

Hannah was about to go to Bruce when there was a terrible explosion of light and sound. The storm?

No, instead, loud voices and heavy footfalls. Men dressed all in black, brandishing weapons. It was a dream. A nightmare.

Cricket started screaming and Bruce was yelling at them to get down, get down.

Hannah dropped to the floor, putting her hands behind her head. Then she locked eyes with her brother. His gaze was blank and cold, lidded, the way they were after Libby. Her brother. Someone she loved deeply, truly.

Maybe she never knew him at all. All this time, her brother has been a stranger.

46

CATRINA

I am the puzzle piece that you think will fit but doesn't. The color is a little off, the edges don't sit quite flush. You can't force it. Though you might try.

I float above them, watch my poor, still body, legs akimbo, arms spread like I'm making a snow angel. Blood pours from a wound in my head. I am shattered.

Joshua is wailing, the sound of his voice carrying like a siren.

Joshua was a thief. The cybersecurity expert who was *an expert* at siphoning funds from the accounts of his clients. A little here, a little there—tiny amounts that amounted to a lot which he funneled into a Bitcoin account. He was slowly becoming very, very rich with his stolen funds, about to retire to Costa Rica or someplace warm and cheap. I was hoping to go with him when all was said and done, or so I like to tell myself. That maybe in some other universe there was a happy ending for me. There was something between me and Joshua, a connection. We were family. So, why not cobble together a kind of family with him? Like I said, the enterprise with Mako was my last endeavor to clean up my biological father's biological mess.

Best laid plans and all of that. I've learned my lesson, I think. It was never up to me.

Ah, well.

Cricket's sobs turn to screams. Honestly, I can't believe that little slut killed me. I wouldn't have thought she had it in her.

Bruce rushes for Hannah, who lets out a groan of pain. The only one who is silent is Mako, holding Liza's motionless form. After a moment, he looks up to survey the scene. Is that a smile on his face?

He wins again.

Or so he thinks.

Then the Feds rush in. And even though I failed in ending Mako, it's an end to him for sure.

Now I am above it all. The watcher.

I see Liza being rolled out on a stretcher, lifted into a waiting ambulance.

Mako is led away in handcuffs to a waiting SUV. I'd expected him to be screaming and railing, but he is quiet and pliant. Exhausted. Maybe even relieved.

Sometimes it's a relief to be done with it all, all the lies and bad actions, all the cover-ups, and shady deals. It takes so much energy.

I should know.

Hannah walks back into Elegant Overlook, Bruce beside her. She has been bandaged. Bruce is holding her good hand, a tender arm around her. Hannah is watching her brother. Bruce is talking to her, but she's not hearing him. She's just watching Mako, her face a mask of sadness, disappointment, anger.

Joshua sits in the back of an SUV, his hands cuffed, as well. His face is bruised and bloody, head resting against the glass.

Cricket is alone, standing by the trees, stunned and pale.

She killed me. The handmaiden. The one I had figured as

a princess, easy to manage. But when the going got tough, she picked up the gun and fired.

Who says there are no more surprises?

I float higher.

A woman in white wanders in and out of the trees looking for the lost children she will never find.

Off in the distance, a little girl wades into Tearwater Lake, wailing for a mama who will never come.

"Wow," says my dad. "We always called you kitten. But you're the wolf."

"Oh?"

"You really blew their house down."

I look at them. They're all broken pieces, just like me. Trying to make themselves fit.

"They deserved it," I say. We all deserve what we get, don't we?

"If you say so."

He is all stardust and rain, fading into the night sky, then fading back in.

I watch him. He's beautiful. He was a beautiful man with dark eyes and high cheekbones, a wide, laughing mouth. I wish I'd had his DNA in me. I wish I had been more like him, even though he was a broken piece, too.

And then, just as dawn breaks the horizon, I see him arrive, driving fast, then skidding to a stop.

And for a moment I feel a tug back to that ugly world I left behind.

Henry.

"My sister," I hear him say. "She's here. She needs help."

It's not long after that that they roll me out, too. The coroner's assistant, a tiny, bespectacled redhead, opens the bag for him. Henry stares a moment. Then he drops to his knees and starts to weep. It's not pretty. Men shouldn't cry.

The young woman puts a hand on his shoulder.

"That's her," he says.

"I'm sorry."

I'm sorry, too. But he'll be okay. He's one of the good ones. Some of us, maybe most of us, we turned out okay in spite of our biology. And the bad ones? Well, I've rooted them out. I've done my part. A kind of justice has been served.

Boris the pedophile committed suicide.

Marta the enabler had a tragic fall from a roof.

Brad the tech mogul who laundered money for drug dealers ran afoul of clients who ended the relationship the only way they knew how. Decapitation.

Mickey who raped a young girl and then denied it. And there's more.

Mickey's game at Red World was being investigated with the help of his brother-in-law, as a haven for bad men looking to groom and lure young girls and boys into sending nude photos of themselves for sale on the dark web. Mickey who embezzled money; the transfer that he made from his computer tonight the one action the Feds needed to take him down. Mickey who was a workplace predator, with at least six women waiting to come forward.

All of whom confessed on tape to Trina, his assistant.

There are others. I could go on.

Each project has been a subtle long game that had the desired result. Cleaning up the mess my father made.

This final one, it didn't go as planned. To say the least.

But so it goes.

Now that my watch is over, I relinquish control.

"Want to go for a ride, kid?" says my dad.

The Indian gleams and rumbles. He loved that thing. He loved me, too, the best he could. None of us is perfect. Or even close.

"Yeah, Dad. Let's ride."

47

HANNAH

That moment again. When it's all over. Or is it just the eye of the storm? Anyway—it's quiet now, with all the violence behind and ahead.

Here, they can breathe a moment and the sky seems clear, the immediate danger passed, no hint of what's to come except for a thick and eerie stillness.

"They approached me back before Christmas," says Bruce. "I really didn't have a choice."

Bruce is talking about the FBI and how he helped them investigate and arrest her brother for, among other things, money laundering for his investors, embezzlement, tax evasion.

There are also allegations that Red World was being used as a place for predators to groom and lure young kids playing the game into sending nude photos of themselves to sell on the dark web. That company officers knew about this and did nothing to stop it.

None of this jibes with the life she thought they had.

Her husband has been lying to her. She suspected as much. She might have preferred to discover he'd been cheating. That seems so simple now.

And that's the least of it.

Henry, the stranger who arrived as the sun was rising, sits over by the kitchen island. He's on the phone.

"I'm sorry," he says. "I'll be home soon and I'll explain everything."

He's told Hannah things that she can't believe, though on some level she knows they're true. Catrina, Henry, Mako, and Joshua are all related by a sperm donor, someone who it turns out was a monster, a serial rapist and killer who sold his sperm for money. Catrina was on a mission to cleanse the gene pool. Henry was trying to stop her. Joshua was helping her, because she had learned that he was stealing money from his clients. Mako had no idea that the woman he'd hired as his assistant was his half sister.

Hannah's life which felt rock solid, is built on quicksand.

But she is her parents' child. This she knows. She, too, was conceived by sperm donor, it seems. Not the same sperm donor as Mako, but a stranger. She, too, has some half siblings looking for connections. But that door is closed. She canceled her Origins account as soon as she understood the truth. It didn't matter to her that the man she called "Daddy" was not her biological father. He was everything she needed him to be. And she wants nothing more. Sophia is famous for saying: Family is not who you are, it's what you do.

Leo kept her safe, and was always there. He showed her the stars, and was always the first face she saw when she looked out into the audience at school plays, graduations, swim meets.

Now Hannah finally understands what Sophia meant.

There will need to be a conversation, probably many long, hard, and unpleasant conversations. Most of them will be about Mako and who he is, what he's done, what will become of him.

Some of them will be about Sophia and Leo and the choices they made. Sophia will drink. And Leo will be emotionally absent. But they'll get through what comes next together. Hannah believes that.

They are still in the vacation rental. That skull surrounded by bits and pieces of bones. The black eyes stare at her. She hates this place.

Henry comes to sit across from Hannah where she's curled up on the couch.

Cricket has gone to lie down on Hannah and Bruce's bed. Soon they will all go to Liza and be there for her. She is fighting for her life. Liza has lost everything, and whatever mistakes she might have made, she is still family. Hannah will take care of her through whatever comes next.

Hannah is hurt—some bruising, a bandaged injury on her arm where a bullet grazed her but didn't penetrate. She has refused more medical attention. She can't be laid up right now, her family will need her. She'll have to get home to Lou and her daughter, to her parents.

The road ahead is long and dark.

She can see the man in front of her, who is related to her brother, but not to her, is in pain. He rests his forearms on his thighs, his head hanging.

"I'm sorry about your sister," she says. Trina. Mickey's half sister, too.

He looks up and she sees Mako's eyes, Catrina's eyes, it sends a little jolt of recognition through her like it did when she first met Joshua.

"That's—very generous. Considering what has just happened to you."

"Family, right?" she says with a light laugh.

"Yeah. It's messed up."

Bruce stands by the fireplace, staring at the flames. He did what he had to do; she knows this. She married an honest, hardworking man who cares for his family and always, always does the right thing. Like her father—like her *Dad*. She has no idea what her biological father was like and she doesn't need to know. The first thought she had about Bruce was: *he's safe.* She chose him as the foundation on which she wanted to build her life, her family.

She doesn't love that he lied to her and hid this huge thing from her. She doesn't love that he worked with the FBI to take her brother down. But she understands it.

Could she have been trusted with that information? Or would she have worked to save Mako from the fate he had designed for himself? She can't answer that and doesn't want to.

But she's done cleaning up Mako's messes. In fact, she herself has some penance to do. What had Catrina called them—Hannah and Cricket? His handmaidens. That was a painful truth that she would have to face.

Why had she done it?

Hidden Mickey's darkness?

She could say that she was afraid of him, or that she didn't really know what he was capable of. But that wasn't the whole truth. There was more, another layer—a fidelity, a love that let her see past his darkness to the squalling, helpless infant within. She wanted, in some great sense, to take care of him. It was a wrong impulse, she knew that. But it was a true one.

Henry is talking, telling her about himself, about Catrina, about how he and a private detective had been investigating and finally realized what she'd been doing. She's listening, trying to understand the winding, twisting path they've all been on, the one that has entwined them all together. A strange and unhappy family.

When Bruce comes to sit beside her, the power finally comes back on. Outside, the rising sun is painting the wet world golden. The storm has passed.

He leans into her, burying his face in her neck. It's the first time she's seen him cry.

Bruce gave the FBI a back door into Mako's network, allowing them to collect evidence against him and some transaction Mako completed tonight gave them the final piece they needed to come and take him down.

But Mako was the agent of his own destruction.

She loves her brother, but he was a bad guy. And if he was going to be punished for things he'd done, then it was his fault, not Bruce's. Bruce hadn't betrayed their family. In a sense, he'd saved them. He'd chosen right over wrong. A thing that Hannah is ashamed to admit she has never been able to do when it came to Mickey.

She wraps her arms around Bruce.

"Forgive me," he whispers.

She already has.

48

HENRY

Christmas 2018

The table is set and Piper is nervous. She's banging around the kitchen, her movements efficient and quick for someone carrying a watermelon in her belly. He passes through and asks what he can do. The air is rich with aromas—the ham in the oven, the potatoes on the stove, the flowers on the table. Music plays softly. Bing Crosby and David Bowie sing the 1977 remix of "The Little Drummer Boy" and "Peace on Earth." Piper's an old soul. She hums along.

"What can I do?" Henry asks, putting his hands on her slender shoulders. He feels some of the tension there relax. He places a kiss on her head and she smells of eucalyptus.

She turns to give him a tired smile; they both know he's not much help in the kitchen.

"Just hang out with the wild man," Piper says, wiping an arm across her brow.

Everyone protested when Piper said she wanted to host

Christmas, but she insisted. He knows that she did it for him. Christmas in their own home with the family they'd built. It meant something to him. In fact, it was everything.

"You got it," he says quickly.

Luke, a born overachiever like his father—is walking early. And he's tearing around the living room like a dervish. He seems to walk only to convey himself between spectacular falls. Henry arrives just in time to keep Luke from crashing into the towering Christmas tree.

"Buddy," says Henry, scooping him up. "Chill."

Luke finally tires himself out and collapses in front of his toys, where Henry joins him to build a castle out of blocks.

The doorbell rings and Piper issues a little shout—she's not ready. But she is. Everything is perfect.

Paul and Gretchen are the first to arrive, laden with bags and bags of gifts, and piles of food. Paul makes two trips from the car, carrying shopping bags and crockery.

"Not enough food, as usual," he says after he drops the final load.

Luke careens into PopPop's arms and Henry breathes a sigh of relief.

"Let's go run around the yard, little man," says Paul. "Tire you out."

Thank goodness for grandparents. Paul never seems to get tired of playing with Luke.

Miss Gail arrives after a while, carrying her famous cherry pie and offering big soft hugs that everyone joyfully accepts. His aunt Gemma has come downstairs and is in the kitchen with Piper and Gretchen. His aunt has been here for a week already, helping with everything for today. She'll stay on through the New Year to help take care of Luke as his little sister arrives— really any minute now.

When the bell rings again it's Detective West and his wife. Their kids are with their respective in-laws this holiday and Henry has invited them to join his family.

His family. Yes.

After drinks and conversation, they gather at the table and Paul says grace, as he always does.

"We are blessed today in the company of family and friends. We are so grateful for this abundance. May all people everywhere know peace and plenty."

Henry looks around the table, holds the hand of his beautiful wife, while Luke bounces happily in his high chair. The cutlery and glasses glitter. His aunt Gemma is wearing a ridiculously sparkly Christmas sweater replete with Santa heads and flying reindeer and somehow it's perfect.

There is laughter and loud conversation, disagreement, teasing. Luke squalls. Piper looks exhausted. Detective West tells a dirty joke and everyone gets a chuckle out of it except for his wife. *Oh, honestly, honey.* She blushes.

After dinner, Paul and Henry help to clean, then take the overtired and cranky Luke on a walk around the neighborhood. The air is warm—Christmas in Florida—the sky a velvety midnight blue, riven with stars. Porch lights glow, Christmas trees glimmer in big bay windows, bikes lie askew in driveways, basketball hoops are mounted over garages, cars line the streets as people gather to celebrate the day with their families.

Family. It's just a story we tell each other about ourselves, thinks Henry.

If there's darkness in his DNA, Henry doesn't feel it tonight. He doesn't see it in the cherubic face of his boy, who is rubbing his eyes in the arms of his grandfather.

He doubts he'll see it when their baby girl arrives. They've decided to name her Alice, a way to remember his mother. Gemma doesn't like the idea; he can tell by her worried frown. But she hasn't said so. But that's what he and Piper have chosen. An homage. An apology. A kind of forgiveness.

Henry and Paul don't speak, silence the overriding theme of their relationship. Luke points up at the moon which is rising full and bright.

Henry thinks about Catrina and wishes that she was at their table tonight.

But she made her choices. And Henry has made his.

She was right after all. In the end, that's all there is to life. What you create, what you build, what you nurture. It's about biology, genetics, of course.

But most of all, it's about what you do with what you're given.

"Should we head back, son?" asks Paul. Luke has rested his head against Paul's shoulder, finally worn out for the day.

"Yeah," says Henry. "Let's go home."

49

HANNAH

As dusk paints the sky outside a fire show of orange, pink, and purple, and the last light of the day shines on the waters of the Intracoastal, Hannah watches from the big picture window of their new kitchen. She dreads the darkness, the nighttime these days. It's when all the doubts and regrets, fears and worries come to call. During the day she can busy it all away, running around after Gigi and running errands, helping Bruce in her new role at his company as operations director. But at night, when things are quiet, then the demons start to howl.

"It's okay," says Bruce, stepping up behind her. As always, he reads her mood. "Everything will be okay."

"I'm fine," she assures him. And she is. Mostly.

The heat from the oven warms her face as Hannah takes the turkey and places the big pan on the stovetop to cool. Bruce sets the table.

"How many?" he asks.

"I'm not sure," she says. "Set the table for six, just in case." Gigi sits happily on the floor watching *Elf* for the hundredth time on the big-screen television, with Lou knitting quietly on the couch, lovingly answering all Gigi's chatter. *Why is he eating that? Why is he so big? Does his daddy love him?*

"Can I do anything?" calls Lou.

"You're doing it," answers Hannah. "Watching *Elf* with Gigi is the best thing you can be doing right now."

Lou chuckles. "Hard duty. But I'll bear up."

"Oooh! Santa!" chimes Gigi with pure delight.

As Hannah stirs more milk and butter into the mashed potatoes, she is washed with gratitude for her family. But she also feels a terrible void, a dark undercurrent.

Mako is under house arrest, awaiting trial for his crimes.

And Sophia can't forgive Bruce for betraying their family. Leo is more forgiving, but he'll always side with Hannah's mother. At any rate, they have decided to spend their Christmas traveling, away from the news and the stares of their neighbors. Her mother's last Facebook post was from the Netherlands, a lovely picture of her parents smiling at a Christmas market, lights glittering all around them. It filled Hannah with sadness and anger. The consequences of their actions were being borne by others, while they went on their merry way.

It's Hannah's first Christmas without her family of origin. She's trying to stay light and enjoy what they have, but if she's honest, she feels as if she's being punished for the things her brother has done. And he'll always be her brother, no matter how much DNA they actually share.

Apparently, Catrina made provisions for what should happen in the event of her untimely death. She'd kept a detailed journal of her genealogical adventures. It included everything about herself, how she learned about her father and tracked down his progeny.

She'd conducted a detailed investigation into their many crimes, and written detailed confessions about how she'd ended or facilitated the end of each of their lives.

All of this had been kept in a safe-deposit box. The key was kept with her lawyer, who sent it, upon learning of Cat's death, to a freelance journalist, a half sibling Catrina had found through the Donor Sibling Registry. This journalist wrote a long and searing article for *The Atlantic*; apparently there's a book deal to come. It will be entitled *Origins* and will detail Cat's journey, and the journalist's own. It was exactly the kind of book Hannah would read under other circumstances.

"I think we're ready," she says, forcing her voice bright. Bruce comes to help her carry the dishes to the table, while Lou fastens Gigi into her booster chair.

Outside the queen palms sway in the last light of afternoon and Bruce stands to say grace, which they don't always do. It's easy to forget gratitude when times get hard.

"People always say that you can't choose your family. But that's not always true. We do choose. And from those choices we build a life. I am so grateful for the life we have, for this meal, and the comfort in which we can enjoy it. Things are not perfect. We have challenges to face. But who was ever promised perfect?"

They lock eyes across the table, while Gigi chatters.

"My actions have brought us pain and for that I am deeply sorry. But sometimes pain comes when healing begins. I am so grateful that we'll walk into the uncertain future together."

"Amen," says Lou.

"Amen," says Gigi with a laugh. Hannah touches her dear silky curls, her flushed cherub cheeks.

Just as they start to eat, the doorbell rings.

Bruce rises to answer, and Hannah follows.

Cricket stands on their porch, looking fragile and tired. They haven't spoken much.

"I don't have anyplace else to go tonight," she says. And Hannah, of course, welcomes her inside. In the foyer, they stand and embrace for a long time.

About a month ago, Hannah and Cricket went to see Libby Cruz's mother and they told her their side of the story the night

Mako raped Libby. They apologized for their role, and tried to do so without making excuses like they were young, and they didn't know, and they were just trying to save their own skins because of the party.

Libby's mother treated them with more compassion than they deserved.

"Just do one thing for me, girls," she asked as they sat in her living room. "Tell this story so people know what really happened to Libby. So other people will think twice about covering for bad men. Just tell the truth. Because it might help someone else. Because it matters."

They agreed to do just that.

"But remember," Mrs. Cruz said. "Michael hurt Libby; you didn't. And Libby chose to end her life, though depression played a huge role—something she inherited from my side of the family. So forgive yourselves, girls. Move on. And *do better* for yourselves, for your daughter."

So, they did. They each wrote a post on Facebook, explaining what happened, and why they made the choices they had when they were teenagers.

The outpouring was—*epic*, as Mako would have said. Judgment. Rage. Compassion. Understanding. Confessions. They lost friends; received hate mail and death threats. They were amazed by the compassion of strangers and the willingness of many to forgive two teenage girls for their weakness and baseness.

This was another reason why Sophia was barely speaking to Hannah. The good girl. The reliable one, the fixer. The one who covered up and kept secrets. The one who ran in for the rescue. The one who still hadn't been able to bring herself to tell her mother about Boots. She finally told the truth.

Sophia on the other hand is a locked box.

"Why a sperm donor? Why not tell us? Why keep this secret from us?" Hannah had wanted to know.

"Honestly?" said Sophia. "It's none of your business, Hannah."

"How can you say that?" she'd asked in her mother's kitchen.

Sophia pulled her shoulders back. "I wanted children. Your father wasn't able to give them to me. We made this choice and thought it was better that you never know. Clearly, we were right."

"You were right to lie?" asked Hannah, looking down into her coffee cup.

"We gave you love, support, a home, a life of privilege. What more do you want from us, dear?"

Just the truth, Mom, she thought but didn't say. After all, she couldn't really throw any stones, could she?

"Who left those Origins tests?" Hannah asked that day.

"You really have to wonder?" she said. "It was your brother, of course. He discovered the truth years ago and this was his way of forcing us to face the fact that he knew. When he confronted us the first time, the technology wasn't quite there. It was still unreliable. But now…there are no more secrets when it comes to genetics."

Neither her mother or father had apologized for their choices, for their lies.

"I'll never be sorry that I have you as my daughter, no matter how you came to us," Leo had said. "The rest of it doesn't matter. Michael is who he is. And no matter his crimes, he's still our son."

Now Hannah releases Cricket. "There's always a place for you at our table, Crick. You know that."

Joshua is gone. He disappeared from the hospital that night and no one has heard from him again. Apparently he was a Bitcoin millionaire, and has used that money to facilitate his escape. Cricket swears he ghosted her, that she hasn't spoken to him. Hannah is not sure that she believes her friend.

They've barely seated themselves again when the doorbell rings another time.

"Okay," says Bruce, glancing at her. "Did you invite someone else?"

Hannah nods. When she opens the door, she finds a very

pregnant Liza, holding a pot of stunning white orchids. She and her baby miraculously survived that night, and she and Hannah are close for the first time since Liza met Mako. Though they are no long living together, Liza has decided to stand by Mako and see him through his trial. What happens after that, she isn't certain. A DNA test has concluded that the baby is indeed Mako's, a little boy due in January.

If Catrina's goal was to cleanse the gene pool of her father's DNA, she'd failed.

"I wasn't sure if you meant it when you invited me," she said, "I didn't know if I should come. But here I am."

"Of course I meant it," says Hannah, bringing her inside with an arm around her shoulders. "We're family."

They *were* family. All of them linked through blood or circumstance or choice. Liza would give birth to Hannah's nephew, Gigi's cousin, her half brother's child. And no matter what any of them had done, to themselves, to others, to each other, nothing would ever change that.

Bruce offers grace again for their newly arrived guests. "Family—it's complicated. And yet here we all are, bound imperfectly but indelibly. We offer our gratitude for this bounty, however varied, however fraught. Love, no matter how hard our life's journey, is always the light at the end of the tunnel."

They eat.

Hannah looks at her husband, his strong profile, her daughter's eyes. Some of the sadness she's felt recedes. Whatever comes next, she's proud of them, the family she's made, the one she chose.

★ ★ ★ ★ ★

acknowledgments

I feel as if it should get easier, but somehow it gets harder every year to write these acknowledgments. Or maybe *harder* is not the word. Maybe it just feels more important to get it right. Because this is my—wait for it!—*twentieth* novel. And in this writing life, the amount and quality of people who contribute to the books, their publishing, my life in general (which is indivisible from my writing life most days) continue to grow. I am blessed beyond measure, and I am awed by the task of expressing my gratitude.

My husband, Jeffrey, and our daughter, Ocean Rae, are the rock-solid foundation on which my life is built. I wouldn't be the person I am or the writer I am without them. Jeff, you're the love of my life, my partner in crime, and my best and truest friend. Good job running "the corporation"—and taking care of us in every other way possible. Ocean, you are by far our greatest accomplishment and our deepest source of pride and joy; you're a light bringer, a joy maker, our North Star. Our beloved labradoodle, Jak Jak, is my faithful writing buddy and foot warmer, and a constant reminder to finish up work so we can play.

When I turn in a first draft to my editor Erika Imranyi, the novel I give her represents the pinnacle of my efforts and ability—the literal best I can do. With wisdom, compassion, and insight she helps me find my way from that flawed version to the book that I hoped it would be. It's a journey we take together. And I wish we could publish a draft with the editing notes in the margin—complete with all the back-and-forth, funny comments, and emoji! Meanwhile, the teams at HarperCollins, Harlequin, and Park Row are every author's dream. I can't say enough good things about the amazing teams in the US, Canada, and the UK, from the stalwart copy editors to the visionary art departments to the intrepid marketing and sales teams. Special thanks to Loriana Sacilotto, executive vice president and publisher, and Margaret Marbury, vice president of editorial, for their stellar leadership and unflagging passion. And much gratitude to Nicole Luongo, editorial assistant, and to Emer Flounders, publicist extraordinaire, for their tireless efforts on my behalf.

My agent, Amy Berkower of the sterling Writers House, is my tireless supporter and fearless captain in navigating the big waters of the writing life. I am so grateful for her wisdom, sharp instincts, and passion. Big thanks to her assistant, Meridith Viguet, for her warmth, good humor, and unparalleled skills in all things, and to the amazing international rights group for finding homes for my novels all over the globe. Merci! Danke! Gracias!

How could a writer survive without her friends? Mine cheer me through the good days and drag me through the challenging ones. They are forced to attend book signings year after year, read early drafts of my work, and endure my social media posts. But they still love me! And I love them! Erin Mitchell is early reader, tireless promoter, inbox tamer, voice of wisdom, and pal. Karin Slaughter and Alafair Burke are the village on my iPhone as we talk about all things life, writing, and publishing—mostly through a code of memes and emoji understood only by us. Heather Mikesell has been a longtime early reader, eagle-eyed editor, and bestie. Nothing feels done until she reads it! Jennifer Manfrey is always on standby to dig in deep to some obscure topic over which I'm obsessing. Tara Popick and Marion Chartoff have had the pleasure of dealing with me since college and grade school, respectively. They still answer my calls! It feels like Gretchen Koss and I are old publishing buddies, as if we've known each other for ages, even though we met quite recently. I am so grateful for her support, sense of humor, and tremendous publicity expertise. A big shout-out to Team Waterside—Kathy Bernhardt, Colleen Chappell, Marie Chinicci-Everitt, Rhea Echols, Karen Poinelli, Tim Flight, Jen Outze, and Heidi Ackers, to name just a few—for being my home team, reading, supporting, showing up at events, and being there in every way possible.

My mom, Virginia Miscione, former librarian and avid reader, gave me the gift of loving story in all forms: books, film, television, and theater. She remains one of my earliest and most important readers. I don't usually give my dad, Joseph Miscione, much of a shout-out. In fact, I mainly just give him a hard time for being the guy who told me *not* to pursue my writing dreams but to get a "real job." I usually do this on stage and it always gets lots of laughs—especially when he's there! (It's not bad advice, though. I have succeeded against all odds!) But he and my mom have been the safety net beneath me as I walk that tightrope we call life. Thanks, Mom and Dad, for always being there. And of course, along with my brother, Joe, for shamelessly bragging, facing out books in stores, and always spreading the word.

As always, research was a big part of the writing of this novel. It's kind of a continuum—reading, researching, writing, living. During the pandemic, I spent some beautiful time in parts of Georgia I had never visited and was awed by the quiet and stunning natural beauty of the state. We stayed in some truly gorgeous rental cabins, and it was at one of these luxurious spots where I first had the idea for this novel. Because why would I just enjoy my vacation like a normal person instead of spinning out the darkest possible scenario while lying awake at night wondering who else might have the lock code to the house? You see how it is with me, right? *The Lost Family: How DNA Testing Is Upending Who We Are* by Libby Copeland was a deep dive into all the ways we are giving away our privacy in the search for our origins. Jeanette Stewart, friend and armchair genealogist, helped me to navigate the world of online ancestry research. We spent some fascinating time digging into a dark chapter in my own family's past and found out some truly shocking things. There might be another book in that. Stay tuned!

Finally, a writer is nothing without her readers. Everything I write is for you. Some of you have been with me since the first book. And since this is number twenty, that's a little more than two decades. Wow! I am honored that you are still here with me. I hear from you via email, on my social media accounts. I see your gorgeous faces again and again at my appearances—in person and virtual. It means so very much to me to know that my stories, my characters, my words have found a home in your minds and hearts. Thank you for reading, for buying, for checking out from the library, for reviewing, sharing with friends, and for tirelessly spreading the word. I am grateful for each and every one of you.

Happy reading!

Questions for Discussion

1. In the prologue, a Secret Santa leaves a DNA testing kit for Hannah and her family. Everyone has a different reaction and opinion about the gift. Discuss each character's reaction and what it might say about them.

2. It's clear as Hannah and Bruce are heading out to the weekend getaway with Mako, Liza, Cricket, and her new boyfriend that there are already tensions and complicated dynamics at play between members of the group. What did you pick up on right away?

3. At first, Henry's story seems to be unconnected to the crew that's traveling to the remote cabin. Did you have early thoughts on who Henry might be and how he fits into the story? How did they evolve as the story unfolded?

4. There are shifting perspectives on the group gathering inside the cabin. We see them close-up through Hannah's

eyes, from just outside the cabin through the point of view of a malicious stranger, and from an even farther distance through Bracken's cameras. What do we learn from each perspective—about the watchers and the watched?

5. At the dinner, Chef Jeff shares the dark history of the house the family is renting. How did you feel about the cabin before and after?

6. What did you make of the use of bone in the decor of the house? The statues upstairs, the chandeliers, and the bone sculpture in the dining room?

7. Chef Jeff brings up the concept of "memento mori." Were you familiar with this phrase? What does it mean to you? How does Hannah feel about it?

8. Hannah, her brother Mako, and their longtime family friend Cricket have a complicated relationship. Discuss how each relates to the other. What role does each person play in the group?

Read on for a sneak peek at The New Couple in 5B,
the next exhilarating thriller
from master of suspense Lisa Unger

overture

You. Standing on solid ground, reaching. Me. On the ledge, looking down. All around me, stars. Stars in the sky, the city spread around me like a field of glittering, distant celestial bodies. Each light a life. Each life a doorway, a possibility. That's the thing I've always loved about my work, the way I can disappear into someone else. I shed myself daily, slipping into other skins. Some of them more comfortable than my own.

"Don't," you say. "Don't do this. It doesn't have to be this way."

I hear all the notes of desperation and fear that sing discordant and wild, a cacophony in my own heart. And I think that maybe you're wrong. Maybe everything I am and everything I've done, has led me here to this teetering edge. There was no other possible ending. No other way.

Sirens. As distant and faint as birdsong. It seems as if, in this city, they never stop wailing, someone always on their way to this emergency or that crisis. Rushing to help or stop or save. From the outside, it seems like chaos. But when you are inside, it's quiet, isn't it? Just another moment. Only this time the worst thing is about to happen, or might, or might not, to us. Every flicker of light, every passing second, just a shift of weight and another outcome becomes real.

"Please." Under the fear, the pleading of your tone, I hear it—hope. You're still hopeful. Still holding on to those other possibilities.

But when I look at you now, I know—and you know it, too, don't you?—that I've made too many dark choices, that there is no outcome but this one. The one that sets us both free right here and right now.

Pounding. They're at the door.

You know what's funny? Even on that day we first met, I knew it would end like this. Not really. Not exactly this, not a premonition, or a vision of the future. But even in the light you shined on me, even as you made me be the person I always wanted to be, there was this dark entity hovering, a specter. The destroyer. You were always too good for me, and I knew I could never hold on to the things we would build together.

Sounds rise and converge—your voice, their pounding, that wailing, the endless honking and whir of movement from this place we have lived in and loved.

The weight of my body, I close my eyes and feel it. The beating of my heart, the rise and fall of my breath. I tilt and wobble on the edge, as you move closer, hands outstretched.

"We'll be okay," you whisper. At least I think that's what you say. I can hardly hear you over all the noise. Your eyes, like the city below me, a swirling galaxy of lights.

You're close now, hand reaching.

Just one step forward or backward.

Which one?

Which one, my love?

ACT I

the inheritance

*Look like the innocent flower,
but be the serpent under it.*
William Shakespeare
Macbeth
Act 1, Scene 5

1

Sometimes the smallest things are the biggest.

Like the slim rectangular box that sits at the bottom of my tote. Maybe just six inches long and two inches wide. Light, flimsy, its contents clatter when shaken. But it's a whispering presence, a white noise buzzing in my consciousness.

Max, dapper in a houndstooth blazer and thin camel cashmere sweater, peers at the oversize menu, considering. As if he isn't going to order the penne ala vodka and salad he always does. I hold mine, as well, perusing my options. As if I'm *not* going to get the pizza margarita, no salad. The tony Italian restaurant on Broadway across from my publisher's office is packed, silverware clinking, conversations a low hum. Lots of business being done over sparkling waters and tuna tartar.

Outside the big picture window, beside which we sit, the river of traffic flows, horns and hissing buses, the screech of brakes, the occasional shout from annoyed drivers. Beneath all of that, I feel it, the presence of that slim box, so full of possibility.

The waitress takes our expected orders, deposits Max's usual bottle of Pellegrino. I'm a tap water girl, but he pours me a glass, always the gentleman. I note his manicured nails, buffed and square, the white face of his Patek Philippe. No smart watch for him. Max appreciates timepieces for their elegant union of form and function.

"So," he says, placing the green bottle on the white tablecloth.

I don't love the sound of that word. Max and I have known each other a long time. There's a heaviness to it, a caution.

"So?"

"Your proposal."

That's why we've met for lunch, to discuss the proposal I've submitted for my new book.

He slips my proposal out of the slim leather folder he's laid on the table between us.

"There's a lot to like here."

That's publishing code for *I don't like it.* How many times did I say the same thing to authors I was editing?

I have always been a writer, scribbling in the nooks and crannies of my days, my foray into publishing just a stop on the road to the writing life. But Max never wanted to be anything else more than an editor, the one who helped talented writers do their best work.

"But?" I venture. He lifts his eyebrows, clears his throat.

Max and I met when we were both editorial assistants, fresh out of the Columbia Publishing Program. We were so eager to enter the world of letters, literature geeks seduced by what we imagined was the glitz and glamour of the industry. He climbed the corporate ladder, while I stayed up late, got up early, holed up on weekends to complete my first book.

By the time I had finished my first draft, Max was a young star editor at one of the biggest publishing companies in New

York, the first person I asked to read my manuscript; he was the first person to say he believed in me, the first editor to buy something I'd written and to make me what I'd always wanted to be. A full-time writer.

He runs a hand through lustrous dark hair, which he wears a little long, takes off his tortoiseshell glasses. "I don't know, Rosie. There's just something—lacking."

I feel myself bristle—lacking? But underneath the crackling of my ego, I think I know he's right. The truth is—I'm not *that* excited about it. The belly of fire that you need to complete a project of this size, honestly, it's just not there.

"There was so much fire in the first one," says Max, holding me in the intensity of his gaze. He's so into this—his job, this process. "There were so many layers—the justice system, the misogyny in crime reporting, the voices of the children. It really grabbed me, even in the proposal you submitted. I could see it. It was fresh, exciting."

"And this isn't." I try and probably fail to keep the disappointment out of my voice.

He leans in, reaches a hand across the table. "It *is*. It's just not *as* exciting. The first book, it was a success, a place from where we can grow. But the next book *needs to be* bigger, better."

Bigger. Better. What's next? That's the mantra of the publishing industry.

"No pressure," I say, blowing out a laugh.

My first true-crime book was about the violent rape of a young Manhattan woman, the travesty of justice that followed where a man was wrongly convicted and the real criminal went free, then continued on to rape and kill three more women. It took me five years to research and write while working a full-time job as an editor. The book did well, not a runaway bestseller but a success by any measure. The moment was right for that book, post Me Too, where society was casting a new light on women wronged by men, looking at older stories through fresh eyes.

It's been a year since the book came out, the paperback about to release soon. I can't take five years to write another one.

Max puts a gentle hand on mine. His touch is warm and ignites memories it shouldn't. His fingers graze my wedding and engagement rings, and he draws his hand back, steeples his fingers.

"Is this *really* what you want to be writing?"

"Yes," I say weakly. "I think so."

"Look," he says, putting his glasses back on. "You've had a lot on your plate."

I'm about to protest but it's true. My husband, Chad, and I had been taking care of Chad's elderly uncle Ivan, who recently passed away. Between being there for Ivan, Chad's only family, in the final stages of his illness, and now managing his affairs, it's been a lot. Scary to watch someone you love die, so sad, sifting through the detritus now of his long and colorful life. Uncle Ivan—he was all we had. I've been estranged from my family for over a decade. His loss feels heavy, something we're carrying on our shoulders. With the temperature dropping and the holidays approaching, there's a kind of persistent sadness we're both struggling under. Maybe it has affected my work more than I realized.

I think of that box in the bottom of my bag, that little ray of light. I am seized with the sudden urge to go home and tear it open.

"Look," he says when I stay quiet. "Just take some time to think about it, go deeper. Ask yourself, 'Is this the story I really want and need to tell? Is it something people need to read?' Make *me* excited about it, too. We have time."

We don't, actually.

The money from the first book—it's running out. Chad has a low-paying gig in an off-off Broadway production. This city— it takes everything to live here. Our rent just went up and we need to decide whether or not we can afford to renew the lease. It's just a one-bedroom, five-story walk-up in the East Village, and we're about to be priced out unless one of us gets paid a significant sum. Chad has an audition for another better-paying job, but things are so competitive, there's no way to know if he even has a chance. It's just a commercial, not something he's excited about, but we need the cash.

Today he's at the reading of Ivan's will. But we don't expect to inherit anything. Ivan died penniless. His only asset the apartment that will go to his daughter Dana.

Did I rush the proposal because I'm feeling desperate? Maybe.

The waitress brings our meal and I'm suddenly ravenous. We dig in. The pizza is good, gooey and cheesy. The silence between us, it's easy, companionable, no tension even though it's not the conversation I was hoping to have. Writers, we only want to hear how dazzling we are. Everything else hurts a little.

"You said there was a lot to like," I say, mouth full. "What *do* you like about it? Give me a jumping-off point to dive deeper."

"I really like the occult stuff," he says, shoving a big bite of penne into his mouth. It's one of the things I love most about Max, his passion for good food. Chad is so careful about everything he eats, either losing or gaining weight for a role. "You kind of glossed over that."

I frown at him. "I thought you didn't like ghost stories."

There were several supernatural elements to my last book—the little girl who dreamed about her mother's death the day before it happened, how one of the children believed he communicated with his murdered sister through a medium. Both of those bits wound up on the cutting-room floor. *Too woo-woo,* according to Max. *Let's stay grounded in the real world.*

"I *don't* like ghost stories—per se," he says now. "But I like all the reasons why people *think* a place is haunted. I like what it says about people, about places, about mythology."

I feel a little buzz of excitement then. And that's why every writer needs a good editor.

The proposal is about an iconic Manhattan apartment building on Park Avenue that has been home to famous residents including a bestselling novelist, a celebrated sculptor and a young stage and screen star. It's also had far more than its fair share of dark events—grisly murders, suicides and terrible accidents. It's a New York story, really—the history of the building, its unique architecture, how it was built on the site of an old church that burned down. I want to focus on each of the crimes, the current colorful cast of characters that resides there, and tell the stories of the people who died there—including Chad's late uncle Ivan, a renowned war photographer.

I'll still have access to the building, even though we're almost done cleaning out Ivan's things. His daughter, from whom Ivan hadn't heard in years, even as he lay dying and Chad tried to call again and again, is now circling her inheritance. She wasn't interested in Ivan, or his final days, his meager possessions. But the apartment—it's worth a fortune. Anyway, I've befriended the doorman, Abi. He is a wealth of knowledge, having worked in the building for decades. I think he's long past retirement age but doesn't seem to have any plans to hang up his doorman's uniform. *Some folks don't get to leave the Windermere, Miss Rosie*, he joked when I asked him how much longer he planned to work. *Some of us are destined to die here.*

"And I like the crimes," Max says, rubbing thoughtfully at his chin. "So I think if we can tease some of those elements out, I can take it to the editorial meeting."

The truth is I'm more excited about revising the proposal than I was about writing the book when I walked in here. He's right. It's not the architecture, the history of the building—it's the darkness, the crimes, the people. The question—are there cursed or haunted places, some energy that encourages dark happenings? Or is it just broken people doing horrible things to each other? A mystery. That's what makes a great story. And story is king, even in nonfiction.

"I'll get right to work," I say. "Thanks, Max."

"That's what editors are for, to help writers find their way to their best book." He looks pleased with himself. "Now, what's for dessert?"

Outside, a loud screech of tires on asphalt draws my attention to the street just in time to see a bike messenger hit by a taxi. In a horrible crunching of metal and glass, the biker hits the hood. His long, lanky limbs flailing, flightless wings, he crashes into the windshield, shattering it into spider webs, then comes to land hard, crooked on the sidewalk right in front of the window beside us. I let out an alarmed cry as blood sprays on the glass, red-black and viscous.

Max and I both jump to our feet. I find myself pressing against the bloody glass as if I can get through it to the injured man. I'm fixated on him, then remembering Ivan, those last shuddering breaths he took.

The biker's eyes, a shattering green, stare. His right leg and left arm are twisted at an unnatural angle, as if there's some unseen hand wrenching his body. I reach for my phone, but Max is already on his. *We've witnessed an accident, on Broadway between fifty-fifth and fifty-sixth, outside Serafina. A man is badly injured.*

He's dead, I want to correct him. But I don't. Once you've seen the look of death, you recognize it right away. It's a kind of vacancy, a light lost, something fled. Those green eyes are empty, beyond sight. A stylish young woman in a long black coat and high heels runs up to the twisted form and drops to her knees while she's talking on the phone.

She puts a tender hand to his throat, checking expertly for a pulse. Then, she starts to scream. Her screaming, so helpless, so despairing—does she know him? *Help. Help. Somebody help him.* Or does she, too, recognize that look? Does it connect her as it does me to every loss she's ever known?

I'm still pressing against the glass, transfixed.

A crowd gathers, blocking the man from sight. In minutes, an ambulance arrives. There's a frenzy of angry honking horns, people frustrated that their trips have been delayed by yet another accident. Max moves over to me, puts a strong arm around my shoulders.

"Are you okay? Rosie, say something."

I realize then that I'm weeping. Fat tears pouring down my cheeks. Turning away from the scene on the street, and into Max's arms, I let him hold me a moment. I take comfort in his familiar scent, the feel of him.

"I'm okay," I say, pulling away finally.

"You sure?" he says, face a mask of concern. "That was—awful."

We sit back down in stunned silence. Time seems to warp. Finally, the man is shuttled away in an ambulance, and the crowd disperses. We're still at our lunch table, helpless to do or change anything. How long did it all take? Someone from the restaurant steps outside, dumps a bucket of soapy water over the blood that has pooled there. Then he uses a squeegee to wash the blood from the window right next to me but instead just smears it in a hideous, wide, red swath.

I get up quickly, almost knocking over my chair. The rest of the diners have gone back to their meals. The show is over; everyone returns quickly to their lives. As it should be, maybe. But I am shaken to my core. So much blood. I feel sick.

"I have to get out of here. I'm sorry."

Max rises, too. He tells the hostess he'll come back for the bill, then shuttles me outside and hails a cab. The traffic is flowing again, and one pulls up right away.

"You're so pale," Max says again, opening the door. He presses a strong hand on my shoulder. "Let me pay the bill and run you home?"

"No, no," I protest, embarrassed to be so rattled. "It's fine."

I just can't stop shaking.

"Call me when you get in," he says. "Let me know you got home safe."

Then I'm alone in the back of the cab, the driver just a set of eyes in the rearview mirror, city noise muffled, Max's worried form growing small behind me. My pulse is racing and my mind spinning.

What just happened? What *was* that?

An accident. One of hundreds that happen in this city every single day. I just happen to have been unlucky enough to witness it.

My father would surely declare it an omen of dark things to come. But he and I don't share the same belief system. I haven't spoken to him in years; amazing that I still hear his voice so clearly.

The cab races through traffic, dodging, weaving, the cabbie leaning on his horn. I dig through my tote and find the little white, blue and purple box, pull it out so that I can put my eyes on it. A pregnancy test.

In the face of death and loss, what do we need most?

Hope.

Life.

I can't get home fast enough.